THE OUTCAST

VOLUME 1

STORY
VAUN WILMOTT

ART
EDWARD GAN

THE OUTCAST

VOLUME 1

story by
Vaun Wilmott

art by
Edward Gan

STAFF CREDITS

toning	**Armand Roy Canlas**
lettering	**Jon Zamar**
graphic design	**Jon Zamar**
cover design	**Nicky Lim**
assistant editor	**Adam Arnold**
editor	**Jason DeAngelis**
publisher	**Seven Seas Entertainment**

Visit us online at www.gomanga.com.

ISBN 978-1-933164-32-8

Printed in Canada

First printing: July, 2007

10 9 8 7 6 5 4 3 2 1

· CONTENTS ·

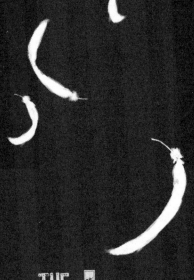

THE OUTCAST

VOLUME 1

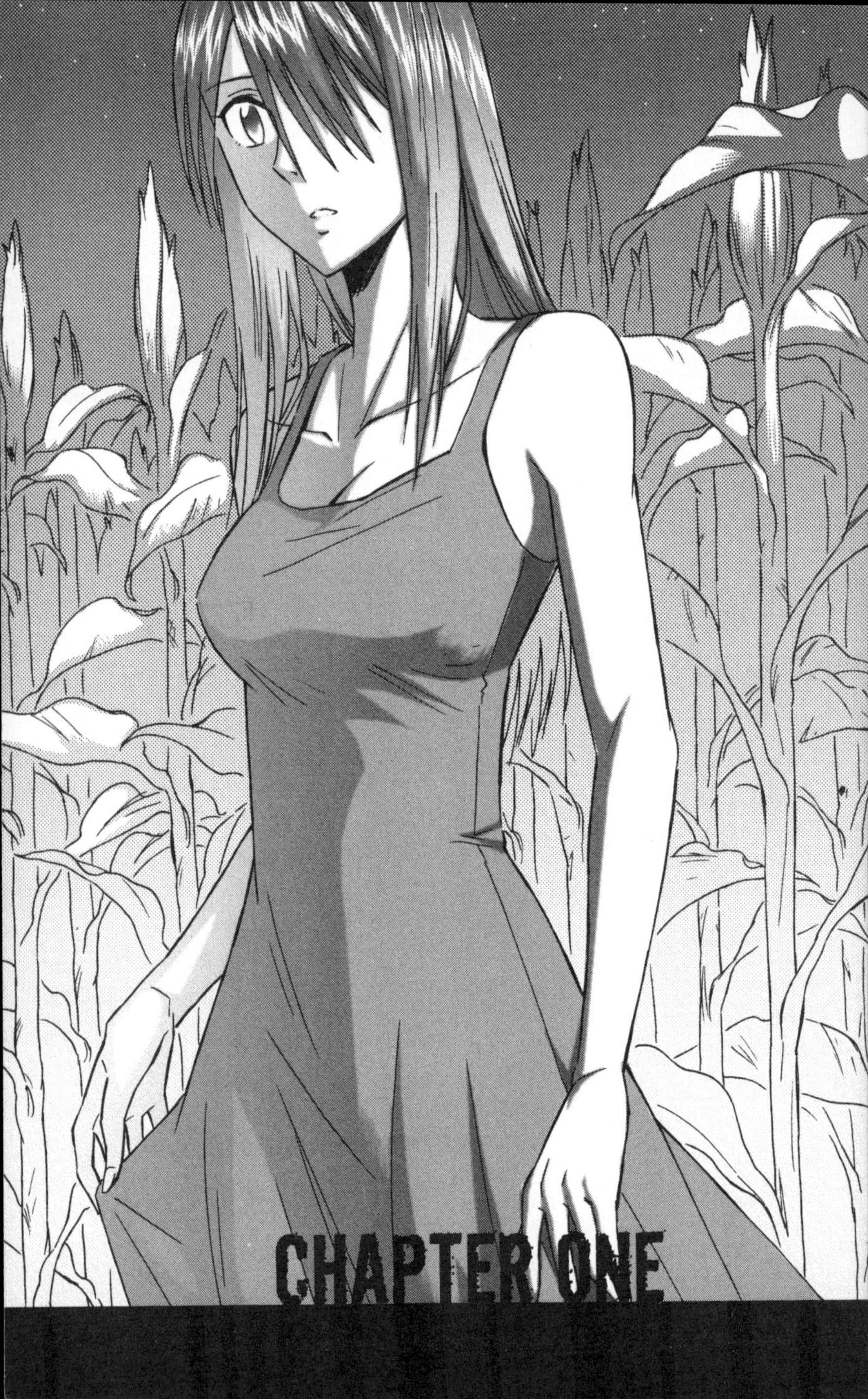
CHAPTER ONE

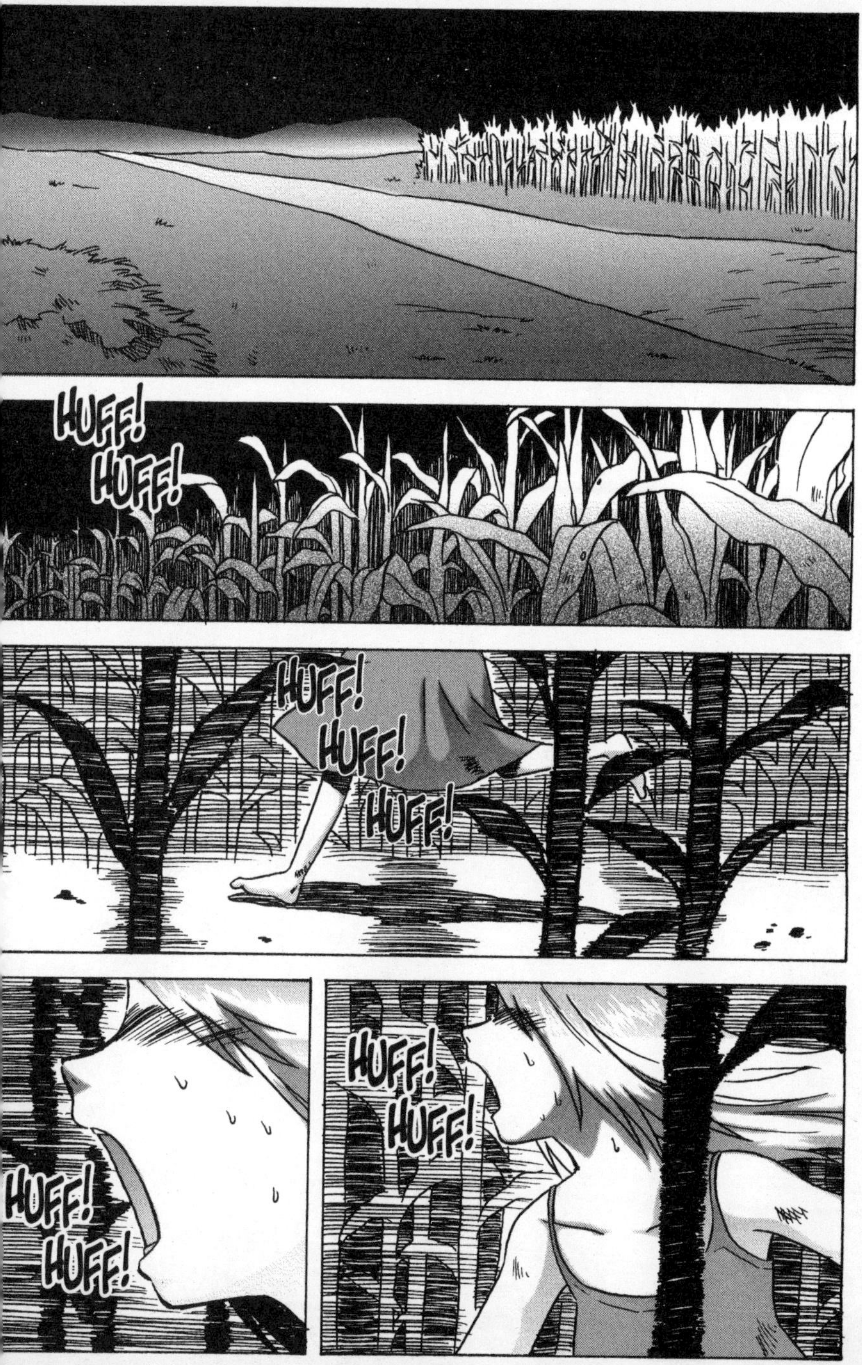
HUFF! HUFF!
HUFF! HUFF! HUFF!
HUFF! HUFF!
HUFF! HUFF!

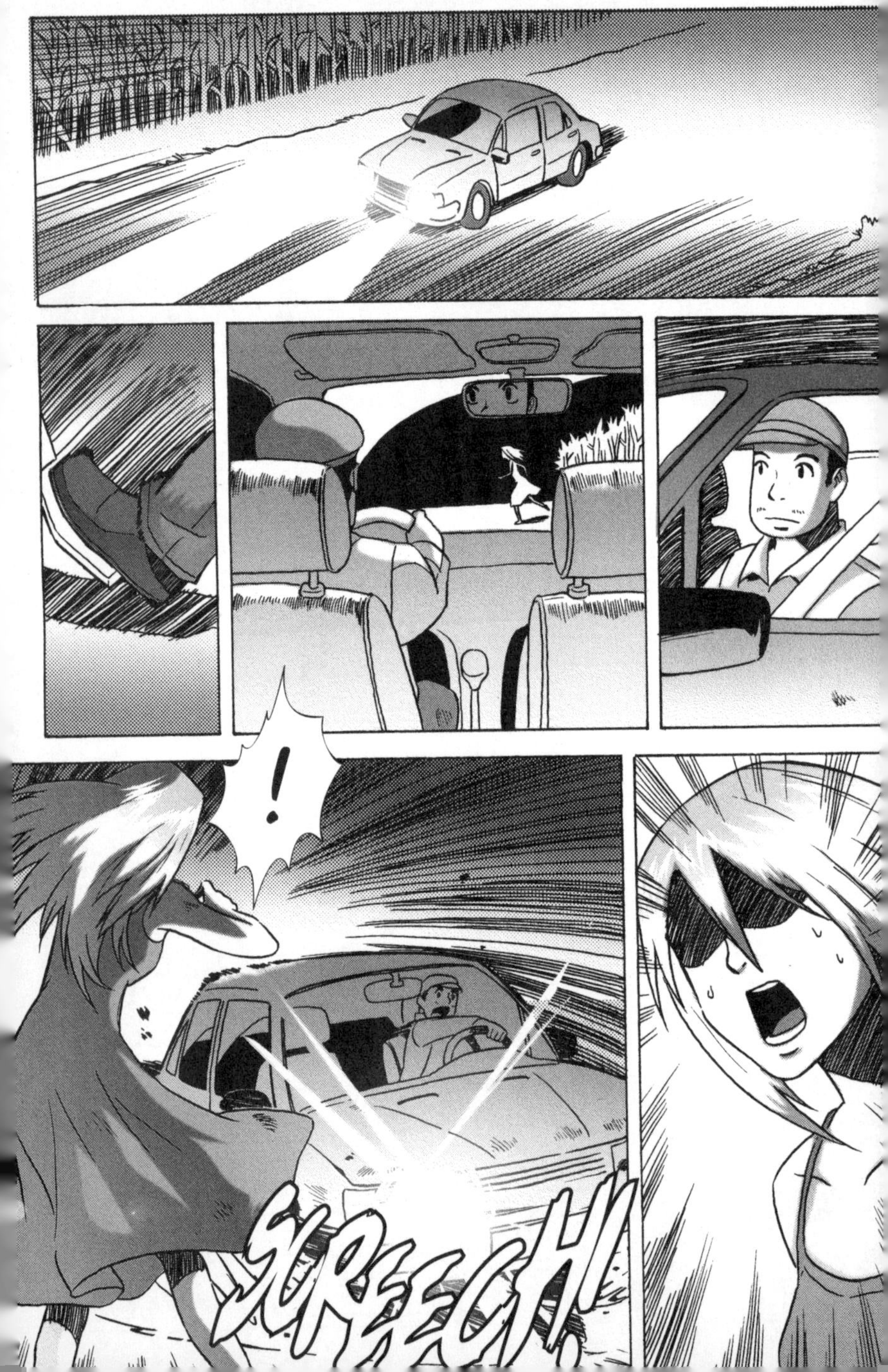
!
SCREECH!

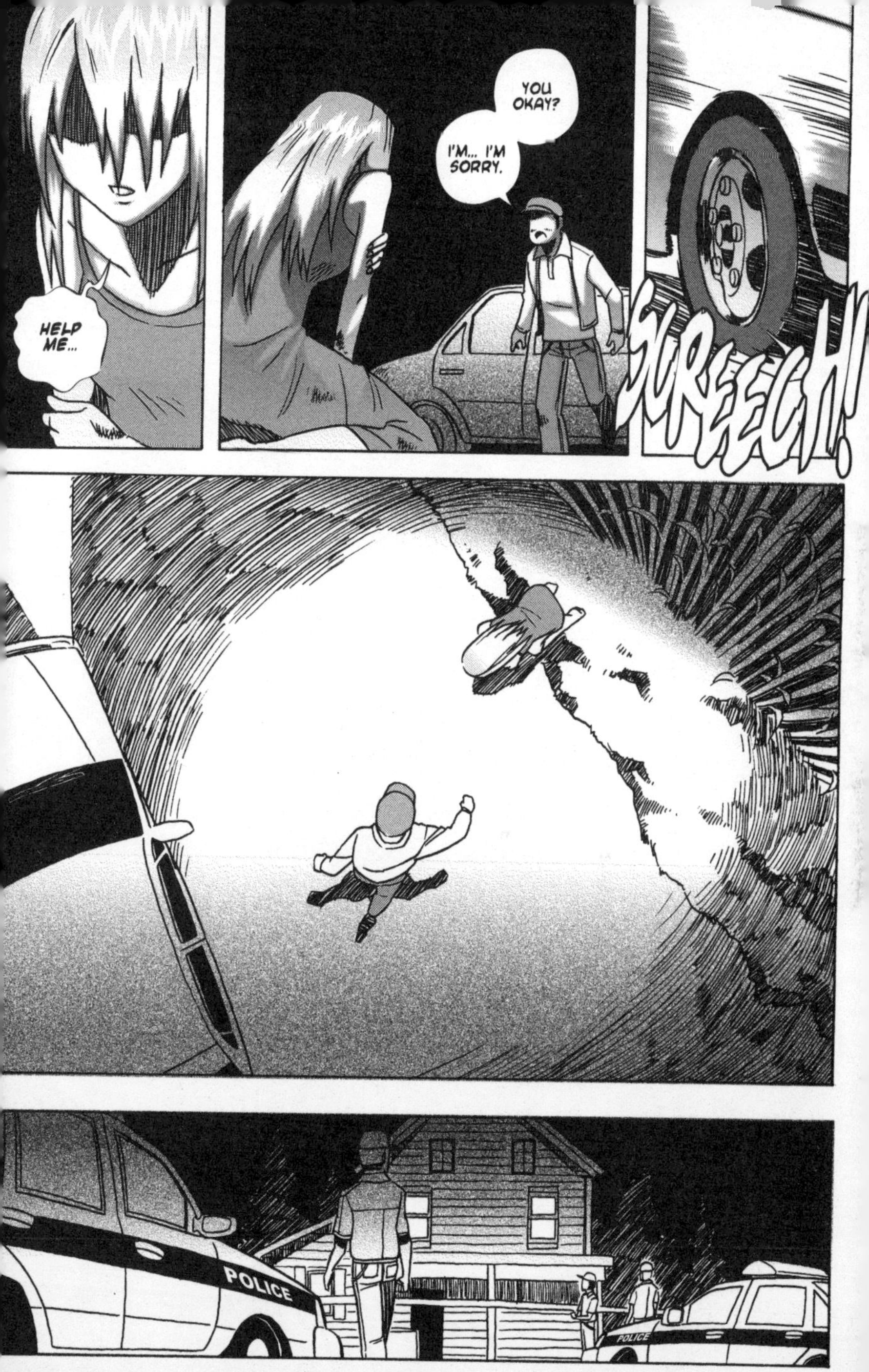
SCREECH!
YOU OKAY?
I'M... I'M SORRY.
HELP ME...
POLICE
POLICE

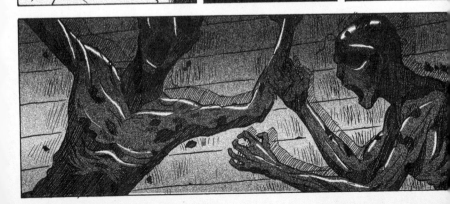

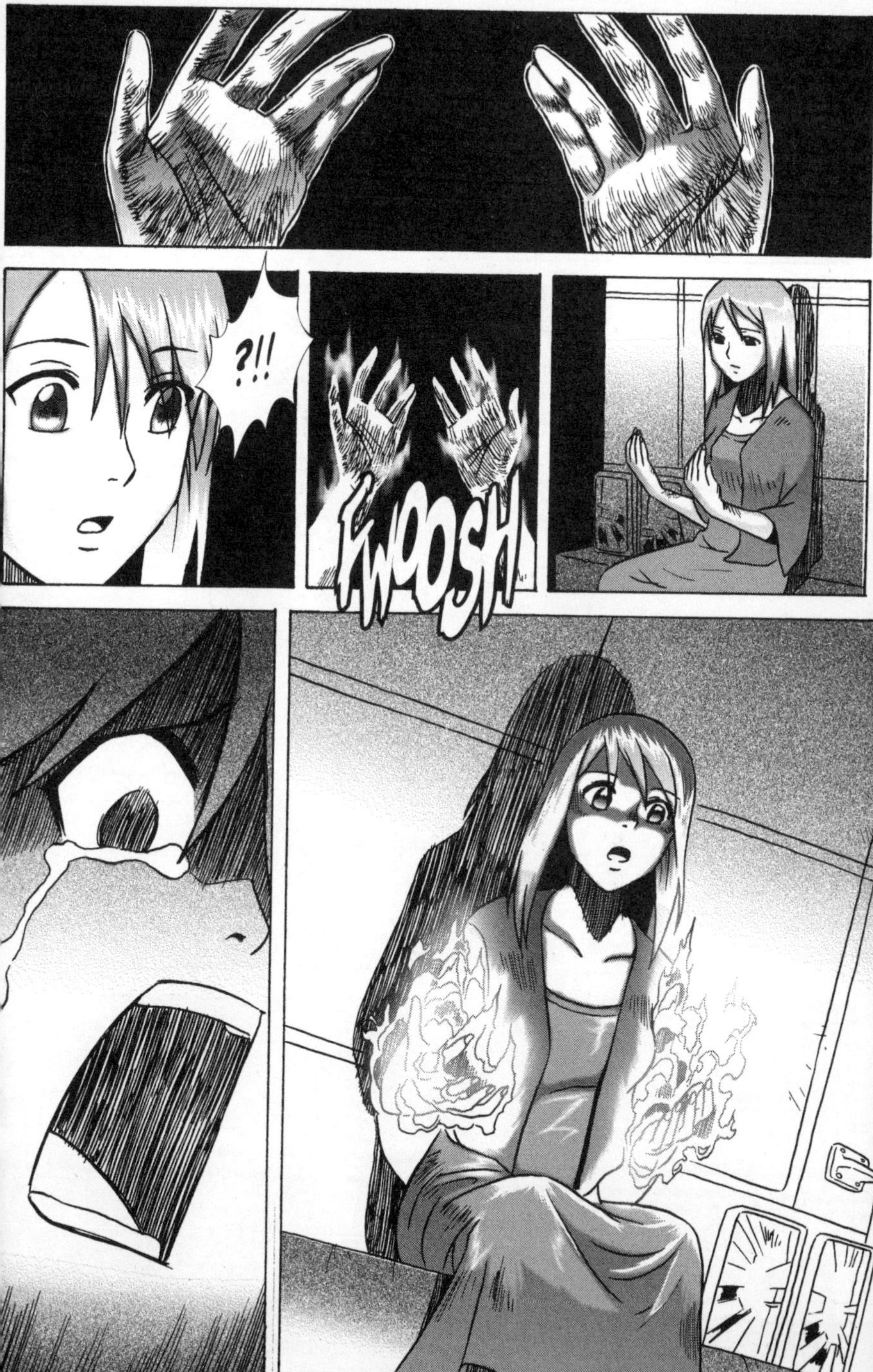
?!!
FWOOSH

AAAAH!
HUFF!
HUFF!

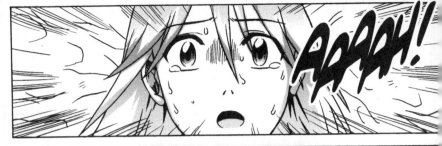

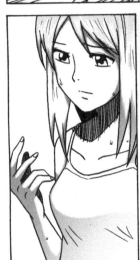

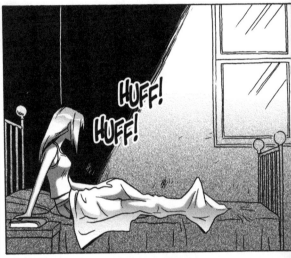

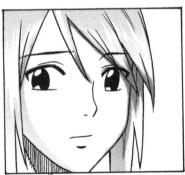

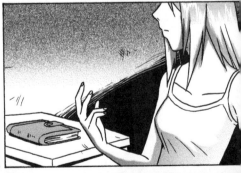

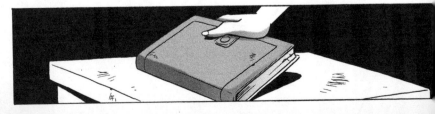

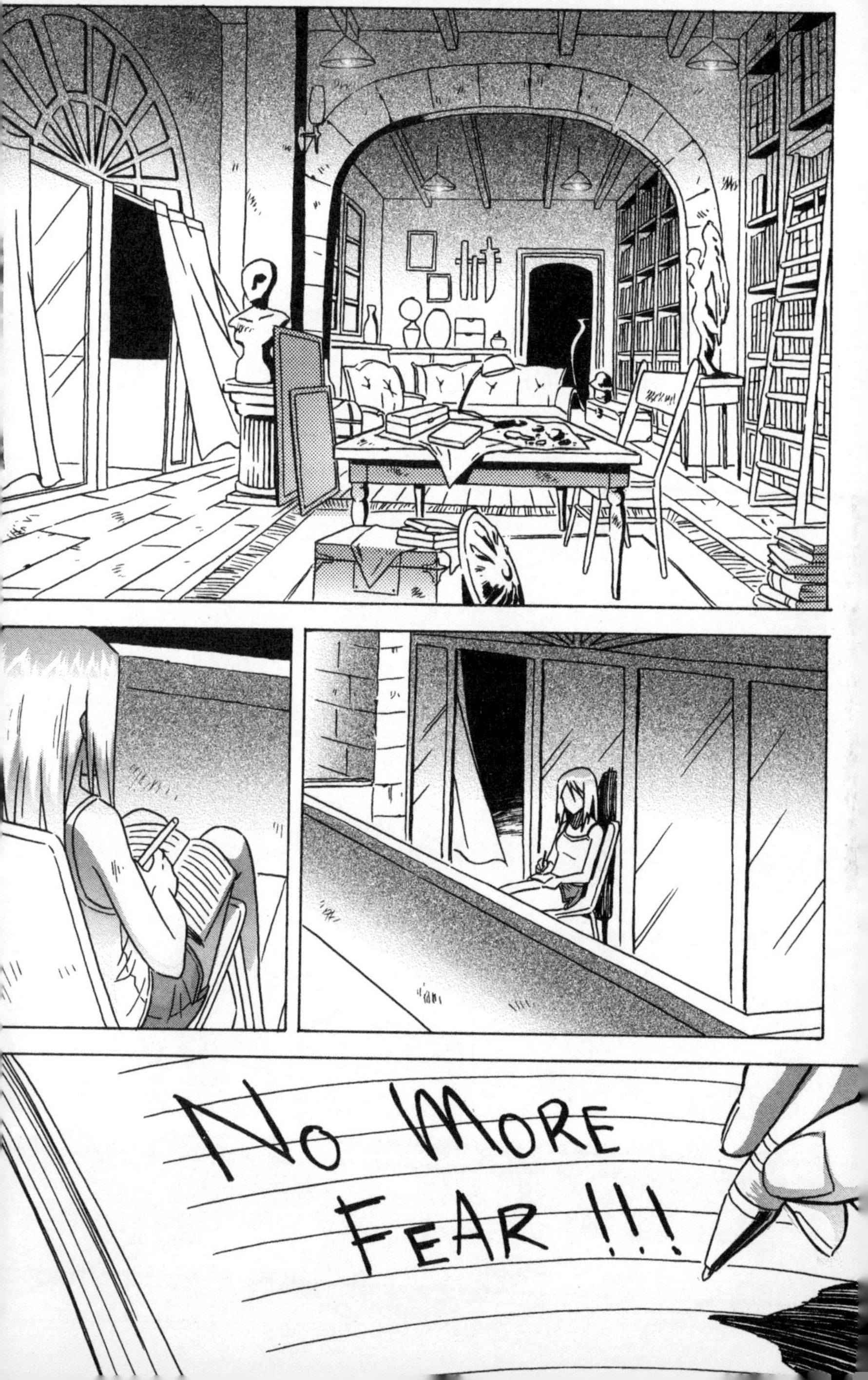
No More
Fear !!!

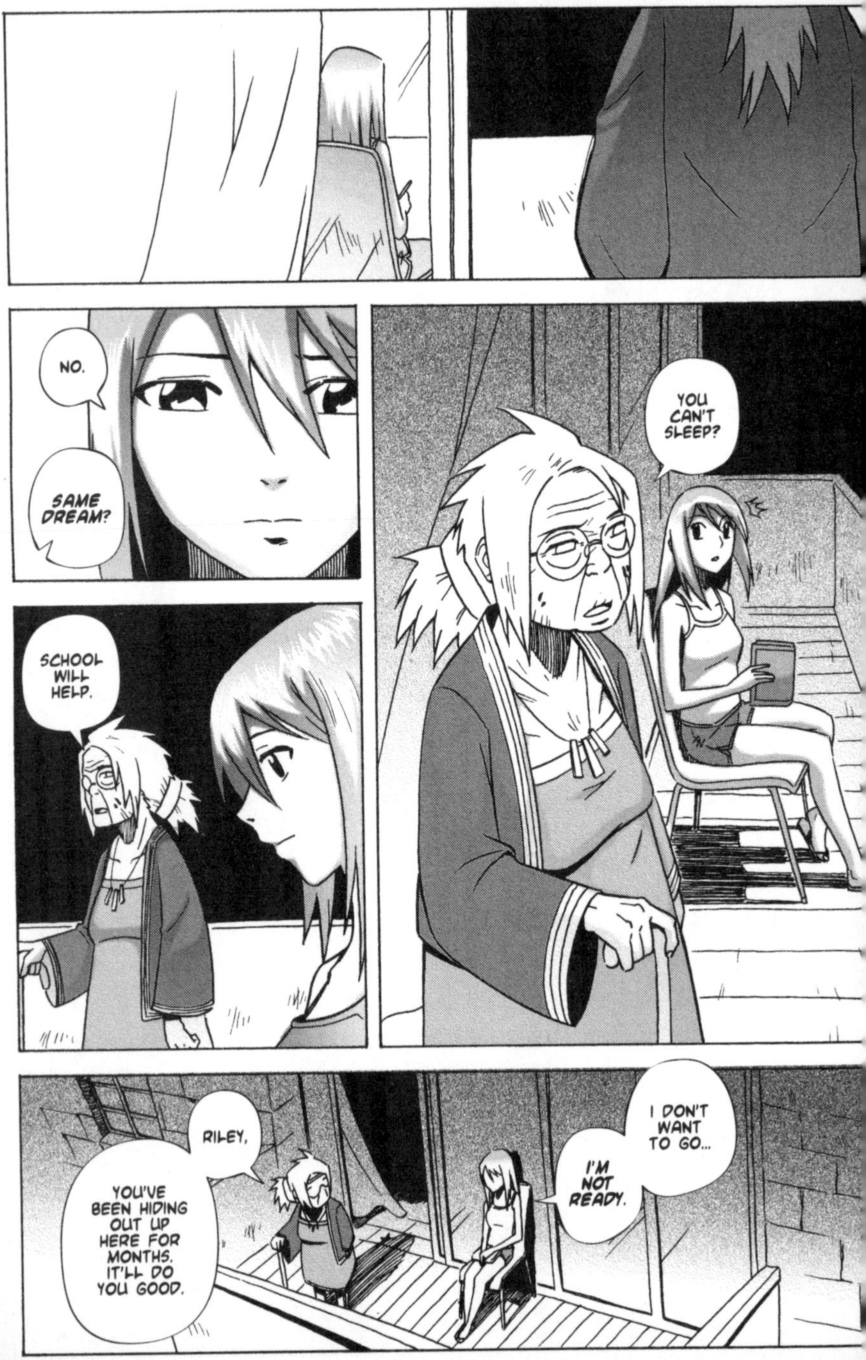
YOU CAN'T SLEEP?
NO.
SAME DREAM?
SCHOOL WILL HELP.
I DON'T WANT TO GO...
I'M NOT READY.
RILEY,
YOU'VE BEEN HIDING OUT UP HERE FOR MONTHS. IT'LL DO YOU GOOD.

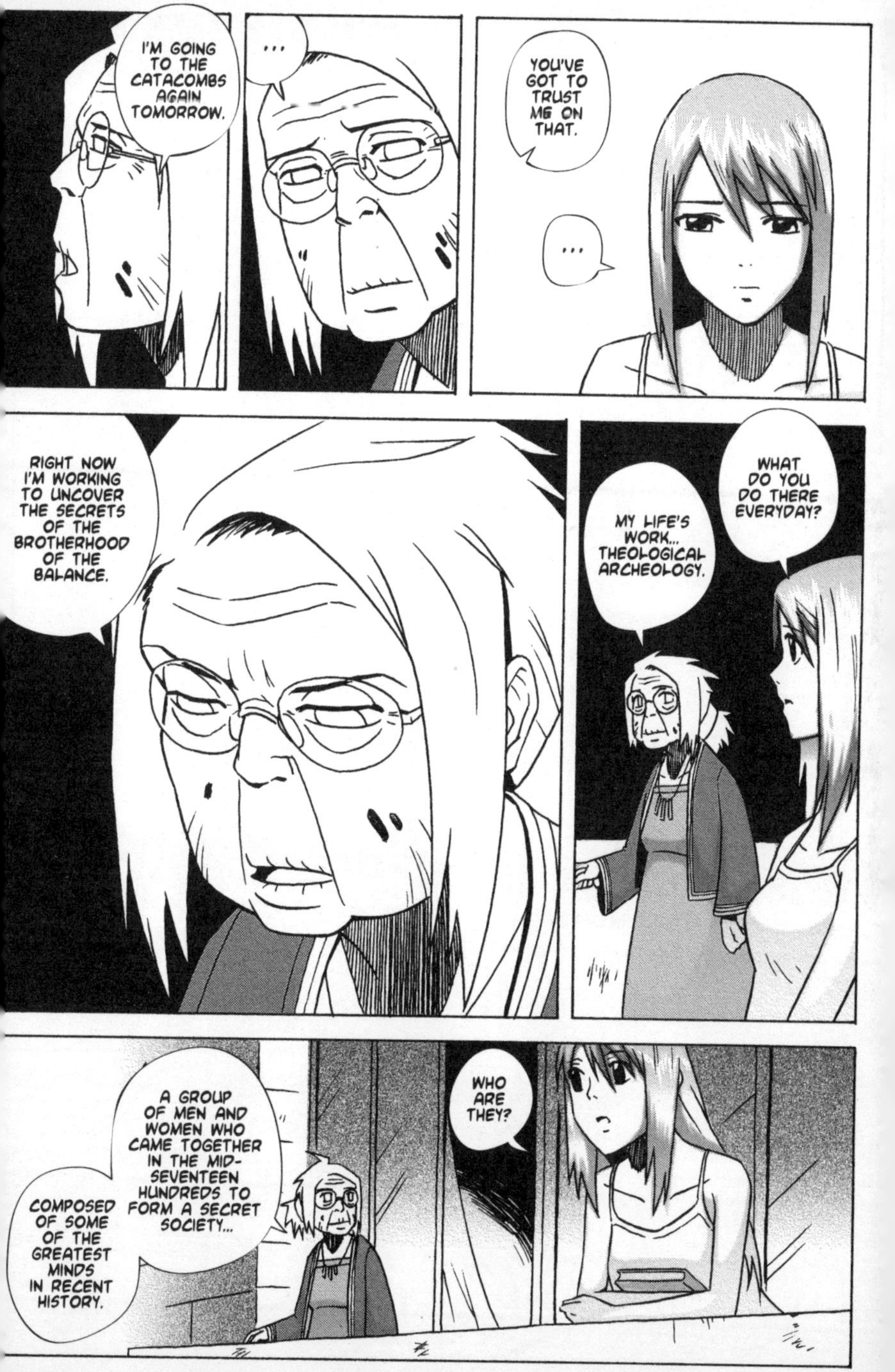
YOU'VE GOT TO TRUST ME ON THAT.
...
...
I'M GOING TO THE CATACOMBS AGAIN TOMORROW.
WHAT DO YOU DO THERE EVERYDAY?
MY LIFE'S WORK... THEOLOGICAL ARCHEOLOGY.
RIGHT NOW I'M WORKING TO UNCOVER THE SECRETS OF THE BROTHERHOOD OF THE BALANCE.
WHO ARE THEY?
A GROUP OF MEN AND WOMEN WHO CAME TOGETHER IN THE MID-SEVENTEEN HUNDREDS TO FORM A SECRET SOCIETY...
COMPOSED OF SOME OF THE GREATEST MINDS IN RECENT HISTORY.

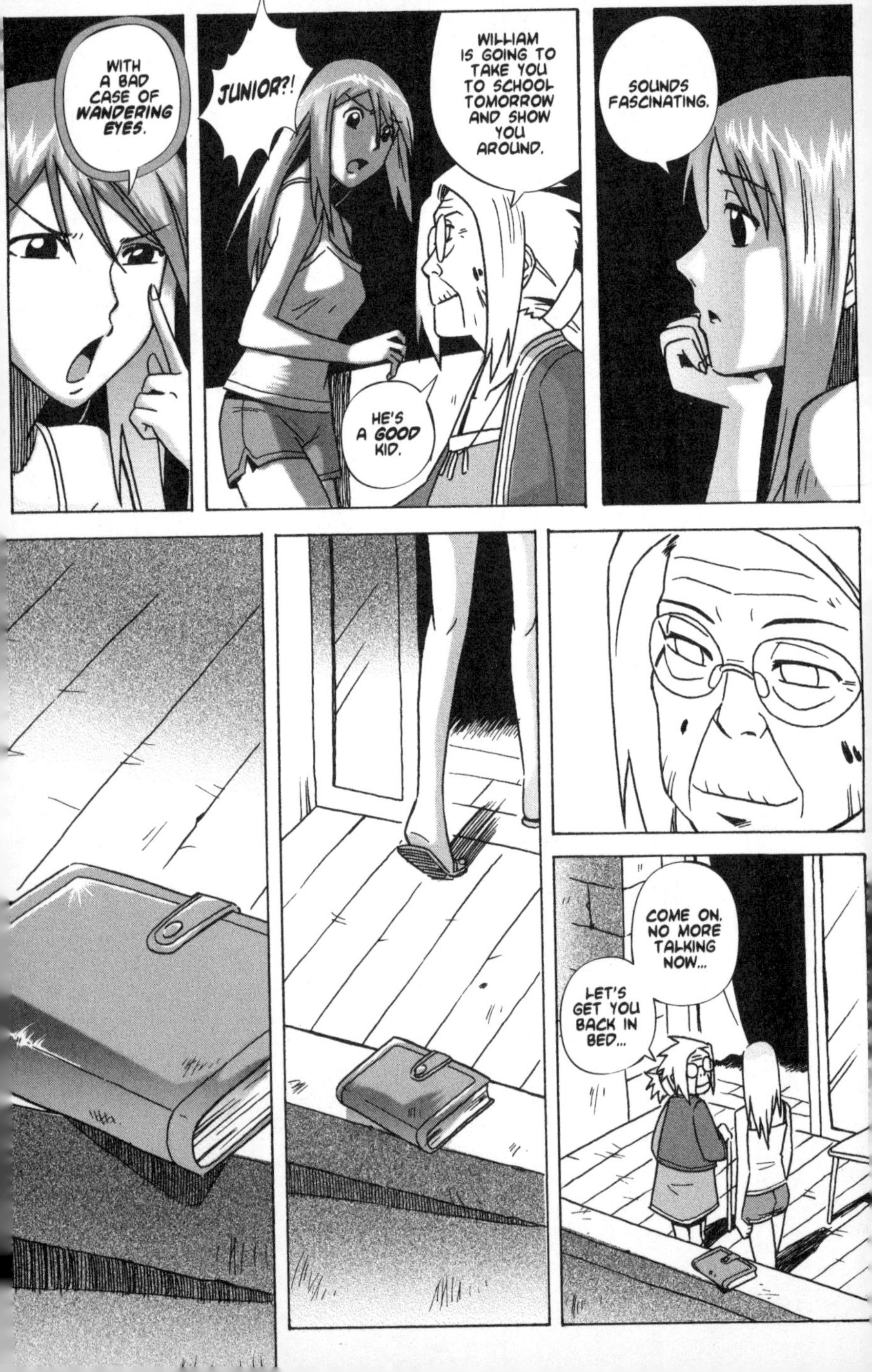
SOUNDS FASCINATING.
WILLIAM IS GOING TO TAKE YOU TO SCHOOL TOMORROW AND SHOW YOU AROUND.
JUNIOR?!
HE'S A GOOD KID.
WITH A BAD CASE OF WANDERING EYES.
COME ON. NO MORE TALKING NOW...
LET'S GET YOU BACK IN BED...

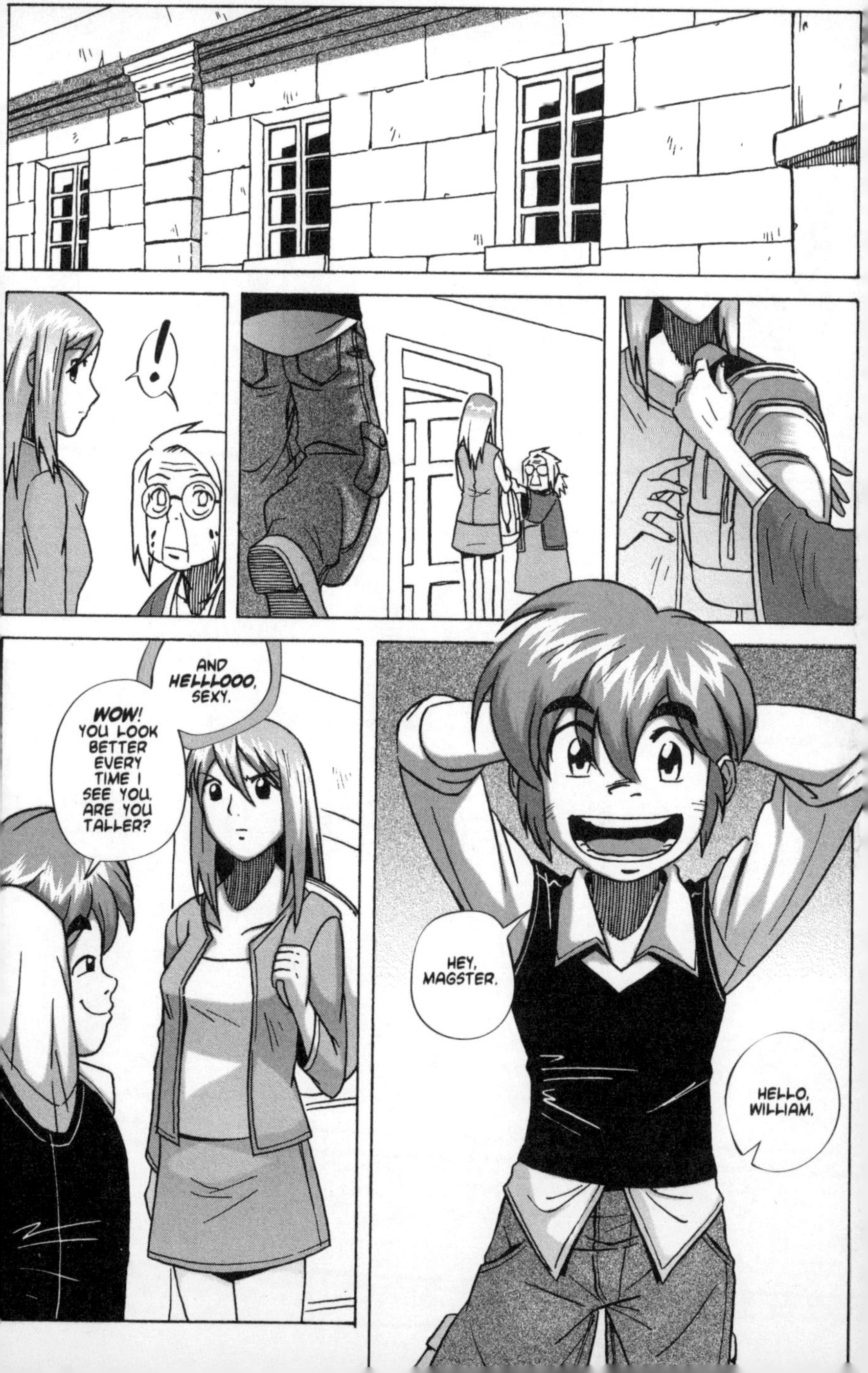
!
HEY, MAGSTER.
HELLO, WILLIAM.
AND HELLLOOO, SEXY.
WOW! YOU LOOK BETTER EVERY TIME I SEE YOU. ARE YOU TALLER?

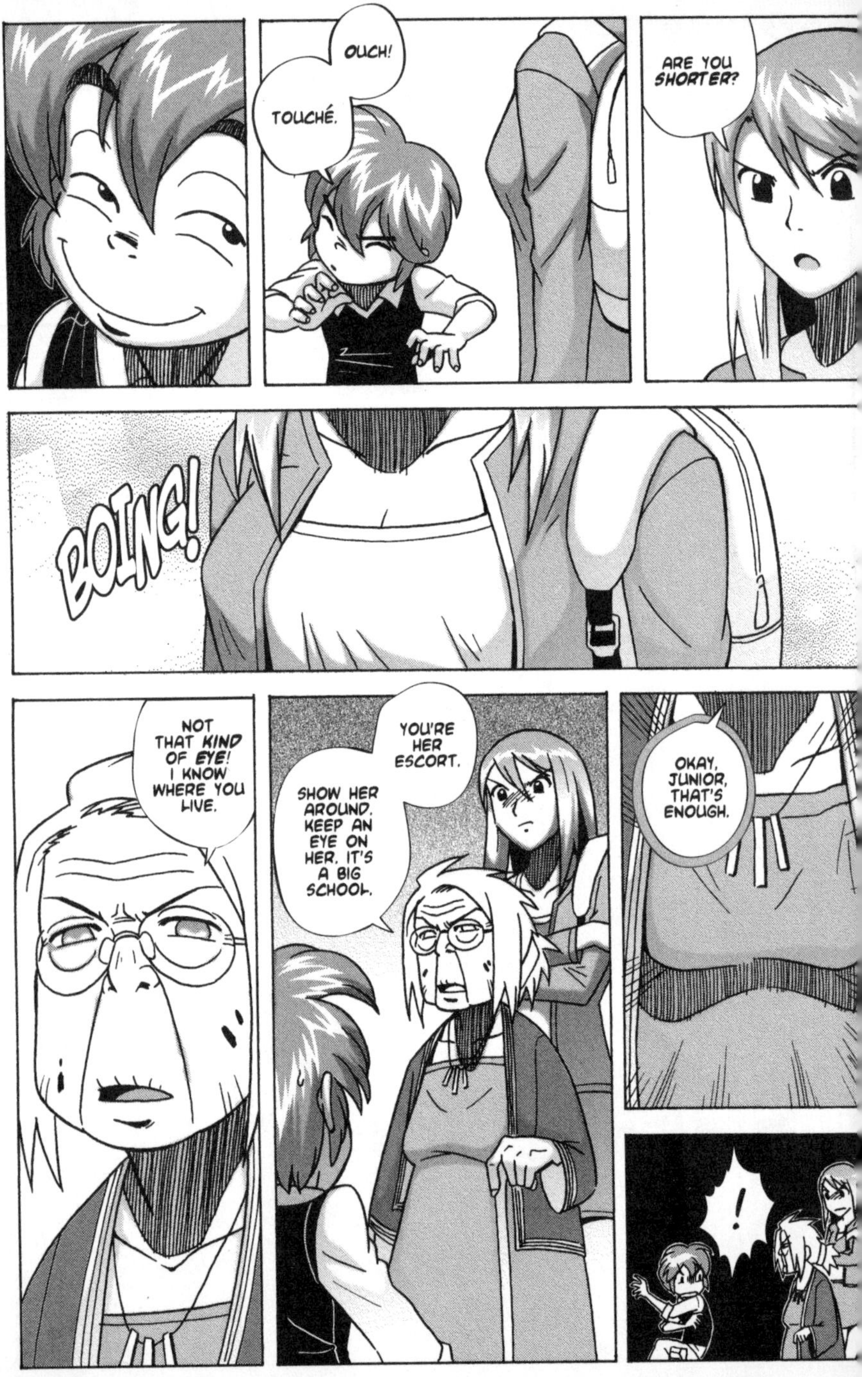
ARE YOU SHORTER?
OUCH!
TOUCHÉ.
BOING!
OKAY, JUNIOR, THAT'S ENOUGH.
!
YOU'RE HER ESCORT.
SHOW HER AROUND. KEEP AN EYE ON HER. IT'S A BIG SCHOOL.
NOT THAT KIND OF EYE! I KNOW WHERE YOU LIVE.

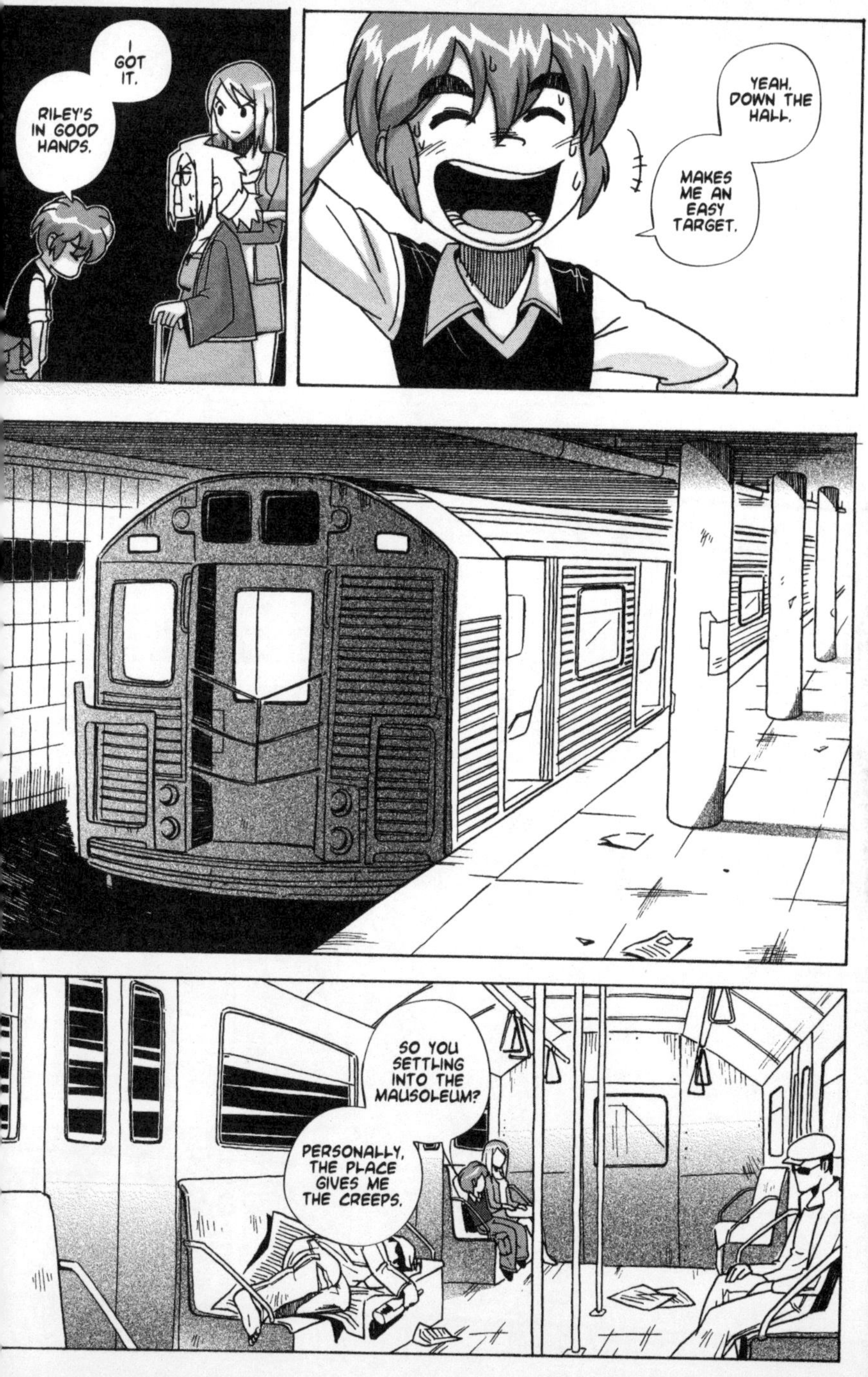
YEAH. DOWN THE HALL.
MAKES ME AN EASY TARGET.
I GOT IT.
RILEY'S IN GOOD HANDS.
SO YOU SETTLING INTO THE MAUSOLEUM?
PERSONALLY, THE PLACE GIVES ME THE CREEPS.

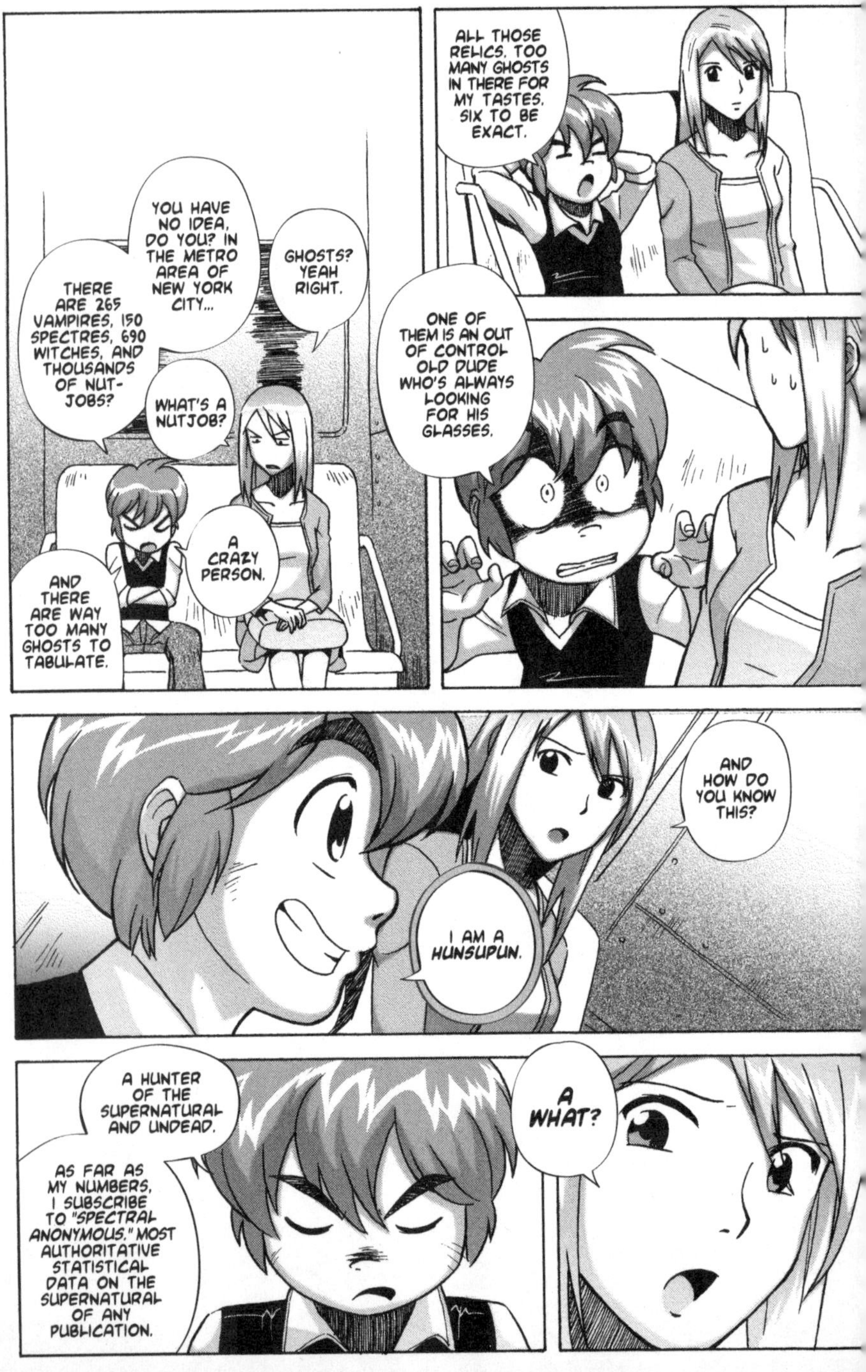
ALL THOSE RELICS. TOO MANY GHOSTS IN THERE FOR MY TASTES. SIX TO BE EXACT.
ONE OF THEM IS AN OUT OF CONTROL OLD DUDE WHO'S ALWAYS LOOKING FOR HIS GLASSES.
GHOSTS? YEAH RIGHT.
YOU HAVE NO IDEA, DO YOU? IN THE METRO AREA OF NEW YORK CITY...
THERE ARE 265 VAMPIRES, 150 SPECTRES, 690 WITCHES, AND THOUSANDS OF NUT-JOBS?
WHAT'S A NUTJOB?
A CRAZY PERSON.
AND THERE ARE WAY TOO MANY GHOSTS TO TABULATE.
AND HOW DO YOU KNOW THIS?
I AM A HUNSUPUN.
A WHAT?
A HUNTER OF THE SUPERNATURAL AND UNDEAD.
AS FAR AS MY NUMBERS, I SUBSCRIBE TO "SPECTRAL ANONYMOUS." MOST AUTHORITATIVE STATISTICAL DATA ON THE SUPERNATURAL OF ANY PUBLICATION.

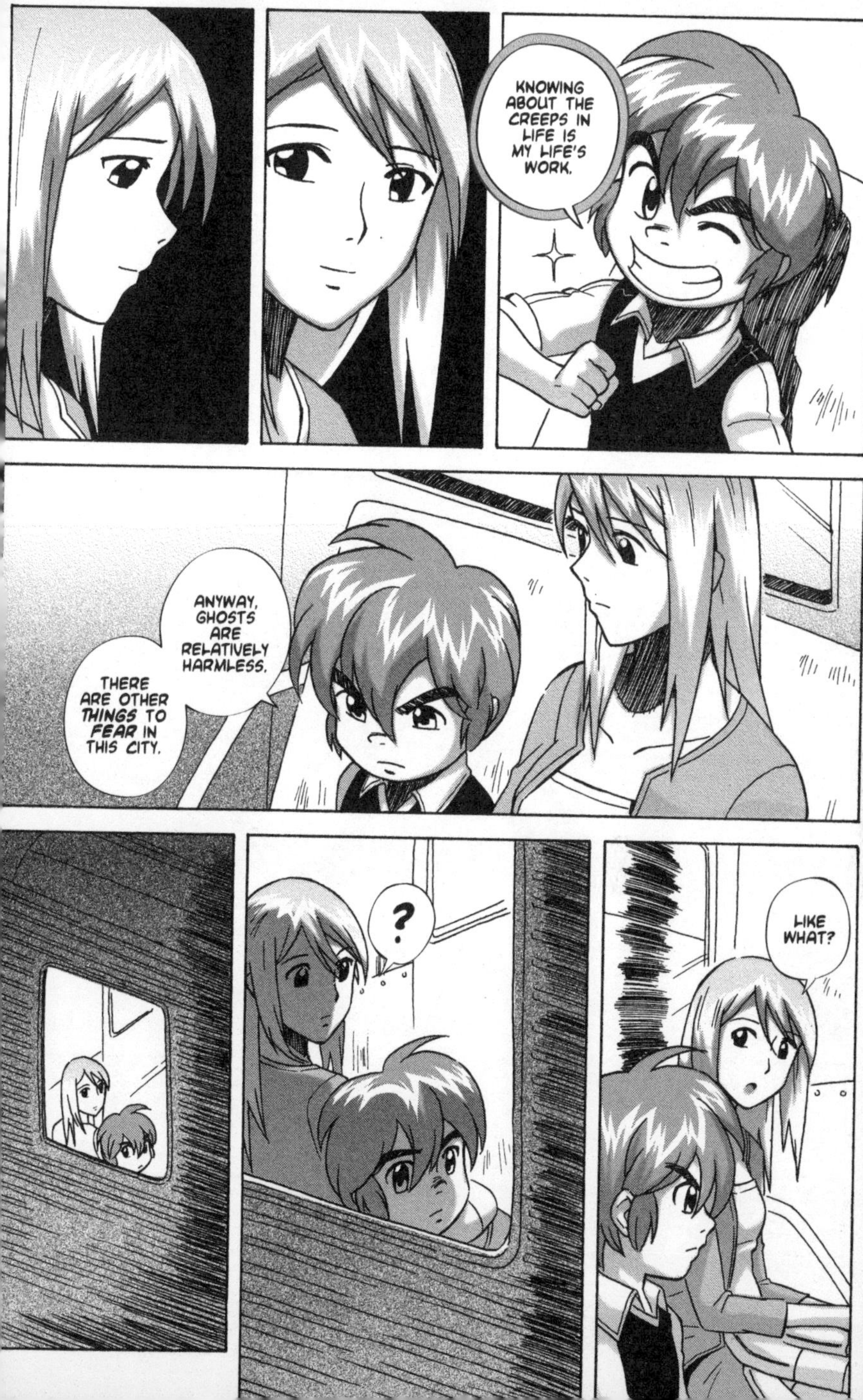
KNOWING ABOUT THE CREEPS IN LIFE IS MY LIFE'S WORK.
ANYWAY, GHOSTS ARE RELATIVELY HARMLESS.
THERE ARE OTHER *THINGS* TO *FEAR* IN THIS CITY.
LIKE WHAT?
?

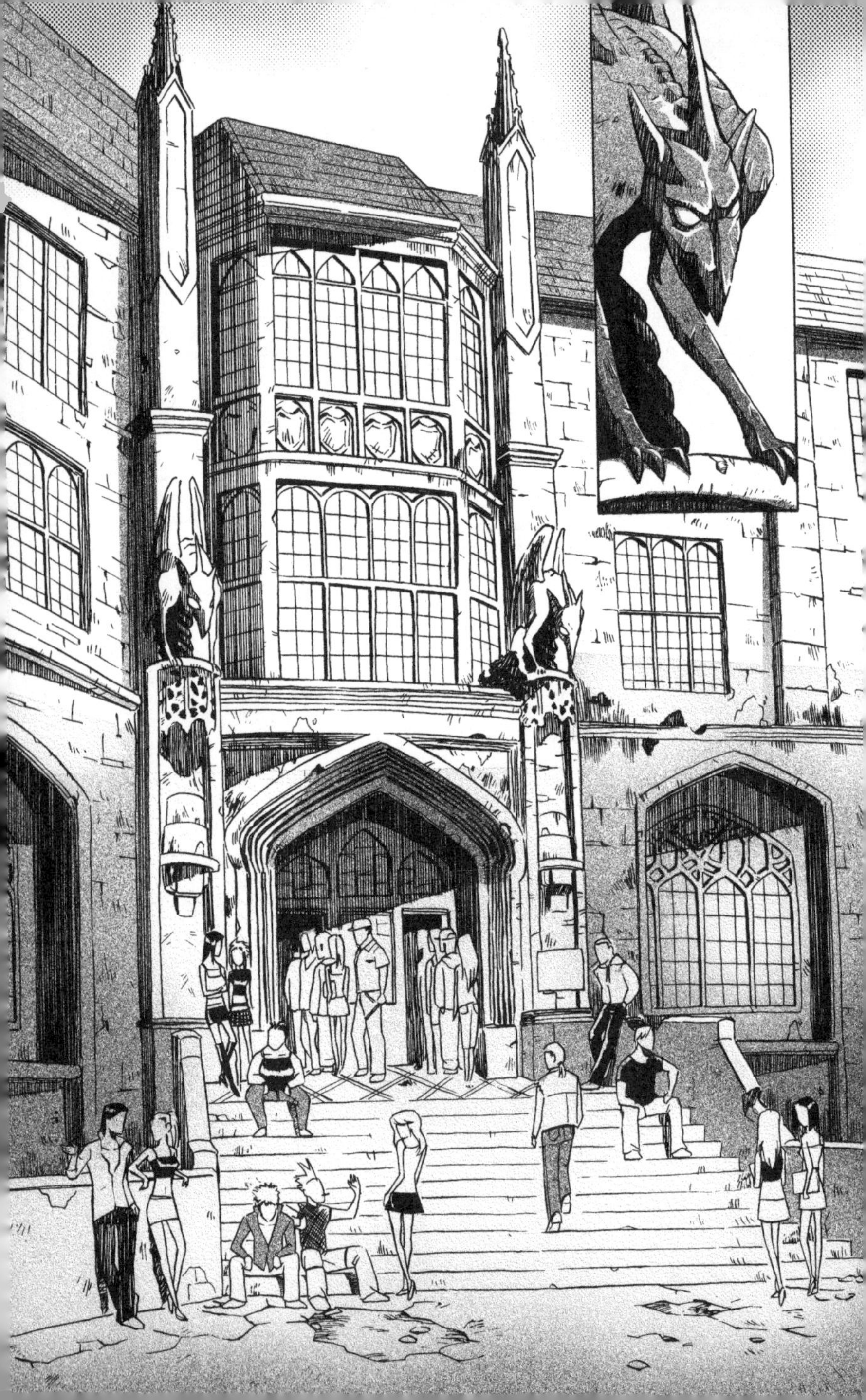

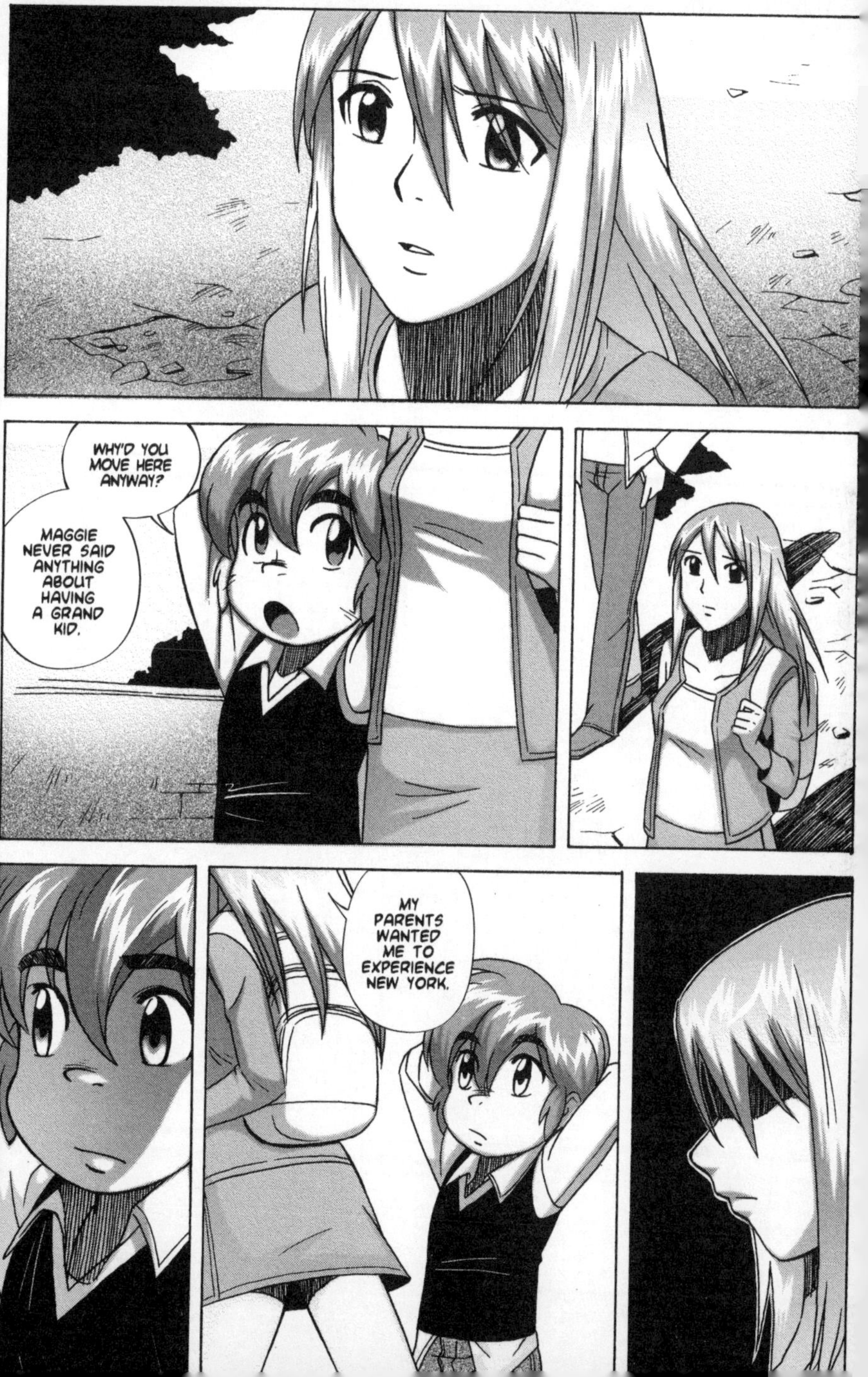
WHY'D YOU MOVE HERE ANYWAY?
MAGGIE NEVER SAID ANYTHING ABOUT HAVING A GRAND KID.
MY PARENTS WANTED ME TO EXPERIENCE NEW YORK.

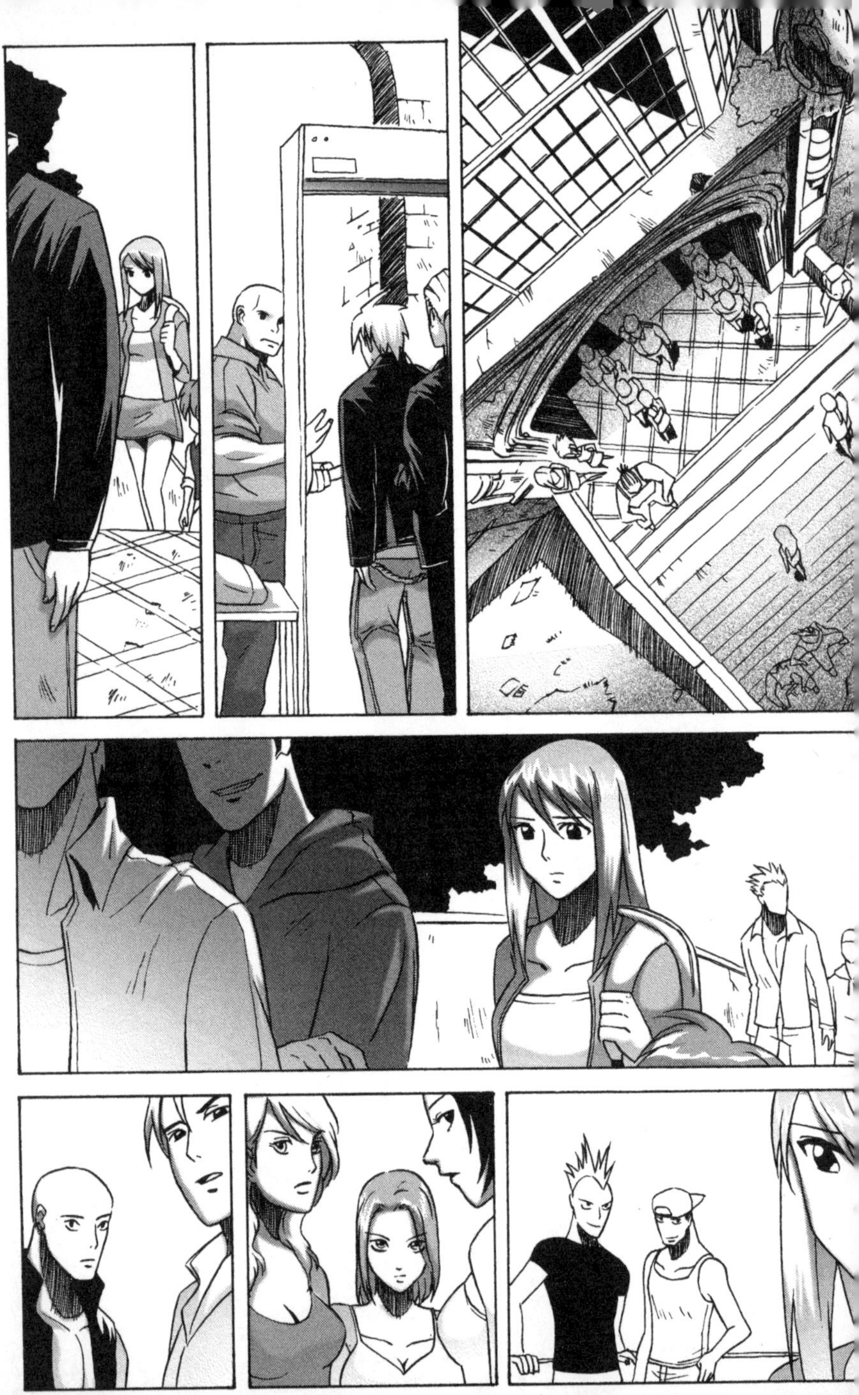

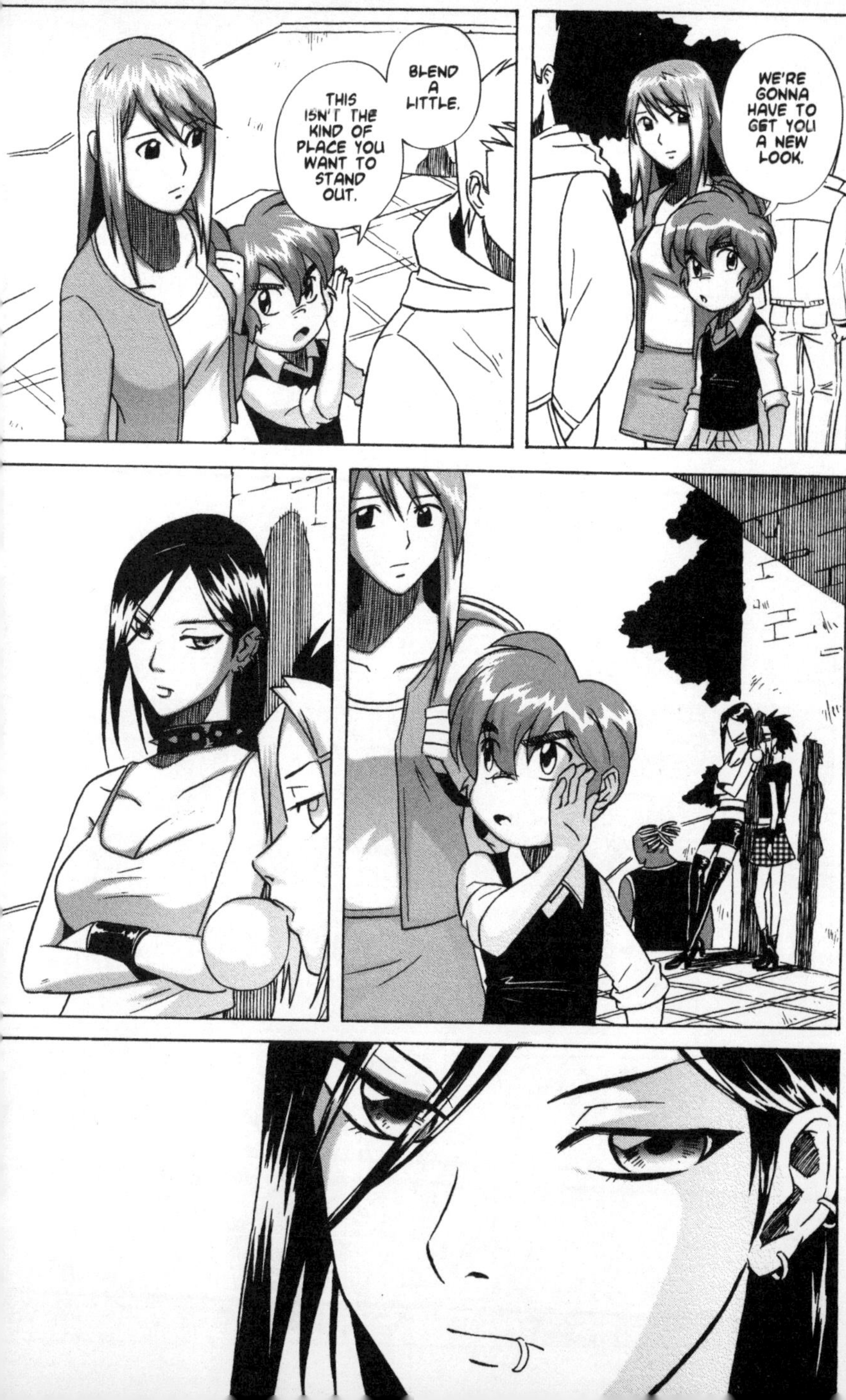
WE'RE GONNA HAVE TO GET YOU A NEW LOOK.
BLEND A LITTLE.
THIS ISN'T THE KIND OF PLACE YOU WANT TO STAND OUT.

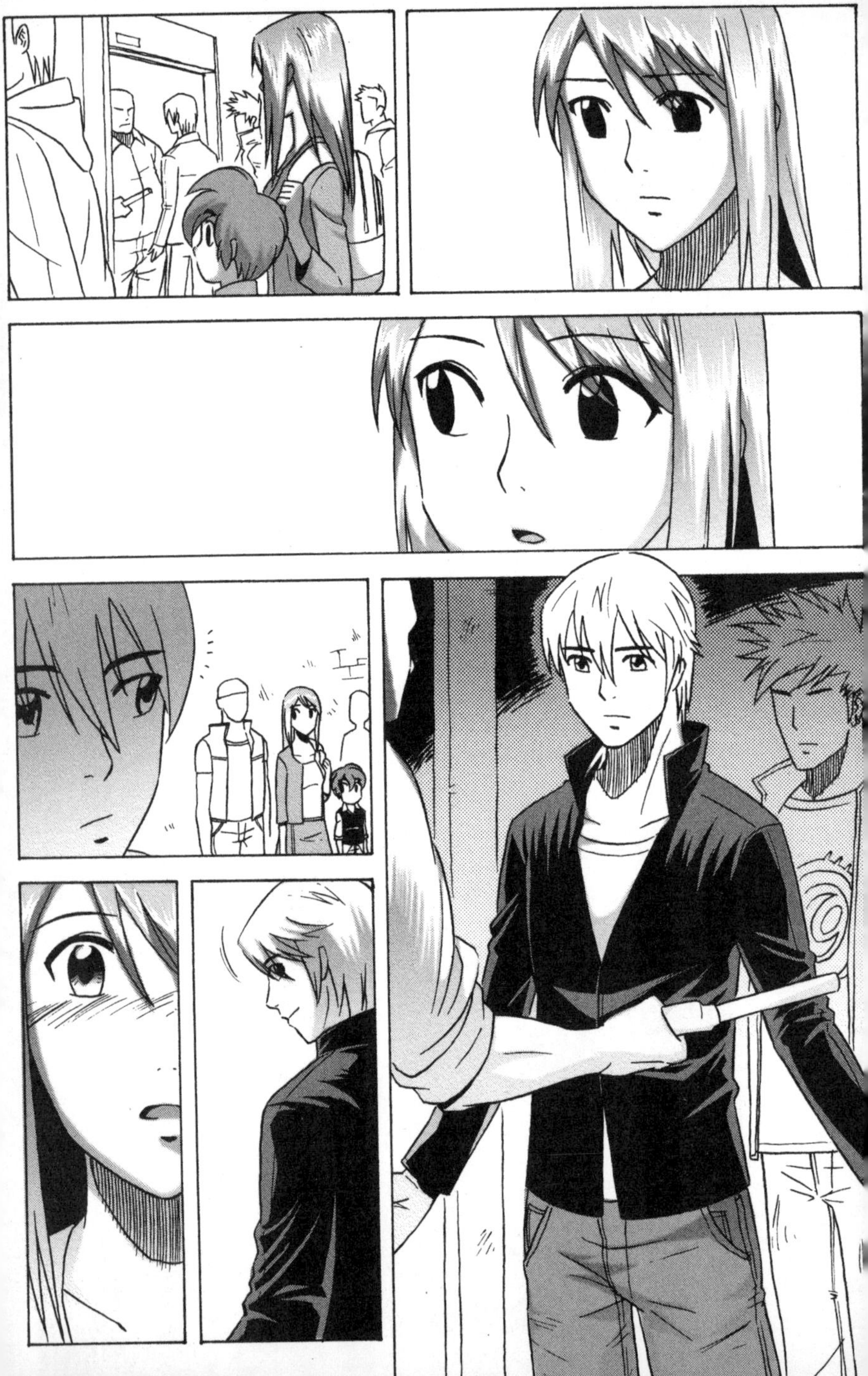

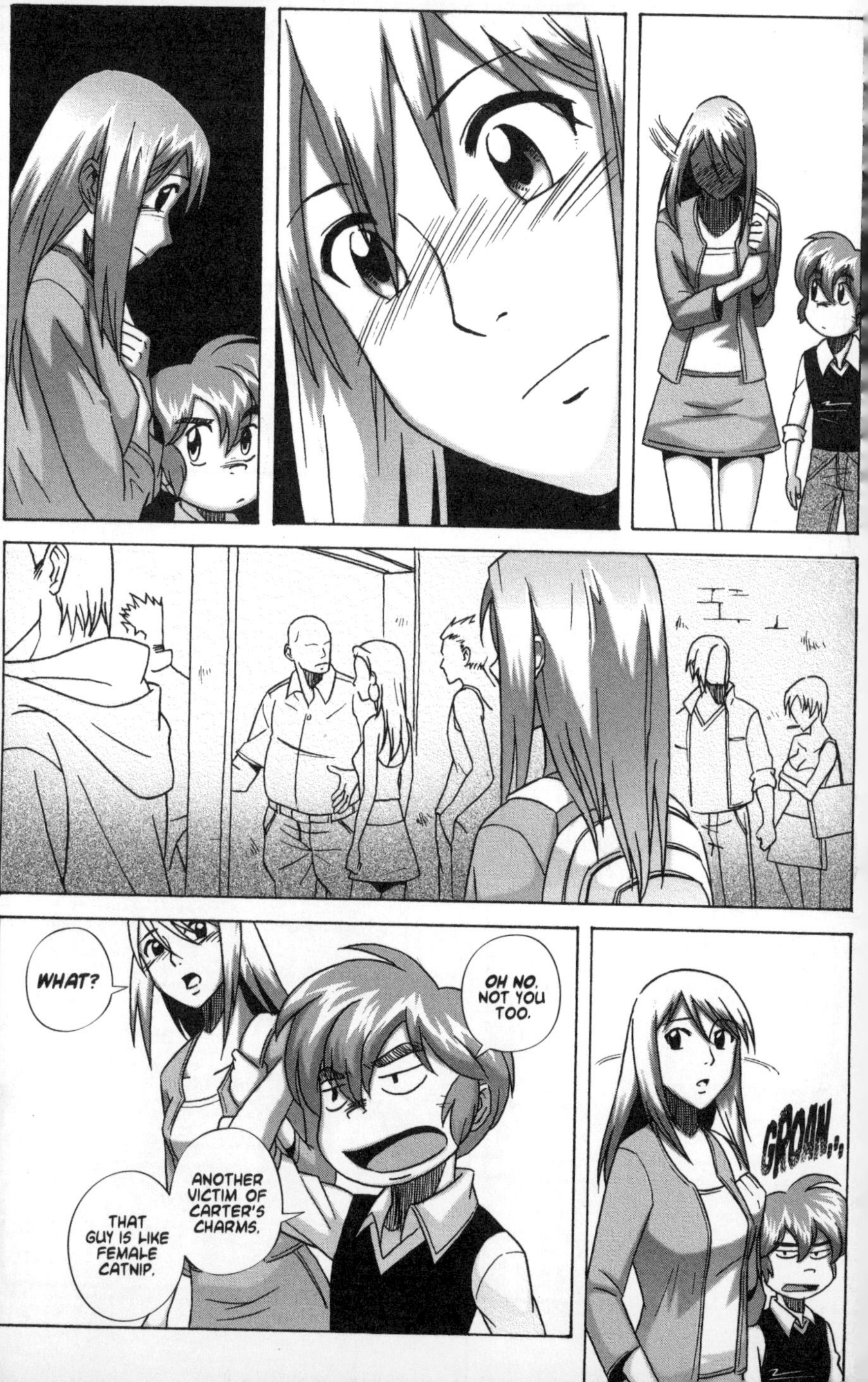
GROAN...
OH NO. NOT YOU TOO.
WHAT?
ANOTHER VICTIM OF CARTER'S CHARMS.
THAT GUY IS LIKE FEMALE CATNIP.

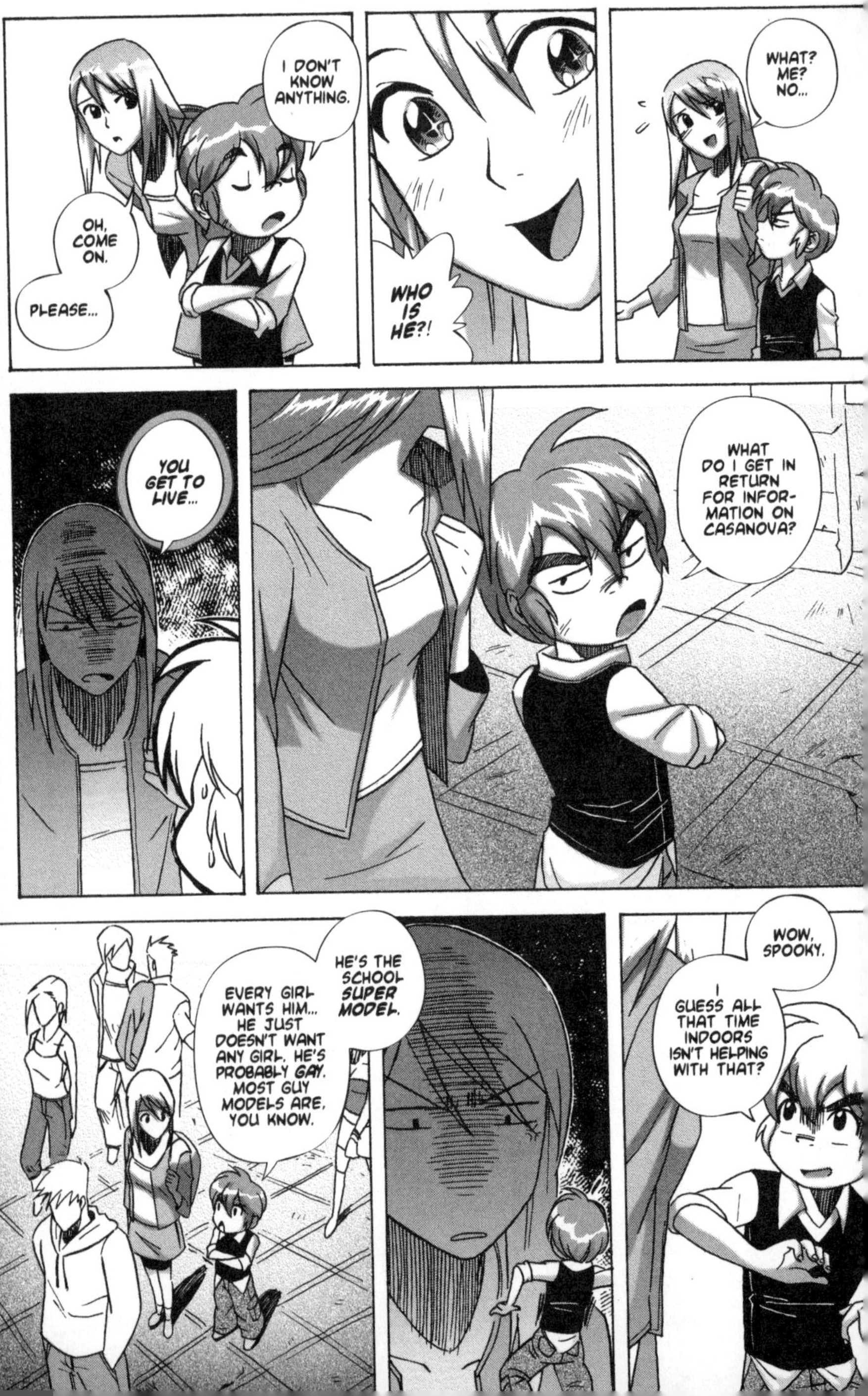
WHAT? ME? NO...
WHO IS HE?!
I DON'T KNOW ANYTHING.
OH, COME ON.
PLEASE...
WHAT DO I GET IN RETURN FOR INFOR-MATION ON CASANOVA?
YOU GET TO LIVE...
WOW, SPOOKY.
I GUESS ALL THAT TIME INDOORS ISN'T HELPING WITH THAT?
HE'S THE SCHOOL SUPER MODEL.
EVERY GIRL WANTS HIM... HE JUST DOESN'T WANT ANY GIRL. HE'S PROBABLY GAY. MOST GUY MODELS ARE, YOU KNOW.

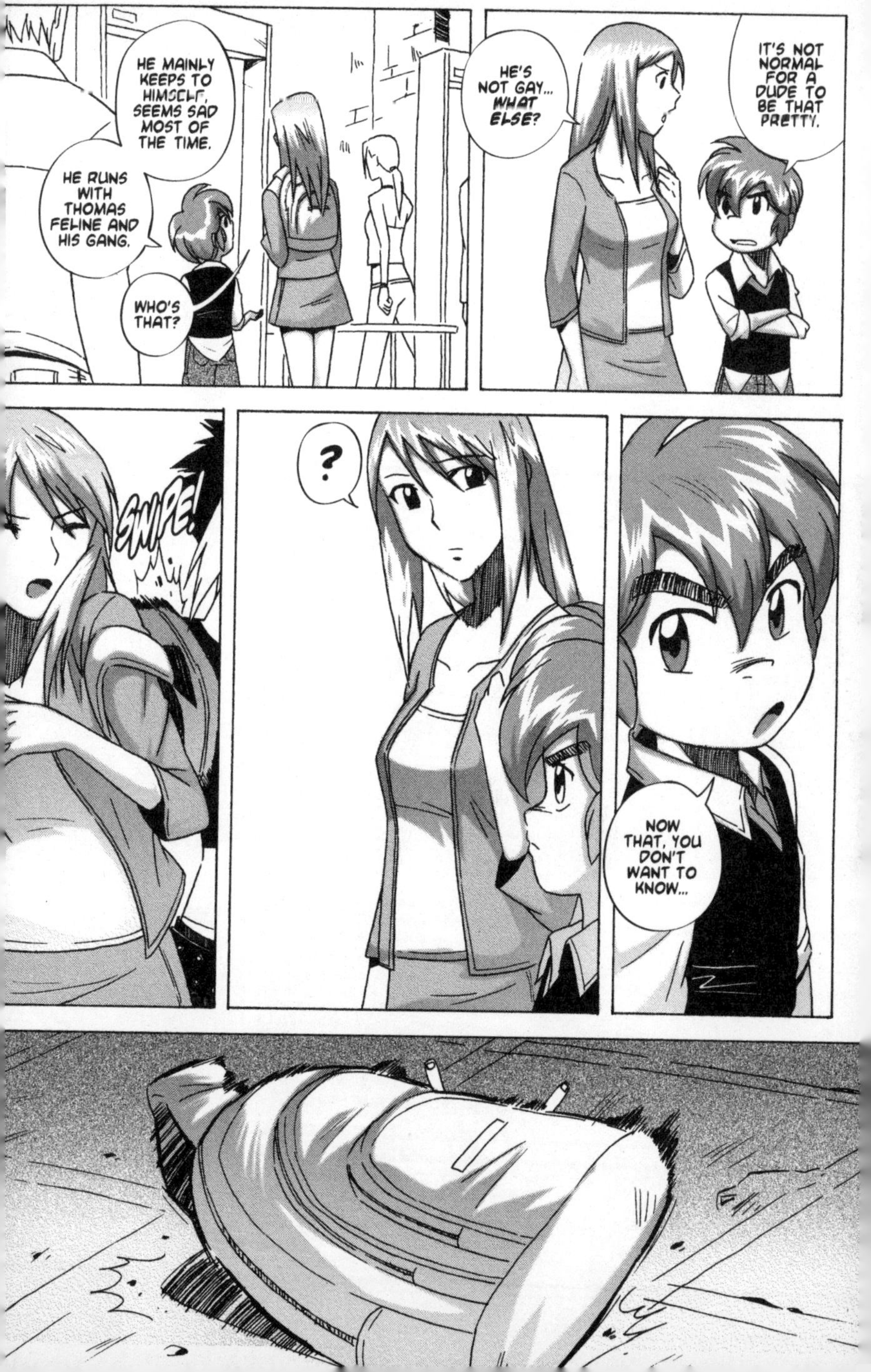
IT'S NOT NORMAL FOR A DUDE TO BE THAT PRETTY.
HE'S NOT GAY... WHAT ELSE?
HE MAINLY KEEPS TO HIMSELF, SEEMS SAD MOST OF THE TIME.
HE RUNS WITH THOMAS FELINE AND HIS GANG.
WHO'S THAT?
NOW THAT, YOU DON'T WANT TO KNOW...
?
SWIPE!

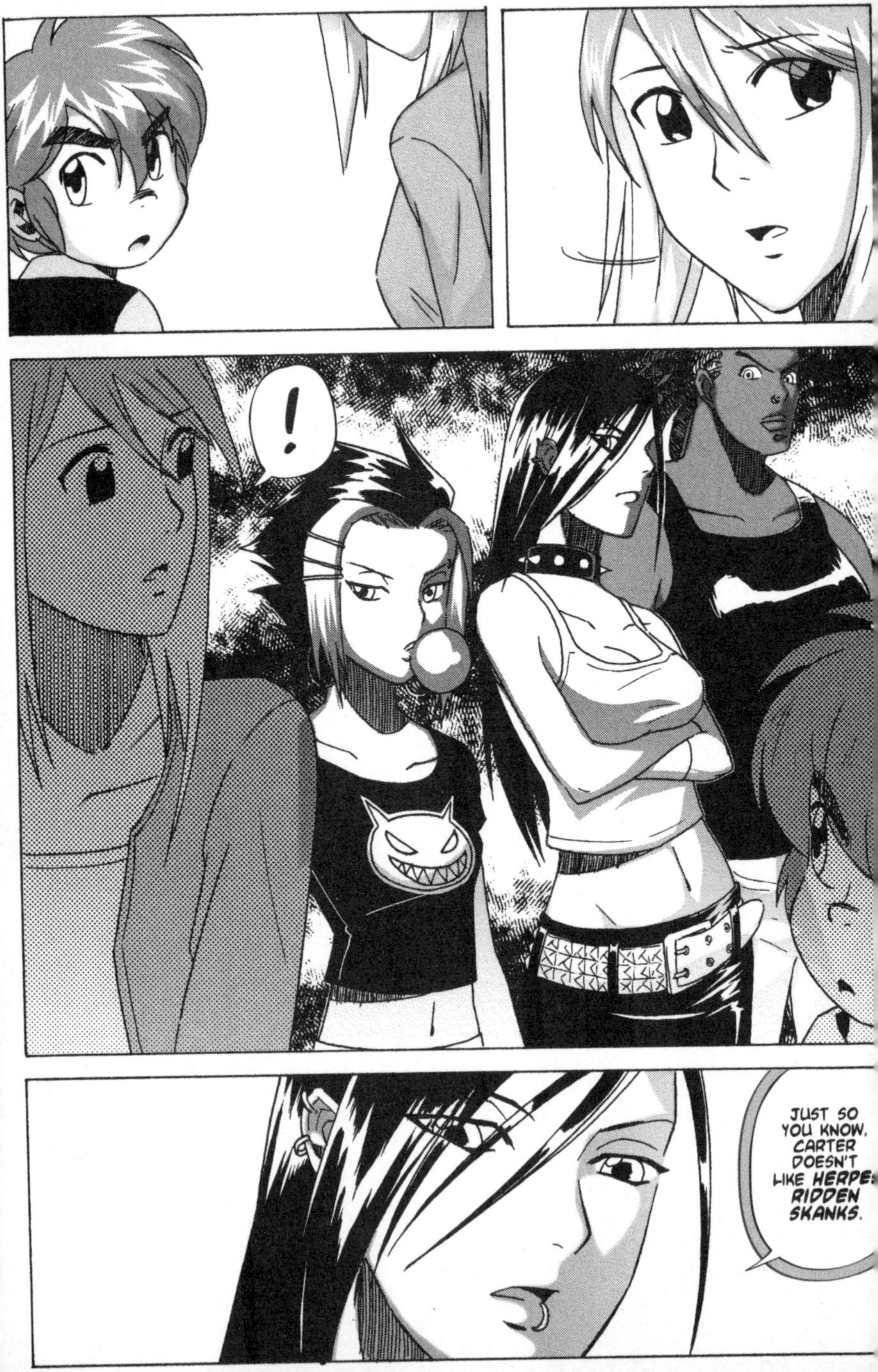
!
JUST SO YOU KNOW, CARTER DOESN'T LIKE HERPE
RIDDEN SKANKS.

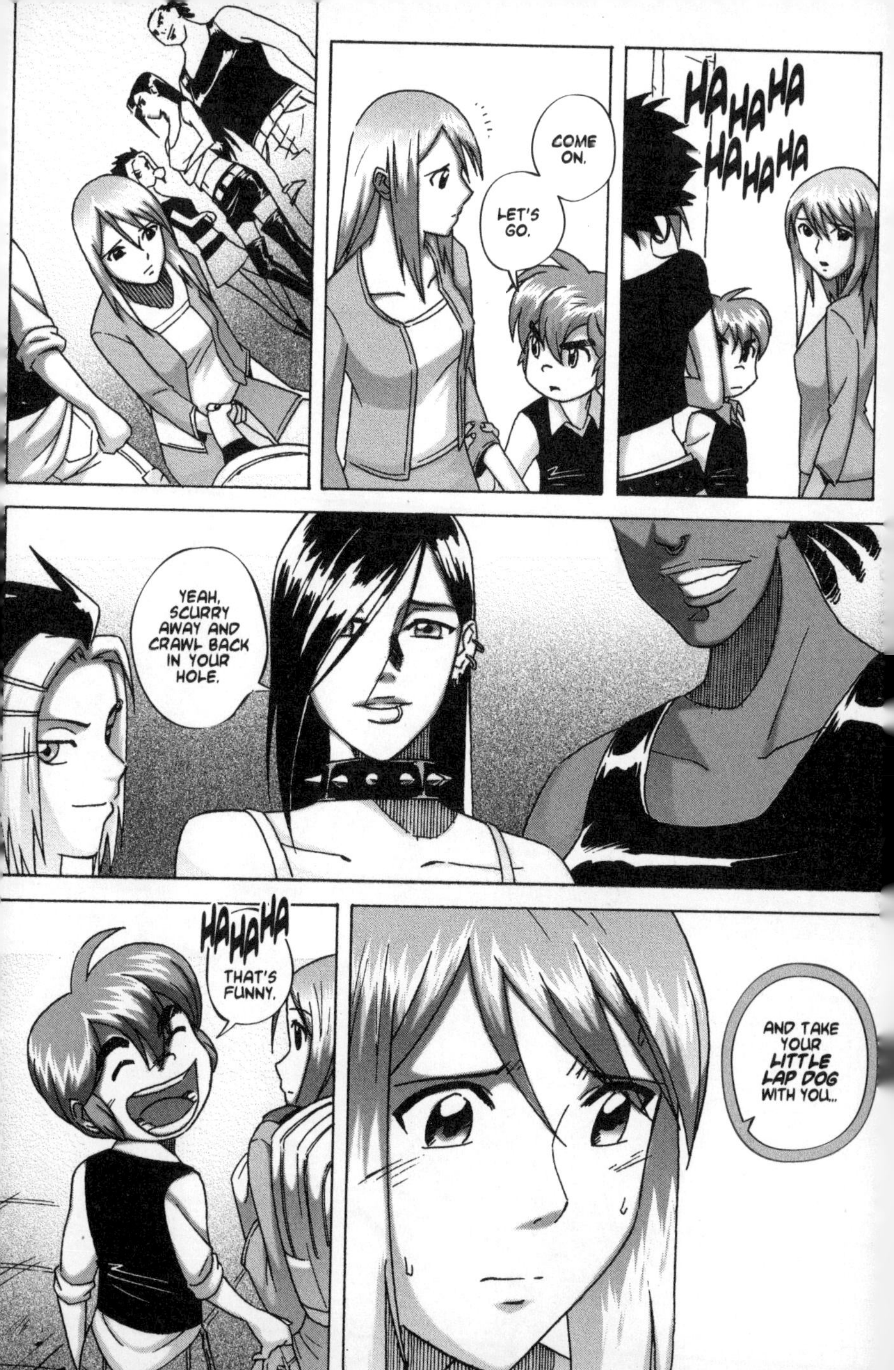
HAHAHA
HAHAHA
COME ON.
LET'S GO.
YEAH, SCURRY AWAY AND CRAWL BACK IN YOUR HOLE.
AND TAKE YOUR LITTLE LAP DOG WITH YOU...
HAHAHA
THAT'S FUNNY.

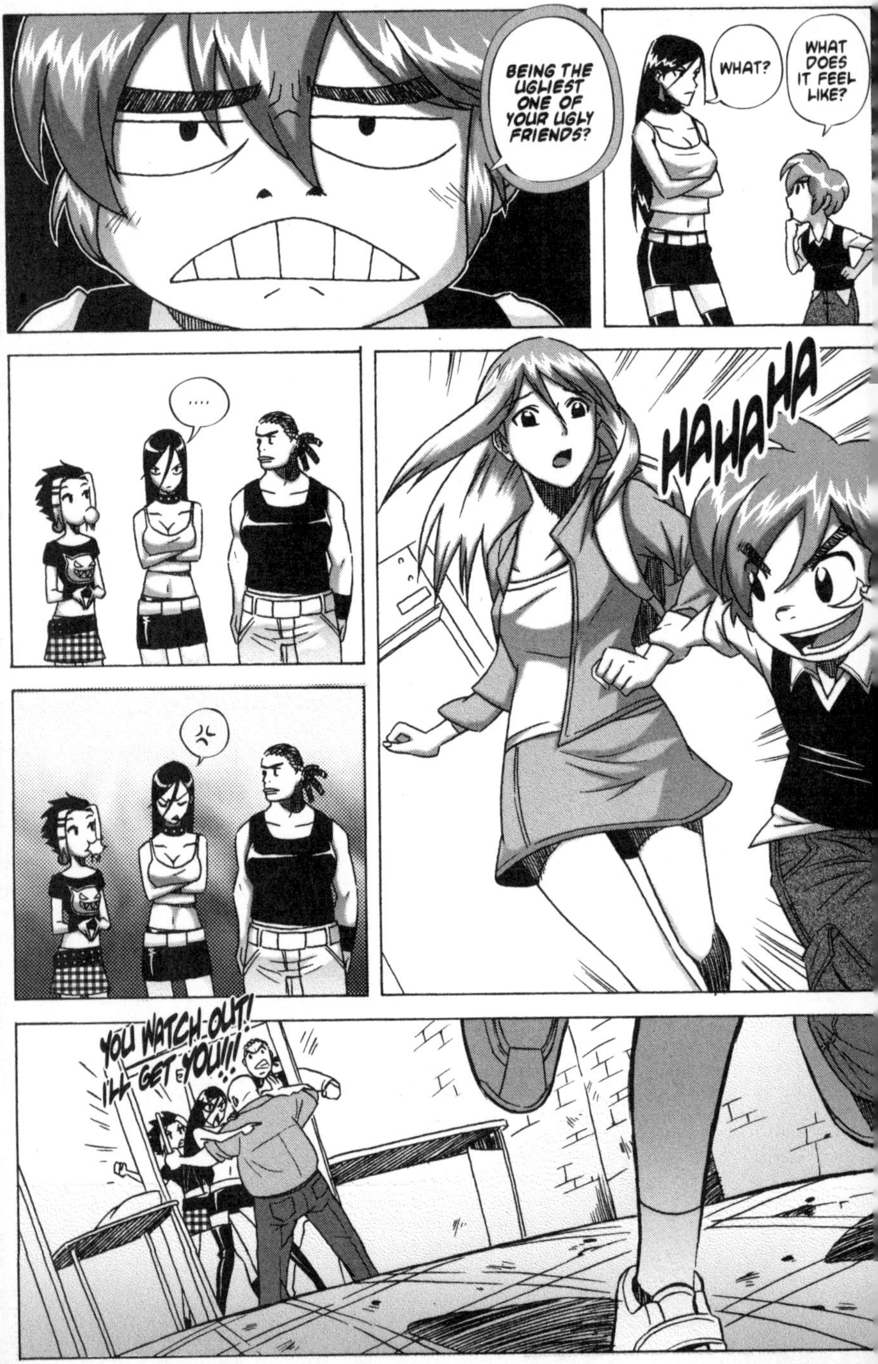
WHAT DOES IT FEEL LIKE?
WHAT?
BEING THE UGLIEST ONE OF YOUR UGLY FRIENDS?
HAHAHA
....
YOU WATCH-OUT! I'LL GET YOU!!!

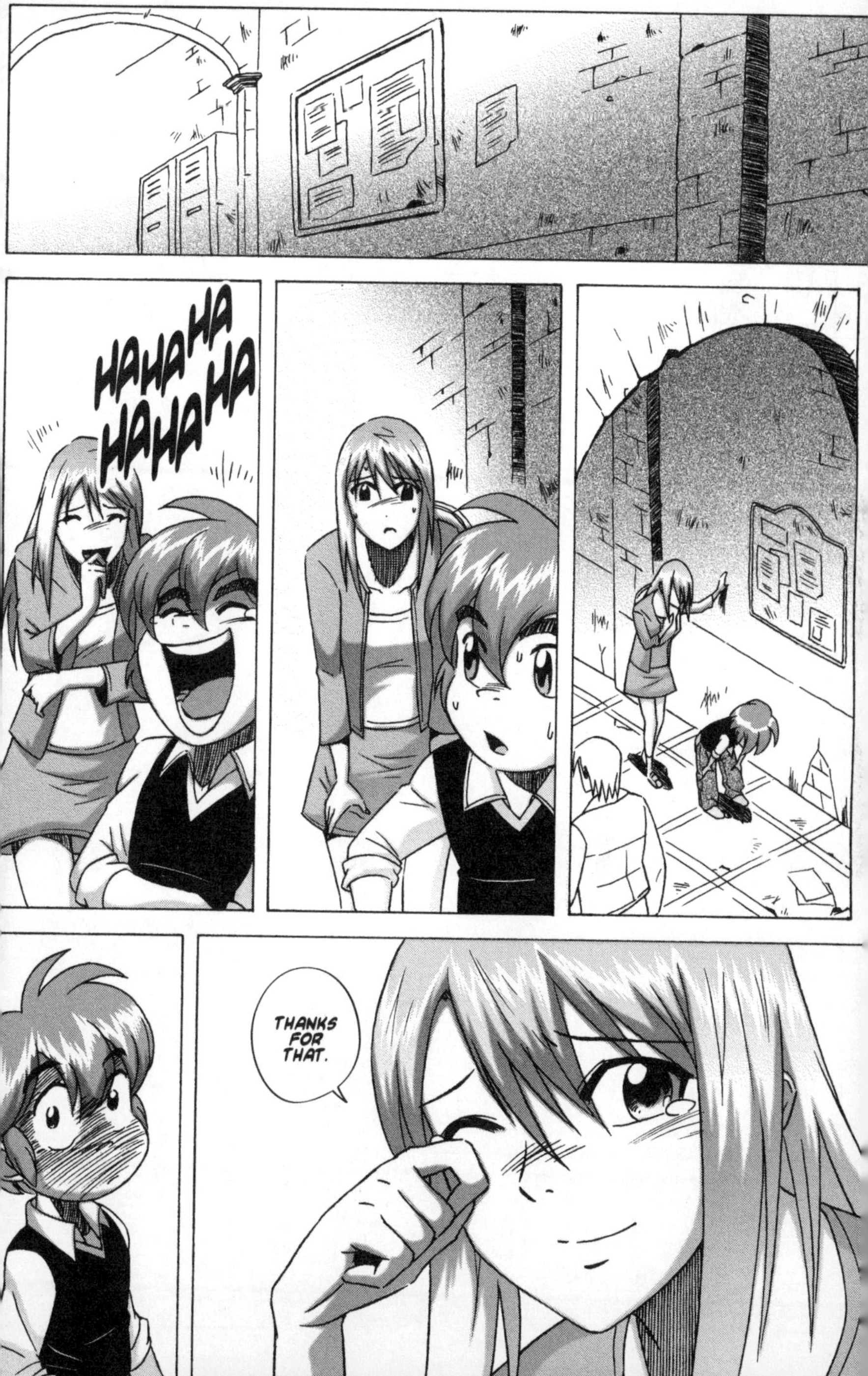
HAHAHA HAHAHA
THANKS FOR THAT.

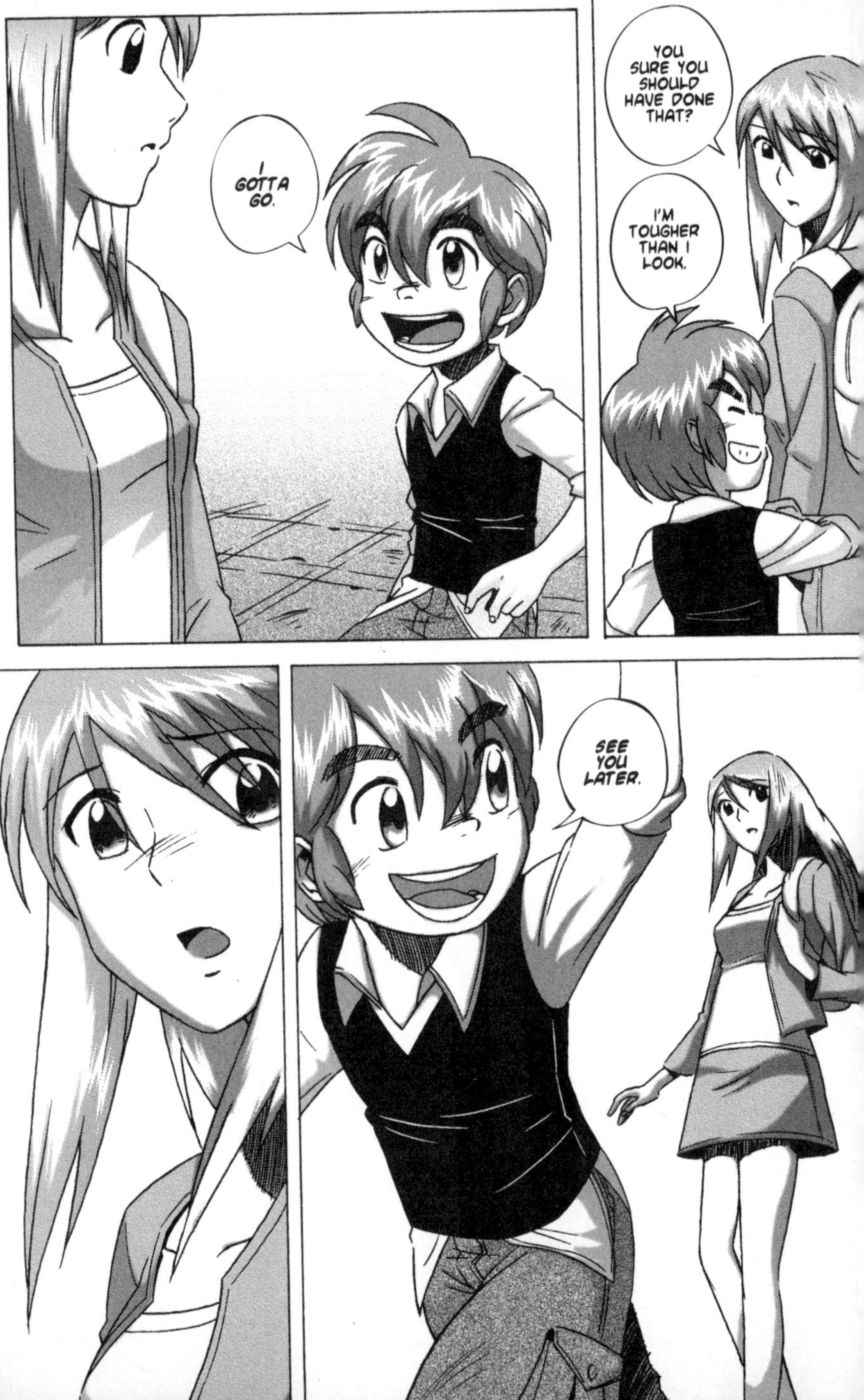
YOU SURE YOU SHOULD HAVE DONE THAT?
I'M TOUGHER THAN I LOOK.
I GOTTA GO.
SEE YOU LATER.

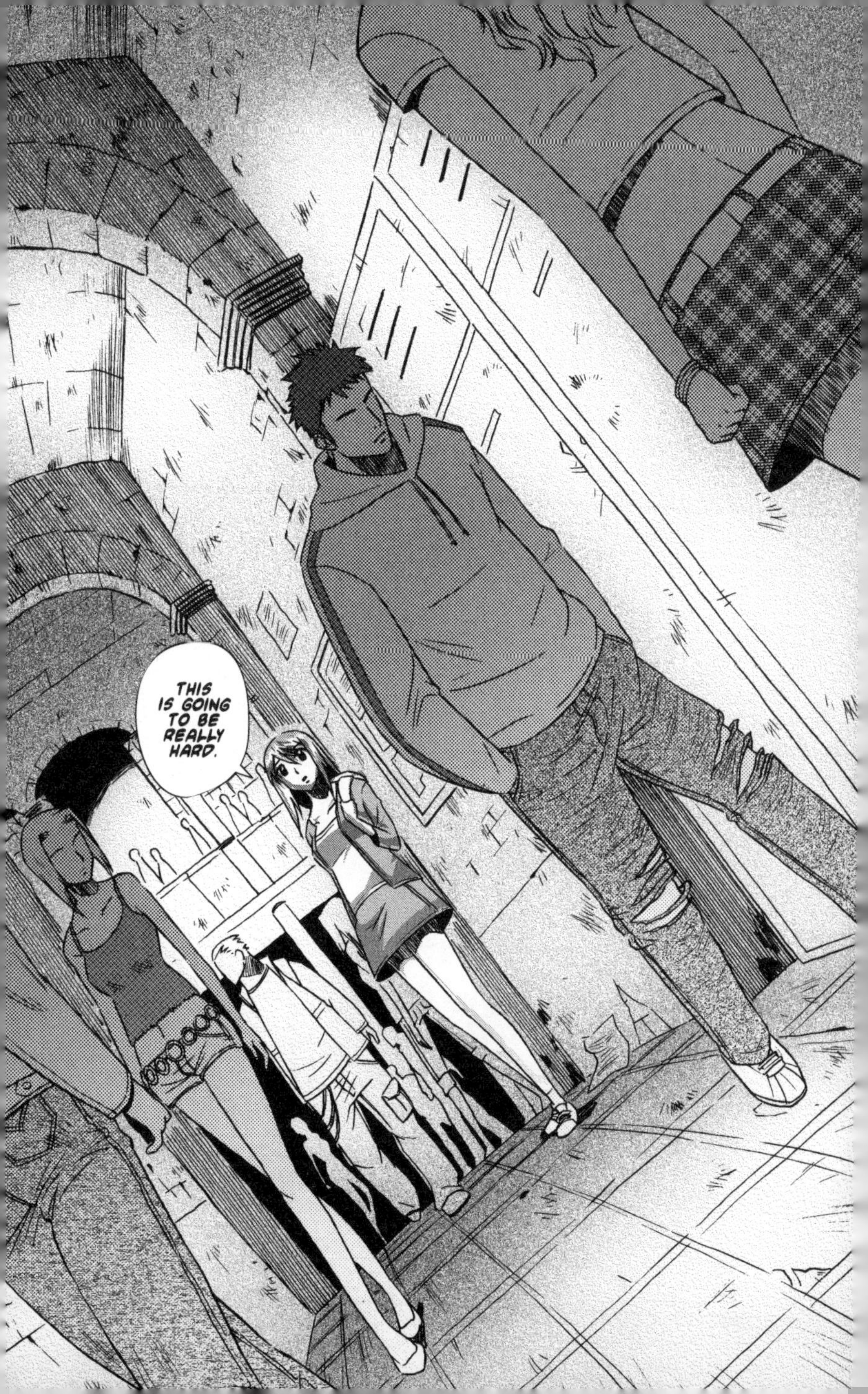
THIS IS GOING TO BE REALLY HARD.

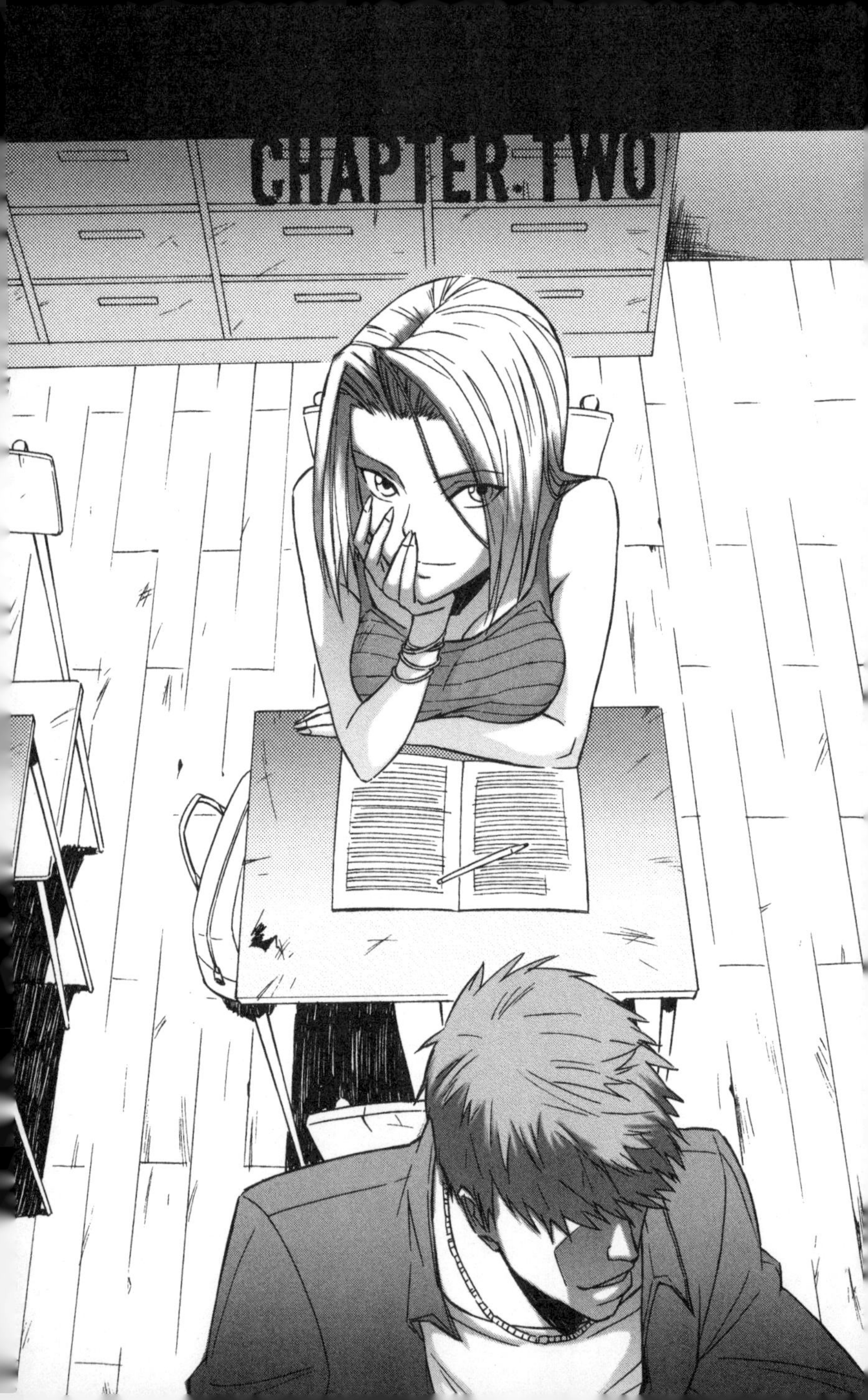
CHAPTER TWO

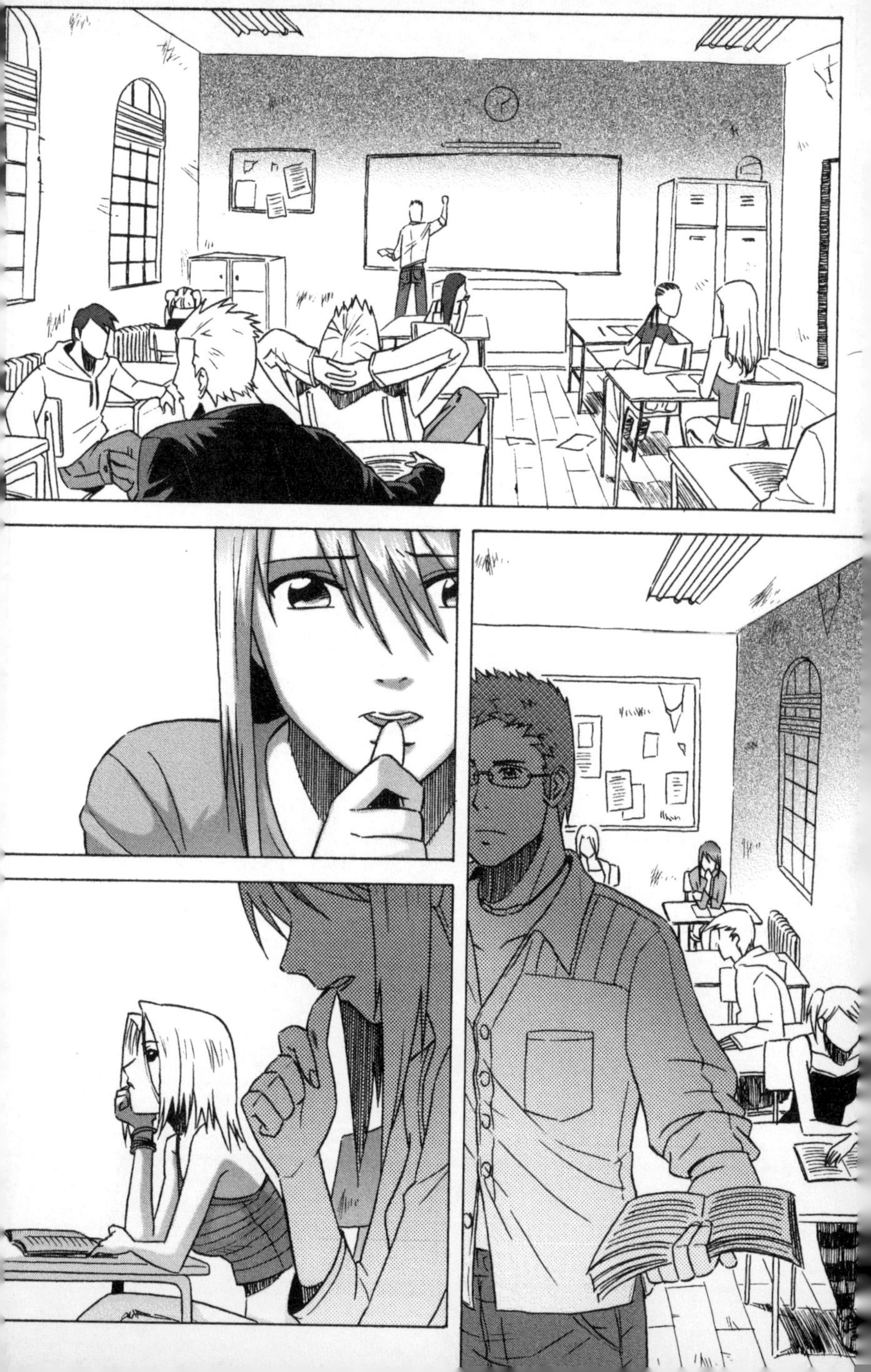

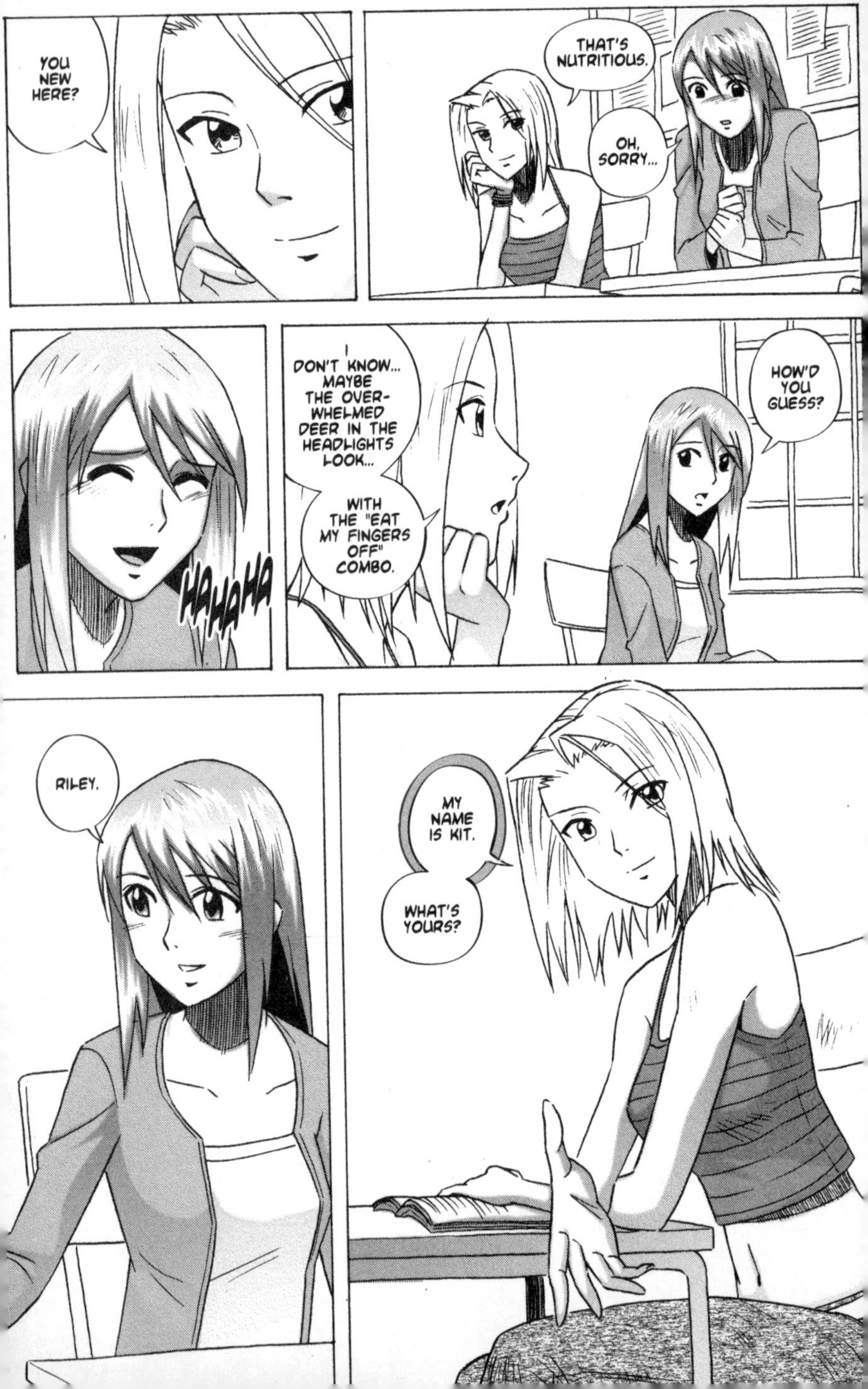
THAT'S NUTRITIOUS.
OH, SORRY...
YOU NEW HERE?
HOW'D YOU GUESS?
I DON'T KNOW... MAYBE THE OVER-WHELMED DEER IN THE HEADLIGHTS LOOK...
WITH THE "EAT MY FINGERS OFF" COMBO.
HAHAHA
MY NAME IS KIT.
WHAT'S YOURS?
RILEY.

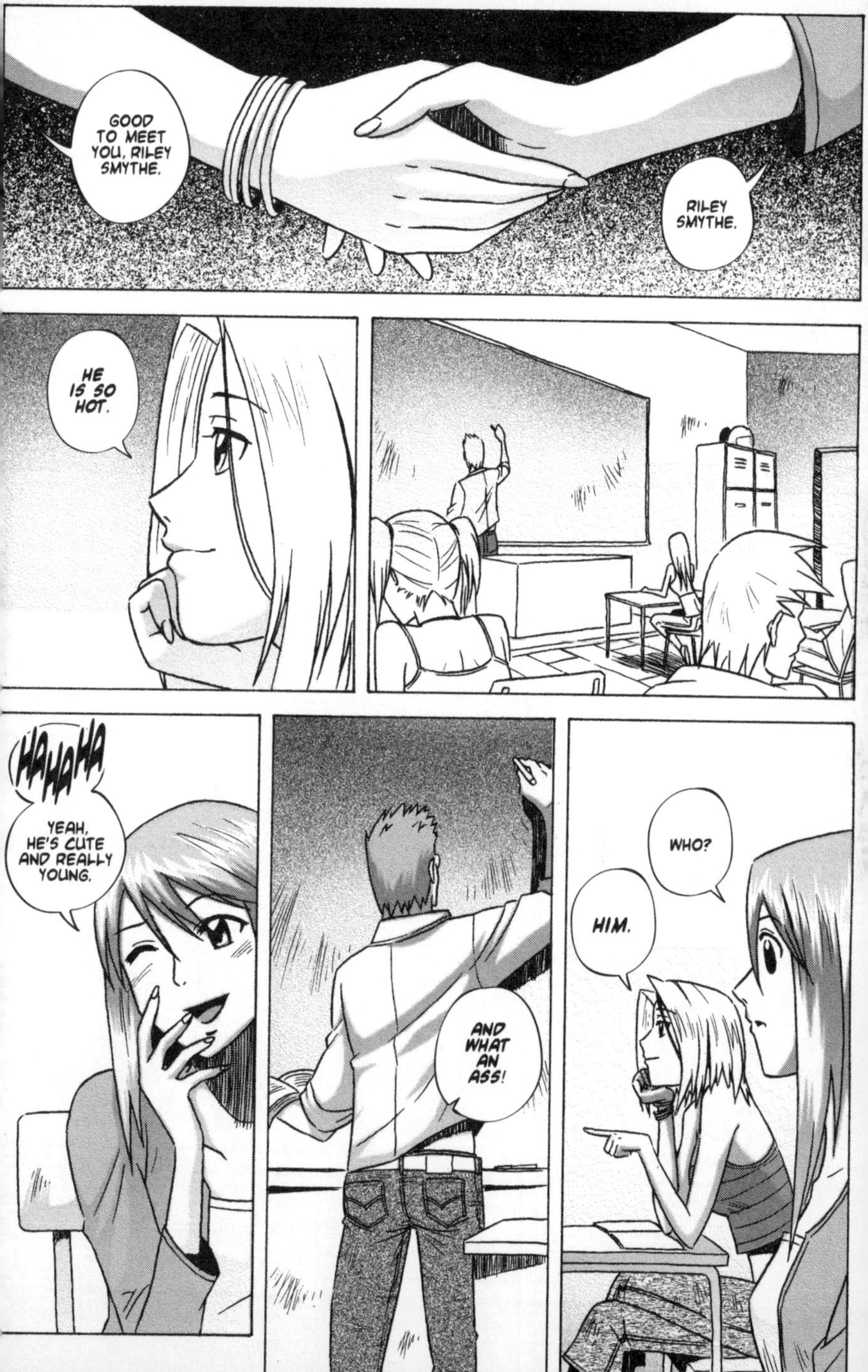
RILEY SMYTHE.
GOOD TO MEET YOU, RILEY SMYTHE.
HE IS SO HOT.
WHO?
HIM.
AND WHAT AN ASS!
HAHAHA
YEAH, HE'S CUTE AND REALLY YOUNG.

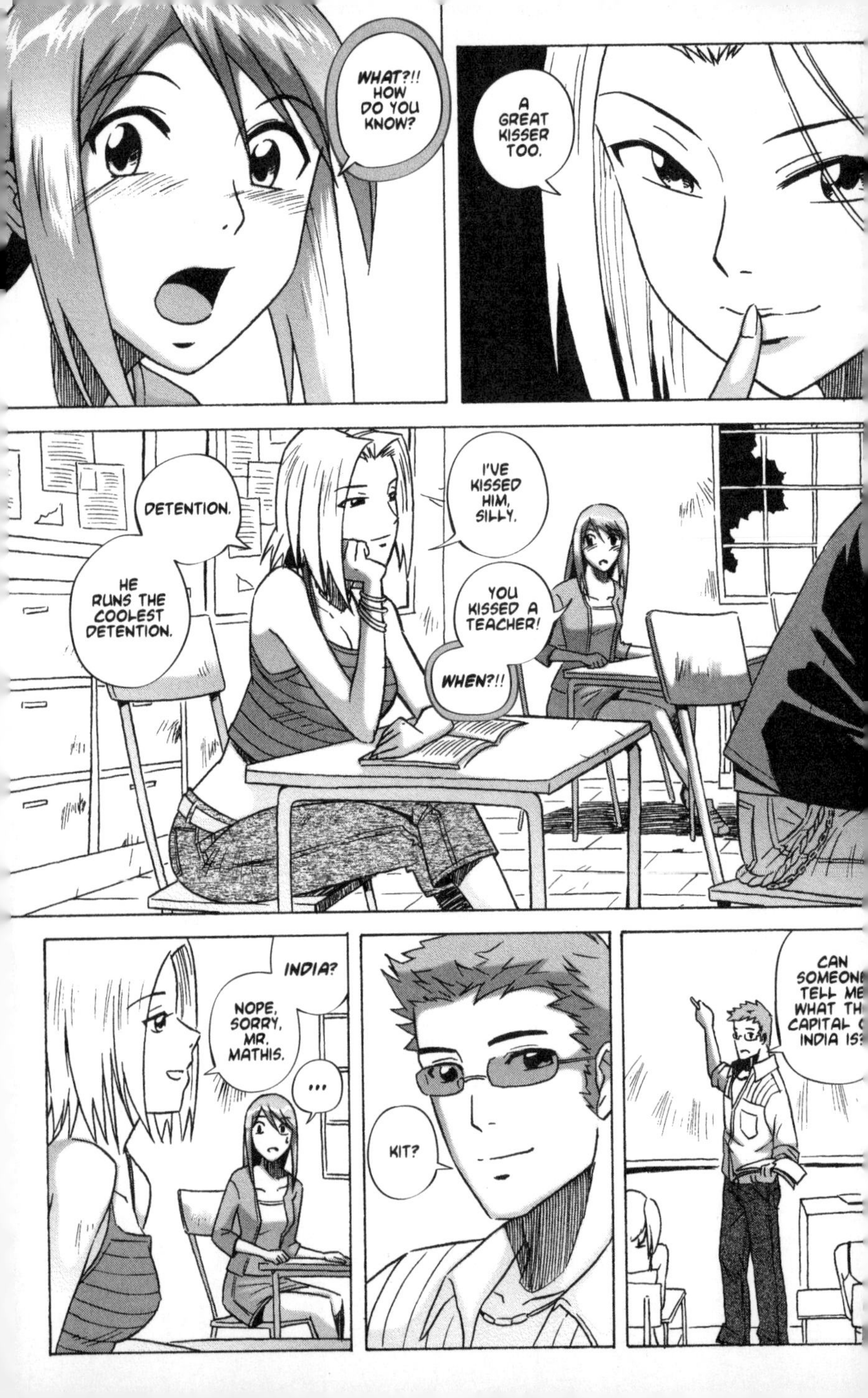
A GREAT KISSER TOO.
WHAT?!! HOW DO YOU KNOW?
I'VE KISSED HIM, SILLY.
YOU KISSED A TEACHER!
WHEN?!!
DETENTION.
HE RUNS THE COOLEST DETENTION.
CAN SOMEONE TELL ME WHAT TH CAPITAL INDIA IS?
KIT?
INDIA?
NOPE, SORRY, MR. MATHIS.
...

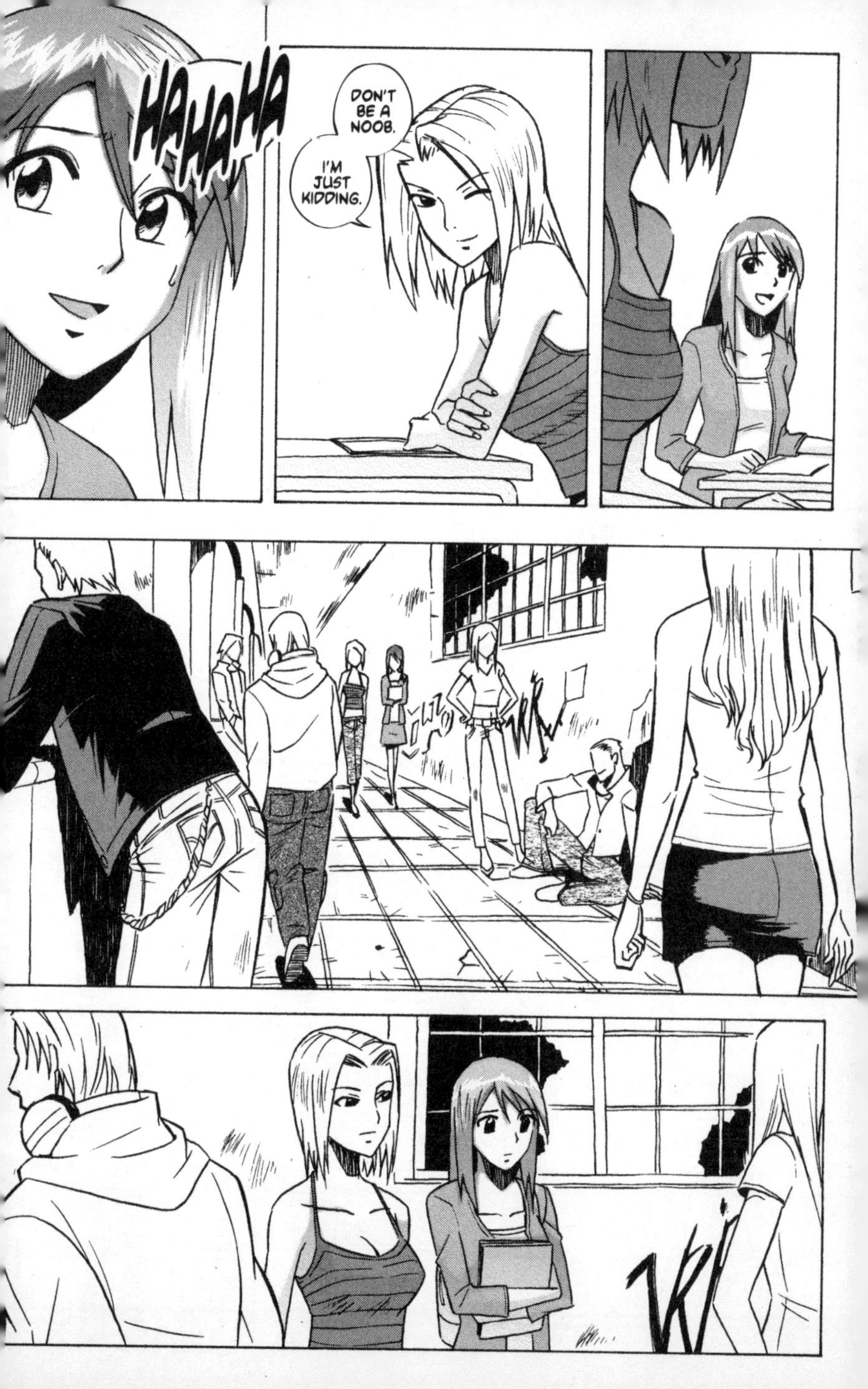
DON'T BE A NOOB.
I'M JUST KIDDING.
HAHAHA

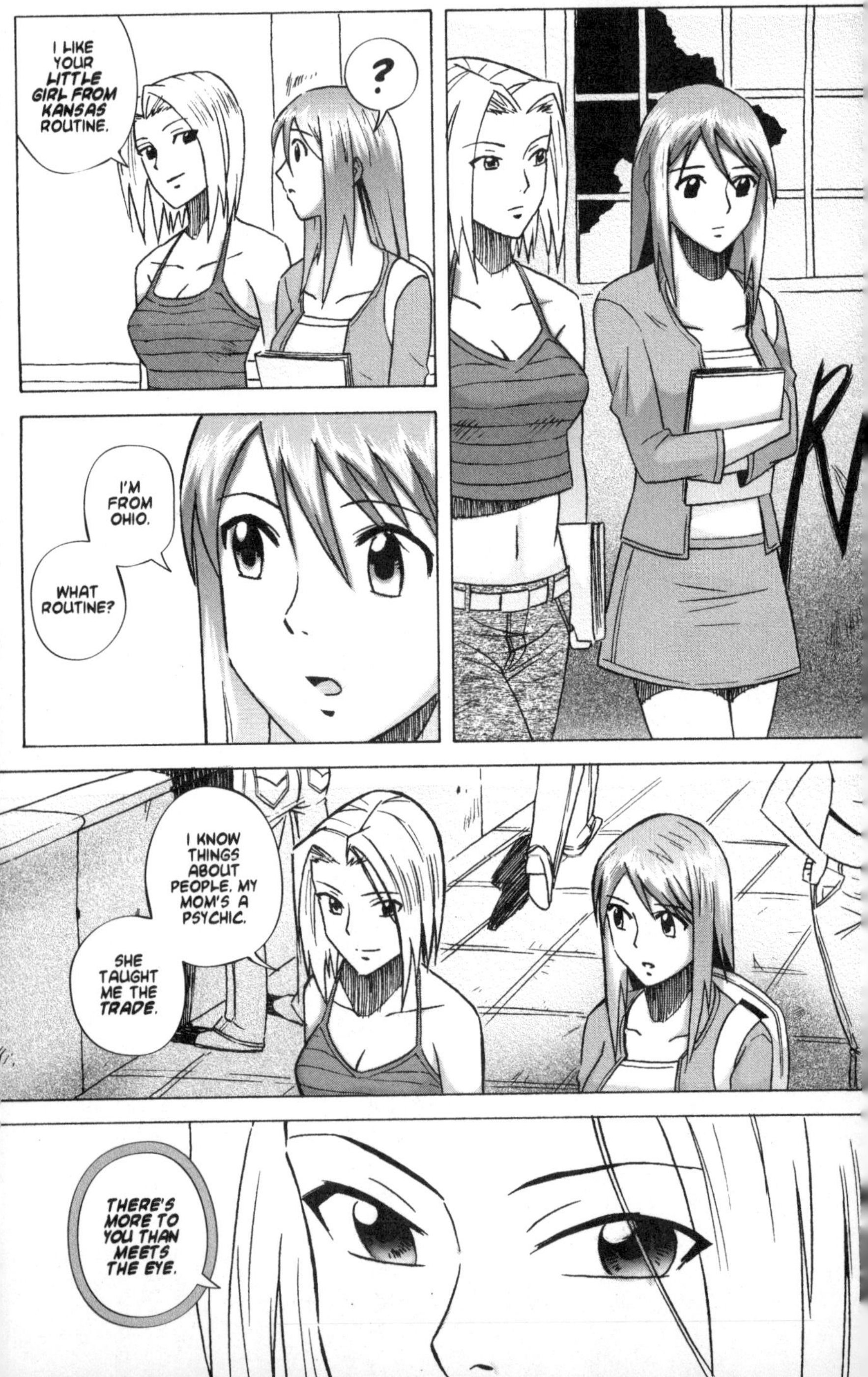
I LIKE YOUR LITTLE GIRL FROM KANSAS ROUTINE.
?
I'M FROM OHIO.
WHAT ROUTINE?
I KNOW THINGS ABOUT PEOPLE. MY MOM'S A PSYCHIC.
SHE TAUGHT ME THE TRADE.
THERE'S MORE TO YOU THAN MEETS THE EYE.

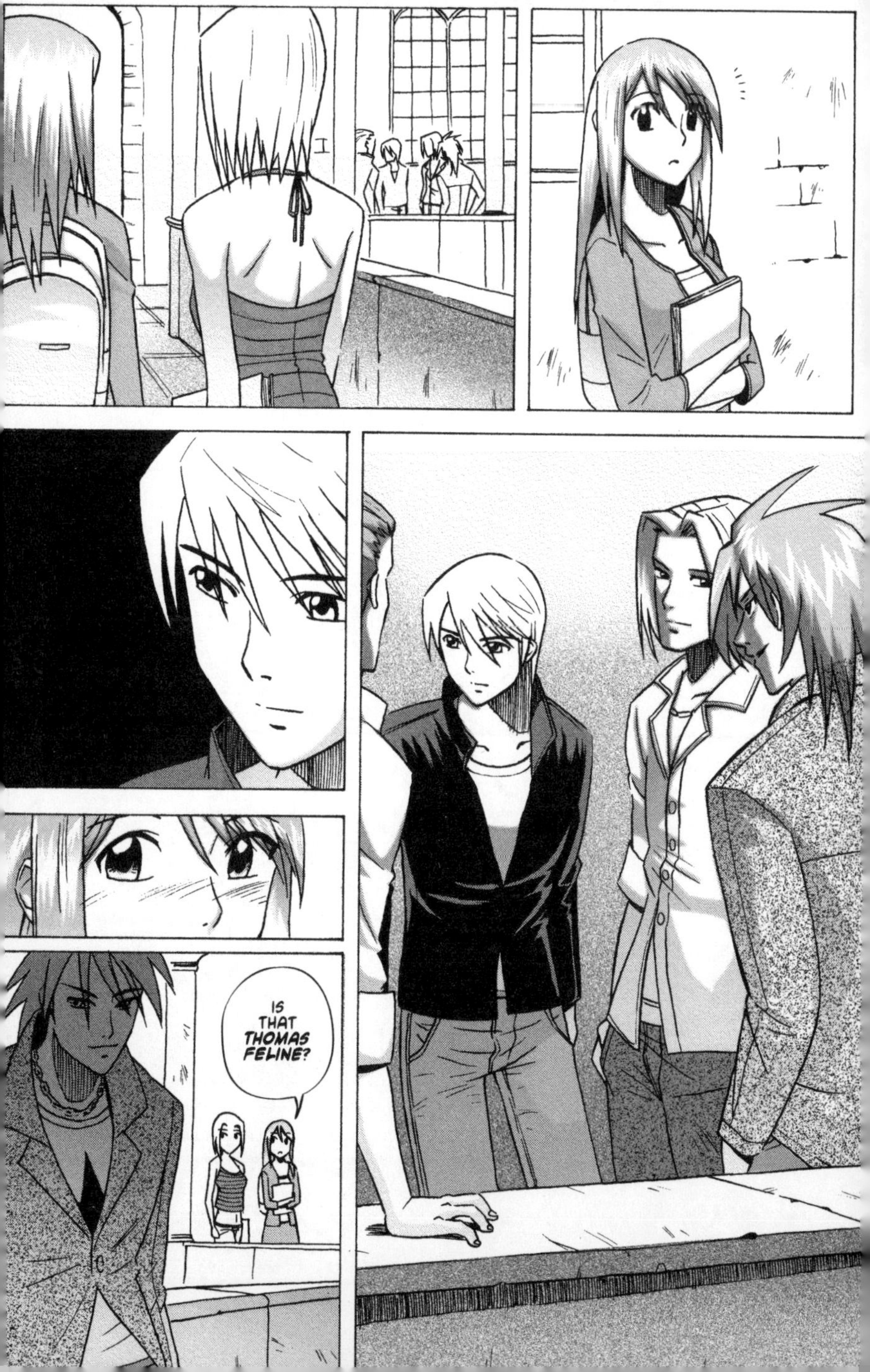
IS THAT THOMAS FELINE?

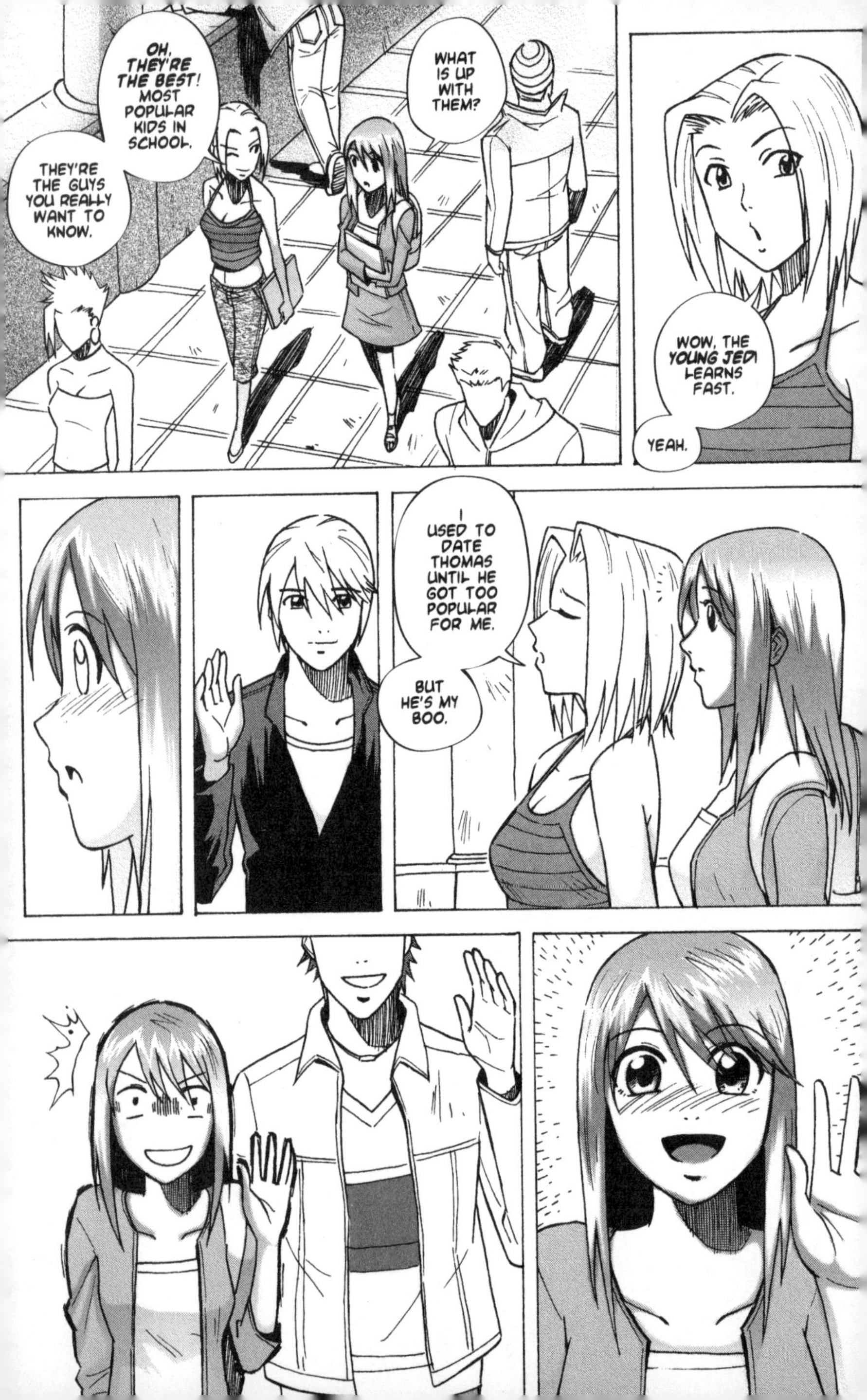
WHAT IS UP WITH THEM?
OH, THEY'RE THE BEST! MOST POPULAR KIDS IN SCHOOL.
THEY'RE THE GUYS YOU REALLY WANT TO KNOW.
WOW, THE YOUNG JEDI LEARNS FAST.
YEAH.
I USED TO DATE THOMAS UNTIL HE GOT TOO POPULAR FOR ME.
BUT HE'S MY BOO.

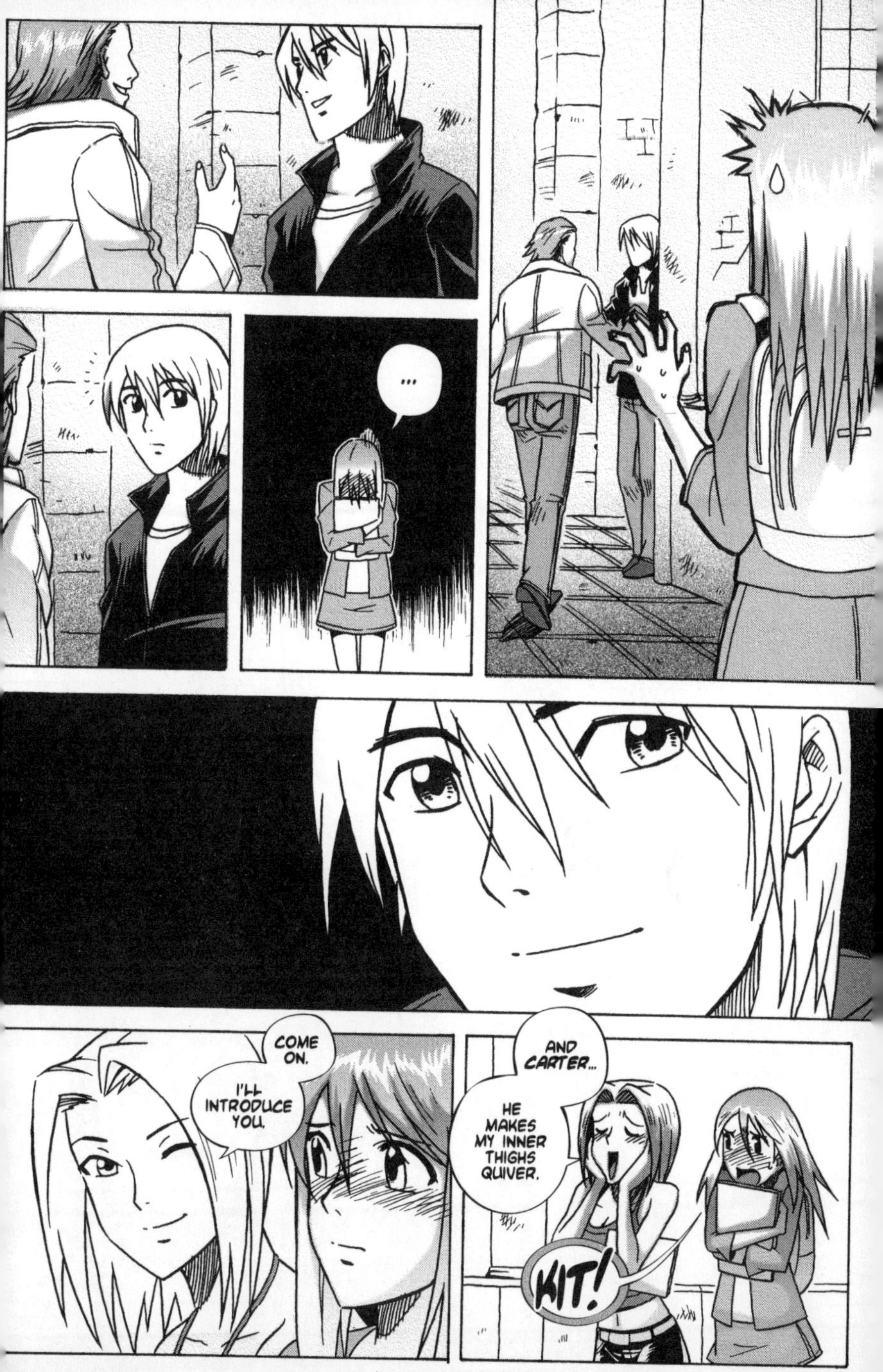
...
AND CARTER...
HE MAKES MY INNER THIGHS QUIVER.
KIT!
COME ON.
I'LL INTRODUCE YOU.

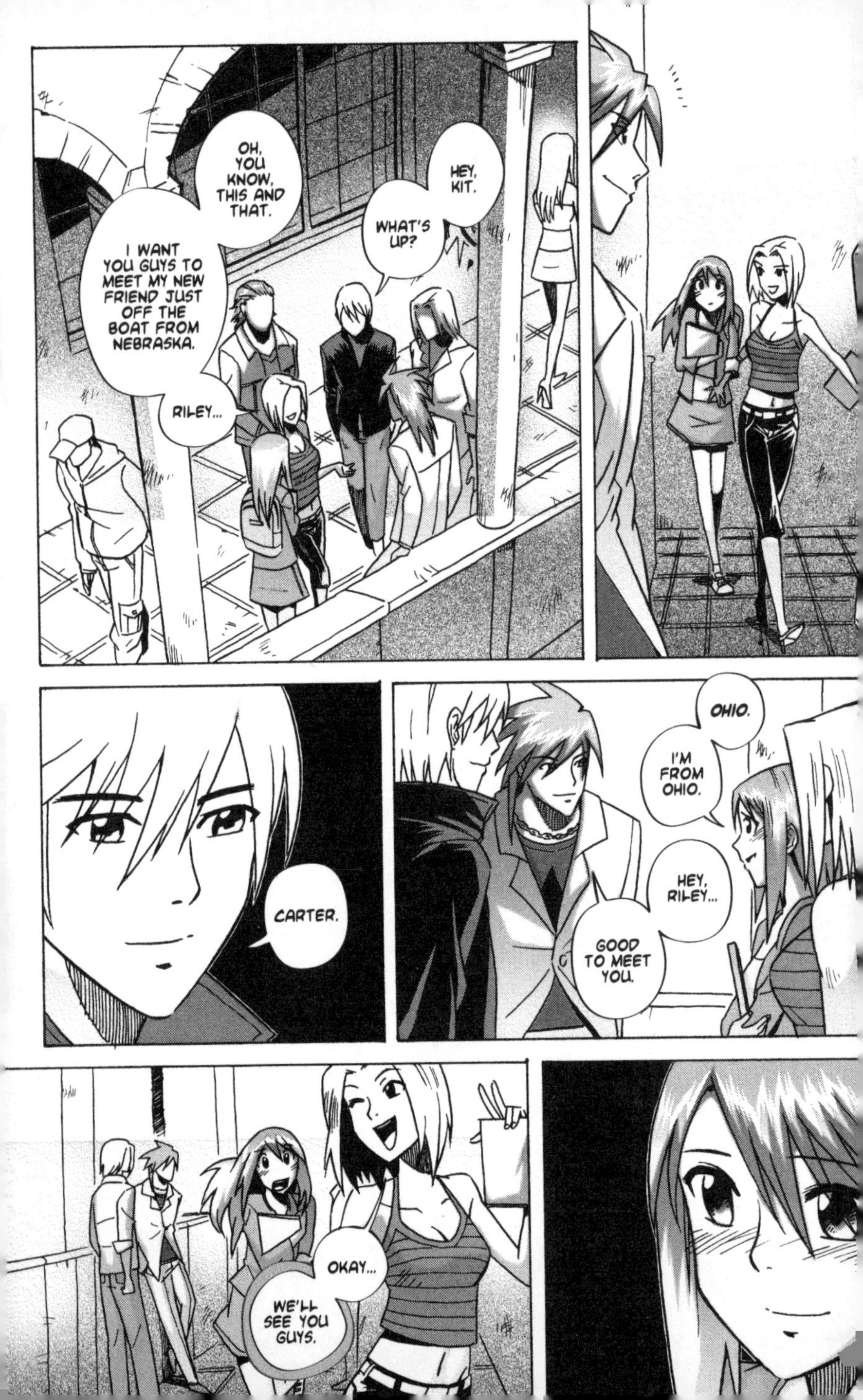
HEY, KIT.
WHAT'S UP?
OH, YOU KNOW, THIS AND THAT.
I WANT YOU GUYS TO MEET MY NEW FRIEND JUST OFF THE BOAT FROM NEBRASKA.
RILEY...
OHIO.
I'M FROM OHIO.
HEY, RILEY...
GOOD TO MEET YOU.
CARTER.
OKAY...
WE'LL SEE YOU GUYS.

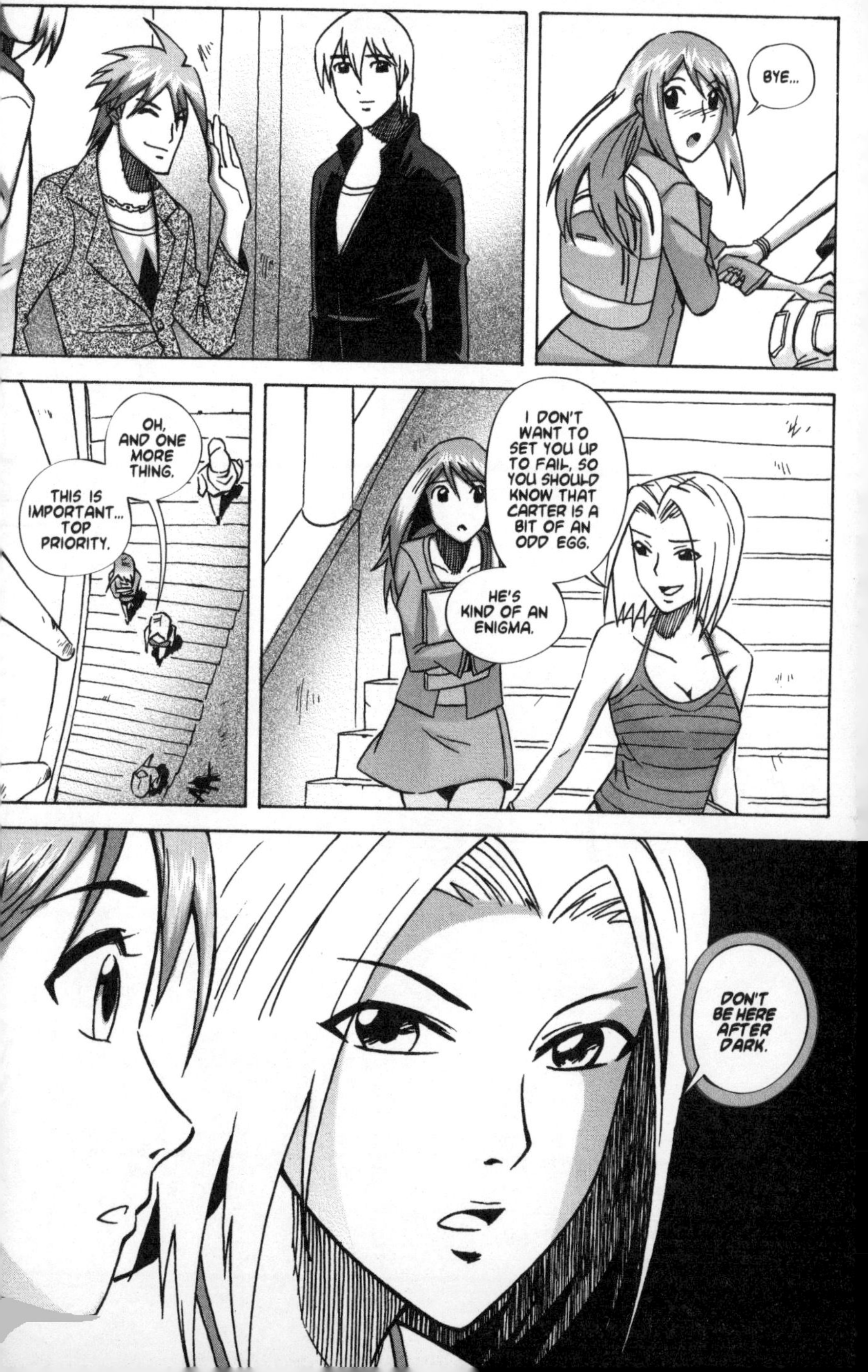
BYE...
I DON'T WANT TO SET YOU UP TO FAIL, SO YOU SHOULD KNOW THAT CARTER IS A BIT OF AN ODD EGG.
HE'S KIND OF AN ENIGMA.
OH, AND ONE MORE THING.
THIS IS IMPORTANT... TOP PRIORITY.
DON'T BE HERE AFTER DARK.

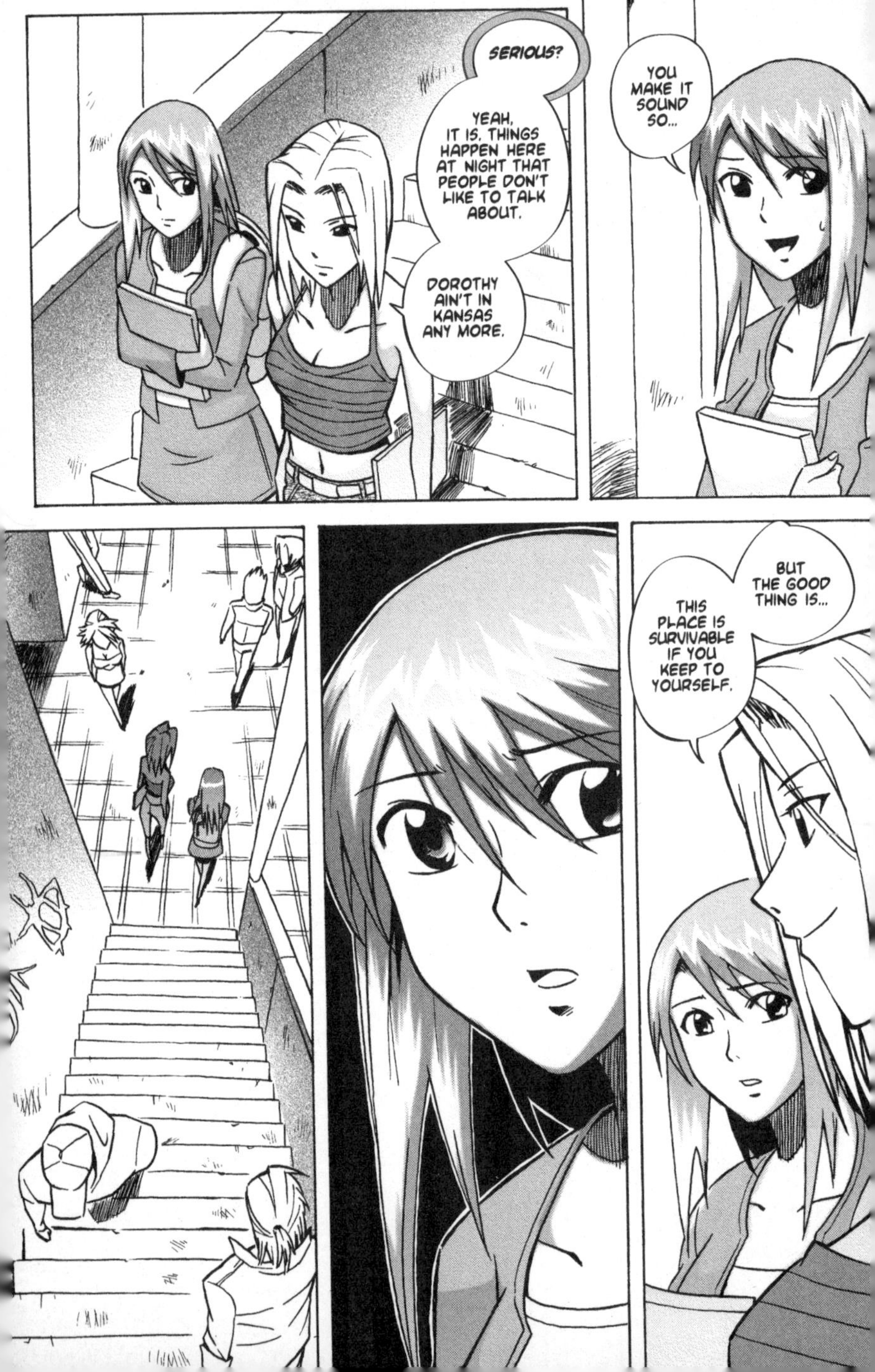
YOU MAKE IT SOUND SO...
SERIOUS?
YEAH, IT IS. THINGS HAPPEN HERE AT NIGHT THAT PEOPLE DON'T LIKE TO TALK ABOUT.
DOROTHY AIN'T IN KANSAS ANY MORE.
BUT THE GOOD THING IS...
THIS PLACE IS SURVIVABLE IF YOU KEEP TO YOURSELF.

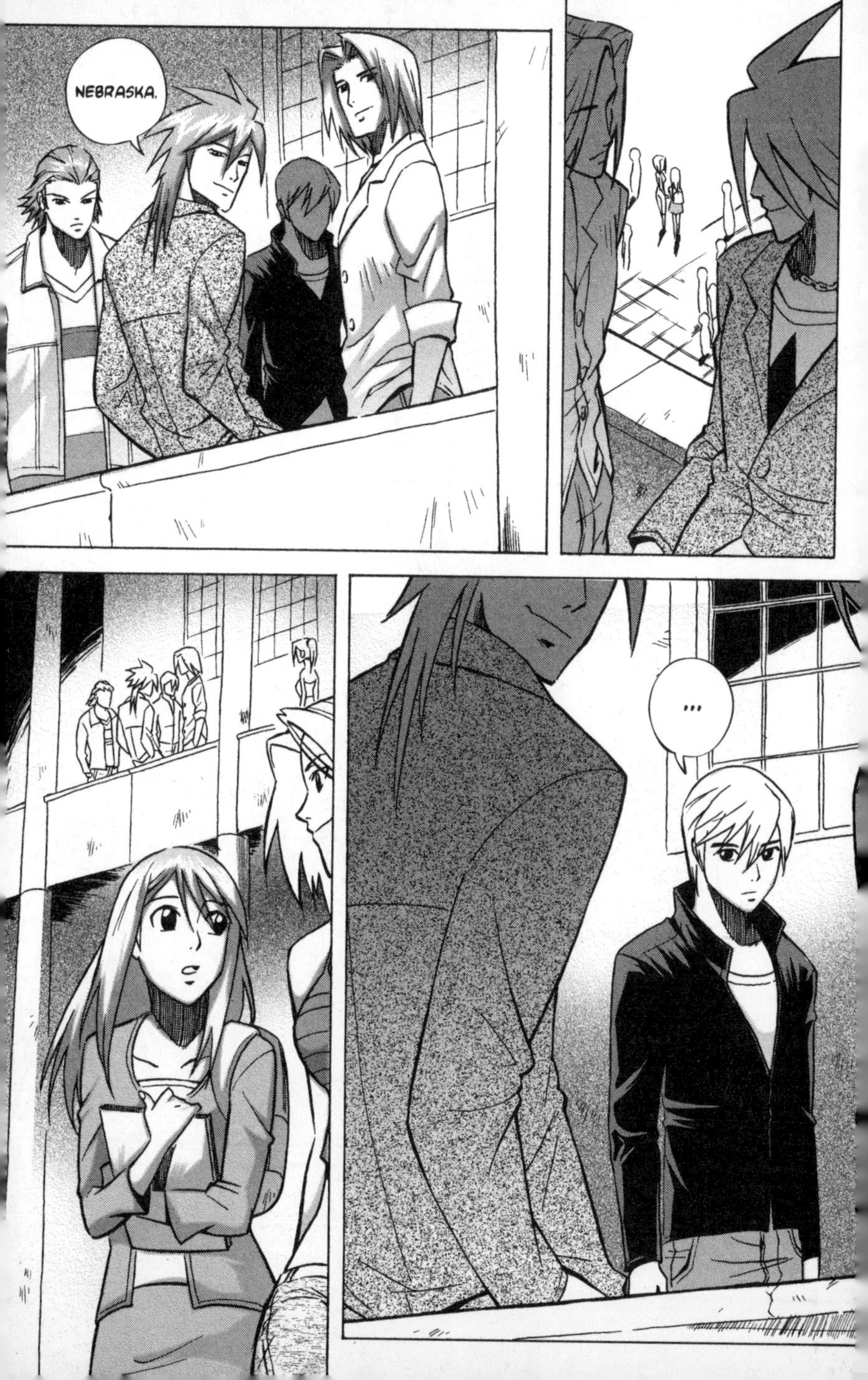
NEBRASKA.
...

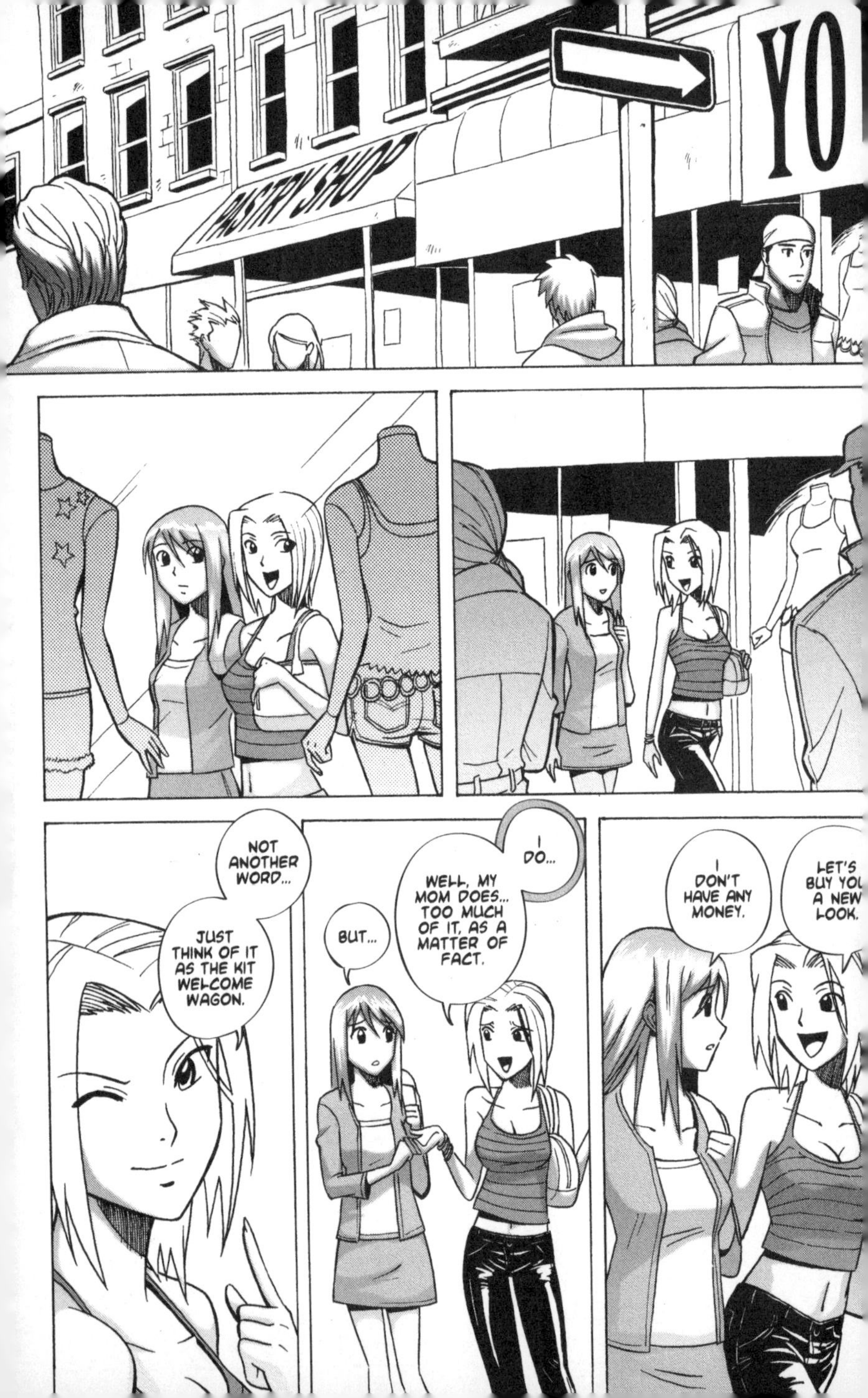
YO
PASTRY SHOP
LET'S BUY YOU A NEW LOOK.
I DON'T HAVE ANY MONEY.
I DO...
WELL, MY MOM DOES... TOO MUCH OF IT, AS A MATTER OF FACT.
BUT...
NOT ANOTHER WORD...
JUST THINK OF IT AS THE KIT WELCOME WAGON.

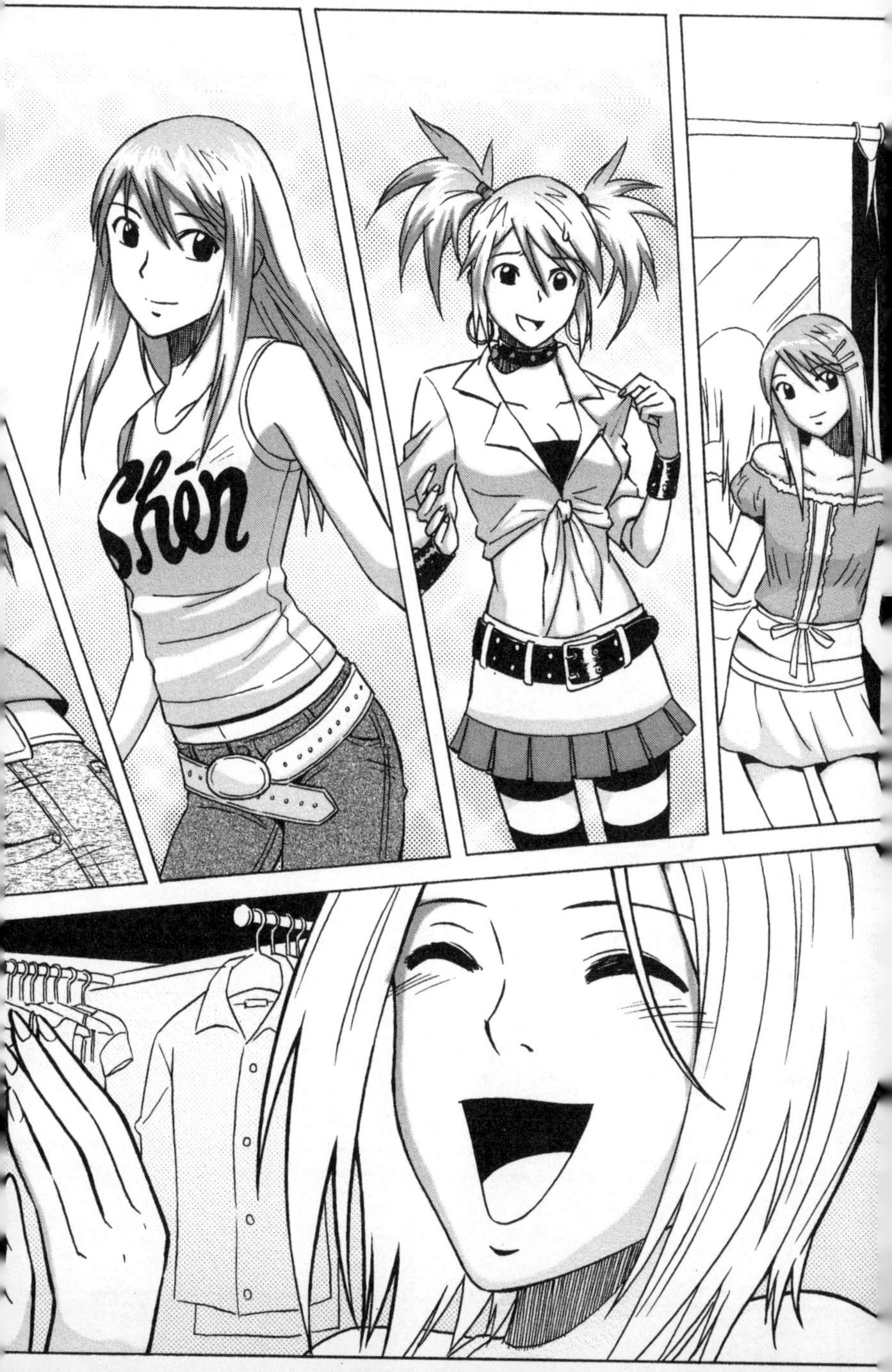
Chén

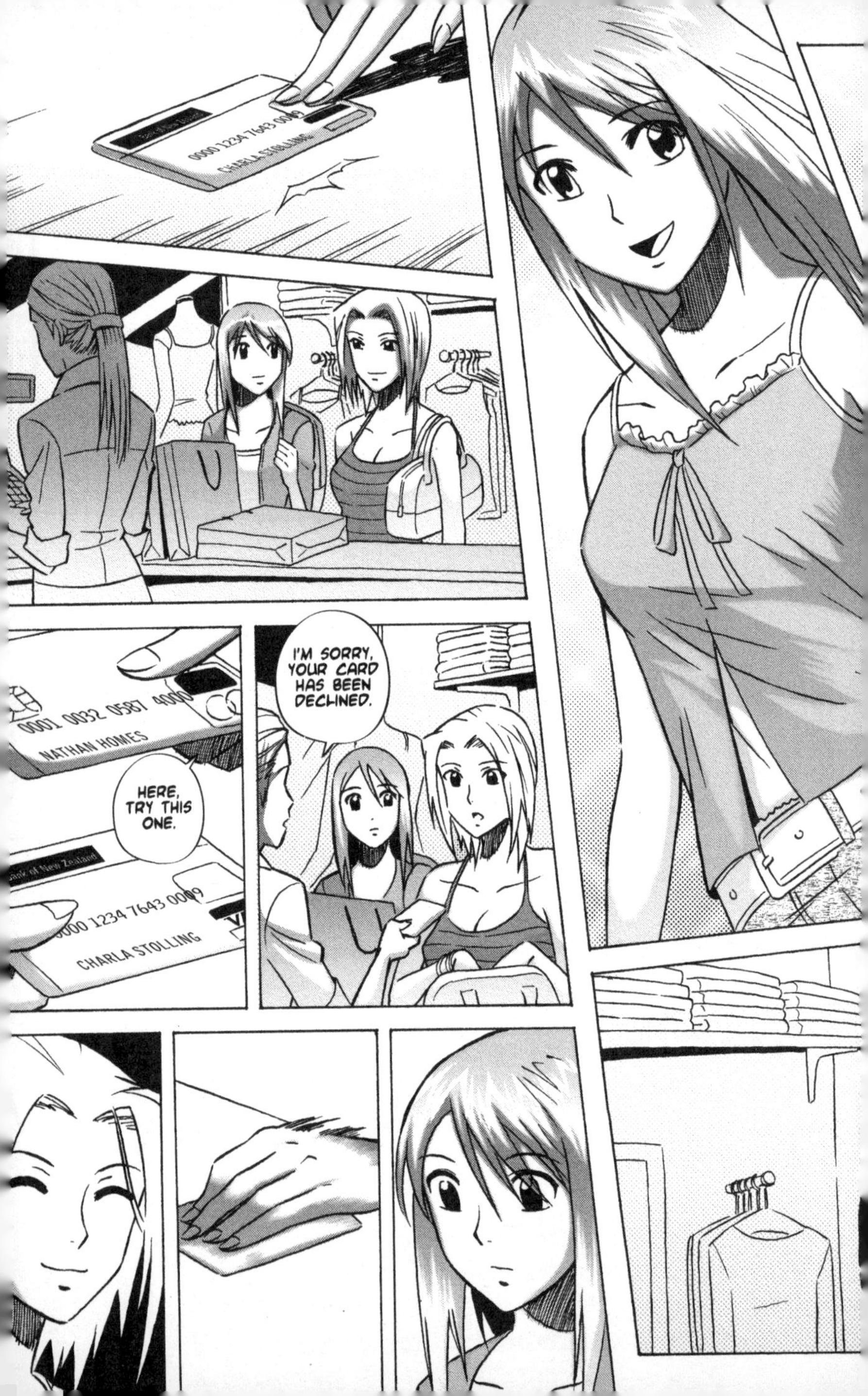
0000 1234 7643 0009
CHARLA STOLLING
I'M SORRY, YOUR CARD HAS BEEN DECLINED.
0001 0032 0587 4000
NATHAN HOMES
HERE, TRY THIS ONE.
Bank of New Zealand
0000 1234 7643 0009
CHARLA STOLLING

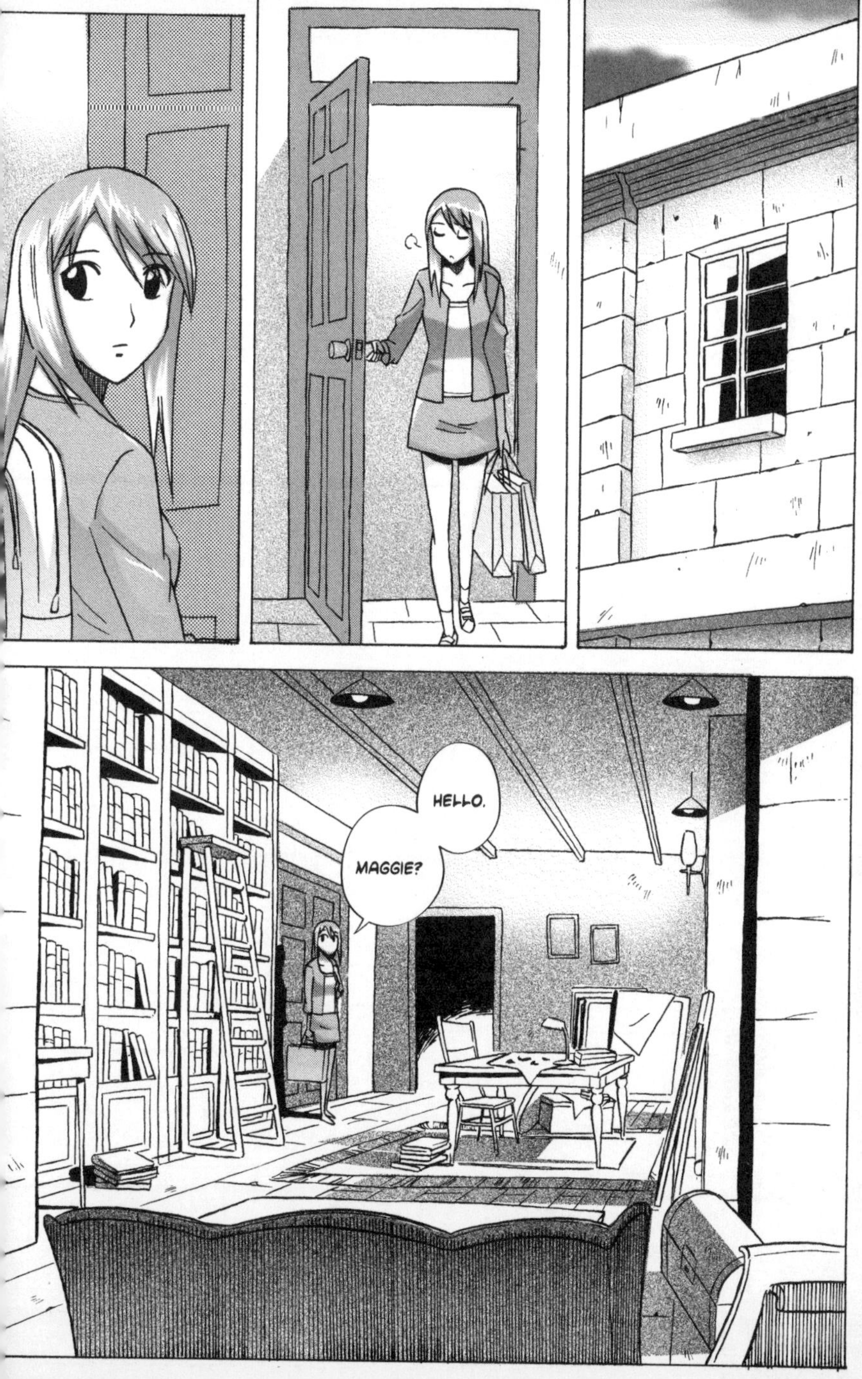
HELLO.
MAGGIE?

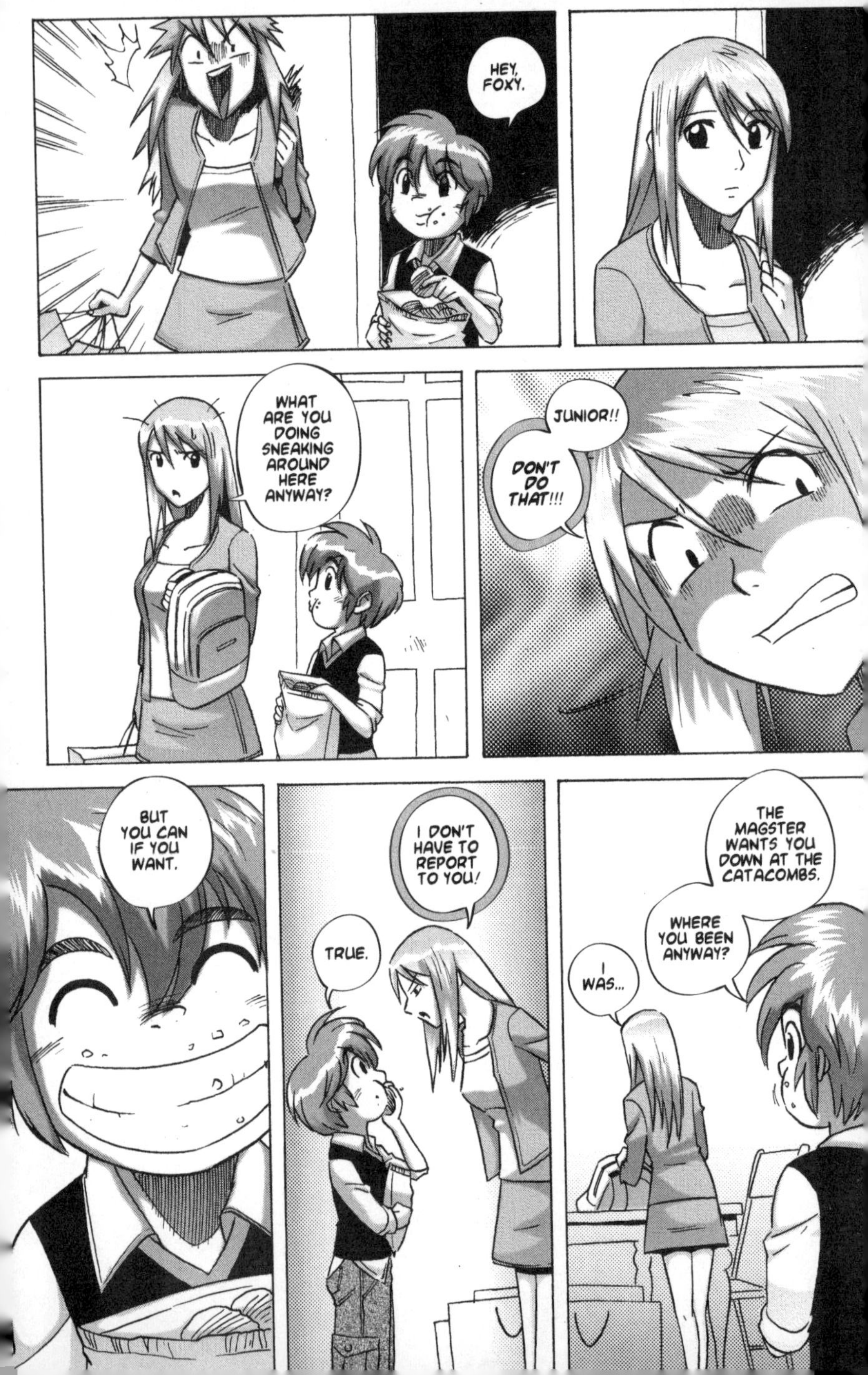
HEY, FOXY.
JUNIOR!!
DON'T DO THAT!!!
WHAT ARE YOU DOING SNEAKING AROUND HERE ANYWAY?
THE MAGSTER WANTS YOU DOWN AT THE CATACOMBS.
WHERE YOU BEEN ANYWAY?
I WAS...
I DON'T HAVE TO REPORT TO YOU!
TRUE.
BUT YOU CAN IF YOU WANT.

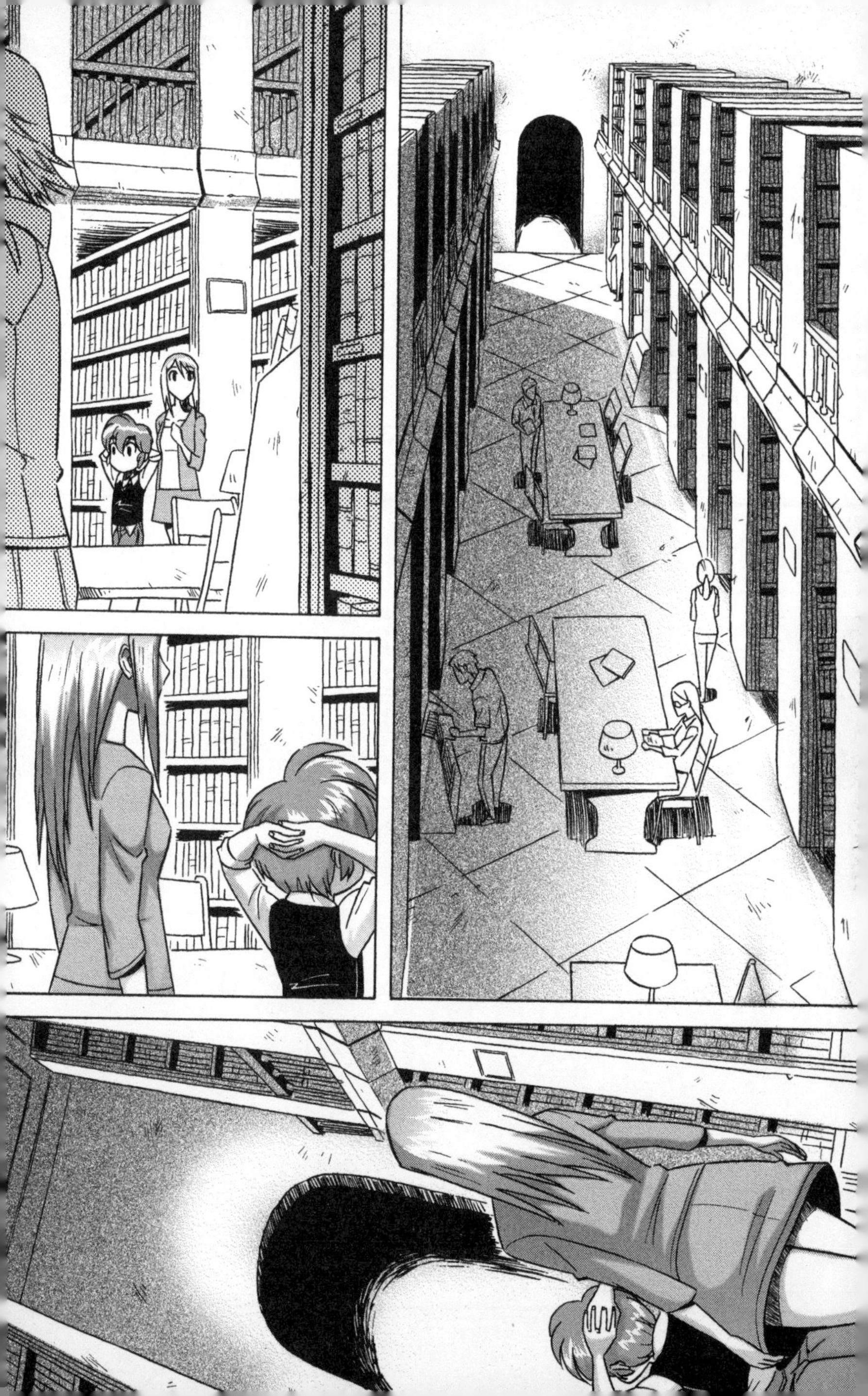

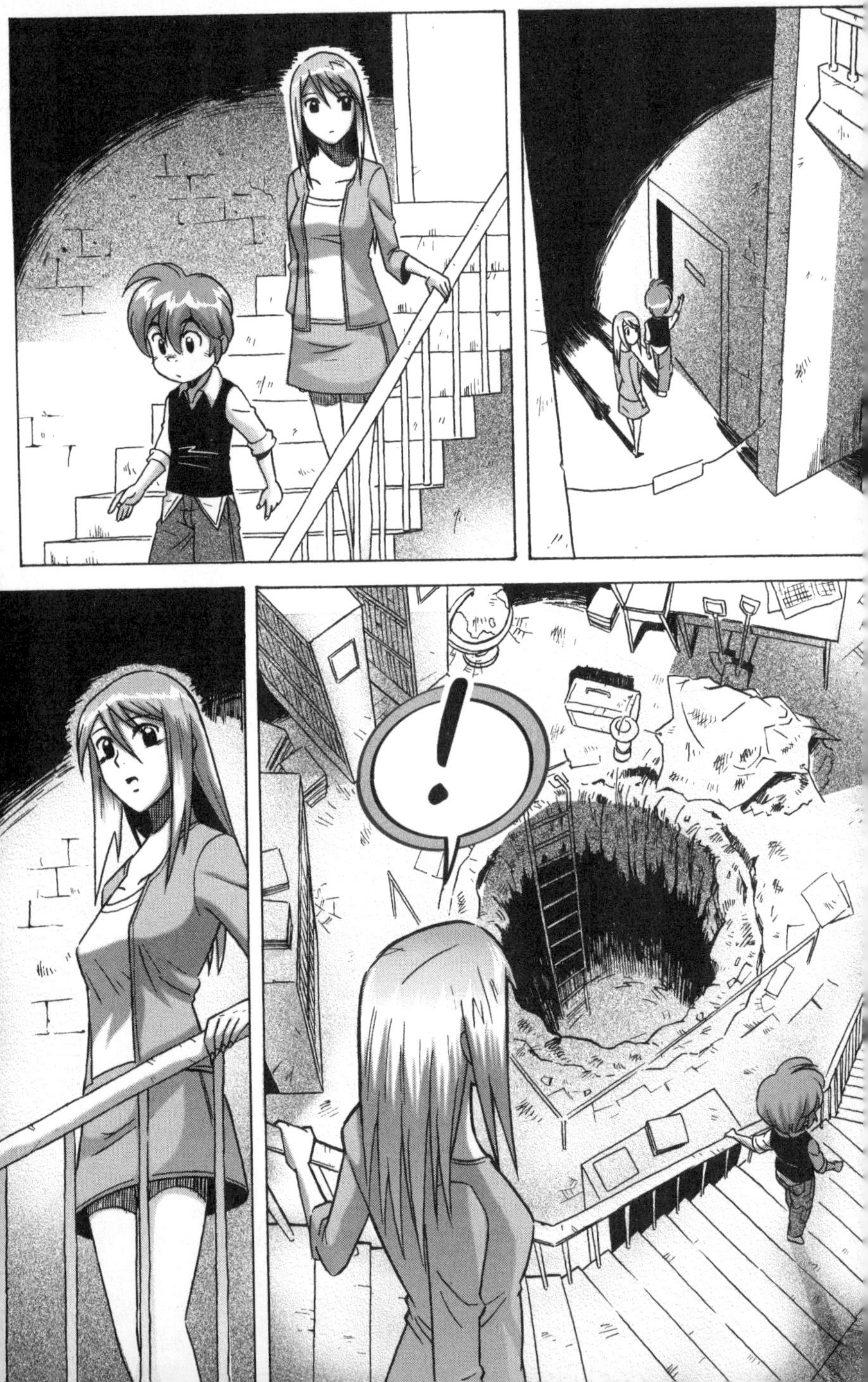
!

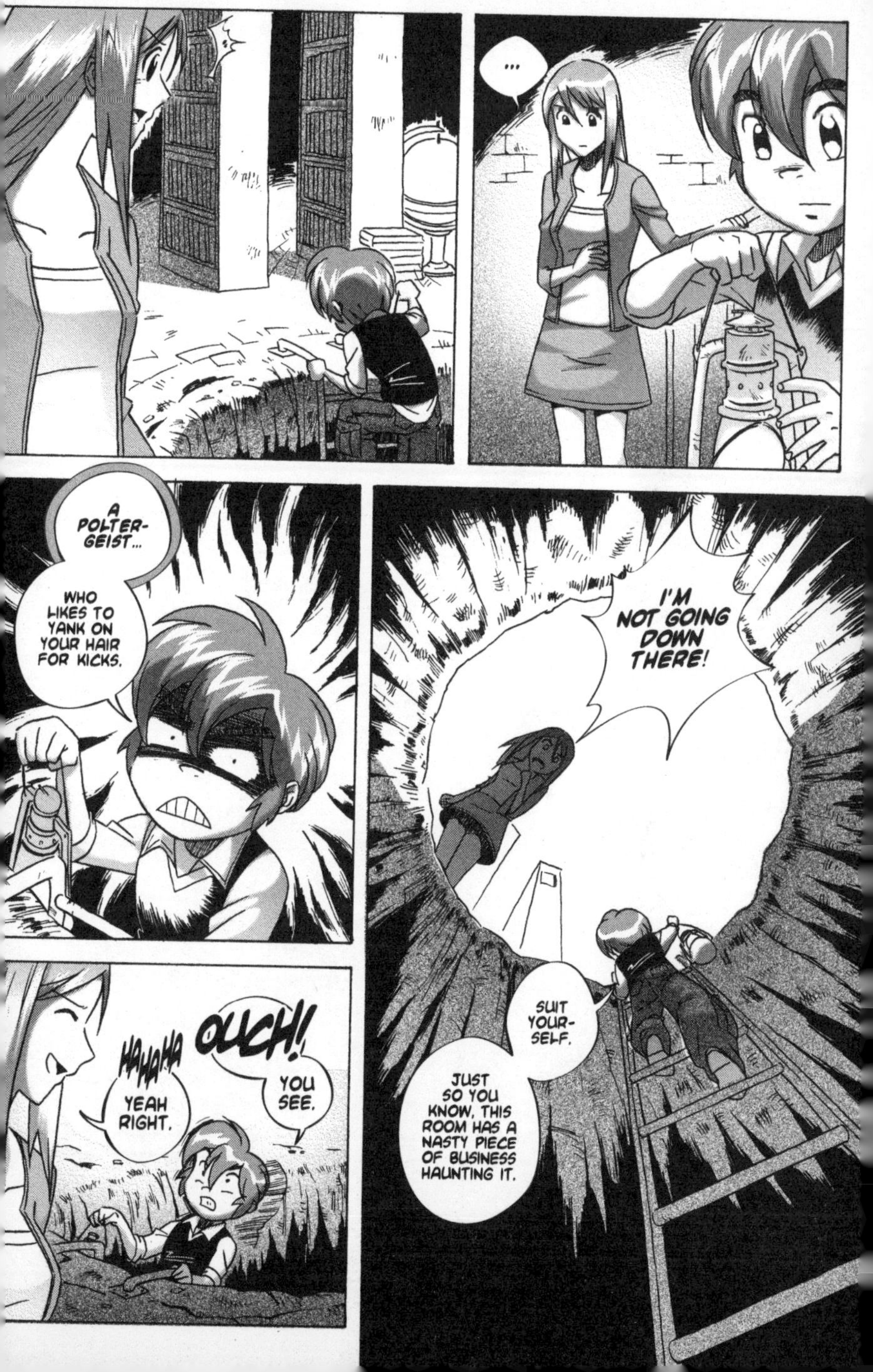
...
I'M NOT GOING DOWN THERE!
SUIT YOUR-SELF.
JUST SO YOU KNOW, THIS ROOM HAS A NASTY PIECE OF BUSINESS HAUNTING IT.
A POLTER-GEIST...
WHO LIKES TO YANK ON YOUR HAIR FOR KICKS.
OUCH!
YOU SEE.
HAHAHA
YEAH RIGHT.

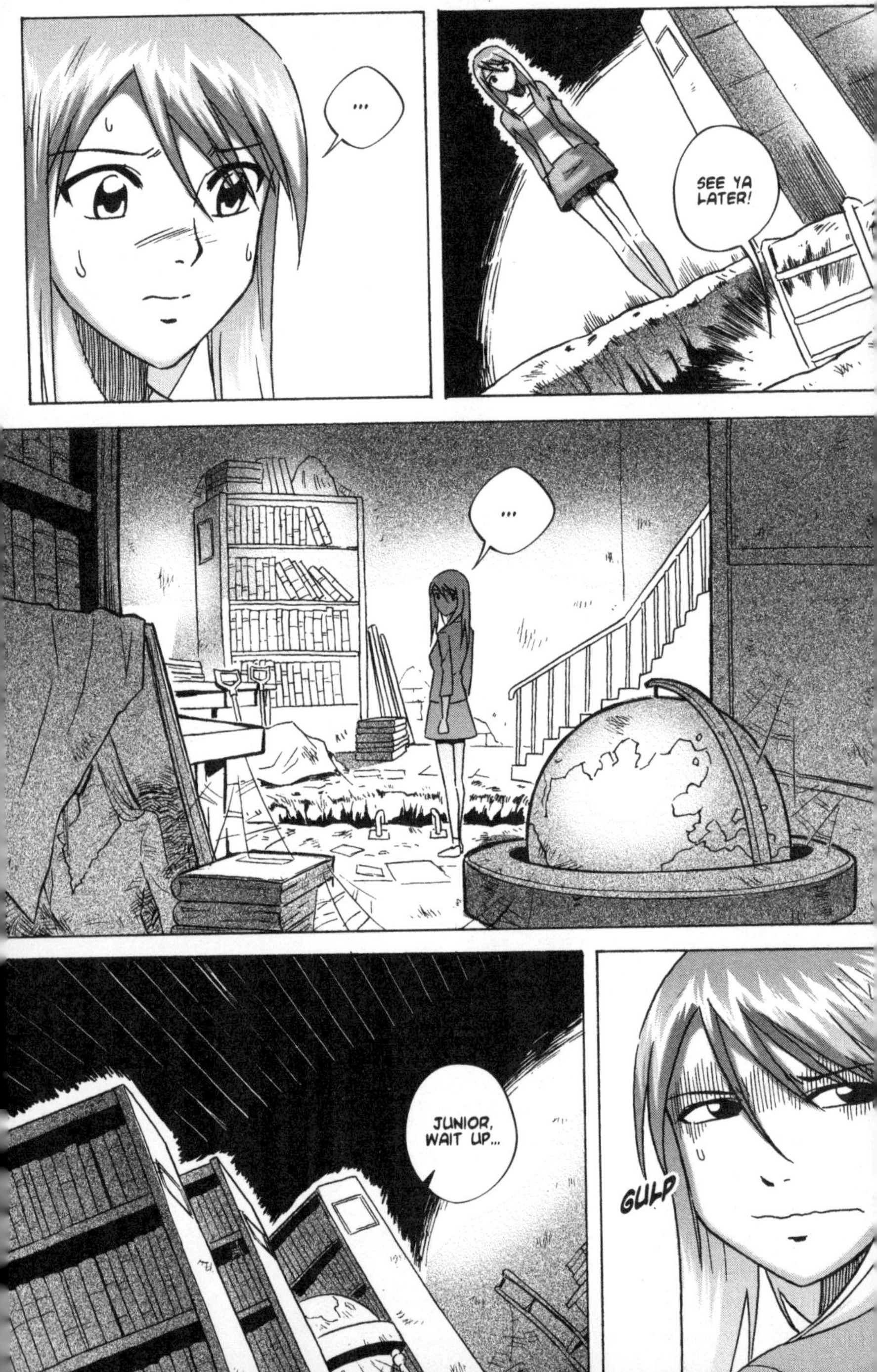
SEE YA LATER!
...
...
GULP
JUNIOR, WAIT UP...

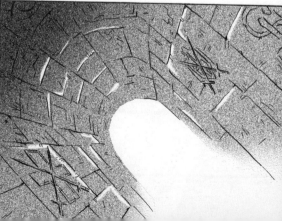

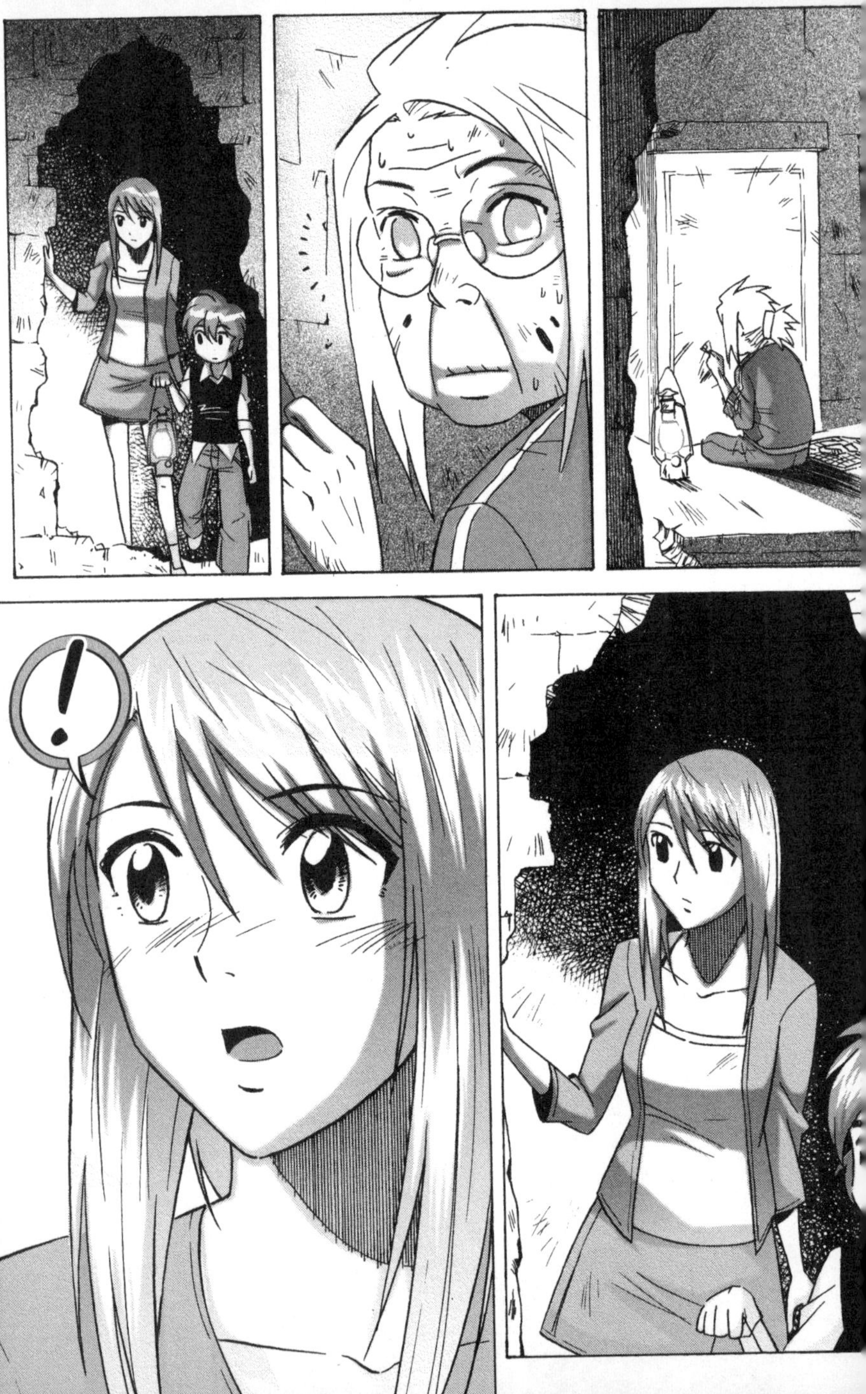
!

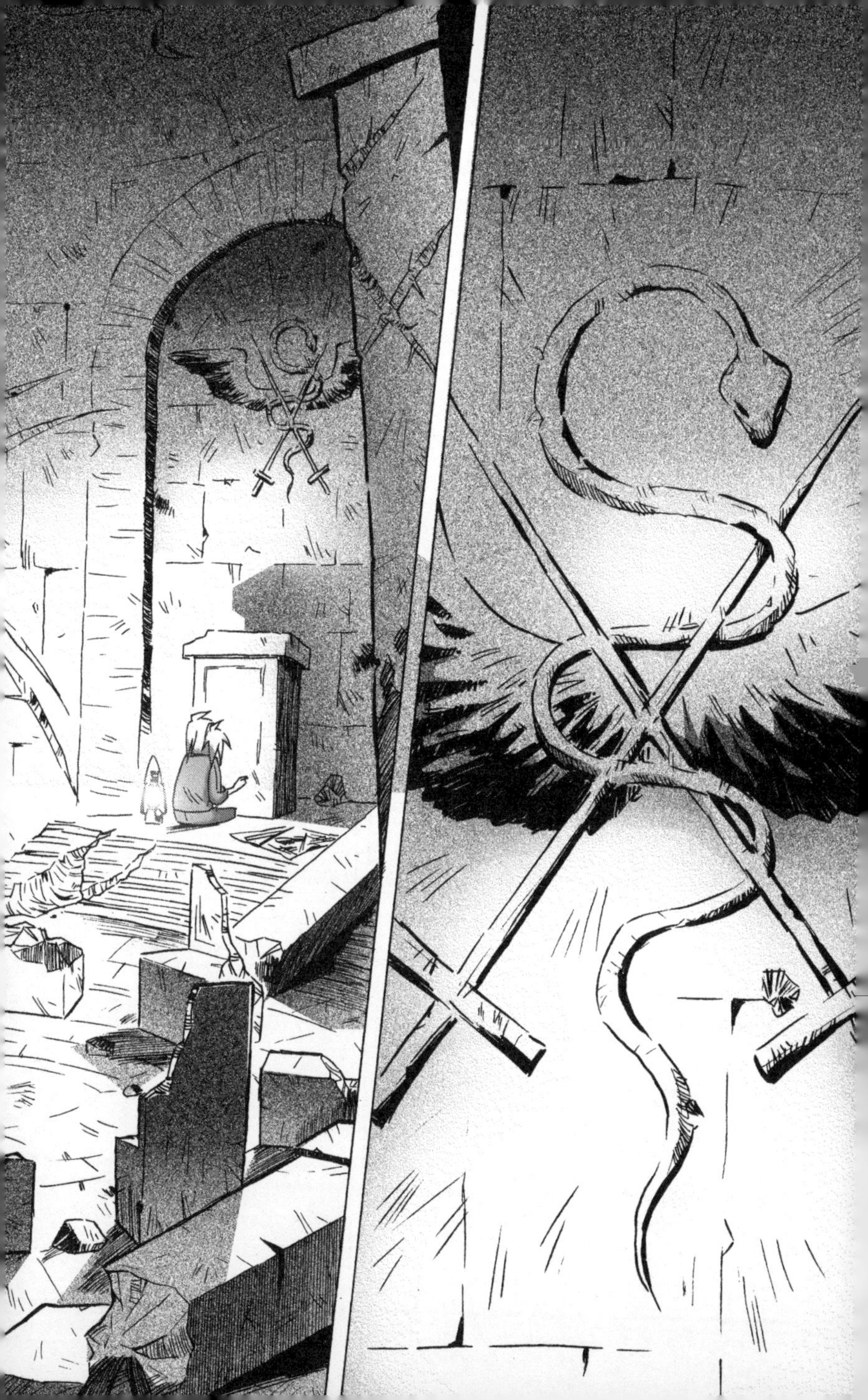

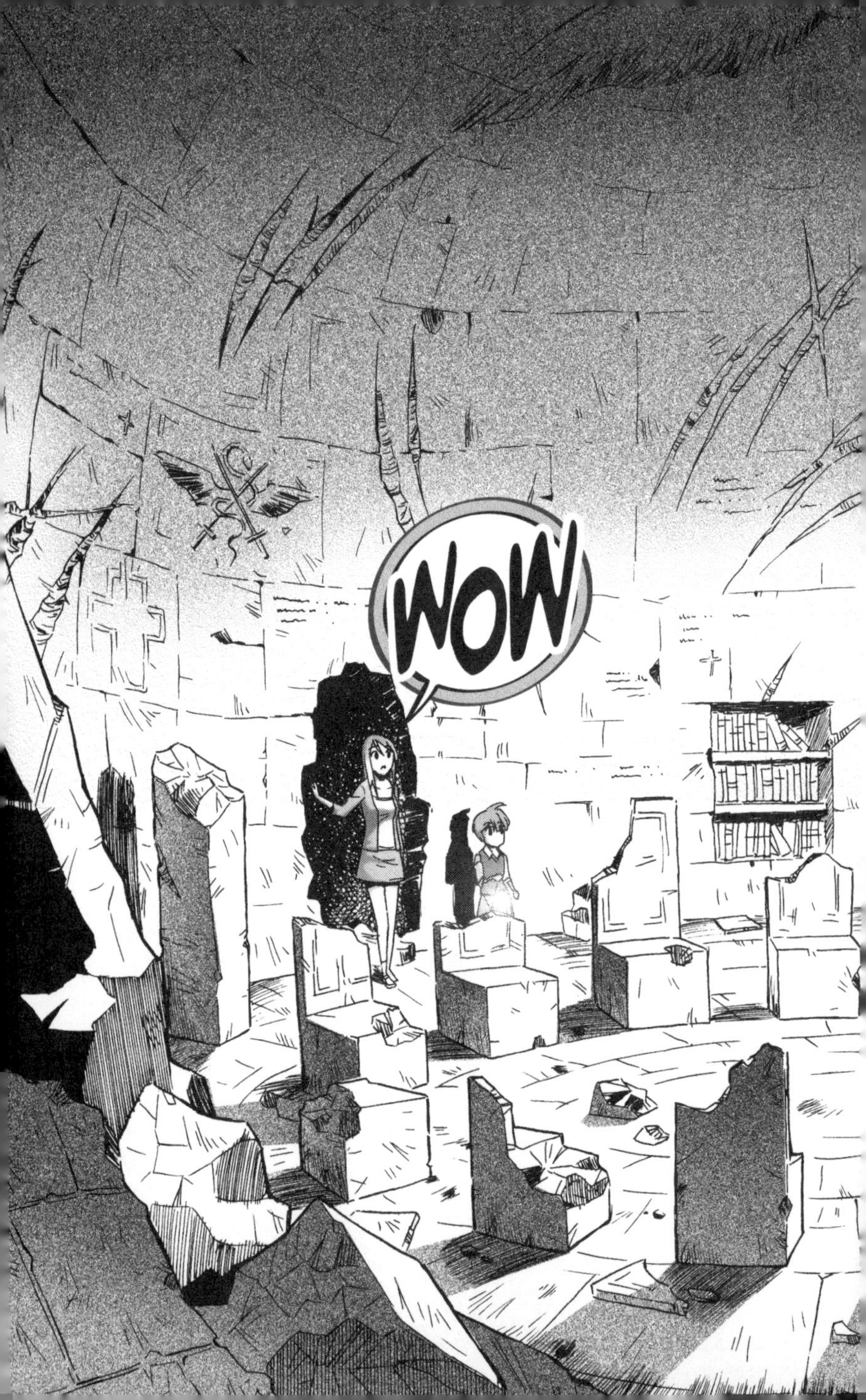
WOW

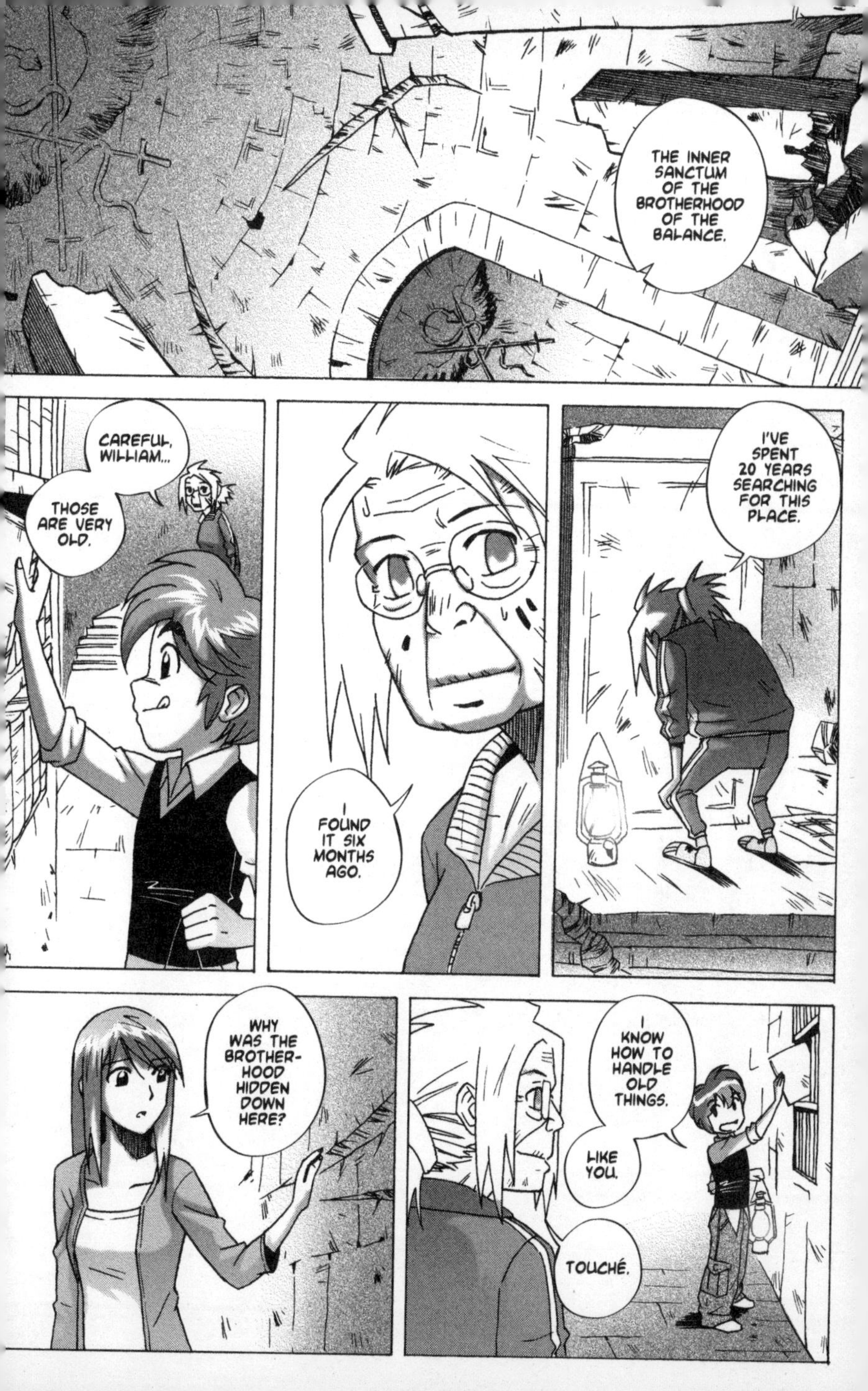
THE INNER SANCTUM OF THE BROTHERHOOD OF THE BALANCE.
I'VE SPENT 20 YEARS SEARCHING FOR THIS PLACE.
I FOUND IT SIX MONTHS AGO.
CAREFUL, WILLIAM...
THOSE ARE VERY OLD.
I KNOW HOW TO HANDLE OLD THINGS.
LIKE YOU.
TOUCHÉ.
WHY WAS THE BROTHER-HOOD HIDDEN DOWN HERE?

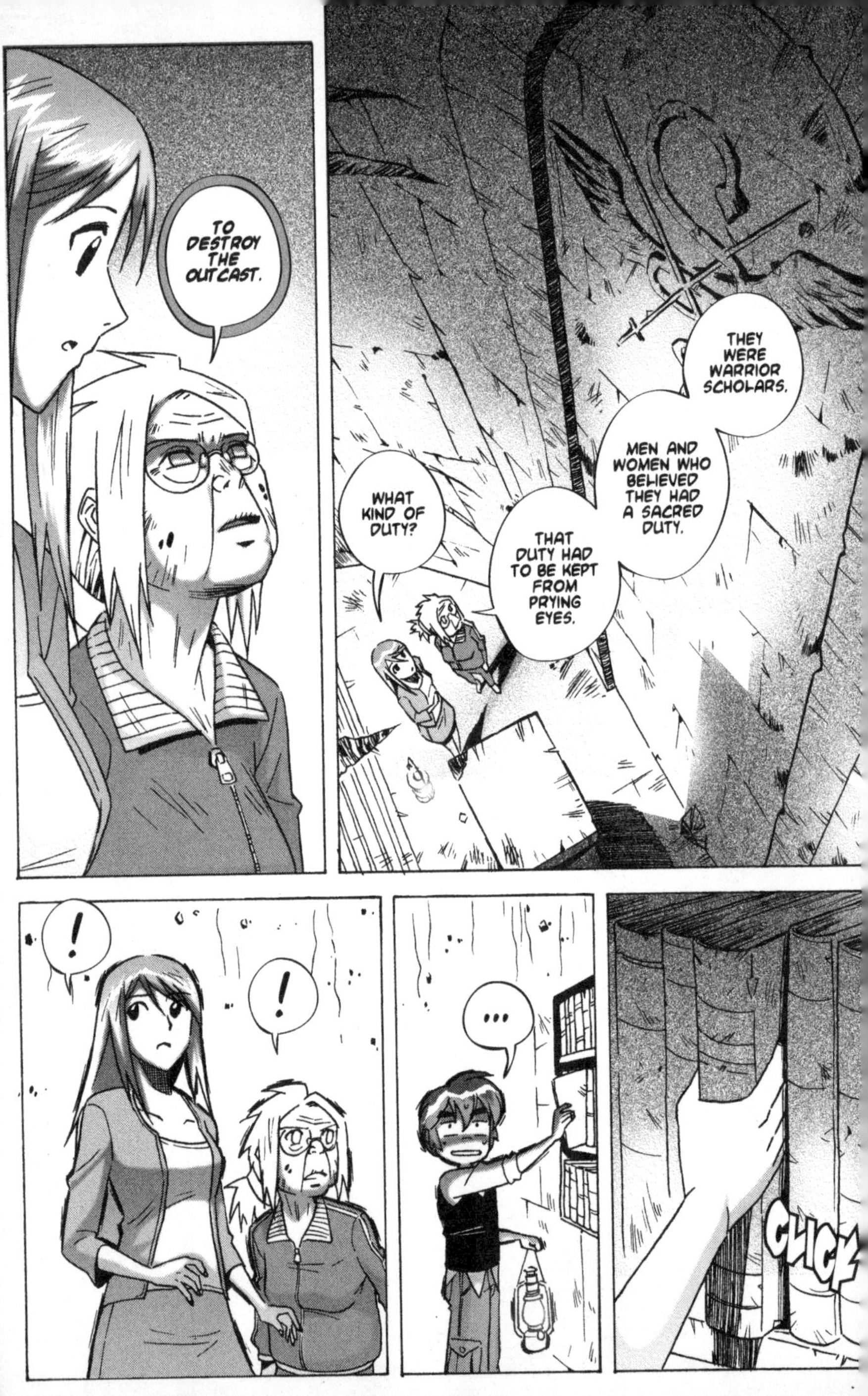
THEY WERE WARRIOR SCHOLARS.
MEN AND WOMEN WHO BELIEVED THEY HAD A SACRED DUTY.
THAT DUTY HAD TO BE KEPT FROM PRYING EYES.
WHAT KIND OF DUTY?
TO DESTROY THE OUTCAST.
CLICK
...
!
!

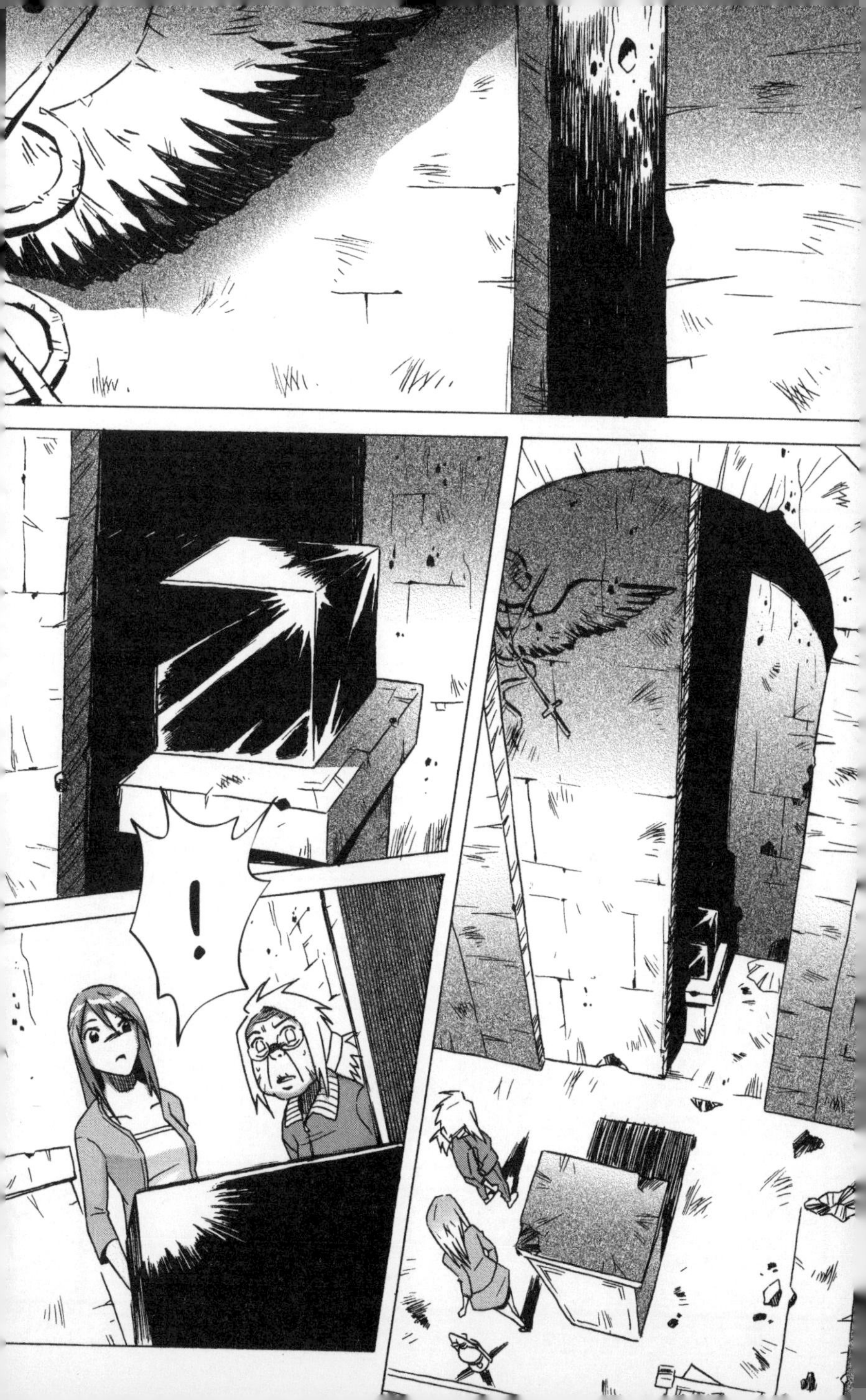
!

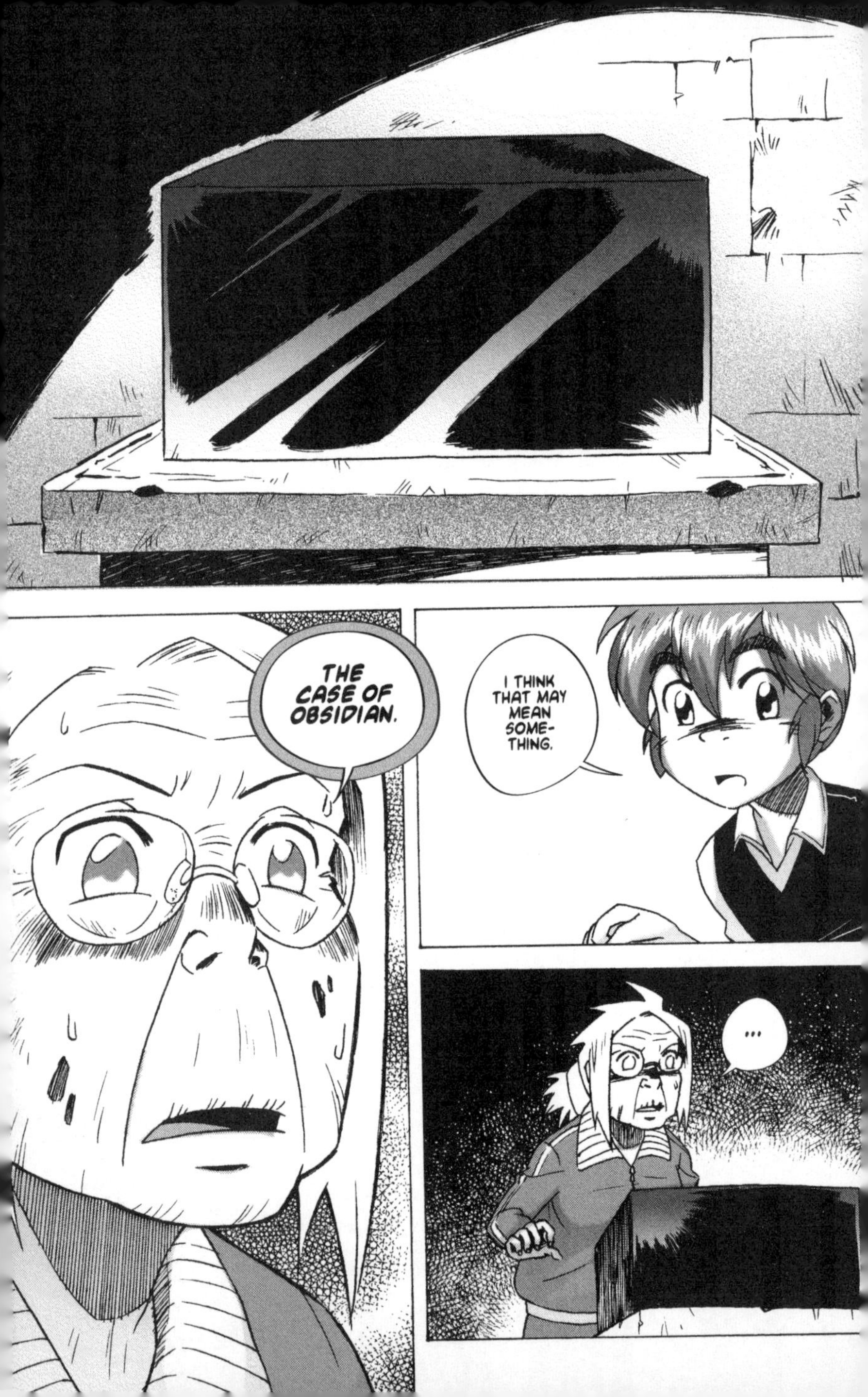
I THINK THAT MAY MEAN SOME-THING.
...
THE CASE OF OBSIDIAN.

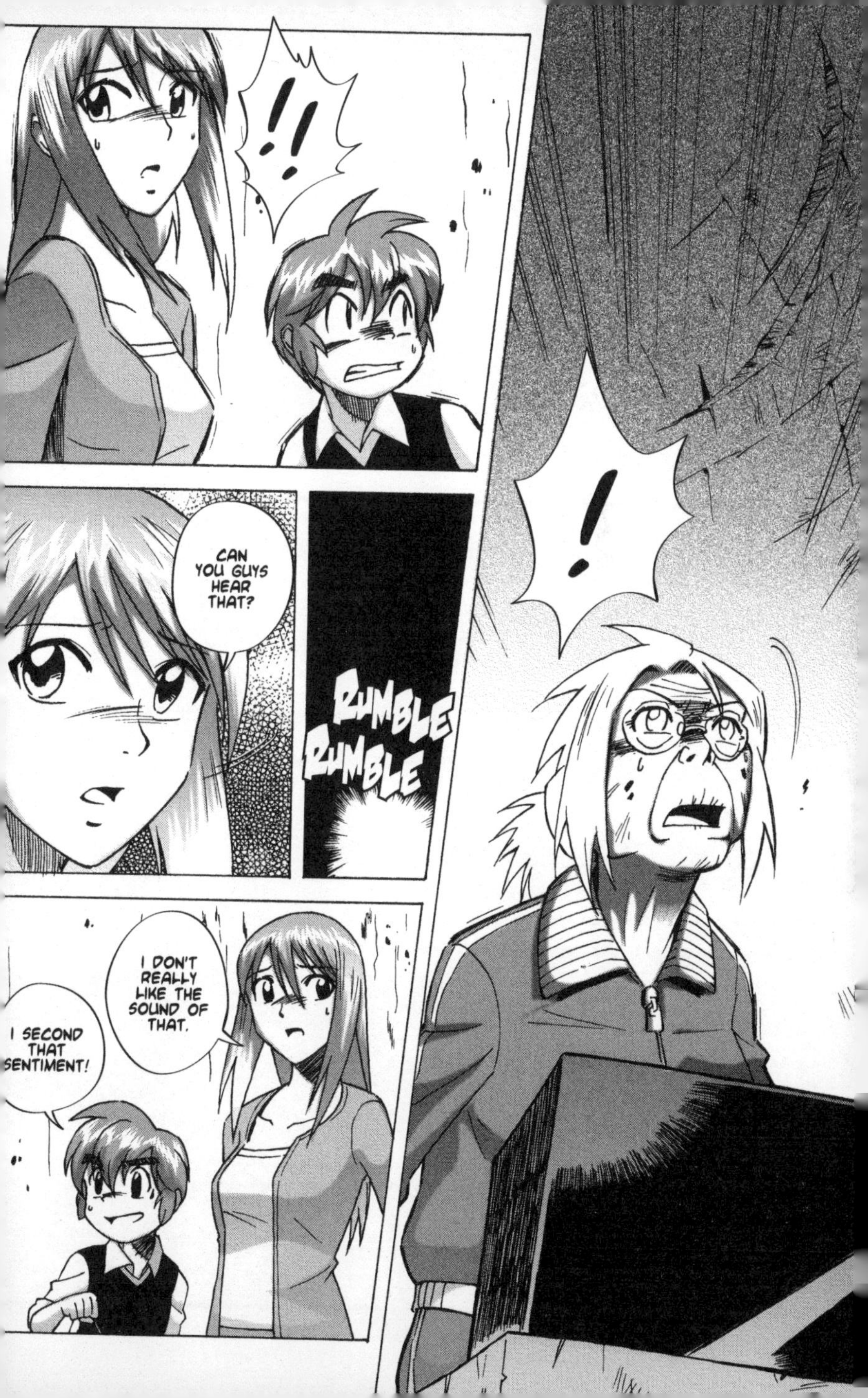
!
!!
RUMBLE RUMBLE
CAN YOU GUYS HEAR THAT?
I DON'T REALLY LIKE THE SOUND OF THAT.
I SECOND THAT SENTIMENT!

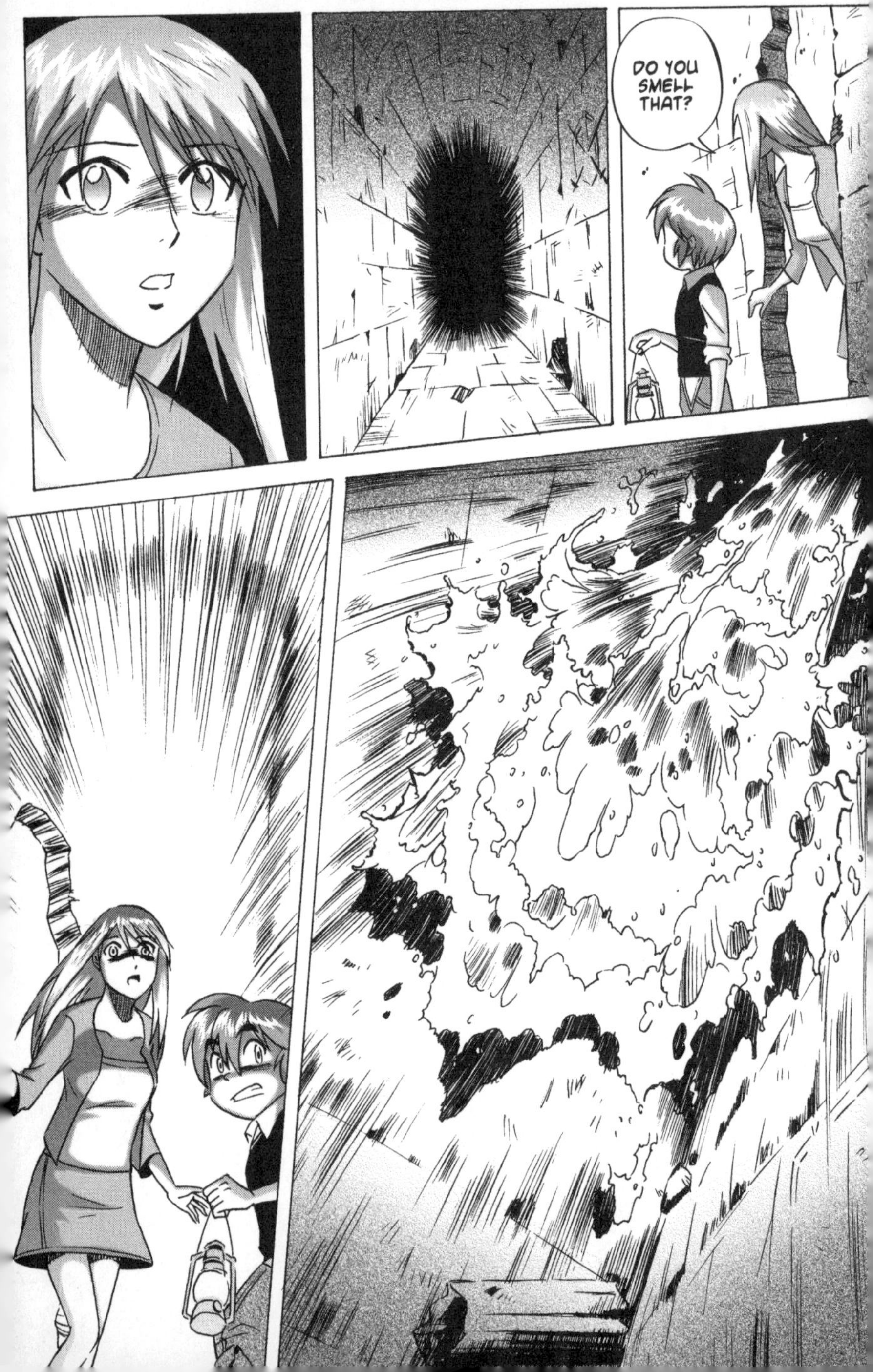
DO YOU SMELL THAT?

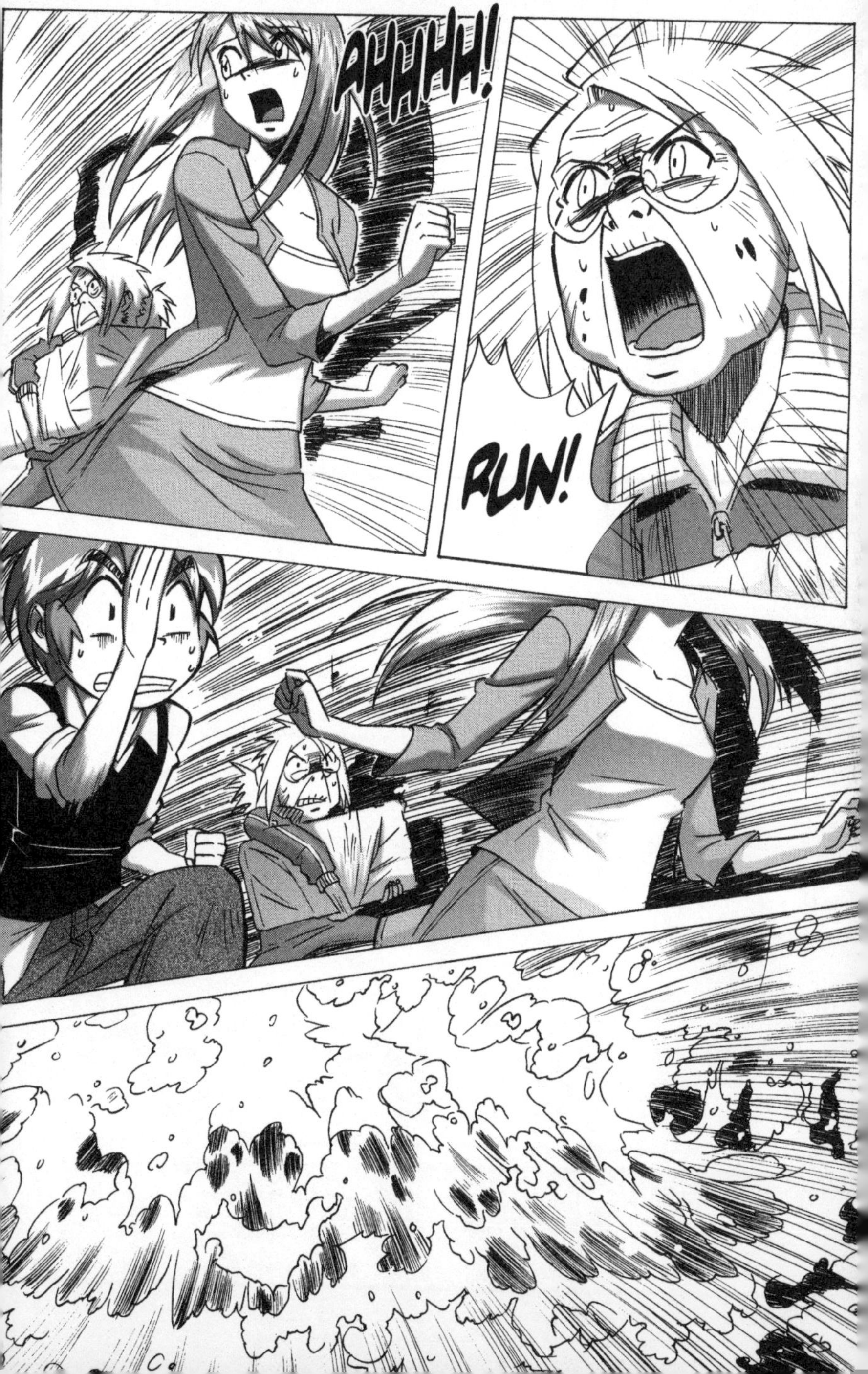
RUN!
AHHHH!

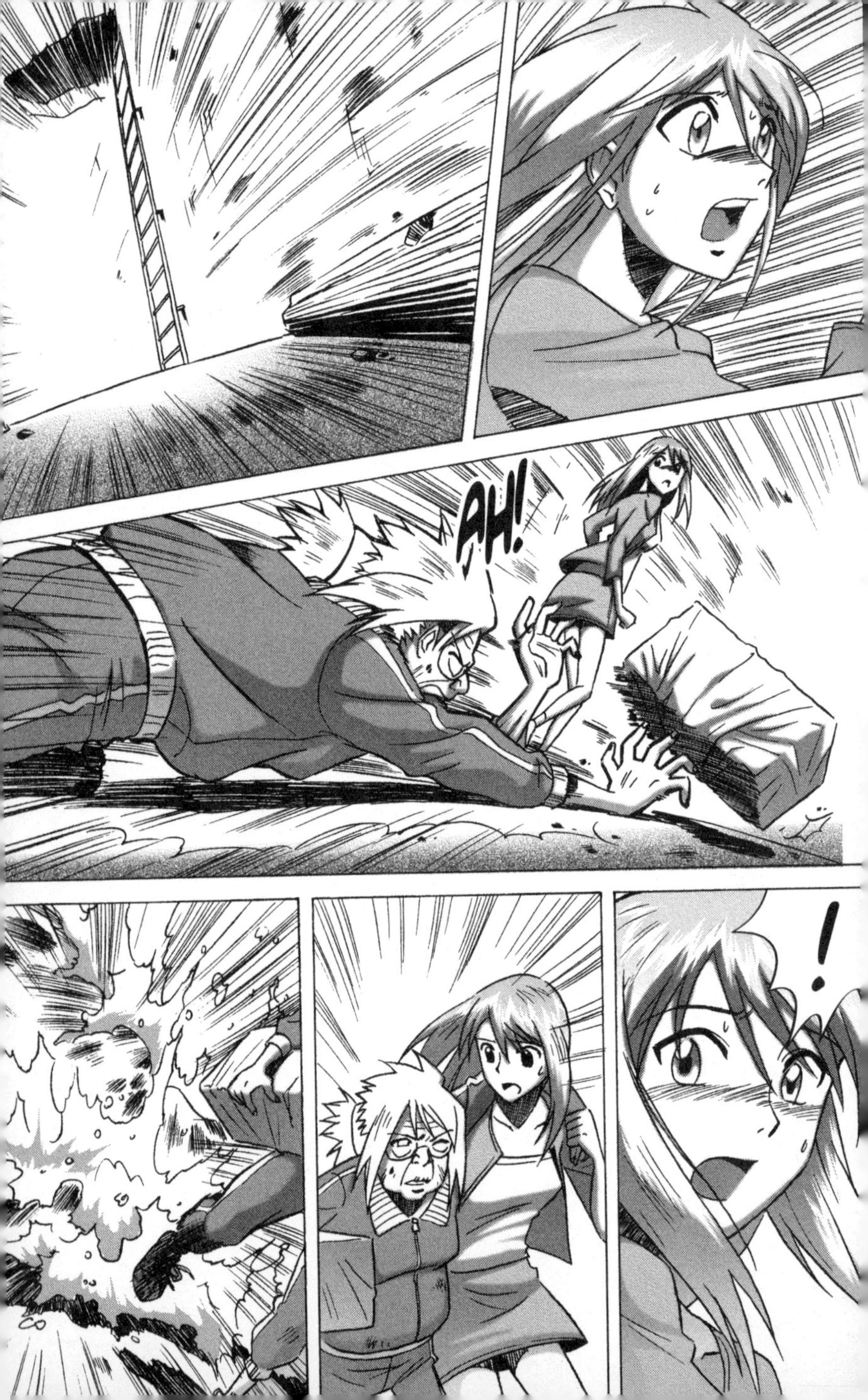
AH!
!

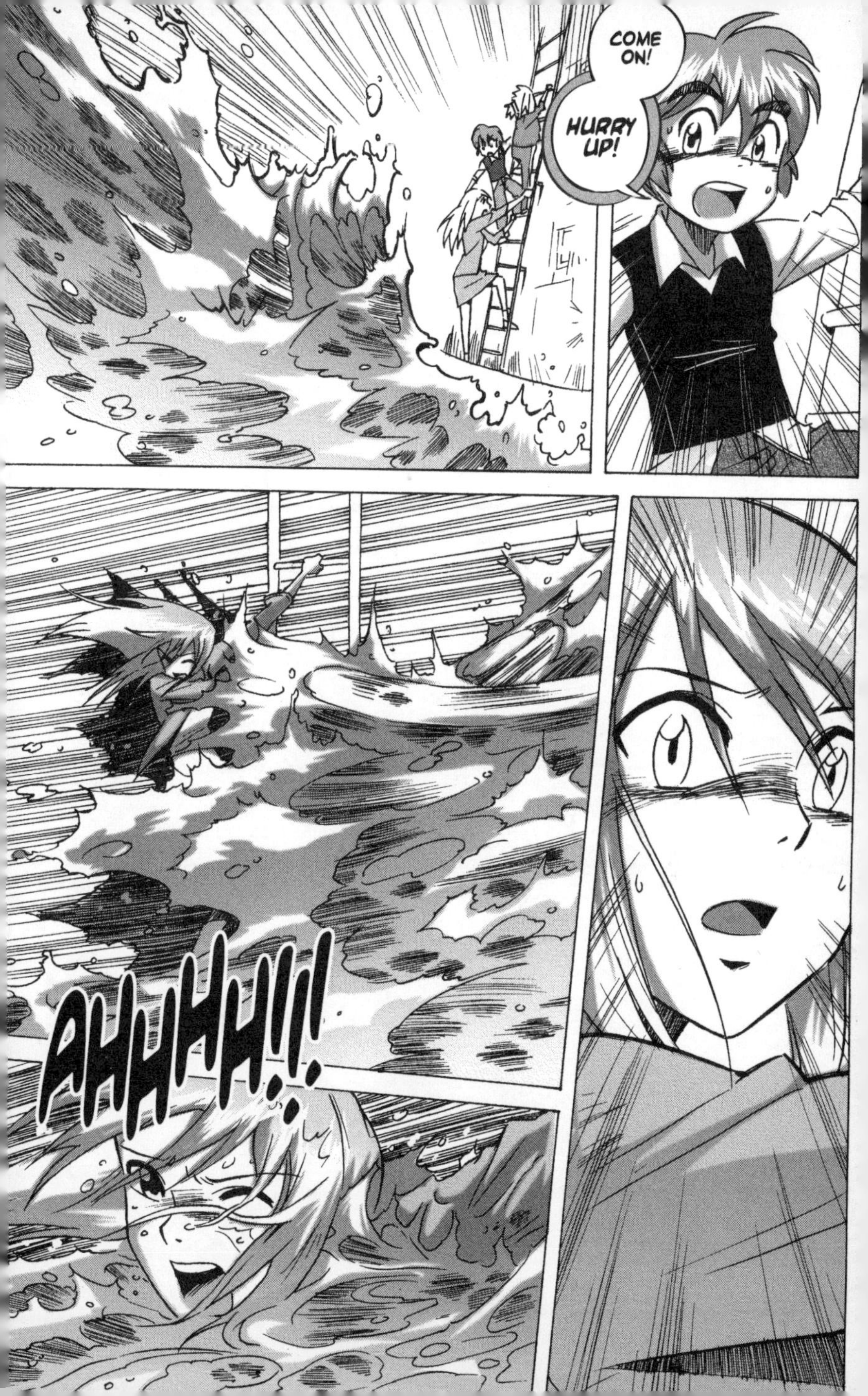
COME ON!
HURRY UP!
AHHHH!!!

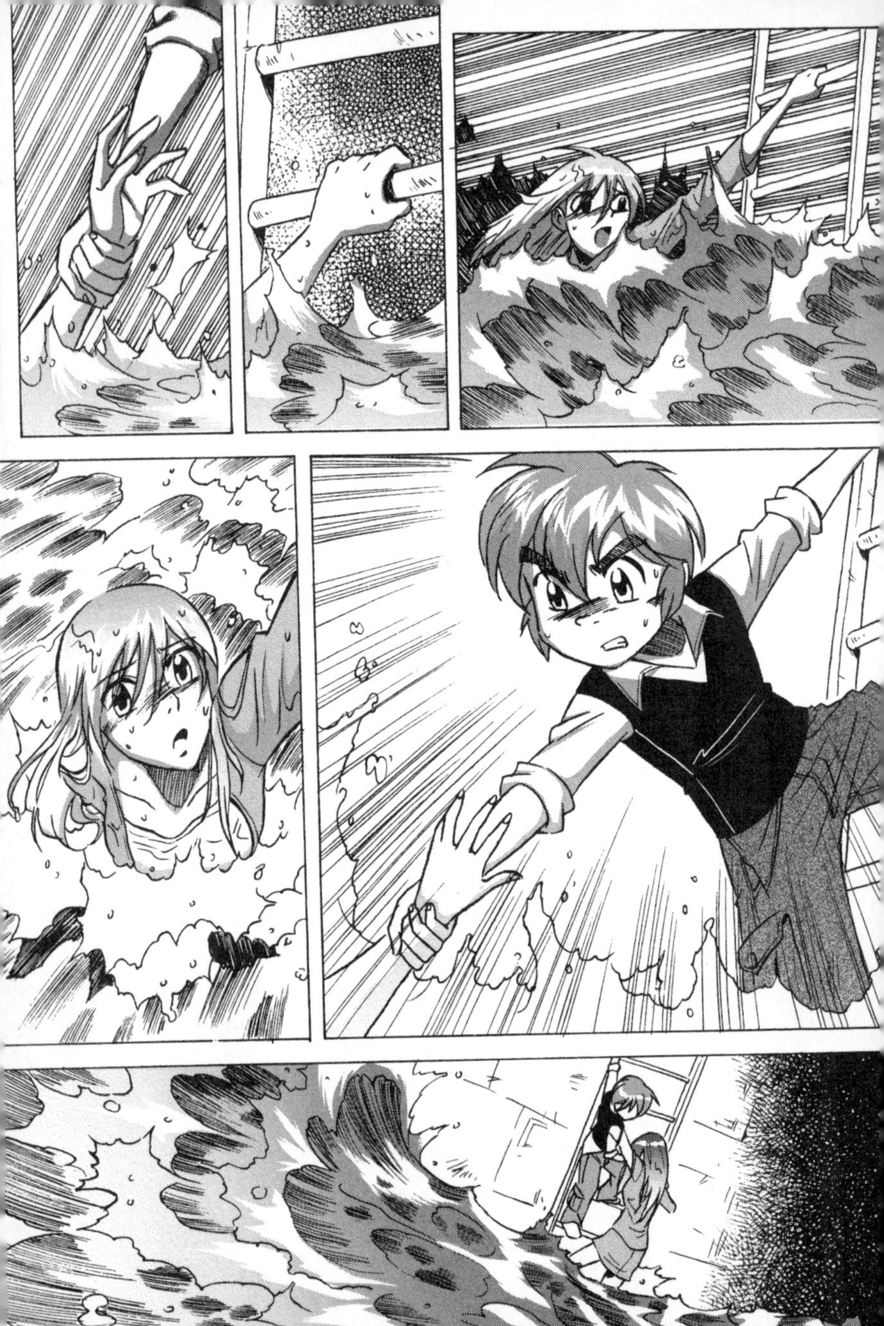

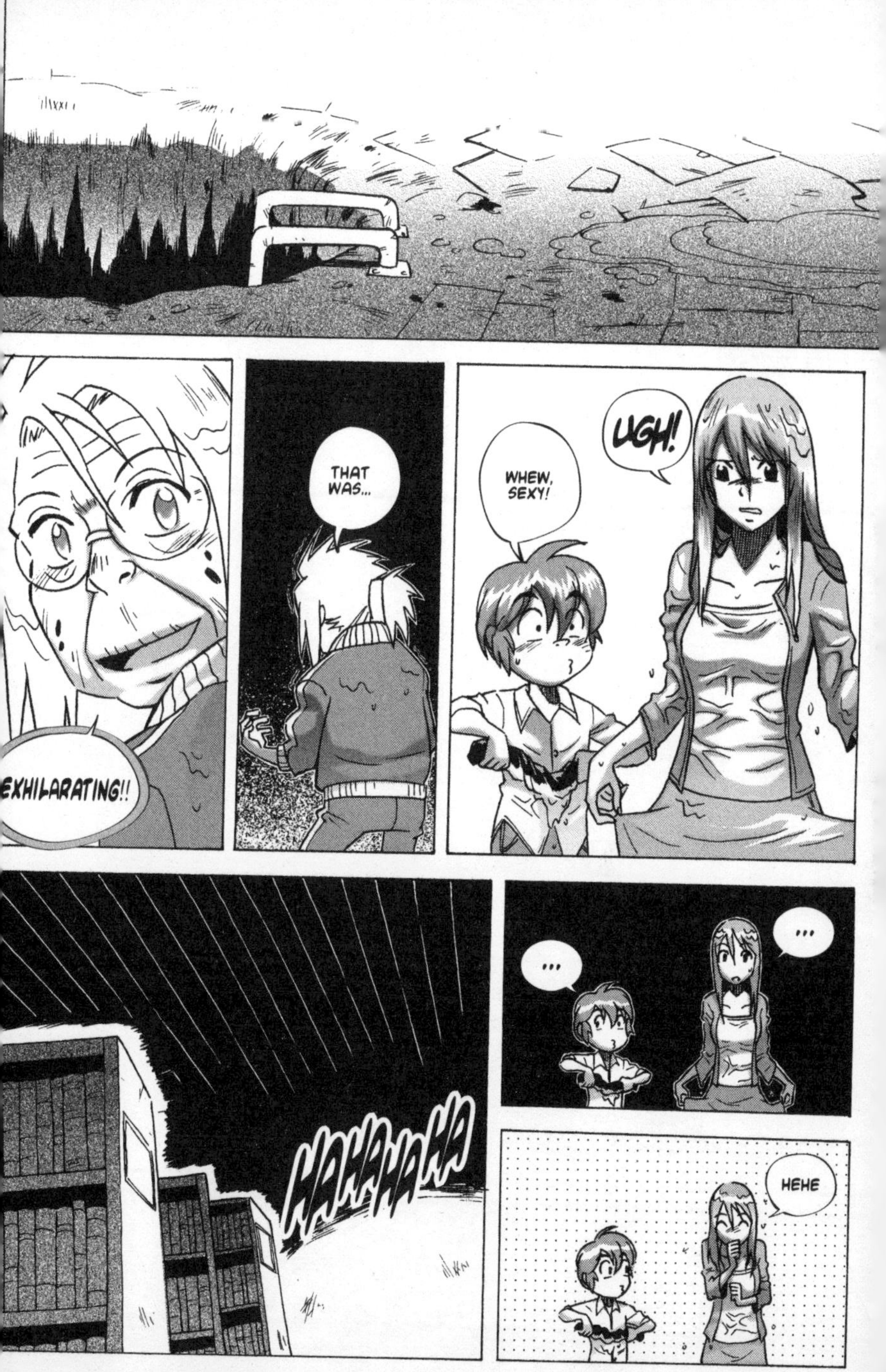
UGH!
WHEW, SEXY!
THAT WAS...
EXHILARATING!!
...
...
HEHE
HAHAHAHA

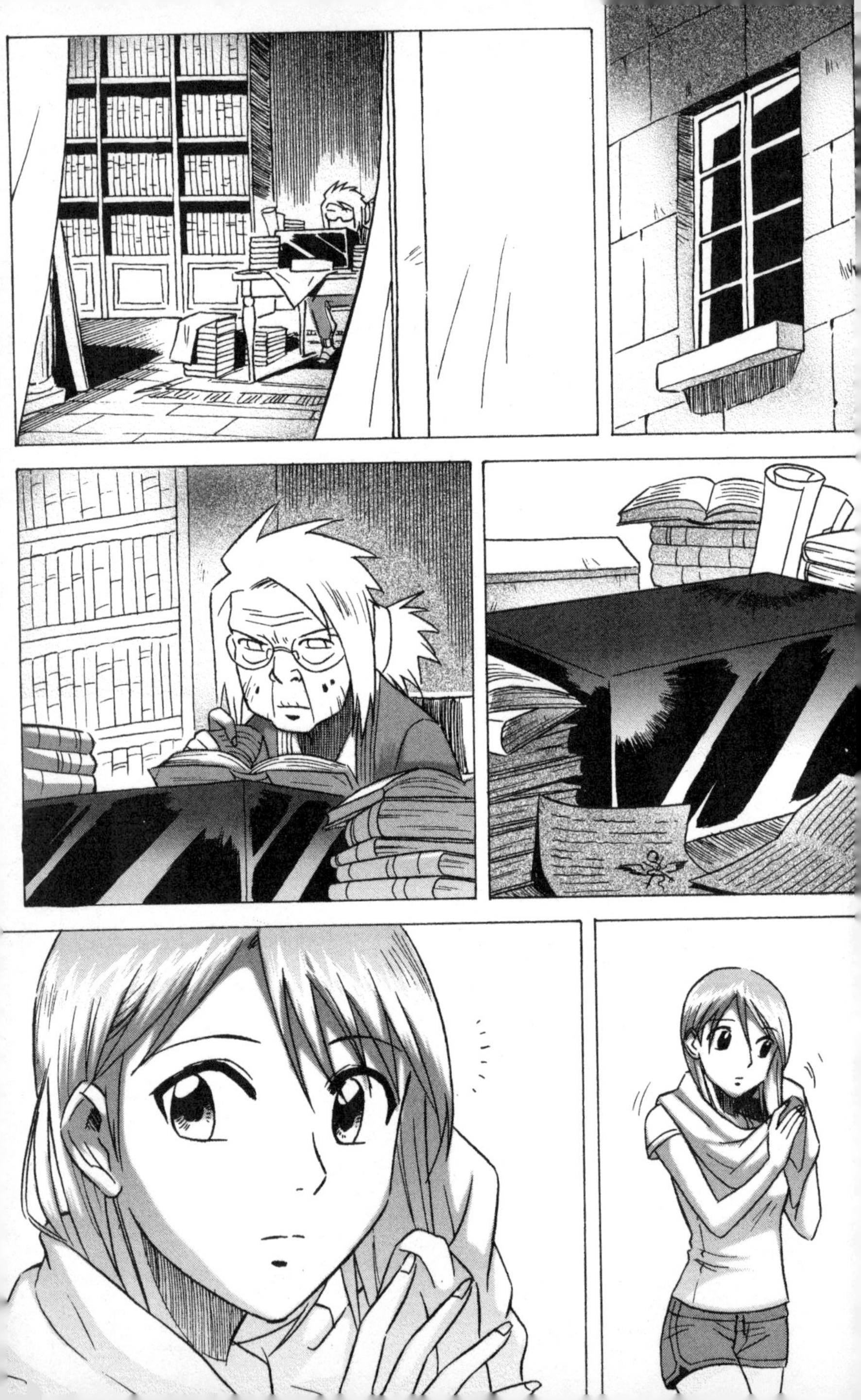

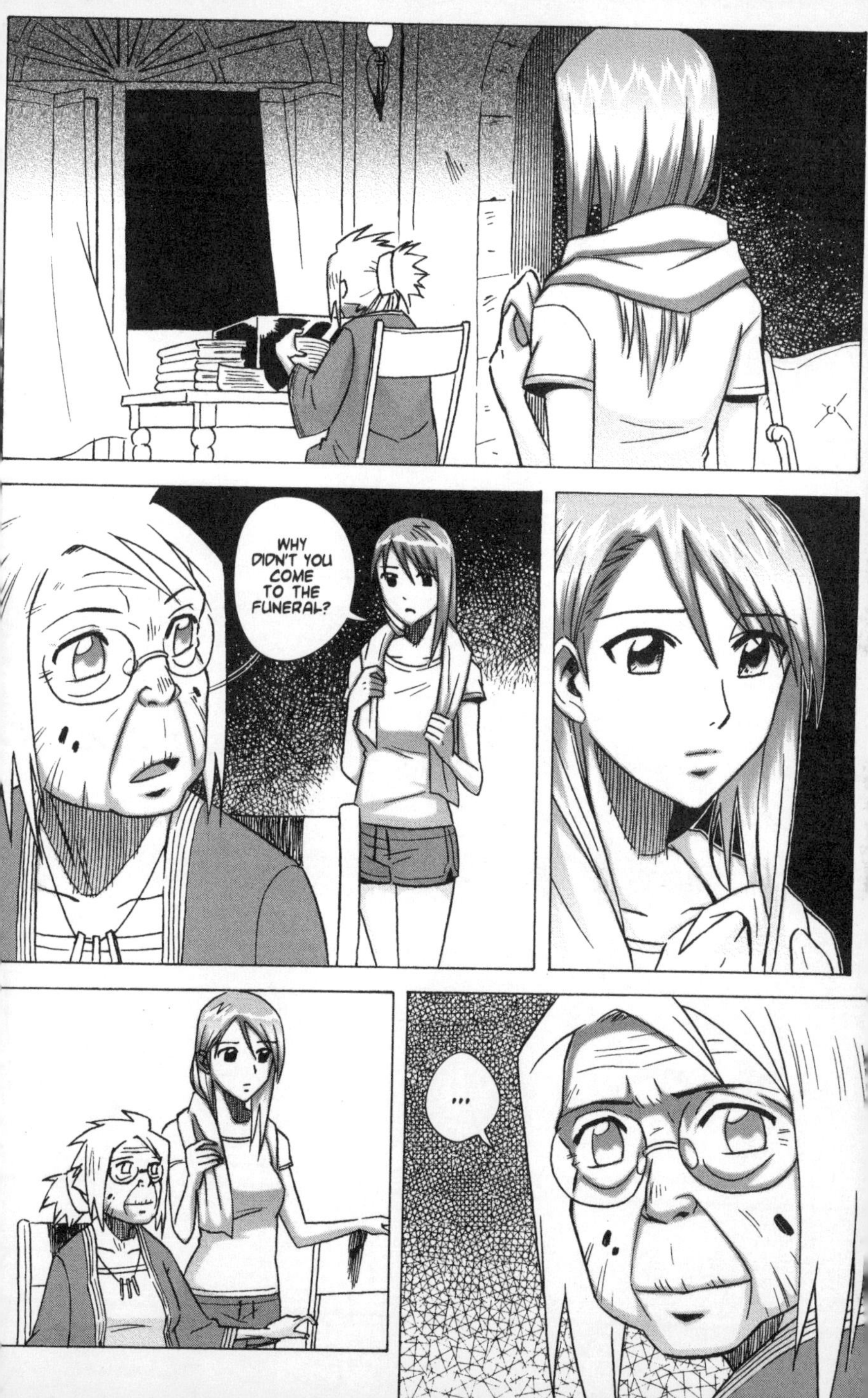
WHY DIDN'T YOU COME TO THE FUNERAL?
...

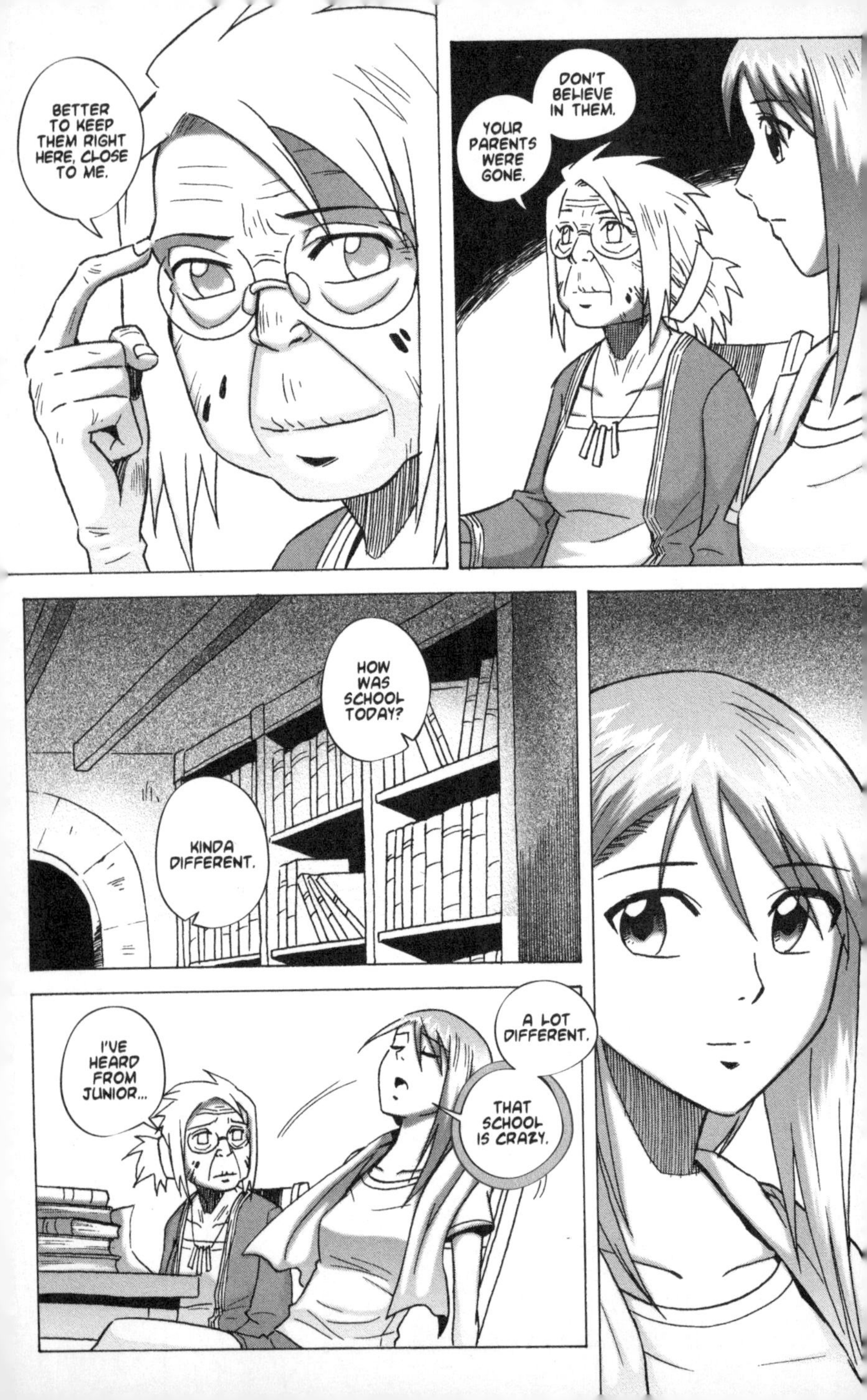
DON'T BELIEVE IN THEM.
YOUR PARENTS WERE GONE.
BETTER TO KEEP THEM RIGHT HERE, CLOSE TO ME.
HOW WAS SCHOOL TODAY?
KINDA DIFFERENT.
A LOT DIFFERENT.
THAT SCHOOL IS CRAZY.
I'VE HEARD FROM JUNIOR...

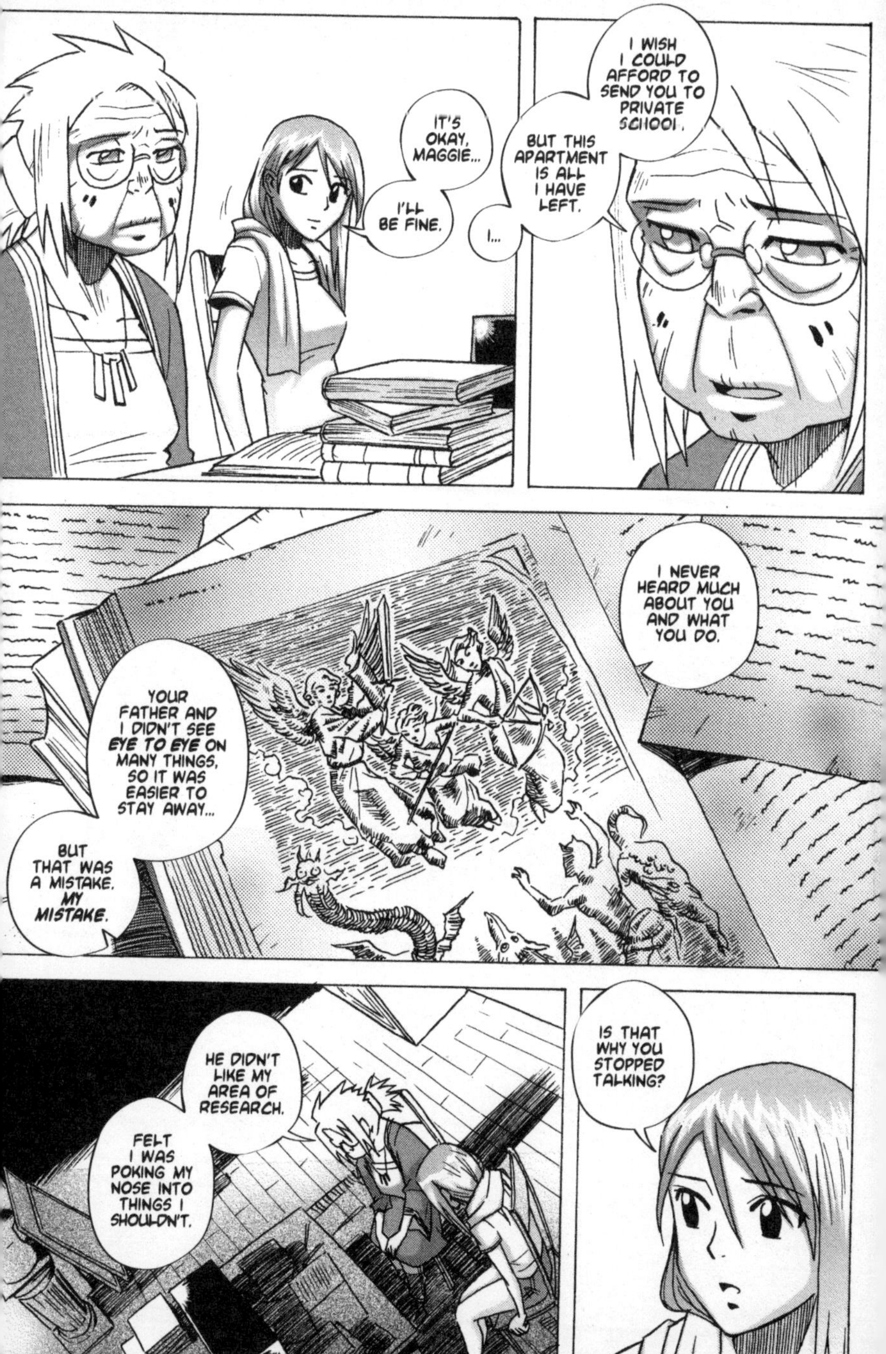
I WISH I COULD AFFORD TO SEND YOU TO PRIVATE SCHOOL.
BUT THIS APARTMENT IS ALL I HAVE LEFT.
I...
IT'S OKAY, MAGGIE...
I'LL BE FINE.
I NEVER HEARD MUCH ABOUT YOU AND WHAT YOU DO.
YOUR FATHER AND I DIDN'T SEE ***EYE TO EYE*** ON MANY THINGS, SO IT WAS EASIER TO STAY AWAY...
BUT THAT WAS A MISTAKE. ***MY MISTAKE.***
IS THAT WHY YOU STOPPED TALKING?
HE DIDN'T LIKE MY AREA OF RESEARCH.
FELT I WAS POKING MY NOSE INTO THINGS I SHOULDN'T.

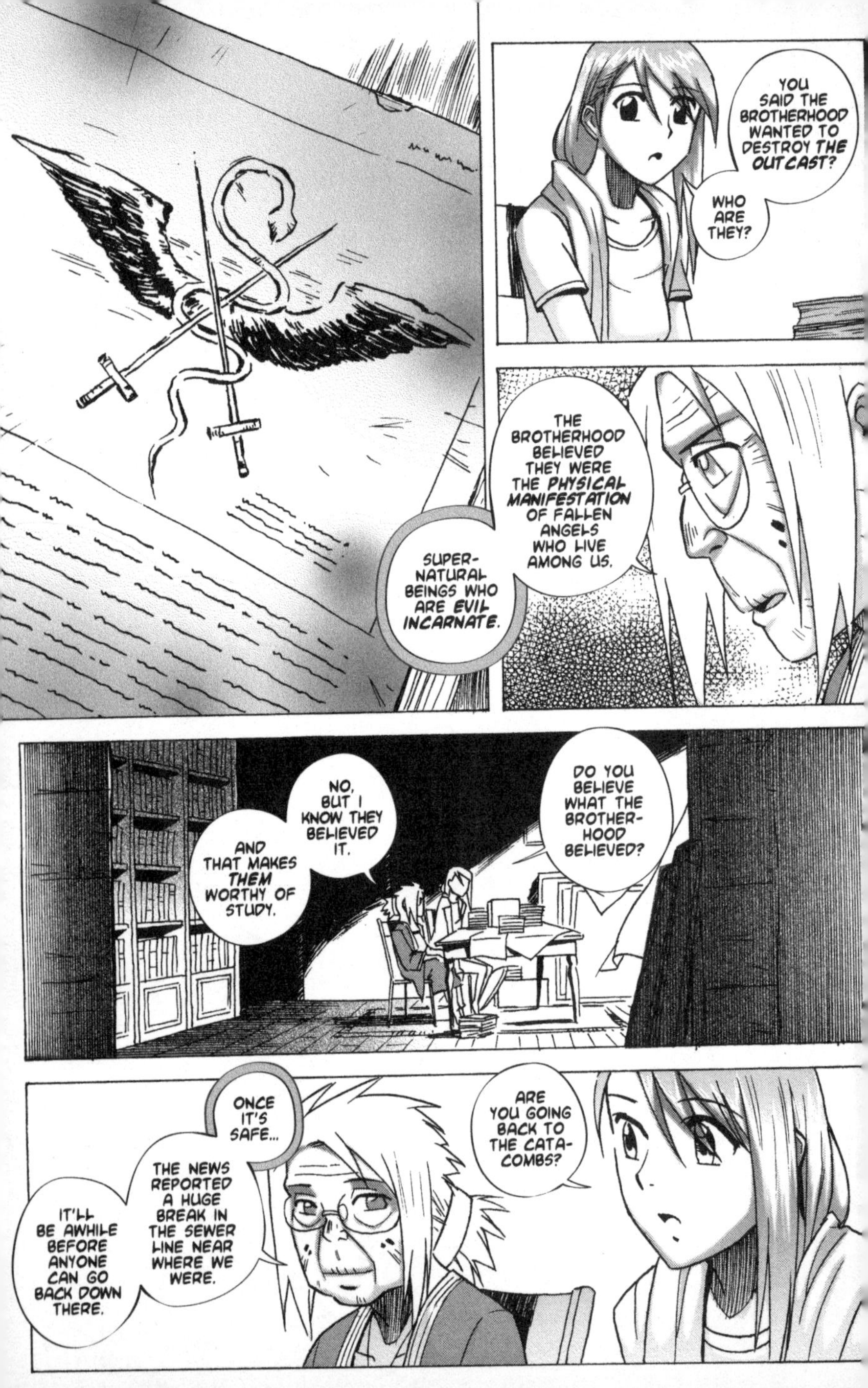
YOU SAID THE BROTHERHOOD WANTED TO DESTROY THE OUTCAST?
WHO ARE THEY?
THE BROTHERHOOD BELIEVED THEY WERE THE PHYSICAL MANIFESTATION OF FALLEN ANGELS WHO LIVE AMONG US.
SUPER-NATURAL BEINGS WHO ARE EVIL INCARNATE.
DO YOU BELIEVE WHAT THE BROTHER-HOOD BELIEVED?
NO, BUT I KNOW THEY BELIEVED IT.
AND THAT MAKES THEM WORTHY OF STUDY.
ARE YOU GOING BACK TO THE CATA-COMBS?
ONCE IT'S SAFE...
THE NEWS REPORTED A HUGE BREAK IN THE SEWER LINE NEAR WHERE WE WERE.
IT'LL BE AWHILE BEFORE ANYONE CAN GO BACK DOWN THERE.

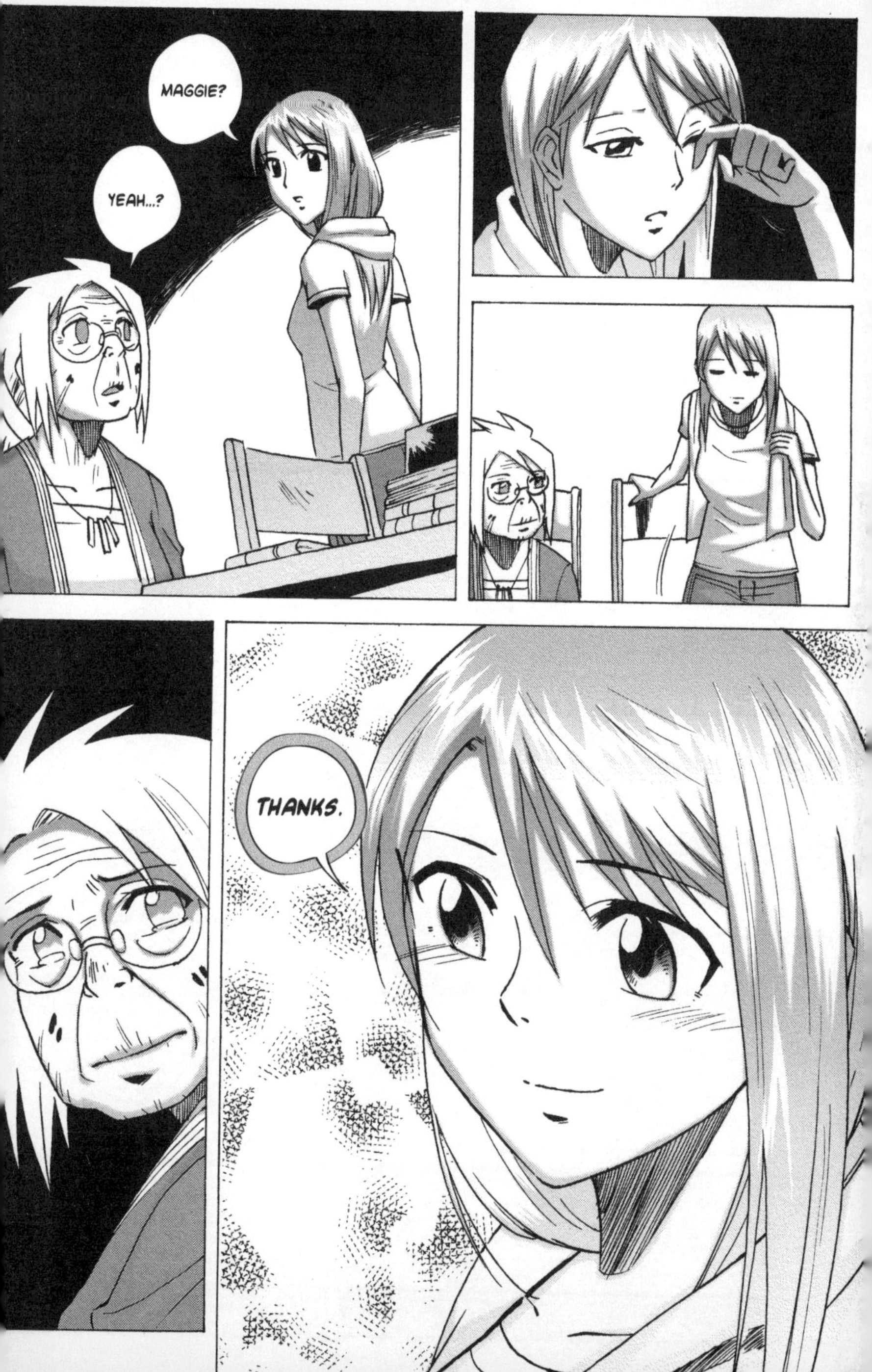
MAGGIE?
YEAH...?
THANKS.

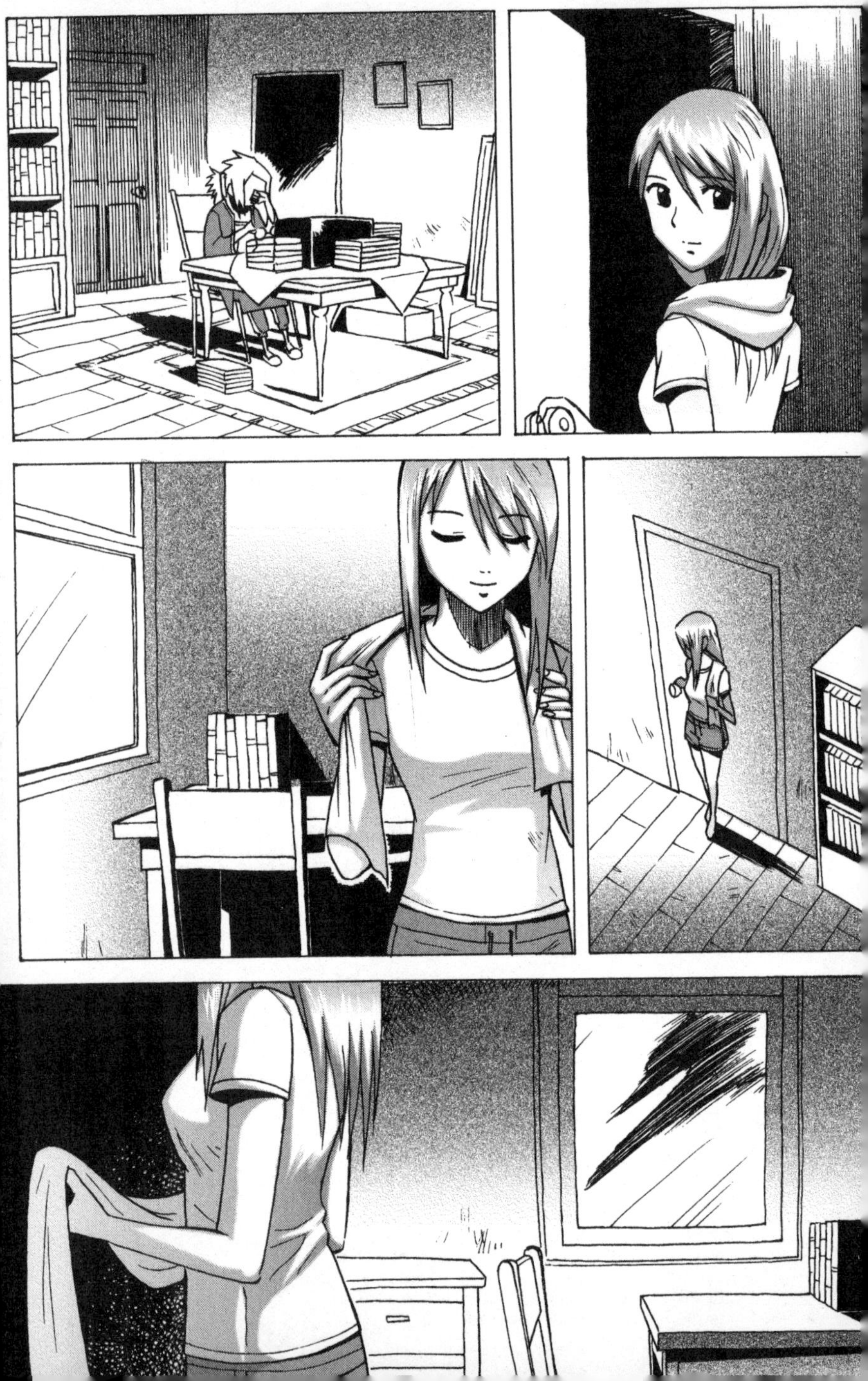

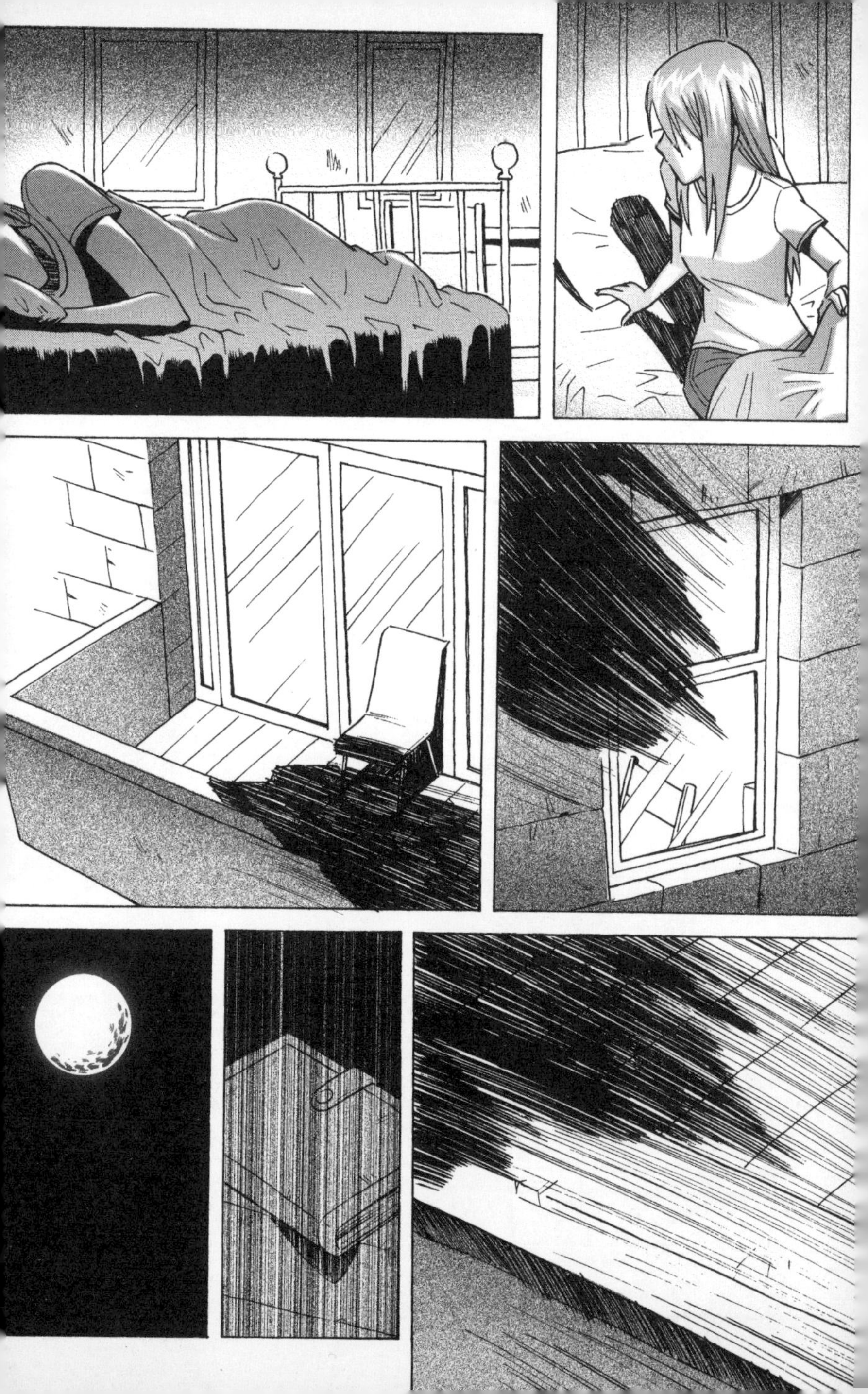

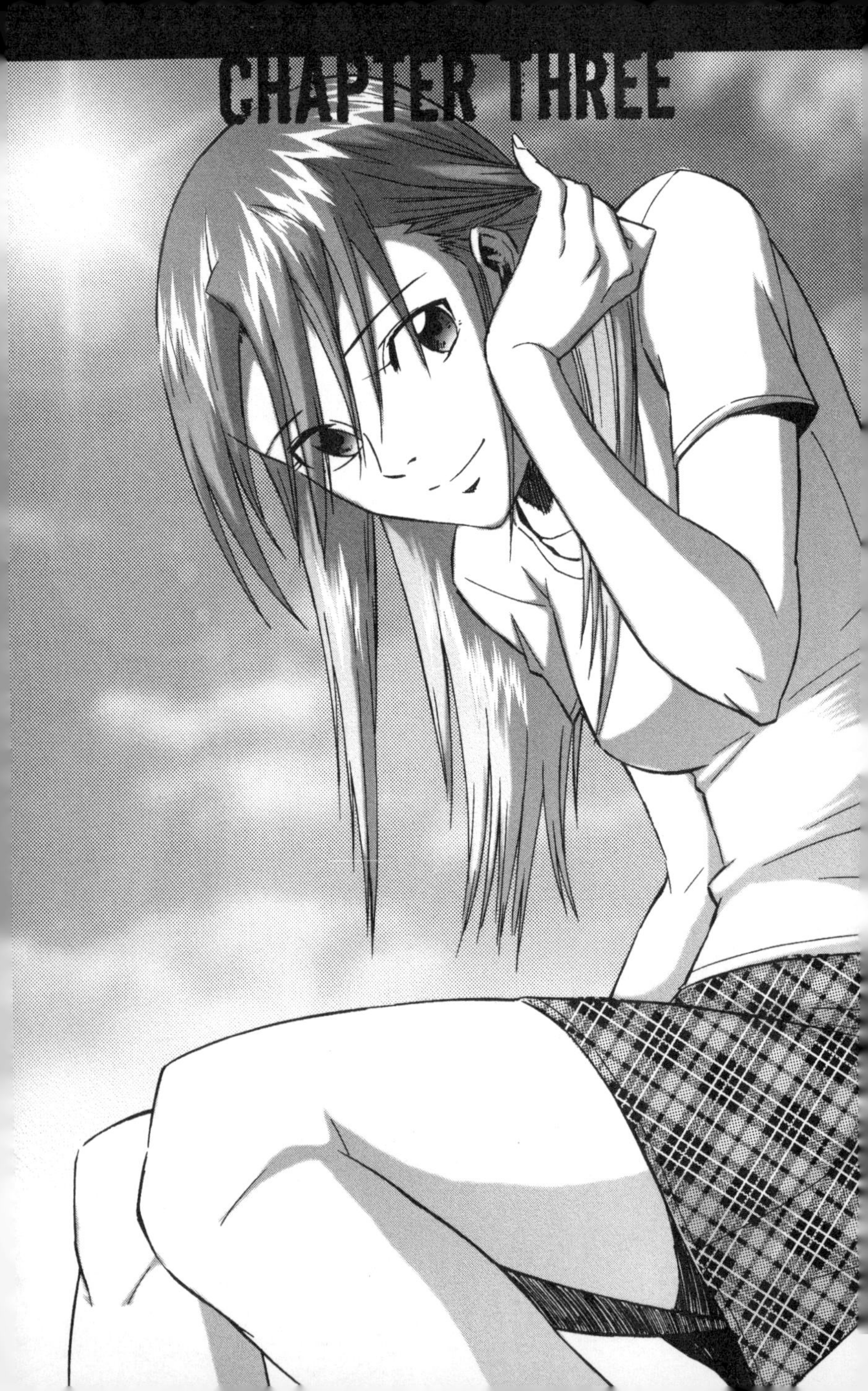
CHAPTER THREE

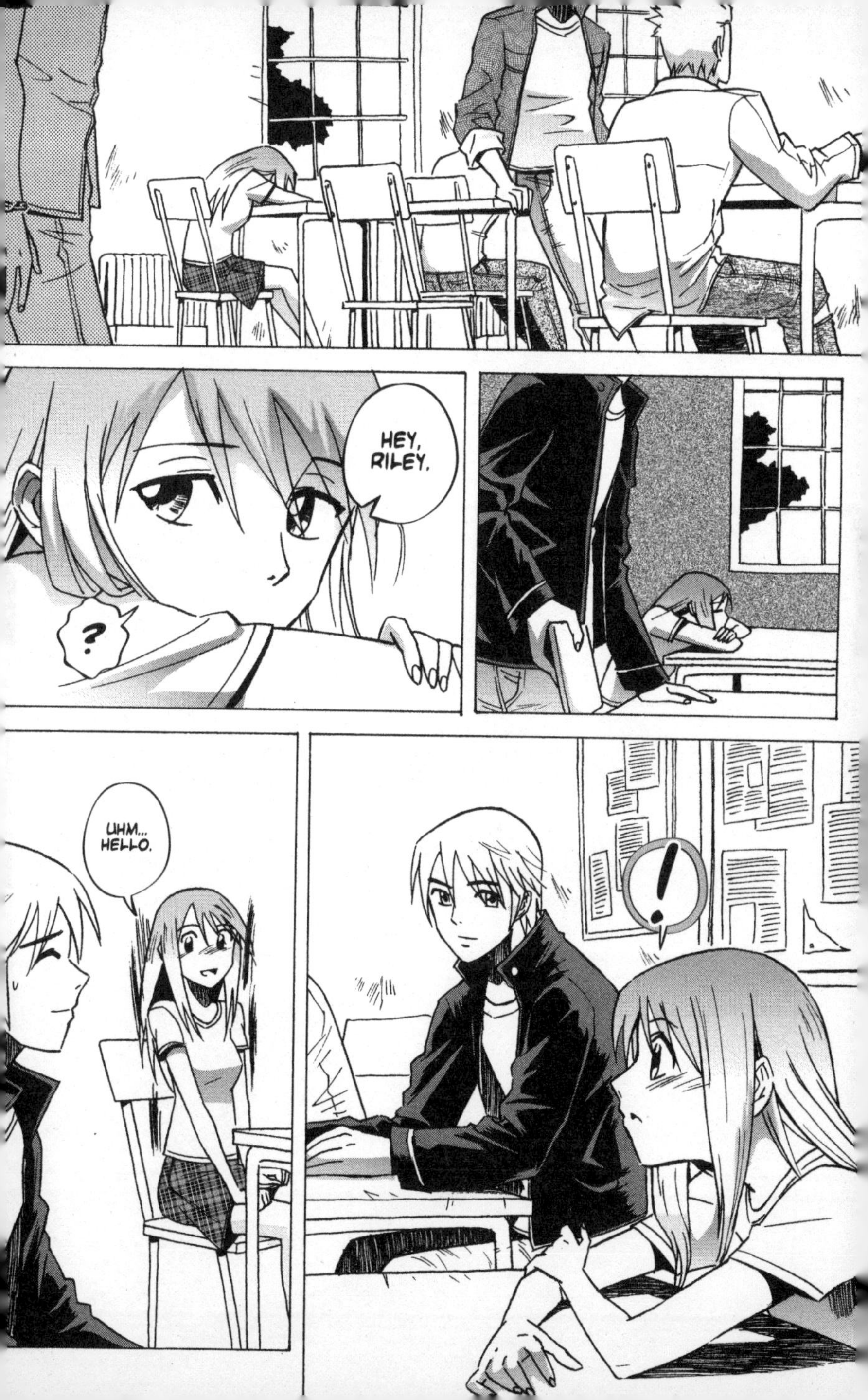
HEY, RILEY.
?
!
UHM... HELLO.

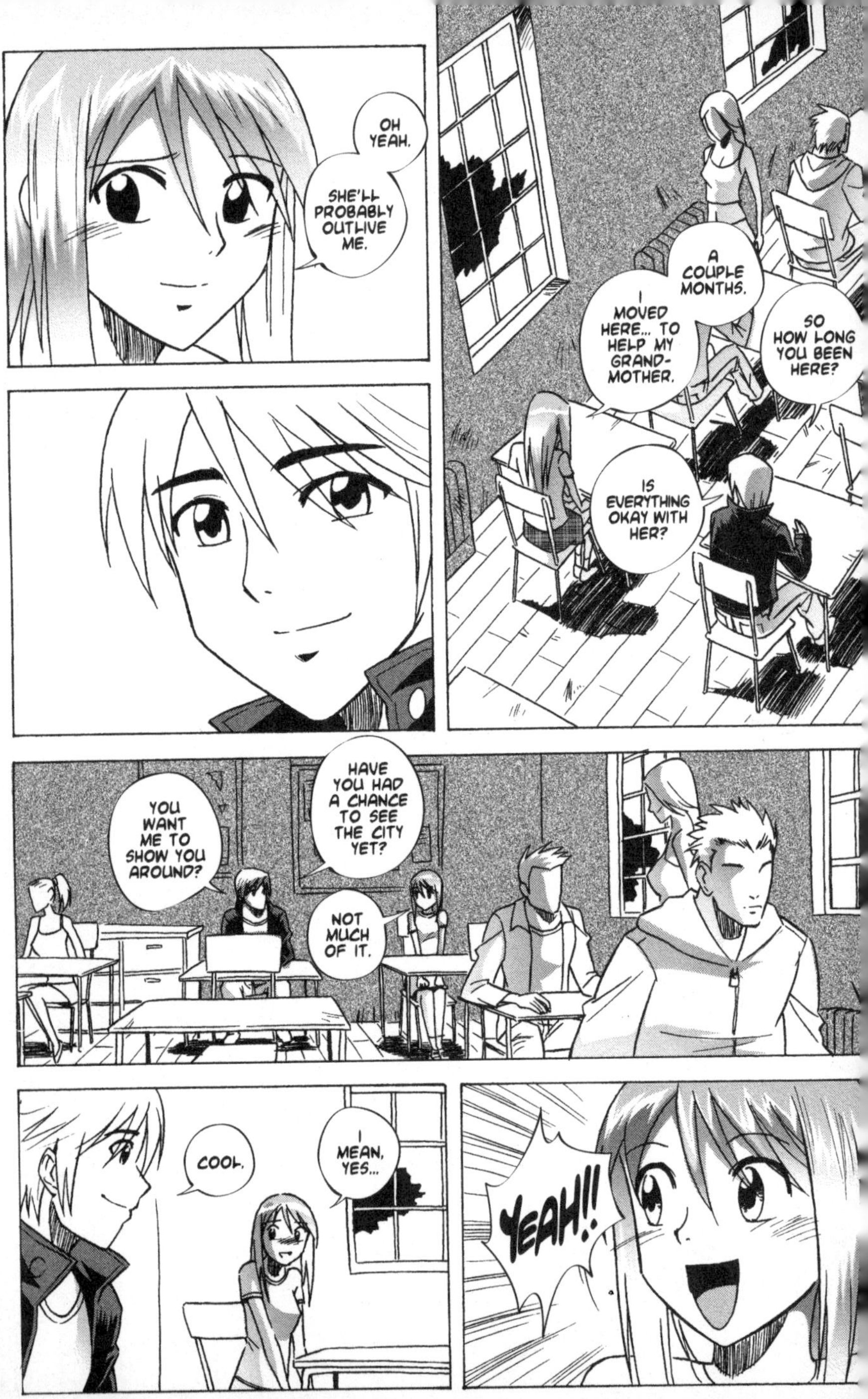
SO HOW LONG YOU BEEN HERE?
A COUPLE MONTHS.
I MOVED HERE... TO HELP MY GRAND-MOTHER.
IS EVERYTHING OKAY WITH HER?
OH YEAH.
SHE'LL PROBABLY OUTLIVE ME.
HAVE YOU HAD A CHANCE TO SEE THE CITY YET?
NOT MUCH OF IT.
YOU WANT ME TO SHOW YOU AROUND?
YEAH!!
I MEAN, YES...
COOL.

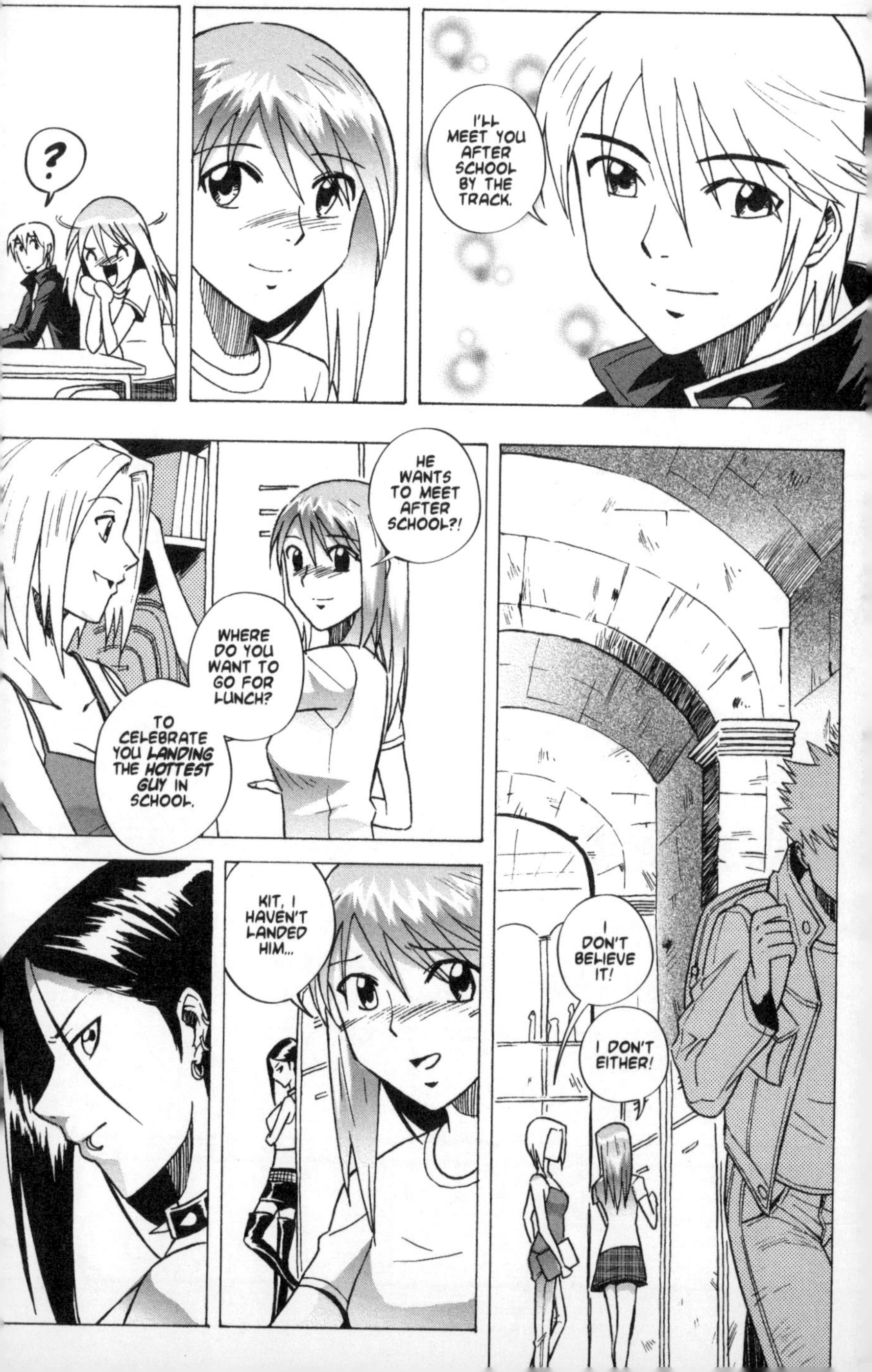
I'LL MEET YOU AFTER SCHOOL BY THE TRACK.
?
I DON'T BELIEVE IT!
I DON'T EITHER!
HE WANTS TO MEET AFTER SCHOOL?!
WHERE DO YOU WANT TO GO FOR LUNCH?
TO CELEBRATE YOU LANDING THE HOTTEST GUY IN SCHOOL.
KIT, I HAVEN'T LANDED HIM...

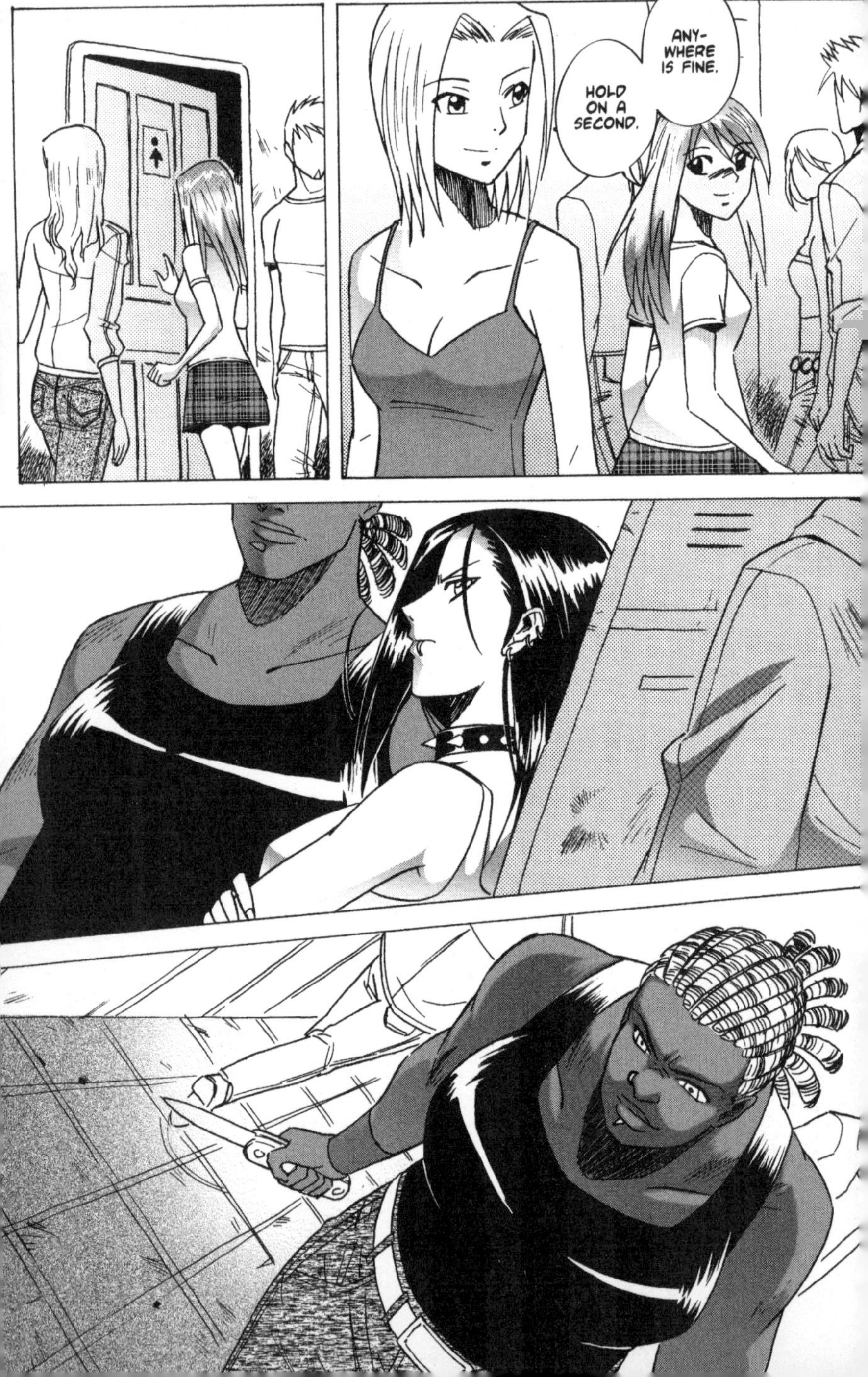
ANY-WHERE IS FINE.
HOLD ON A SECOND.

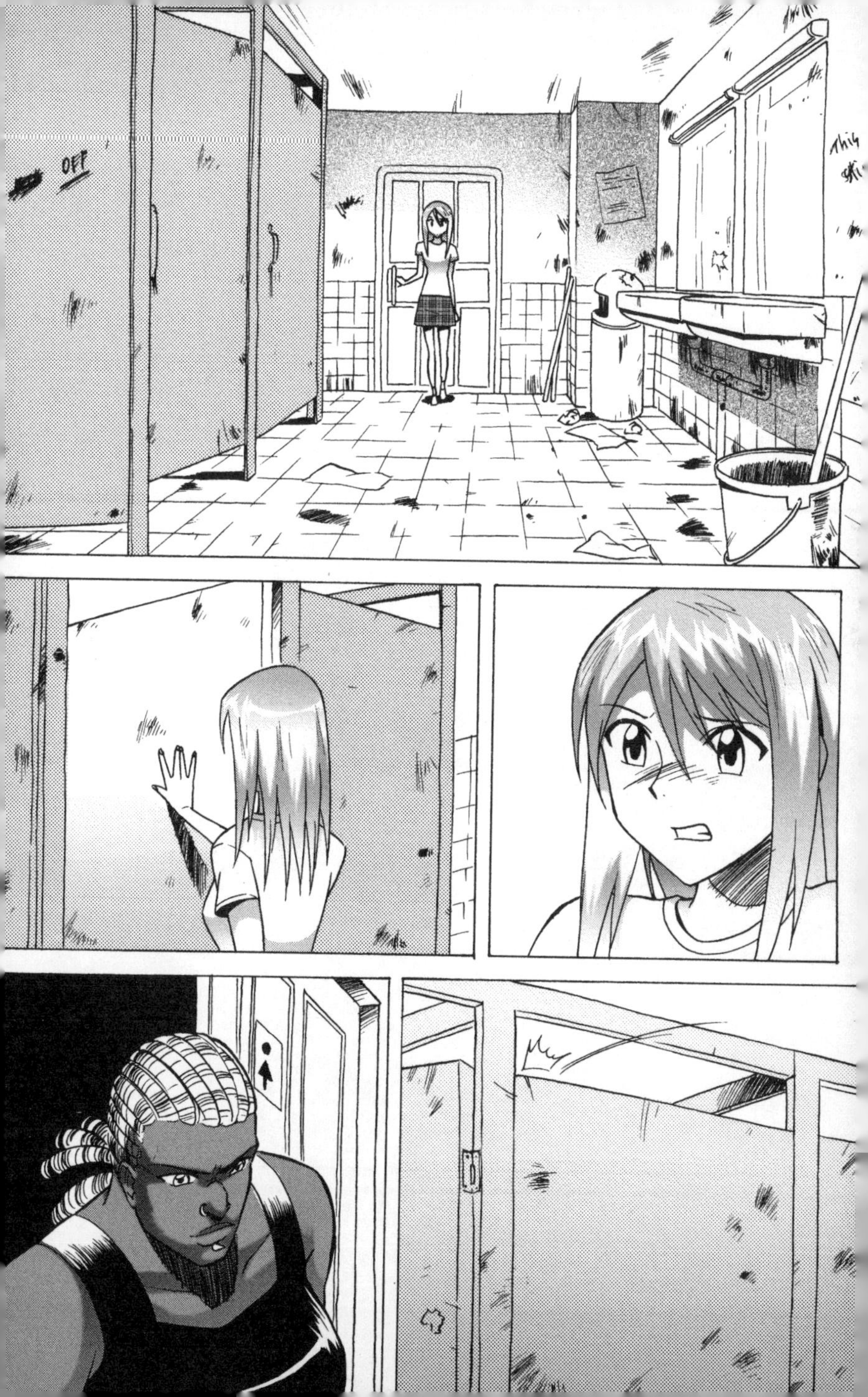
OFF

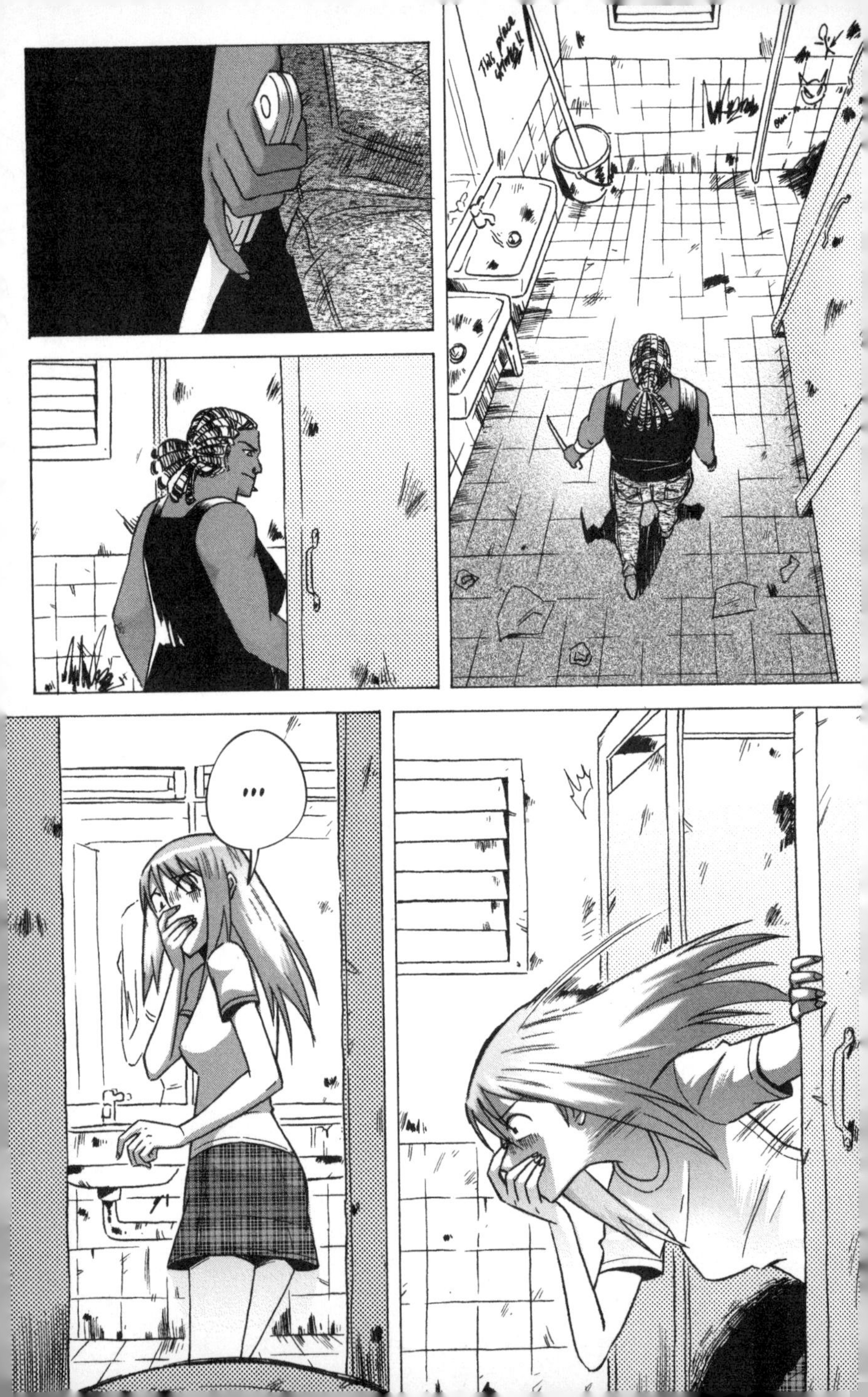
...

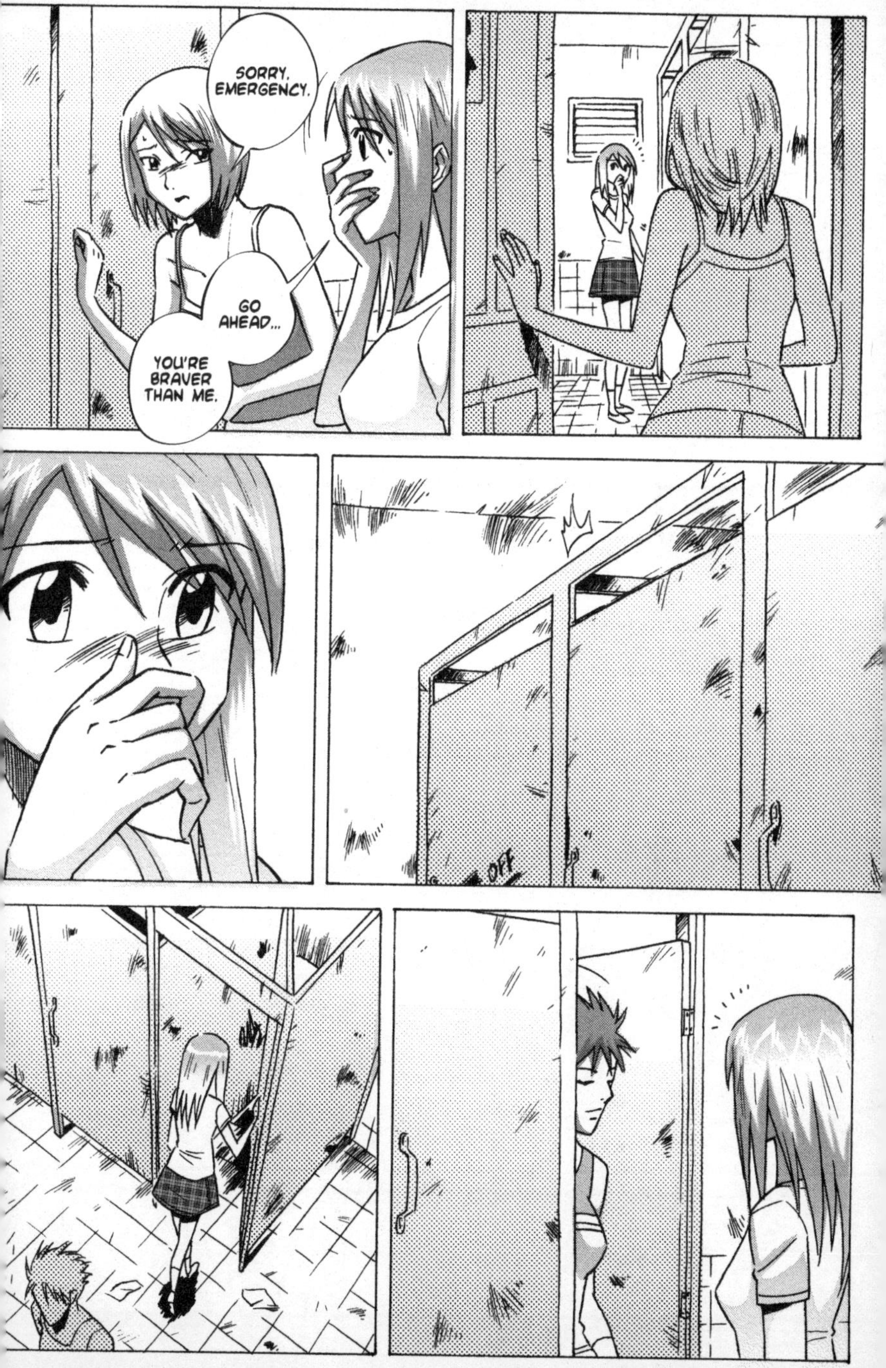
SORRY, EMERGENCY.
GO AHEAD...
YOU'RE BRAVER THAN ME.
OFF

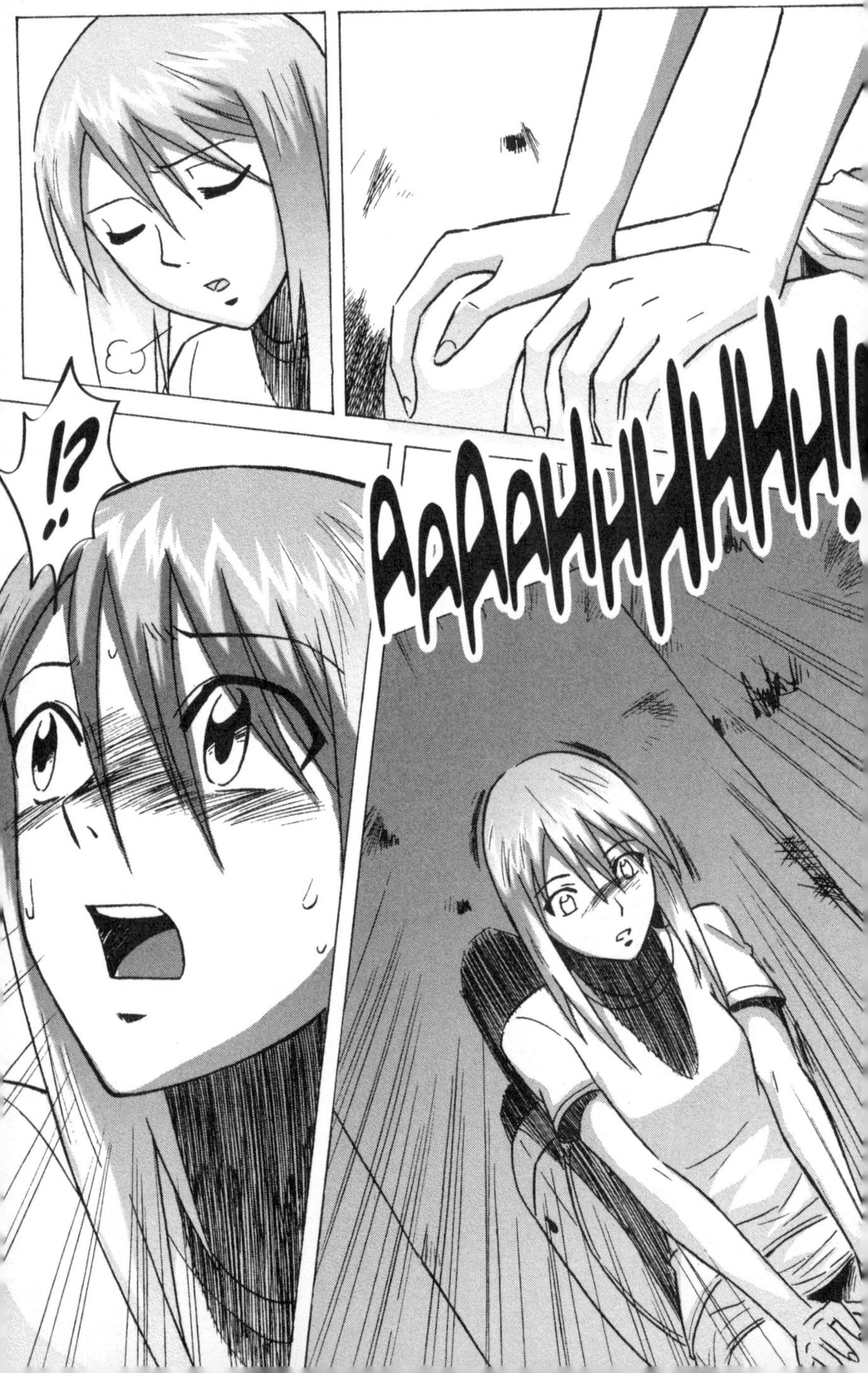

AAAAHHHHHHH!!
!?

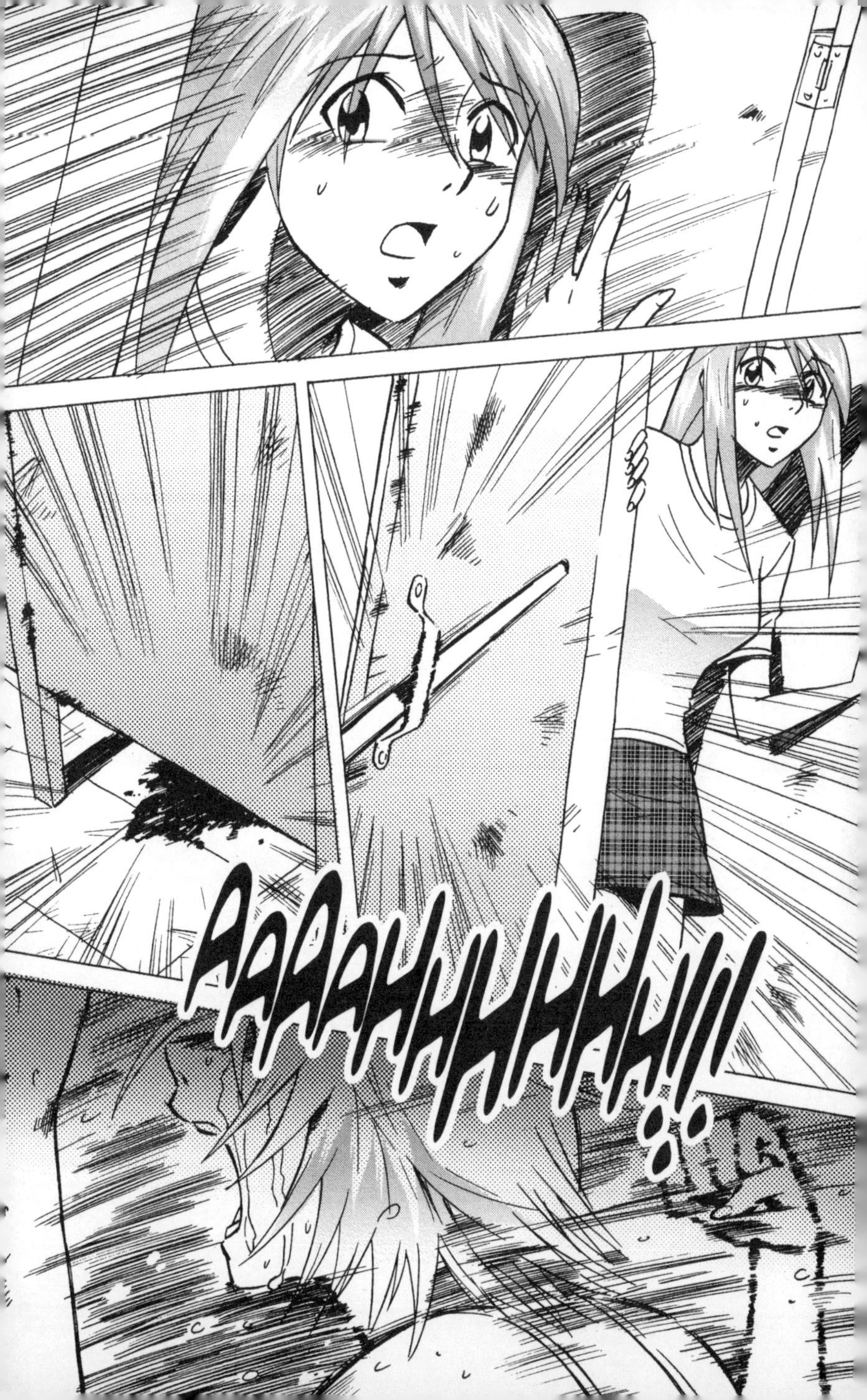
AAAAHHHHHHH!!

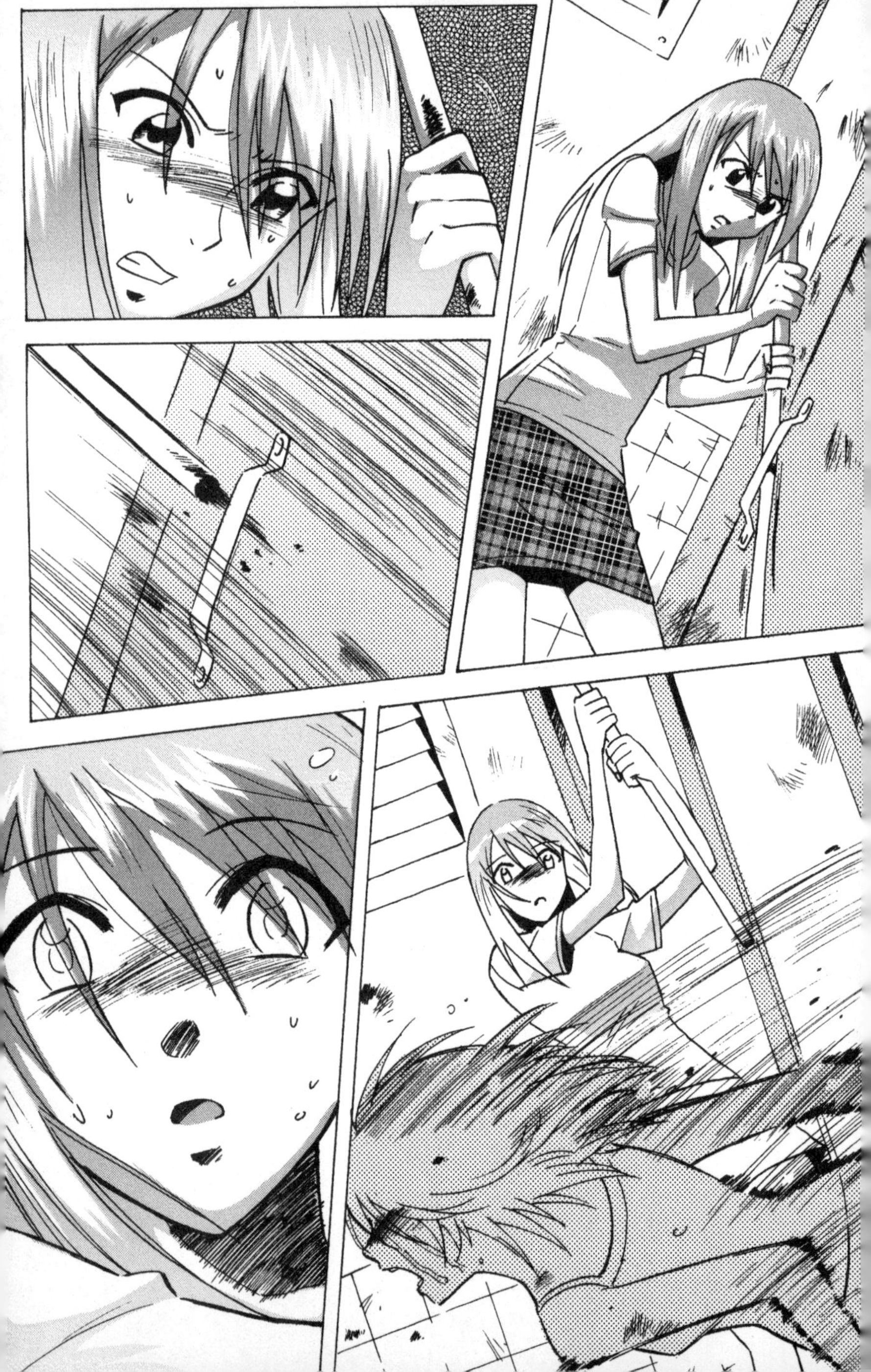

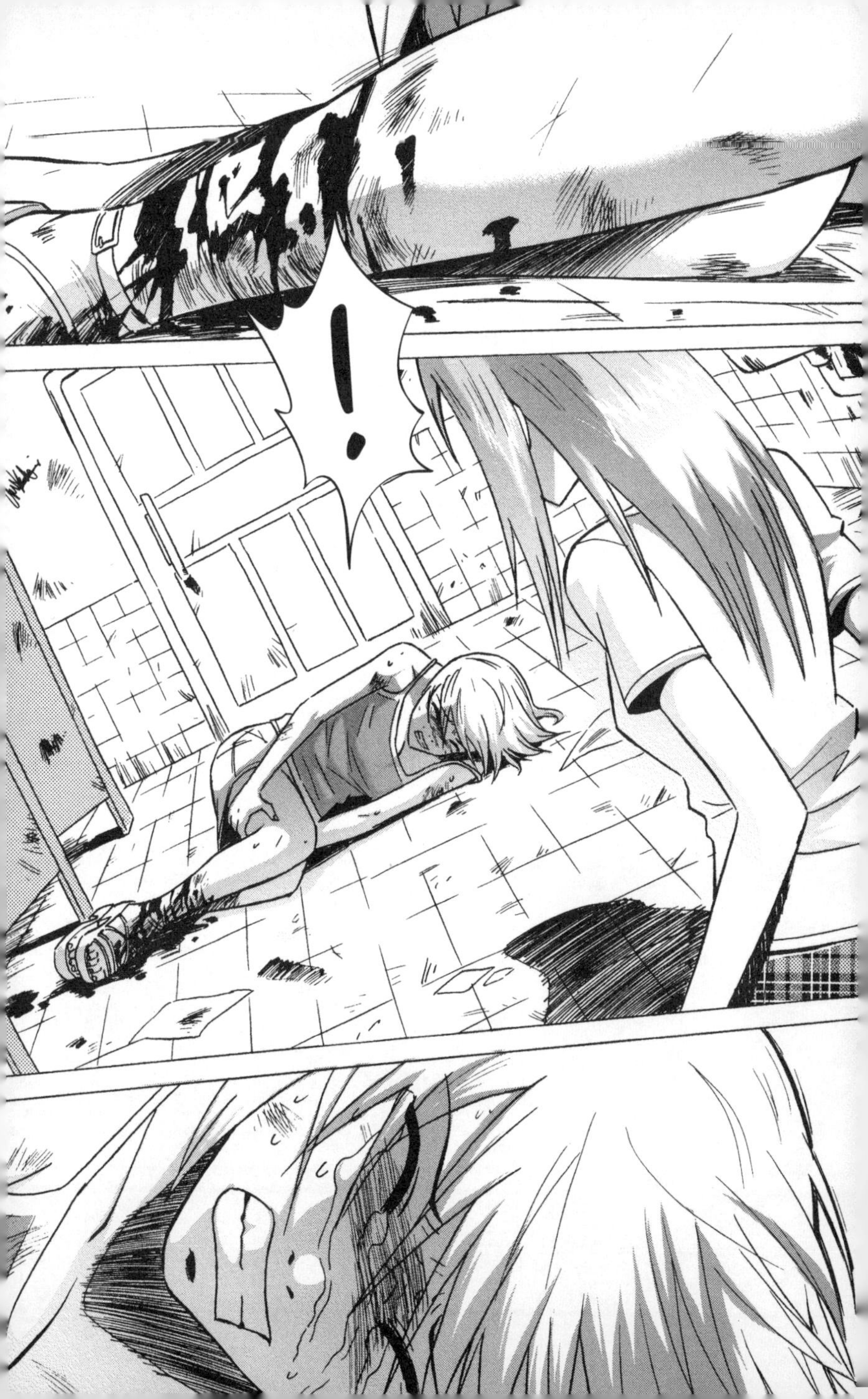
!

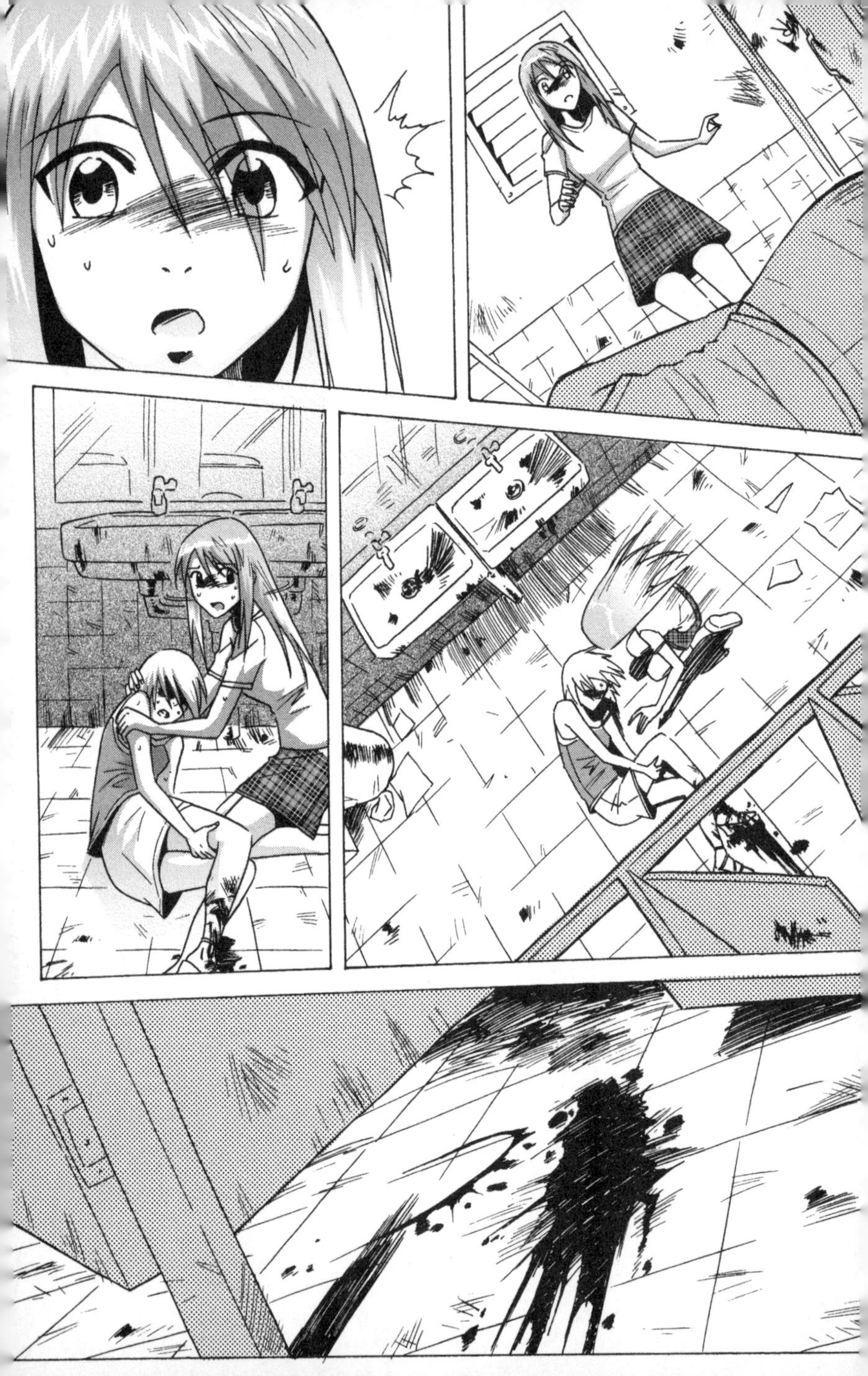

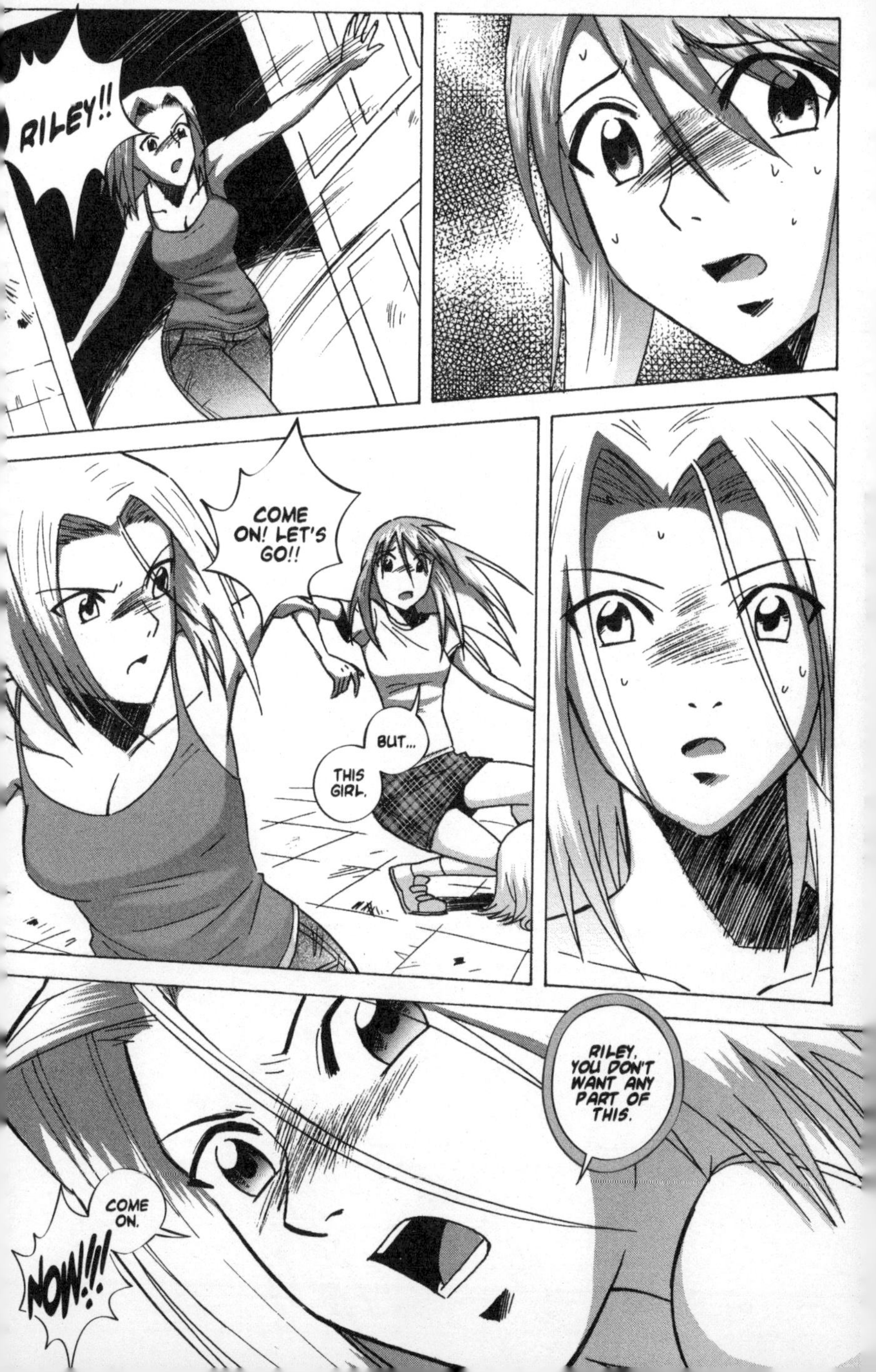
RILEY!!
COME ON! LET'S GO!!
BUT... THIS GIRL.
RILEY, YOU DON'T WANT ANY PART OF THIS.
COME ON.
NOW!!!

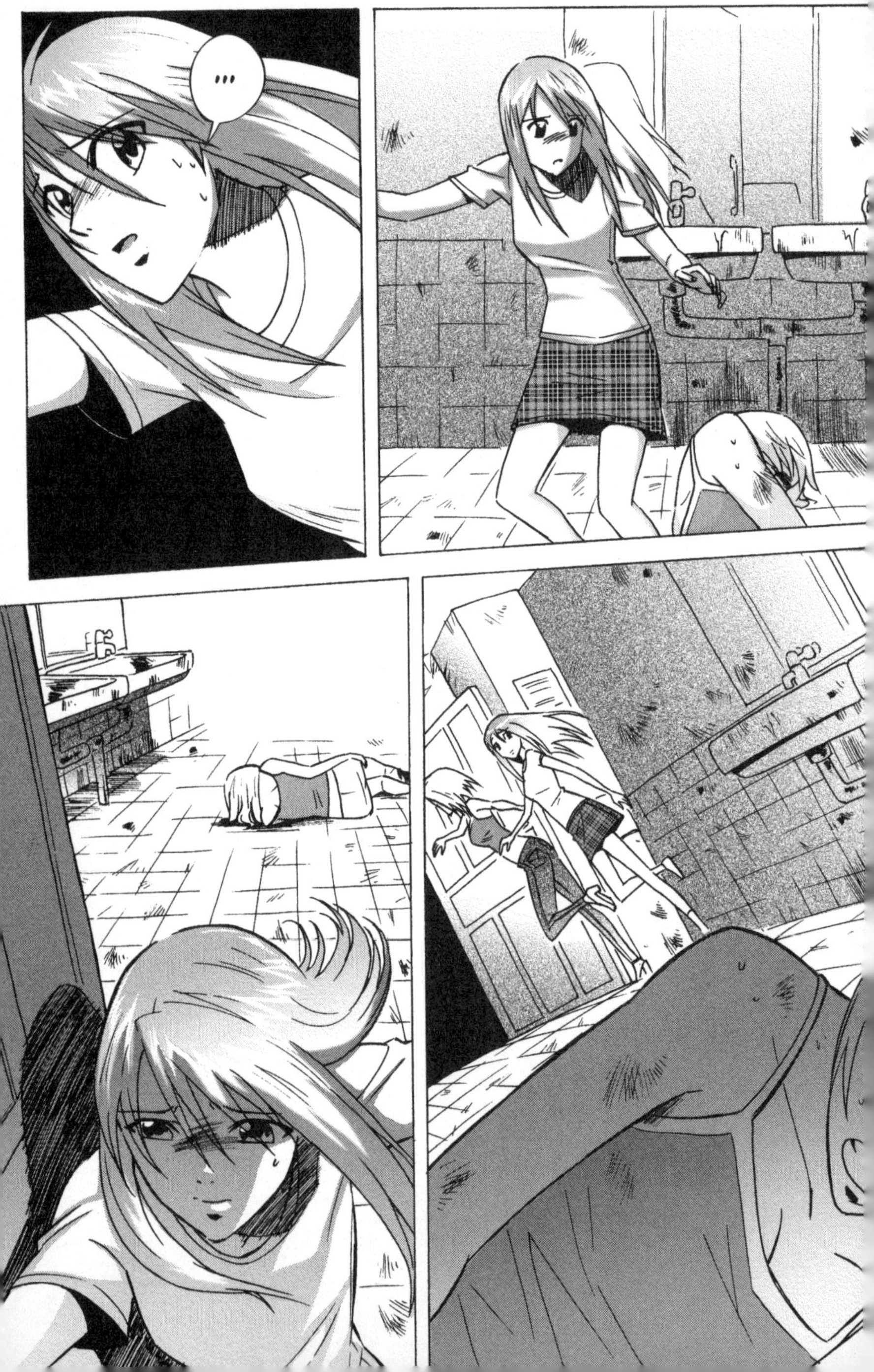
...

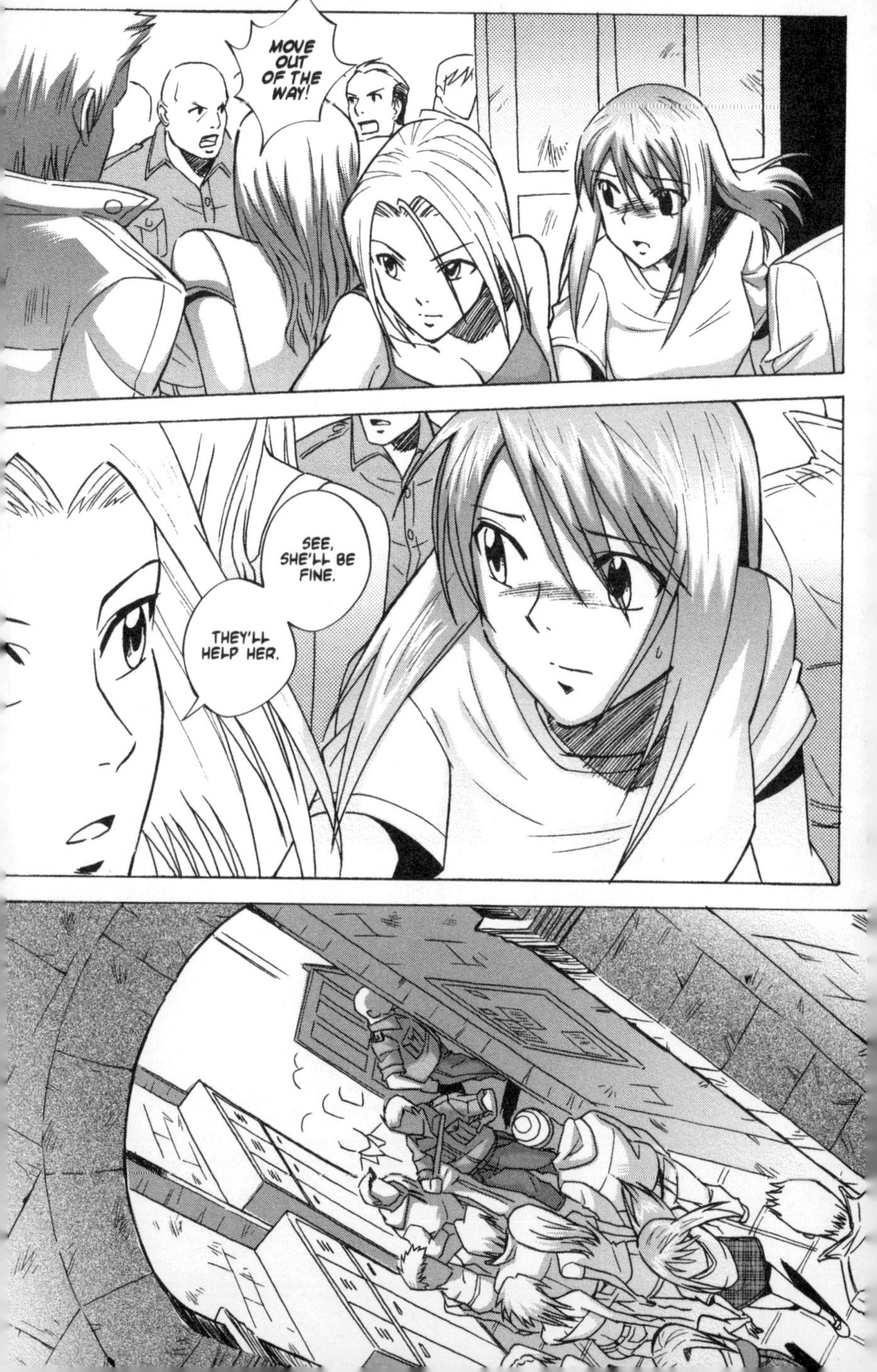
MOVE OUT OF THE WAY!
SEE, SHE'LL BE FINE.
THEY'LL HELP HER.

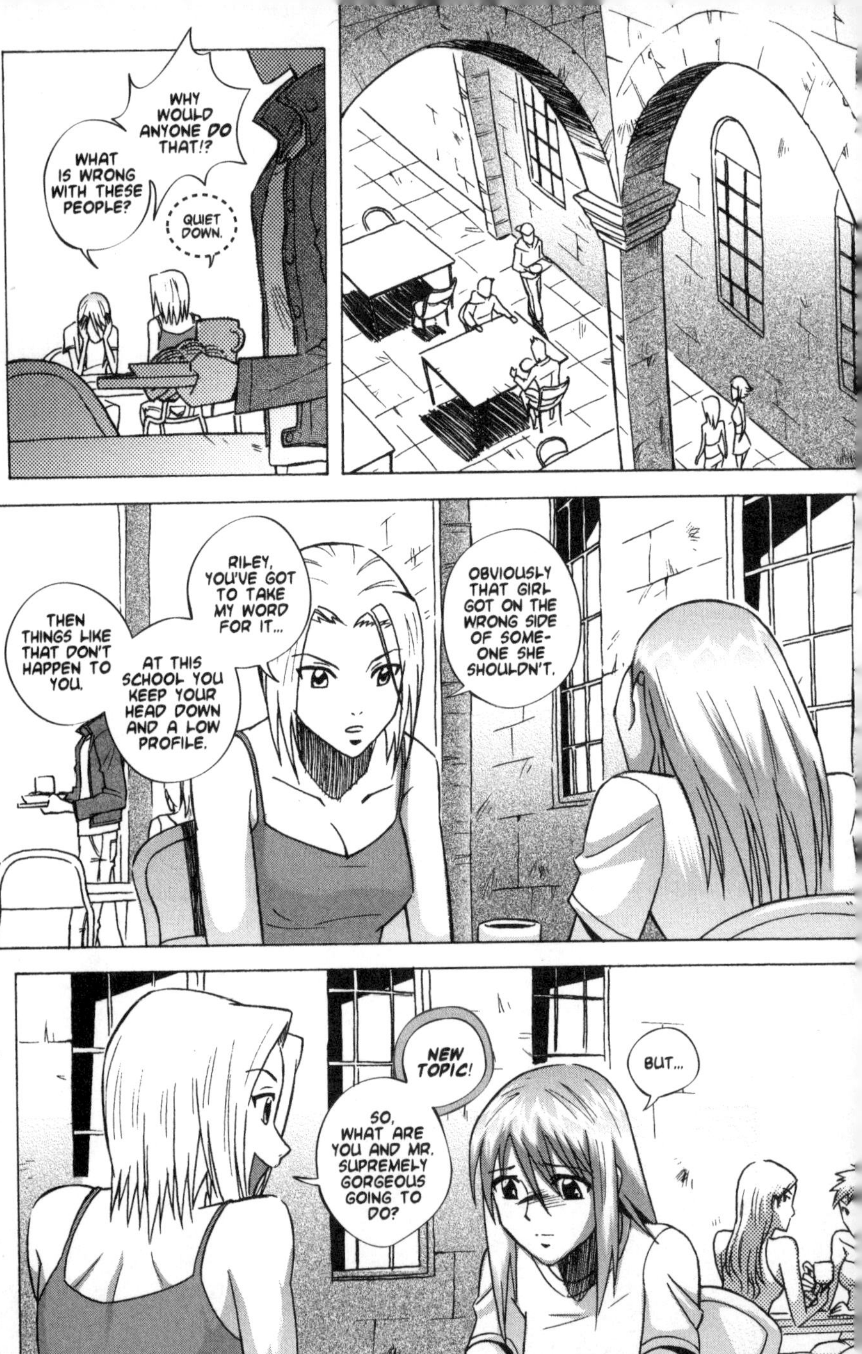
WHY WOULD ANYONE DO THAT!?
WHAT IS WRONG WITH THESE PEOPLE?
QUIET DOWN.
OBVIOUSLY THAT GIRL GOT ON THE WRONG SIDE OF SOME-ONE SHE SHOULDN'T.
RILEY, YOU'VE GOT TO TAKE MY WORD FOR IT...
AT THIS SCHOOL YOU KEEP YOUR HEAD DOWN AND A LOW PROFILE.
THEN THINGS LIKE THAT DON'T HAPPEN TO YOU.
BUT...
NEW TOPIC!
SO, WHAT ARE YOU AND MR. SUPREMELY GORGEOUS GOING TO DO?

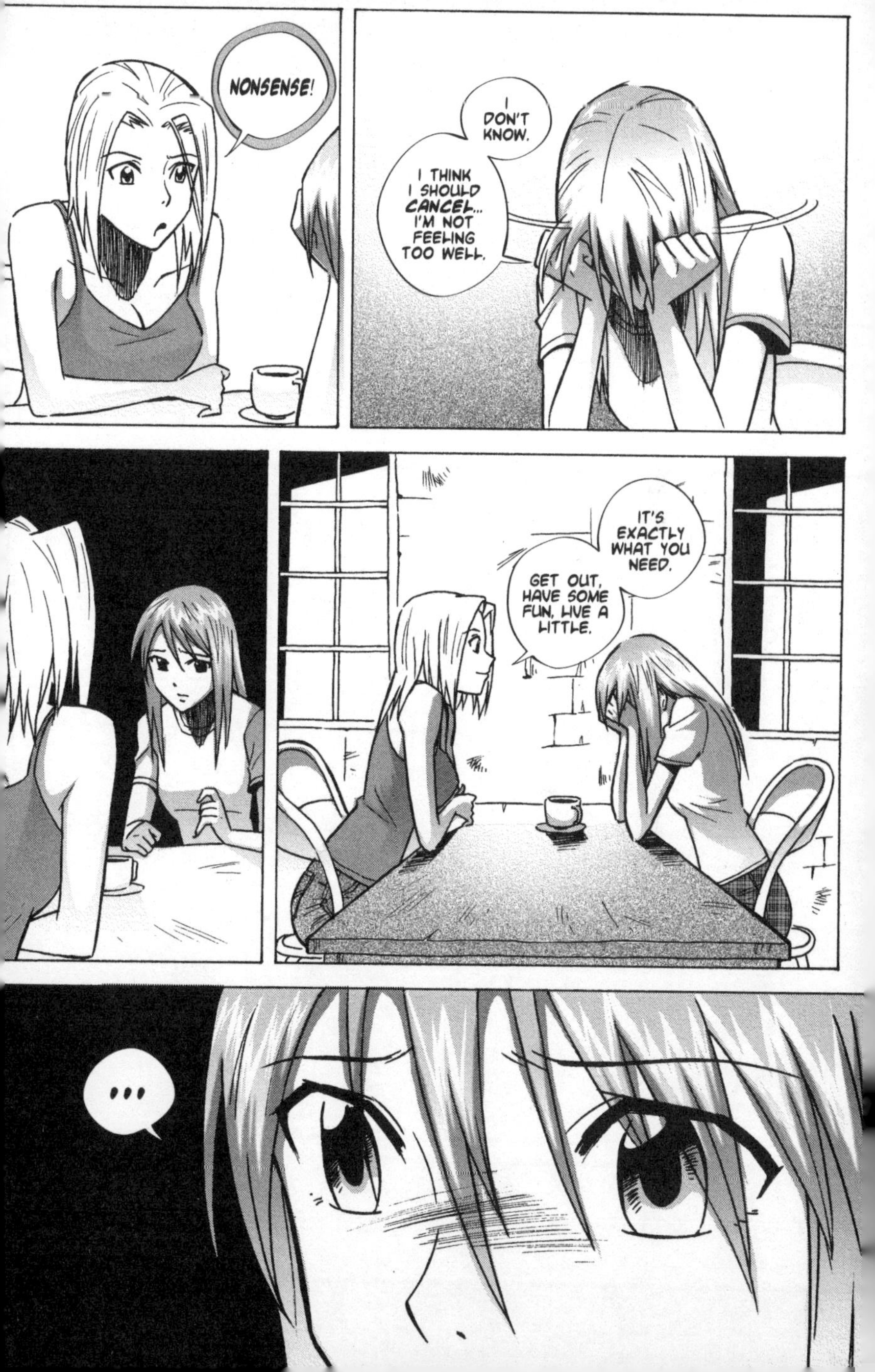
I DON'T KNOW.
I THINK I SHOULD CANCEL... I'M NOT FEELING TOO WELL.
NONSENSE!
IT'S EXACTLY WHAT YOU NEED.
GET OUT, HAVE SOME FUN, LIVE A LITTLE.
...

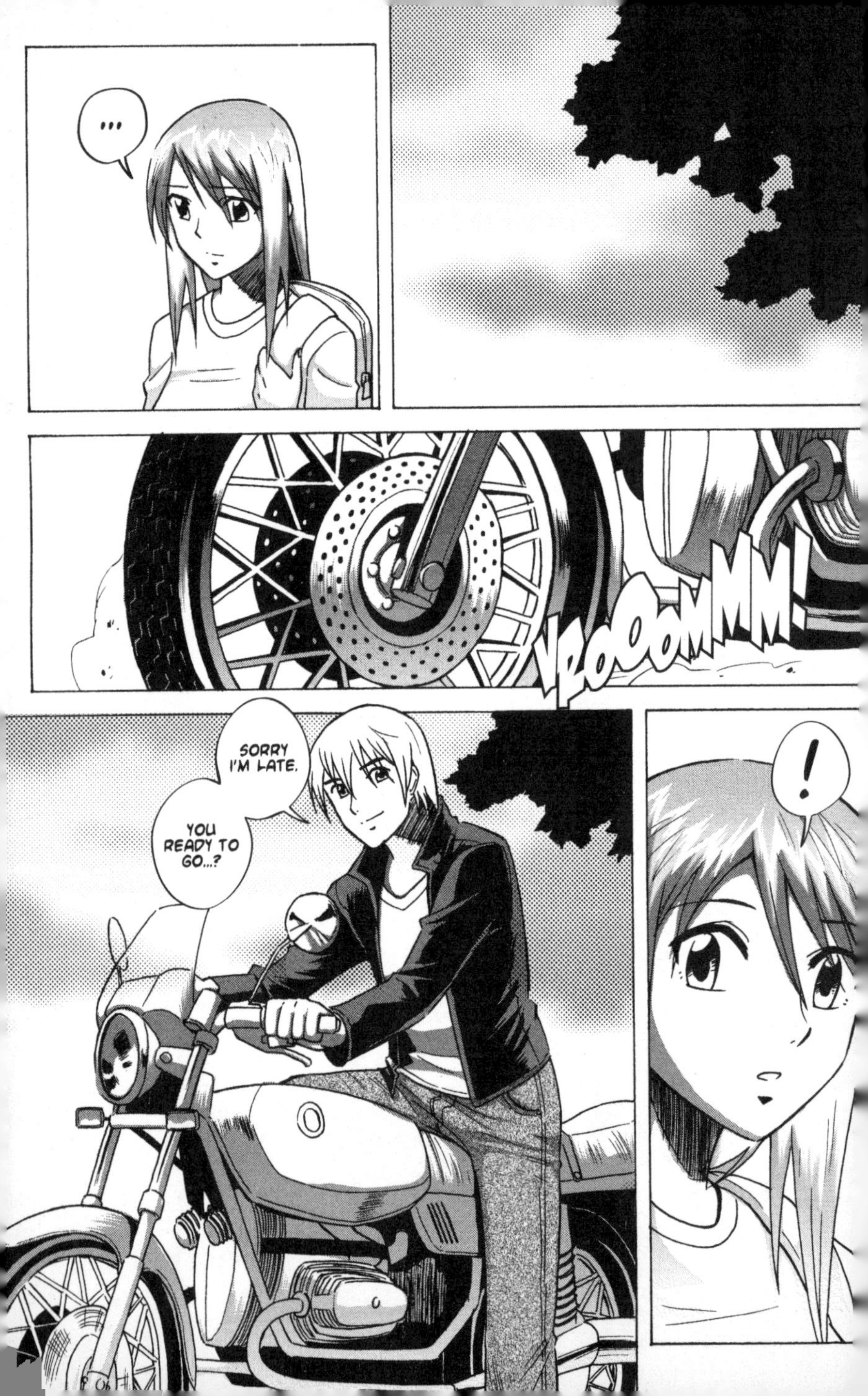
…
VROOOMMMM!
!
SORRY I'M LATE.
YOU READY TO GO…?

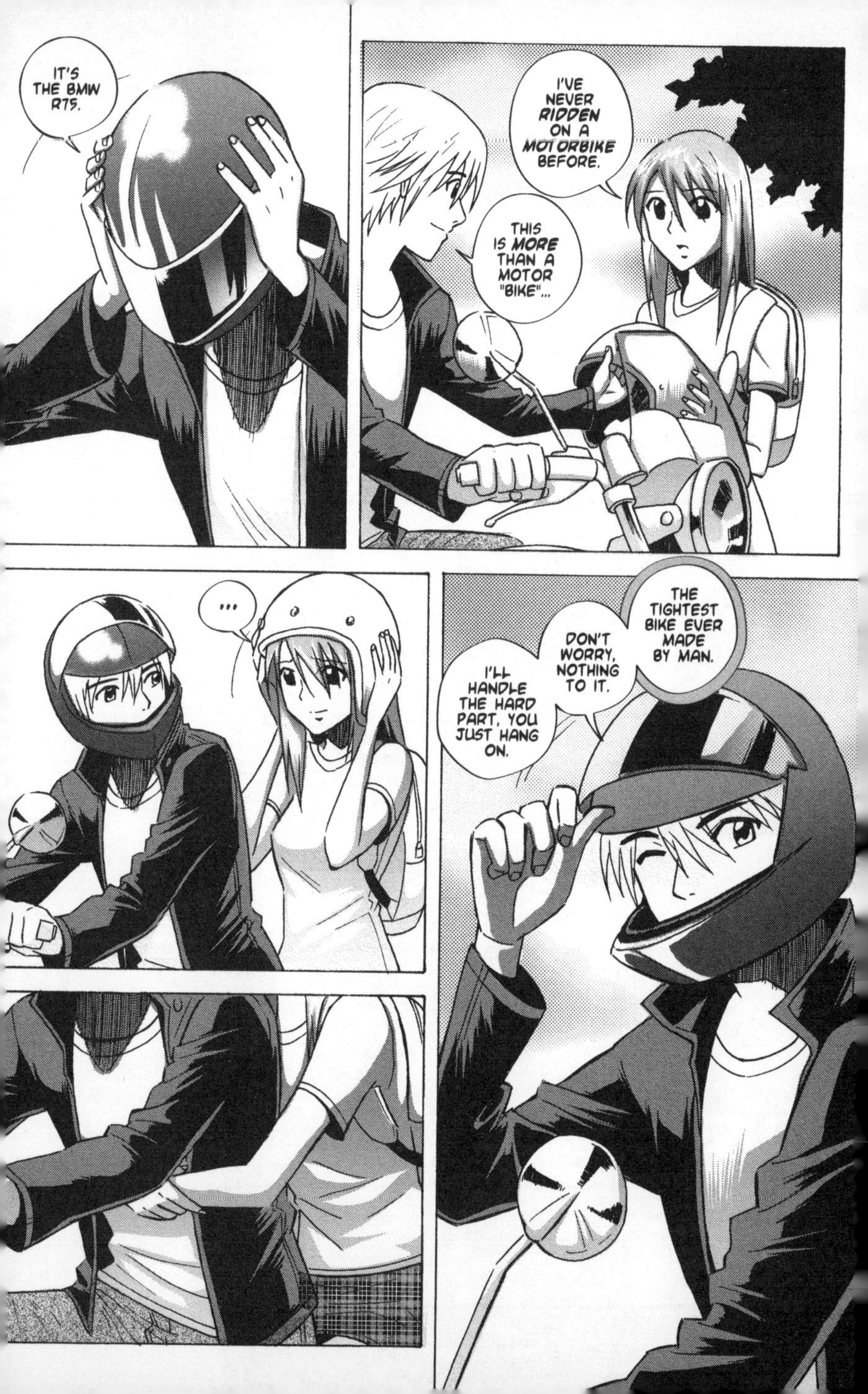
I'VE NEVER RIDDEN ON A MOTORBIKE BEFORE.
THIS IS MORE THAN A MOTOR "BIKE"...
IT'S THE BMW R75.
THE TIGHTEST BIKE EVER MADE BY MAN.
DON'T WORRY, NOTHING TO IT.
I'LL HANDLE THE HARD PART, YOU JUST HANG ON.
...

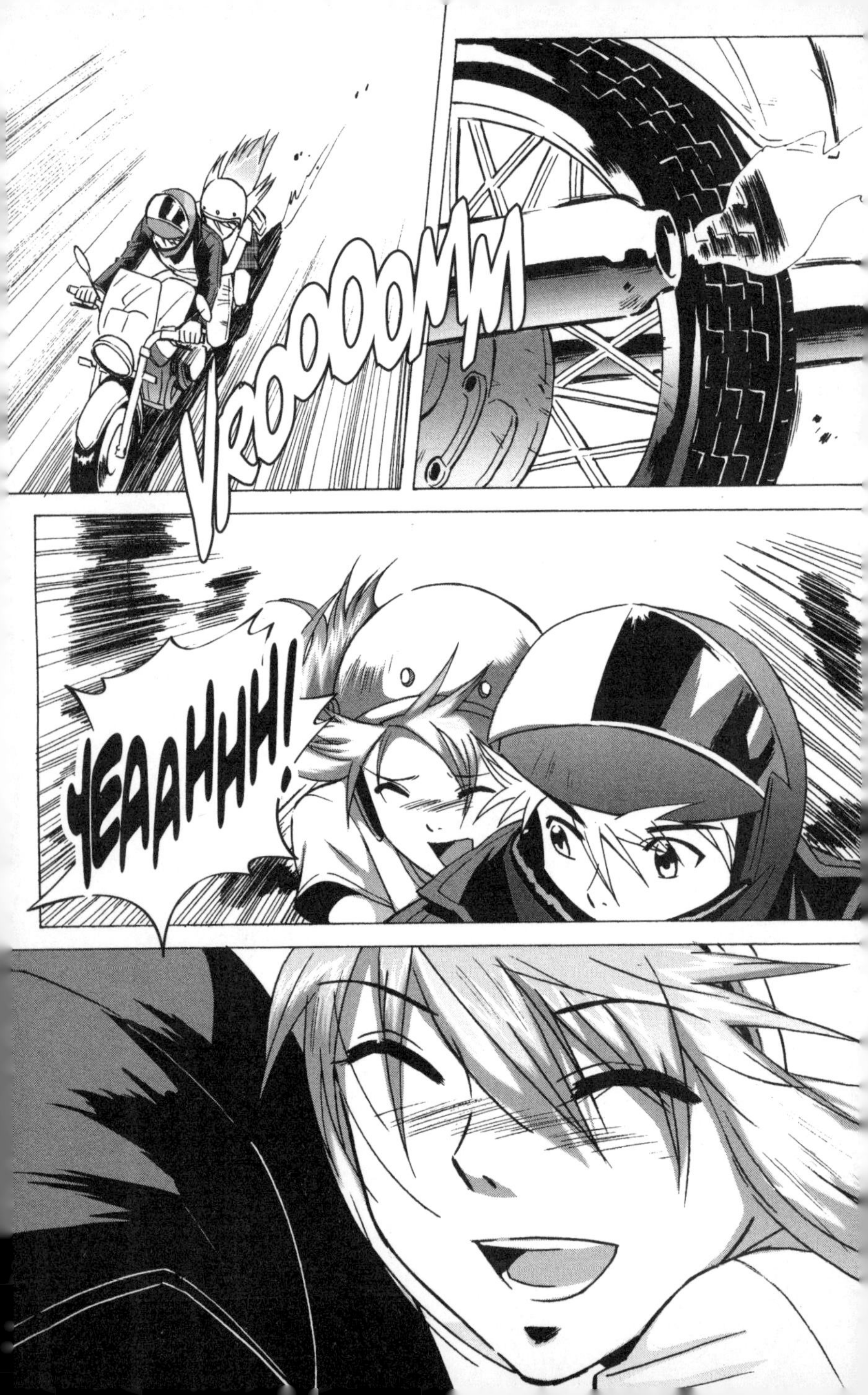
VROOOOMM
YEAAHHH!

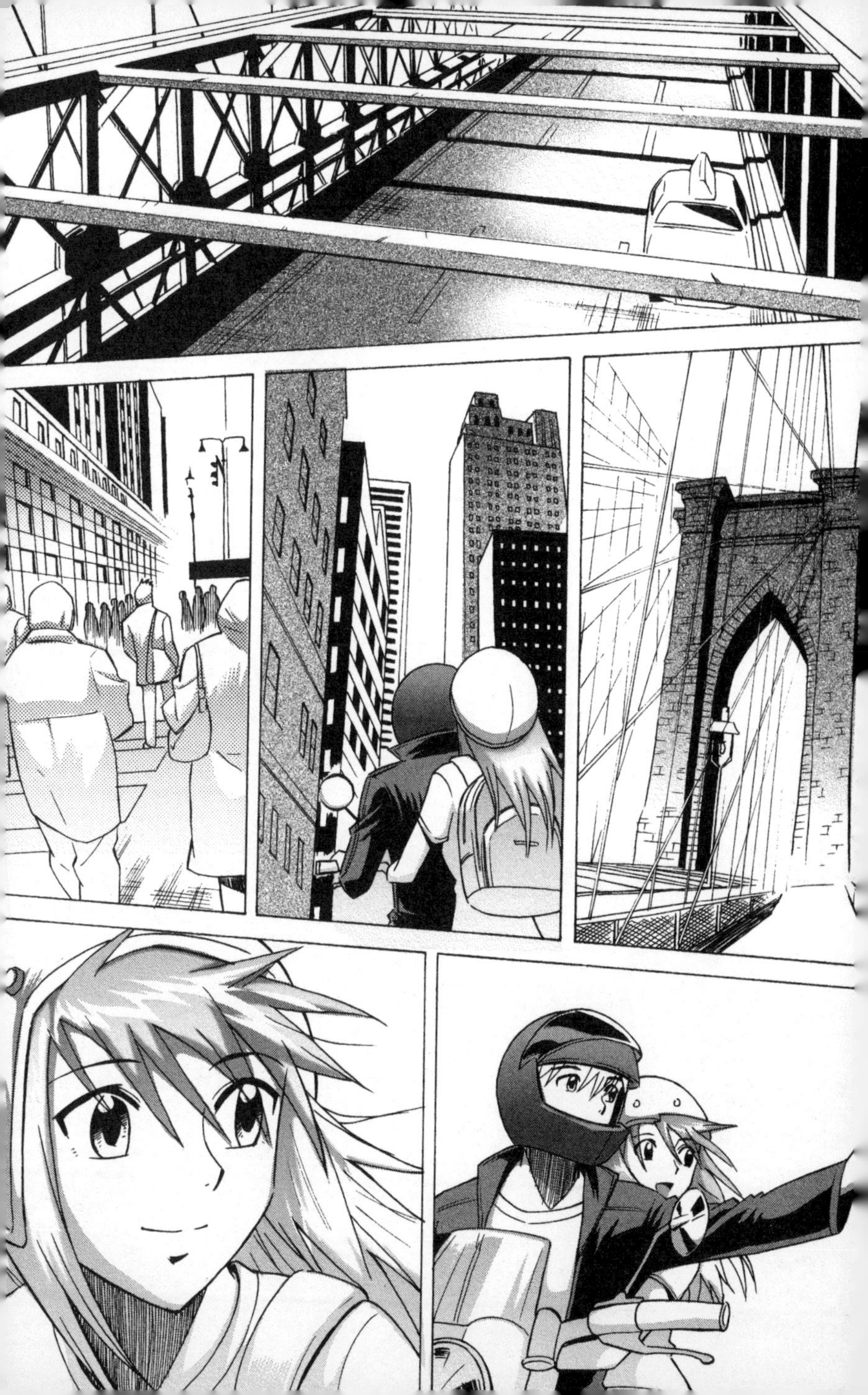

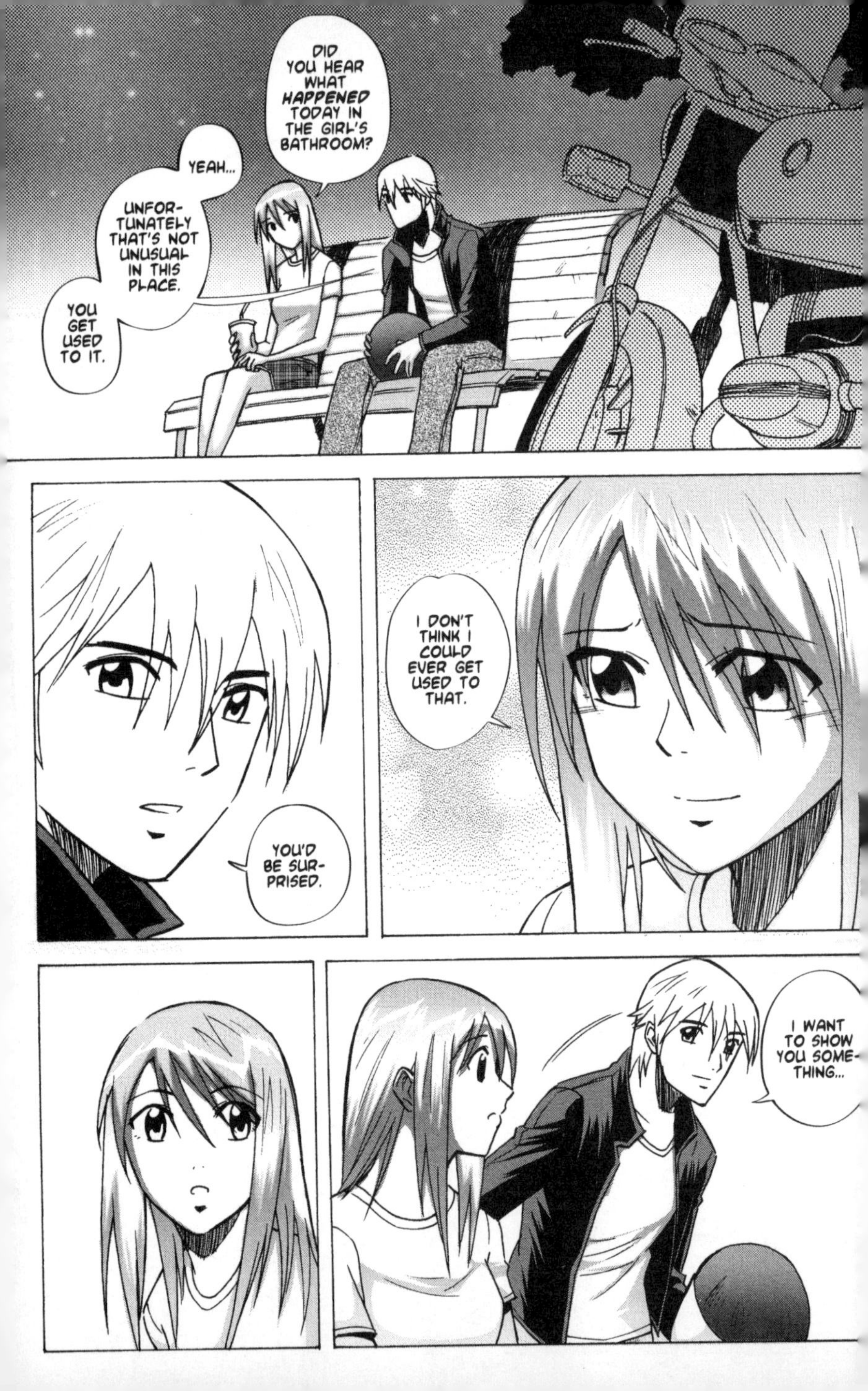
DID YOU HEAR WHAT HAPPENED TODAY IN THE GIRL'S BATHROOM?
YEAH...
UNFORTUNATELY THAT'S NOT UNUSUAL IN THIS PLACE.
YOU GET USED TO IT.
I DON'T THINK I COULD EVER GET USED TO THAT.
YOU'D BE SURPRISED.
I WANT TO SHOW YOU SOMETHING...

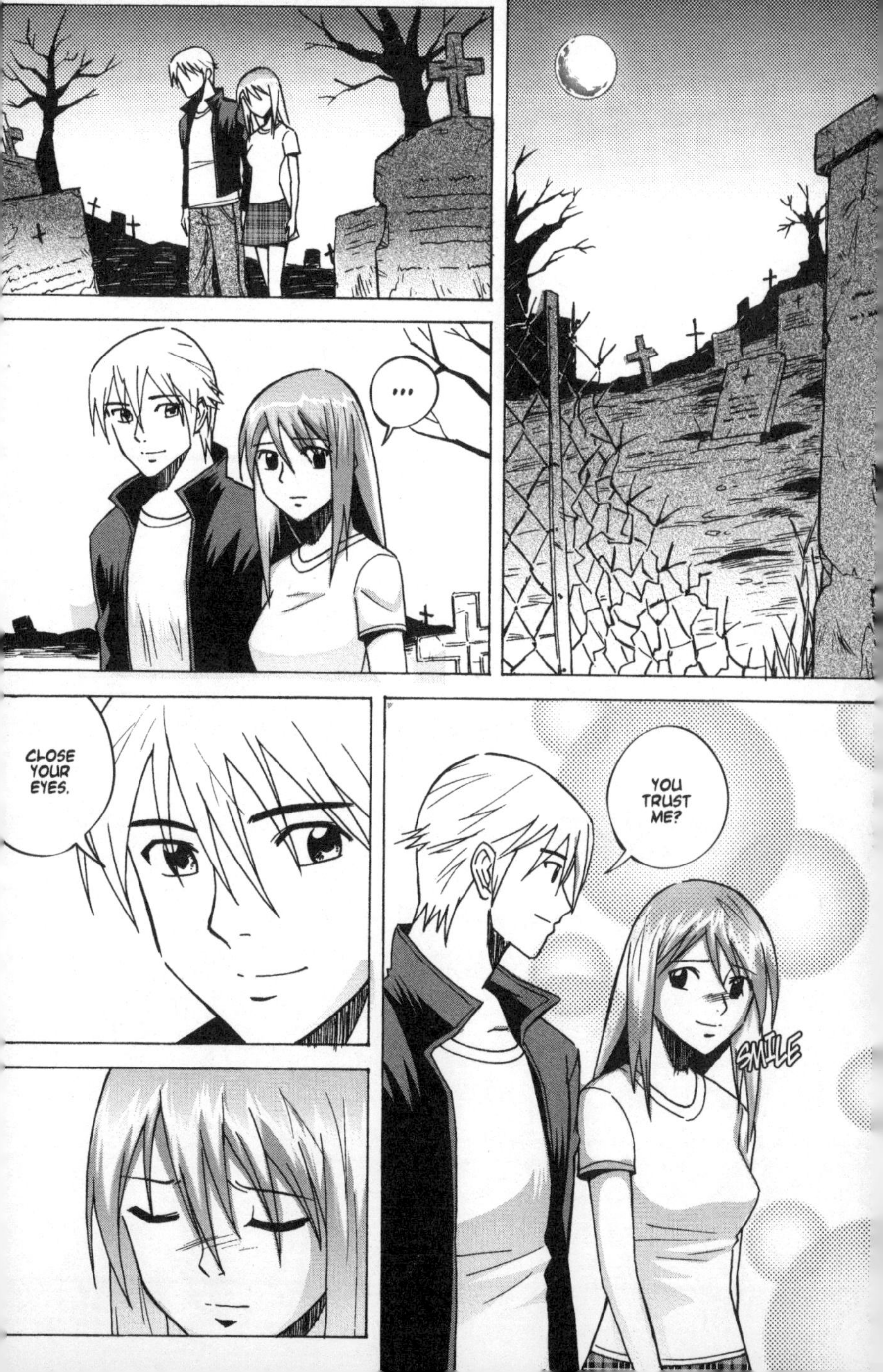
...
YOU TRUST ME?
SMILE
CLOSE YOUR EYES.

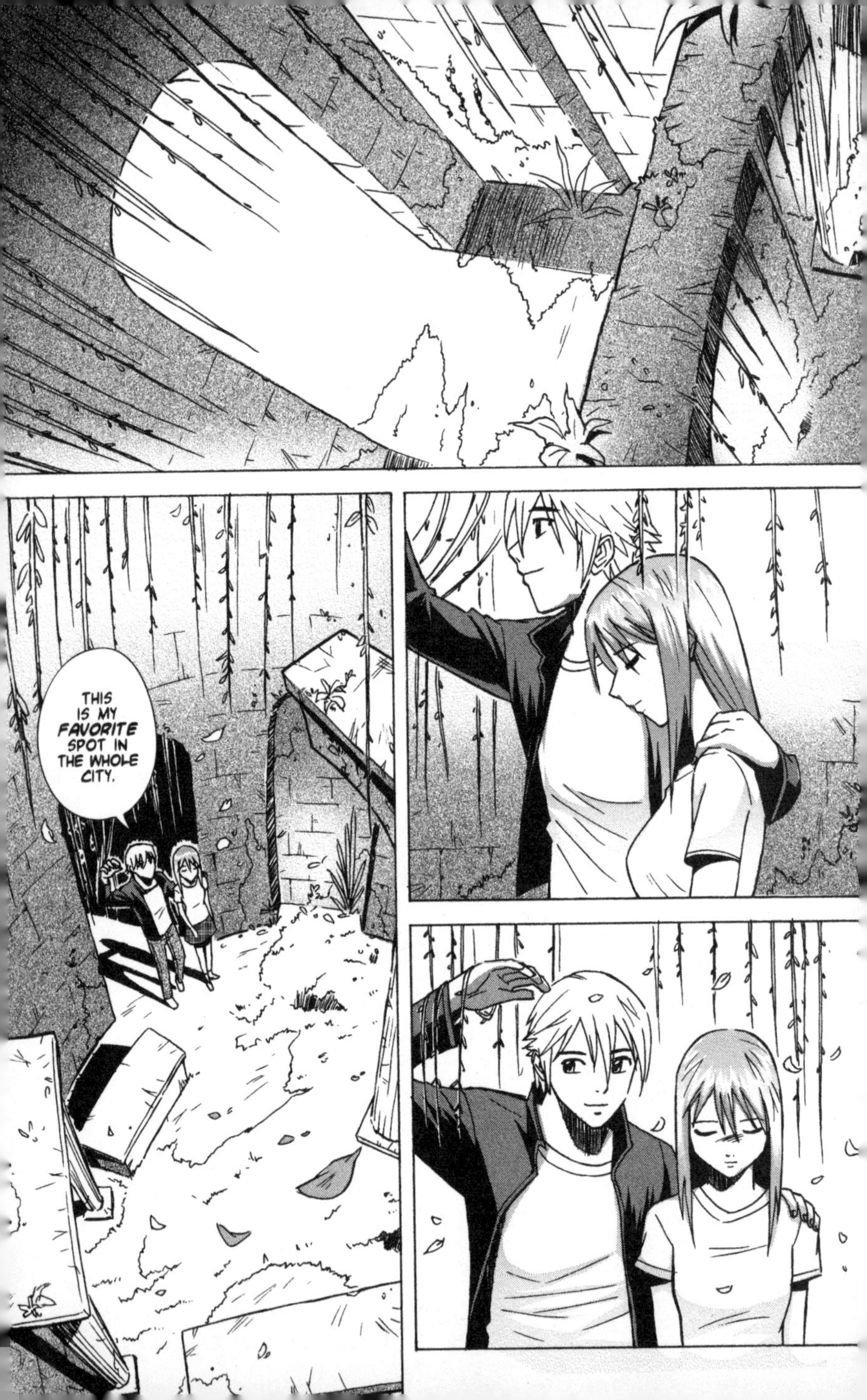
THIS IS MY FAVORITE SPOT IN THE WHOLE CITY.

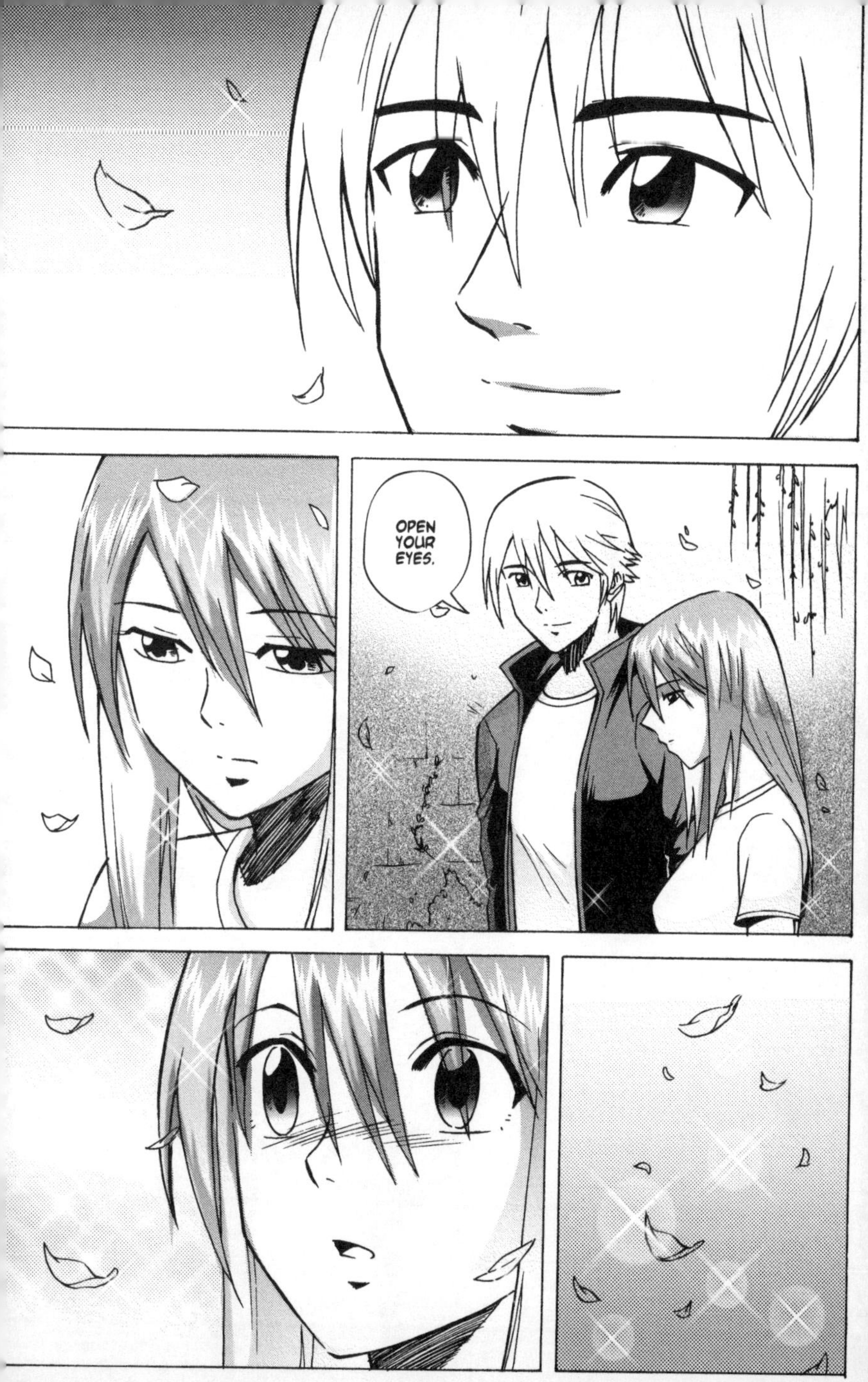
OPEN YOUR EYES.

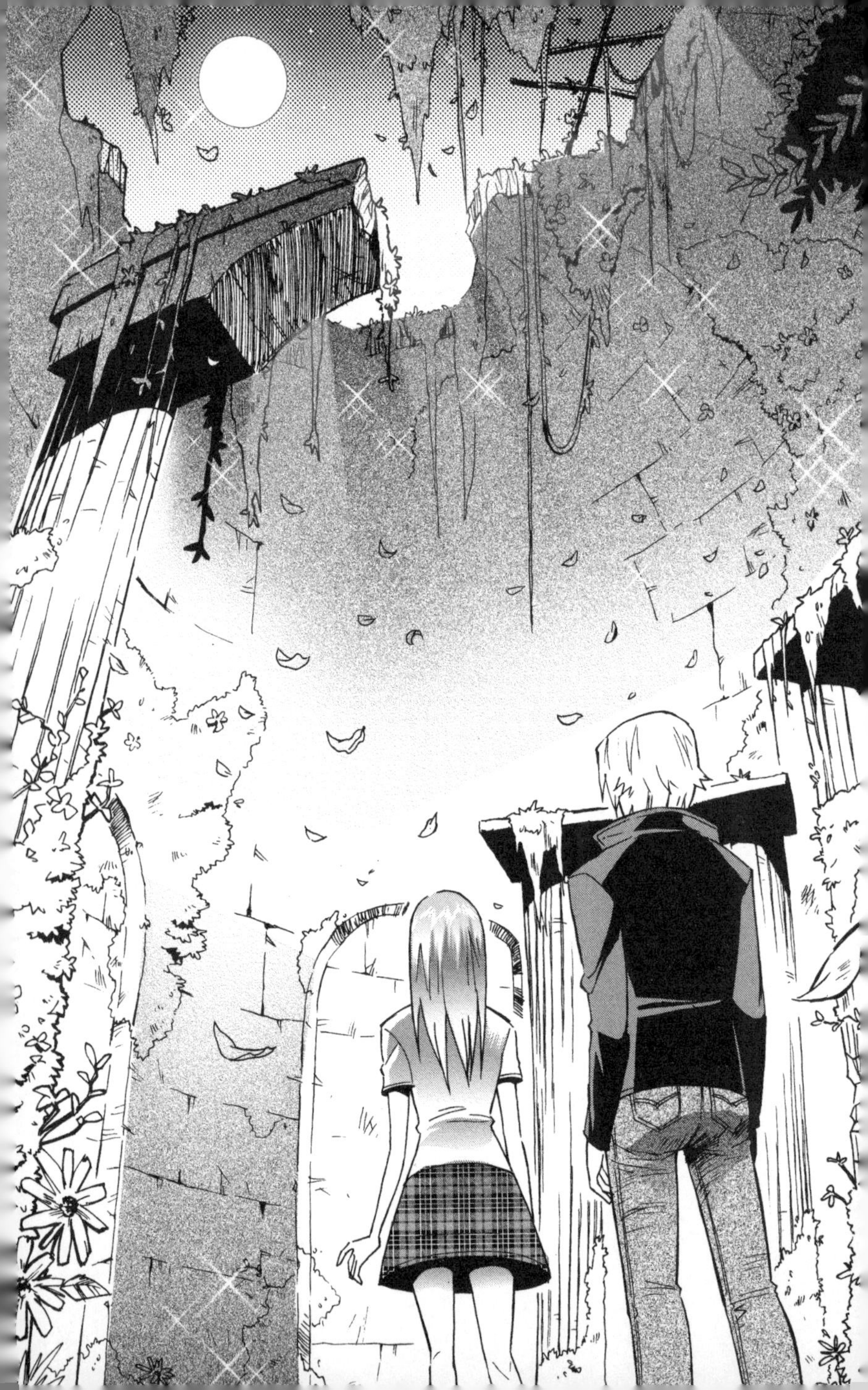

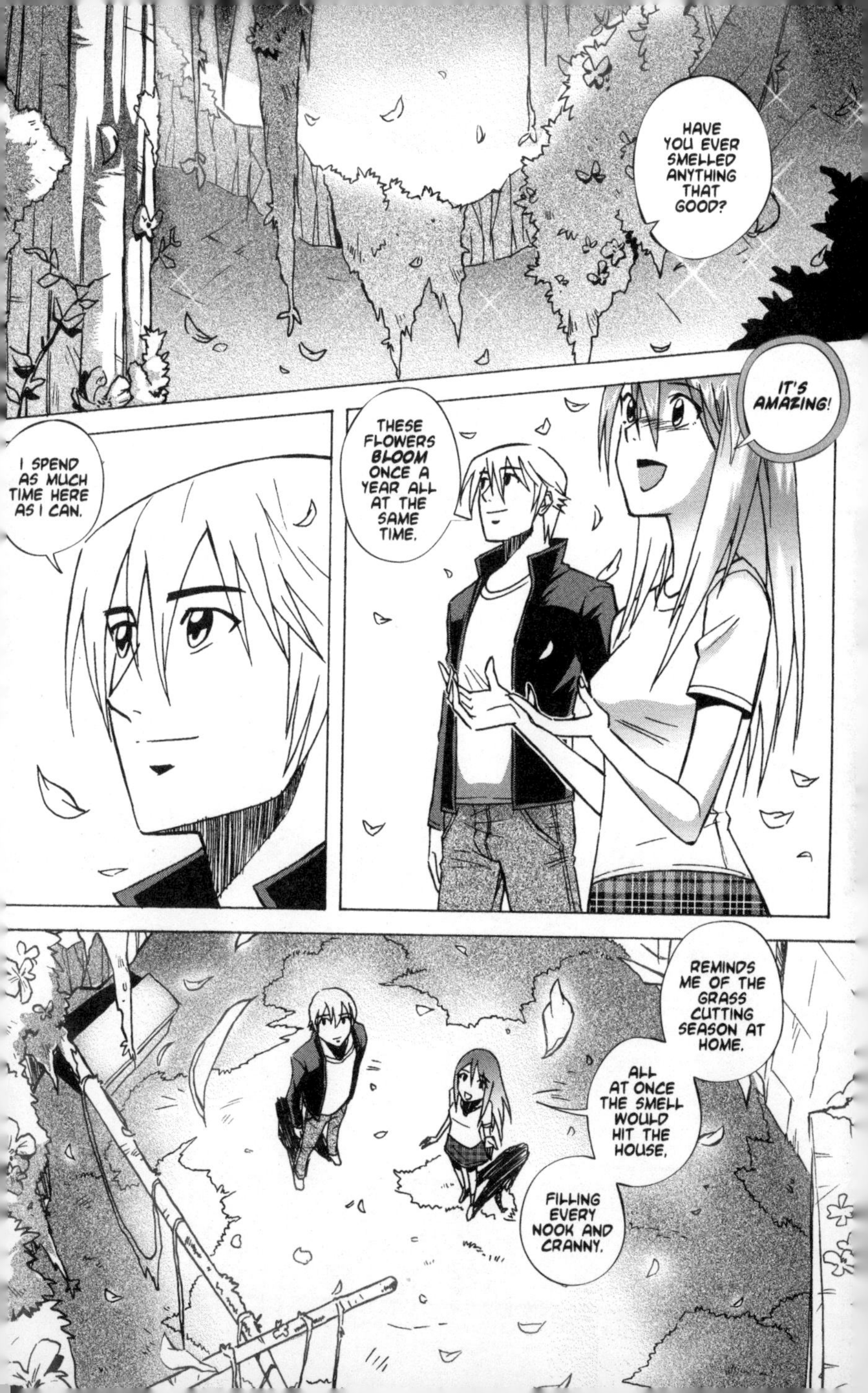
HAVE YOU EVER SMELLED ANYTHING THAT GOOD?
IT'S AMAZING!
THESE FLOWERS BLOOM ONCE A YEAR ALL AT THE SAME TIME.
I SPEND AS MUCH TIME HERE AS I CAN.
REMINDS ME OF THE GRASS CUTTING SEASON AT HOME.
ALL AT ONCE THE SMELL WOULD HIT THE HOUSE,
FILLING EVERY NOOK AND CRANNY.

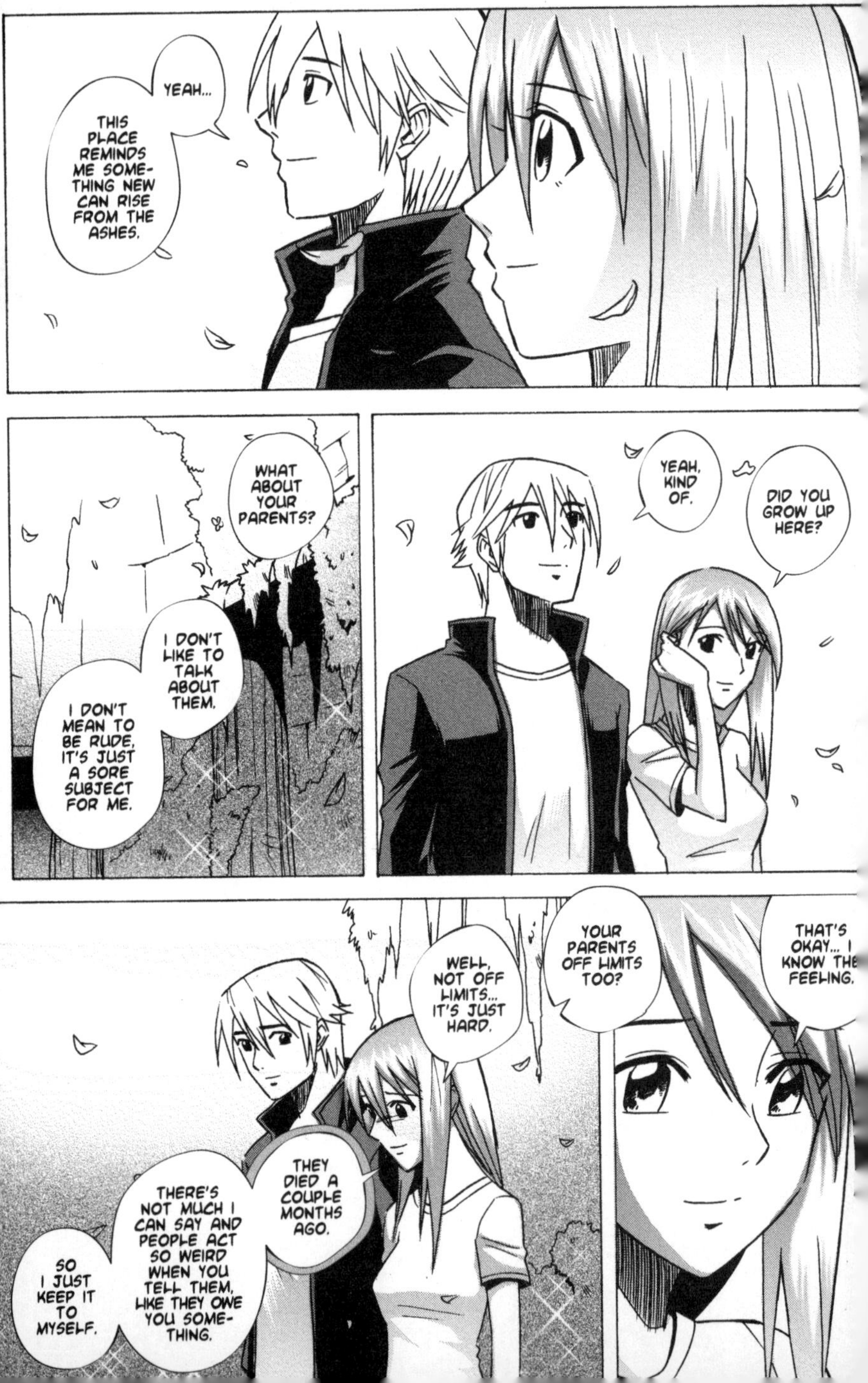
YEAH...
THIS PLACE REMINDS ME SOMETHING NEW CAN RISE FROM THE ASHES.
DID YOU GROW UP HERE?
YEAH, KIND OF.
WHAT ABOUT YOUR PARENTS?
I DON'T LIKE TO TALK ABOUT THEM.
I DON'T MEAN TO BE RUDE, IT'S JUST A SORE SUBJECT FOR ME.
THAT'S OKAY... I KNOW THE FEELING.
YOUR PARENTS OFF LIMITS TOO?
WELL, NOT OFF LIMITS... IT'S JUST HARD.
THEY DIED A COUPLE MONTHS AGO.
THERE'S NOT MUCH I CAN SAY AND PEOPLE ACT SO WEIRD WHEN YOU TELL THEM, LIKE THEY OWE YOU SOMETHING.
SO I JUST KEEP IT TO MYSELF.

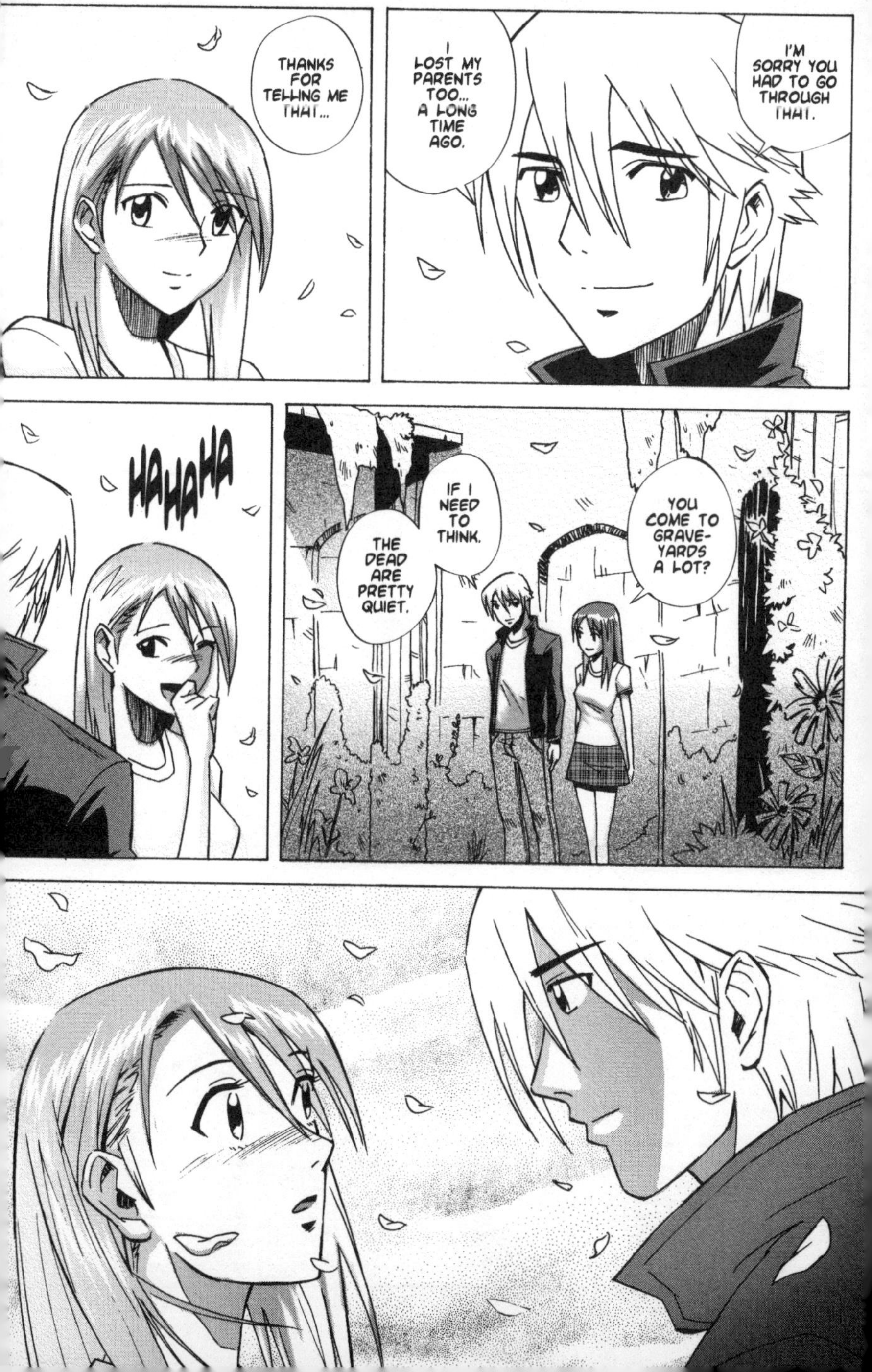
I'M SORRY YOU HAD TO GO THROUGH THAT.
I LOST MY PARENTS TOO... A LONG TIME AGO.
THANKS FOR TELLING ME THAT...
YOU COME TO GRAVE-YARDS A LOT?
IF I NEED TO THINK.
THE DEAD ARE PRETTY QUIET.
HAHAHA

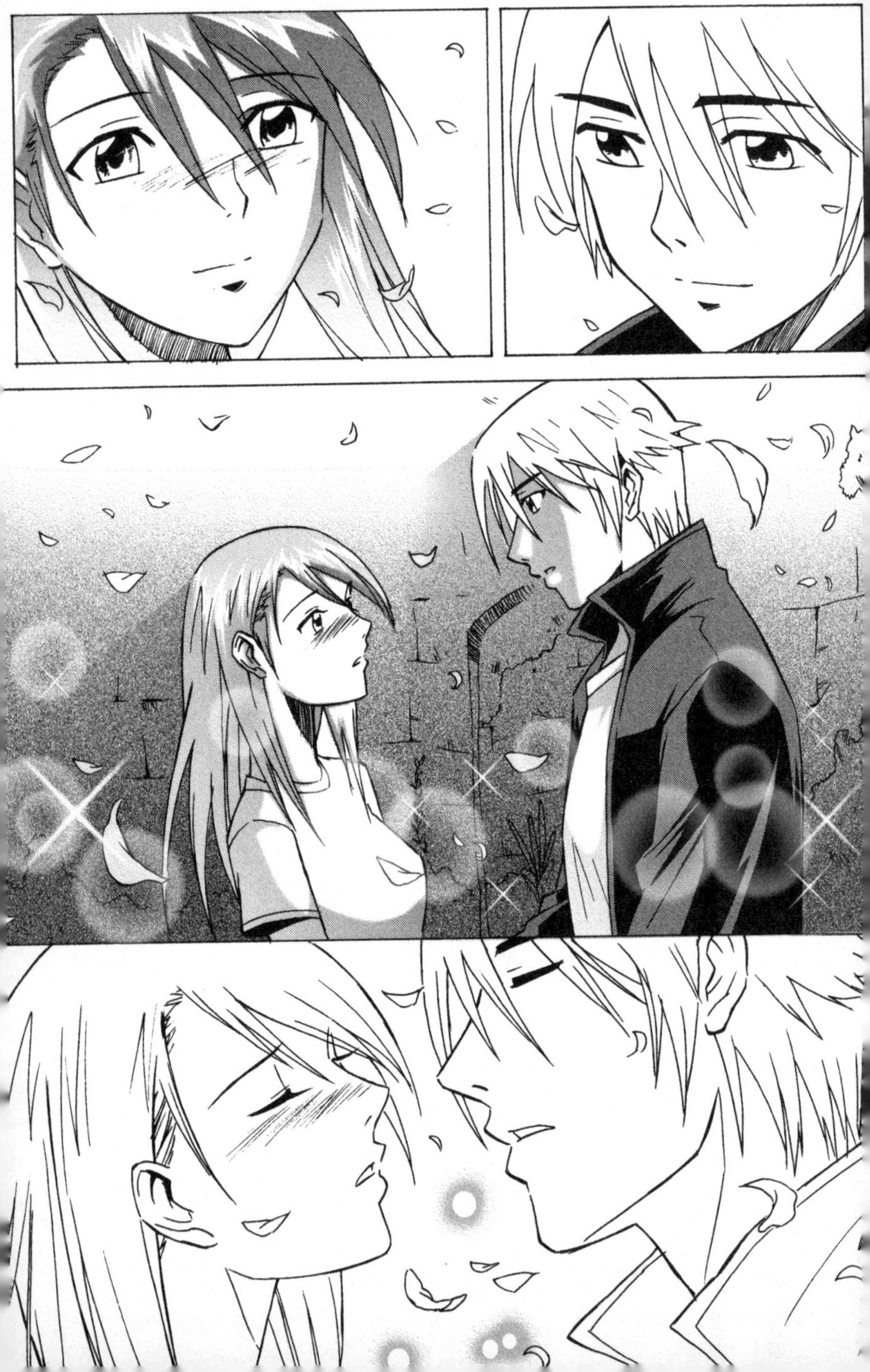

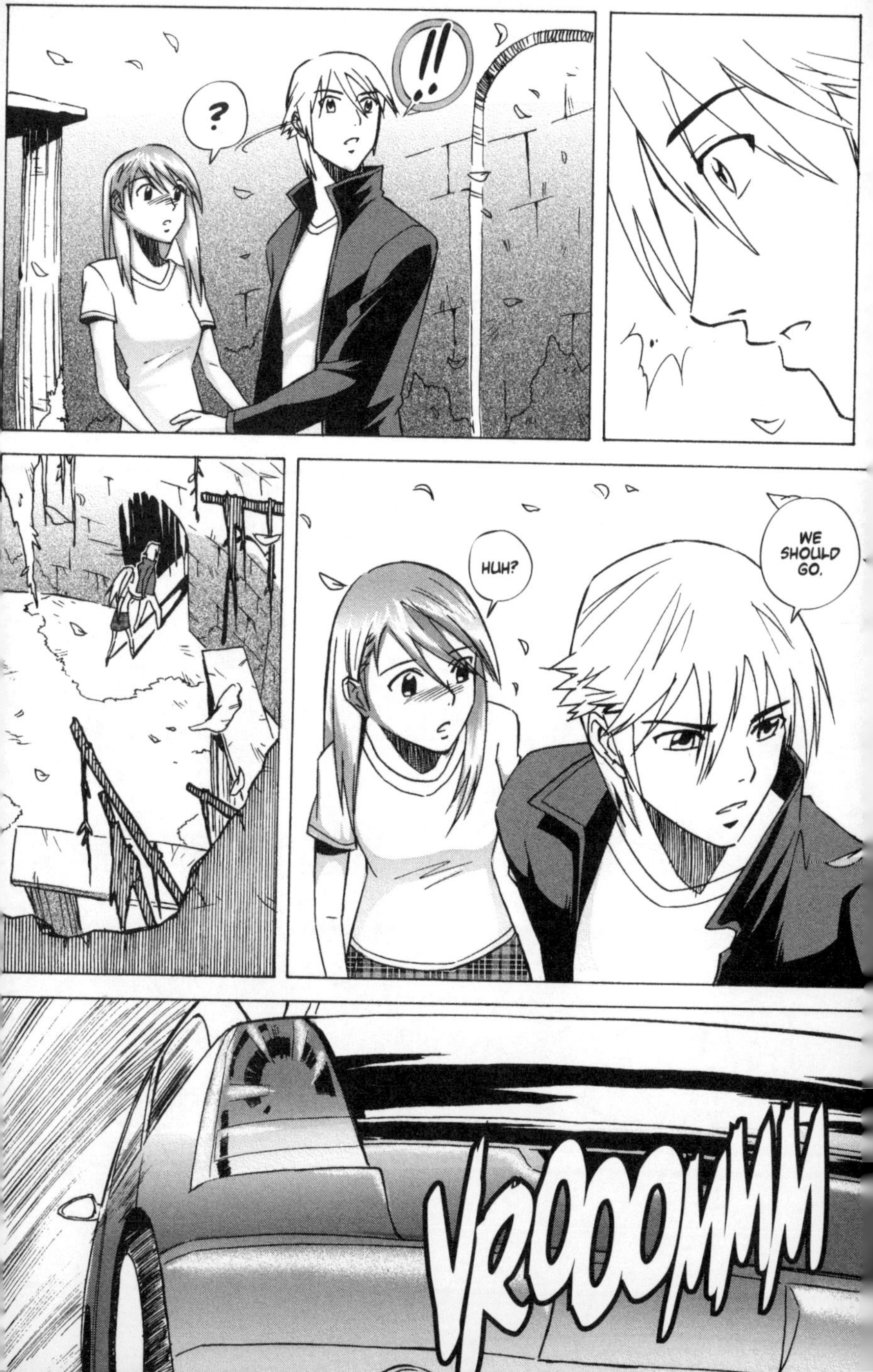
!!
?
WE SHOULD GO.
HUH?
VROOOMMM

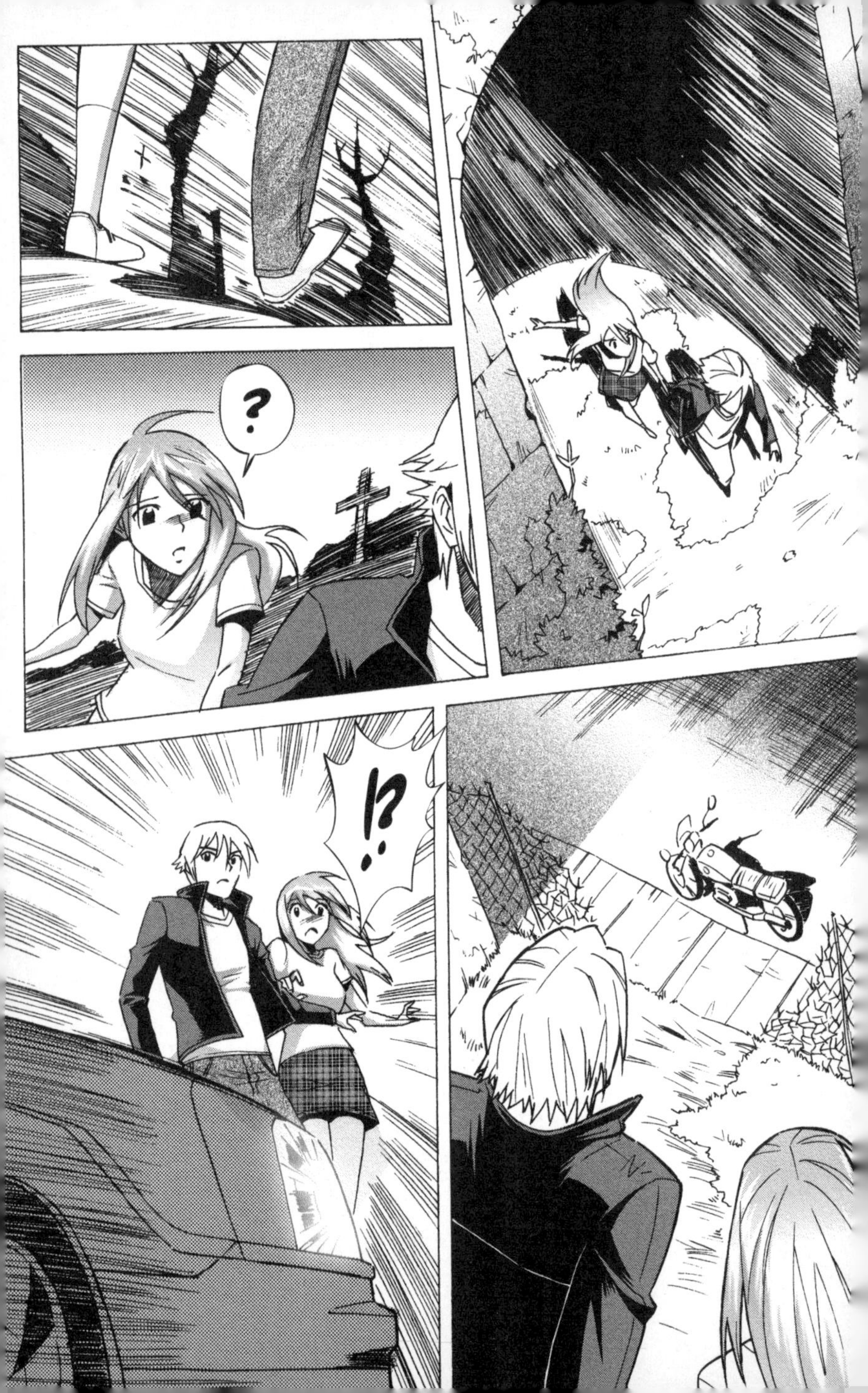
?
!?

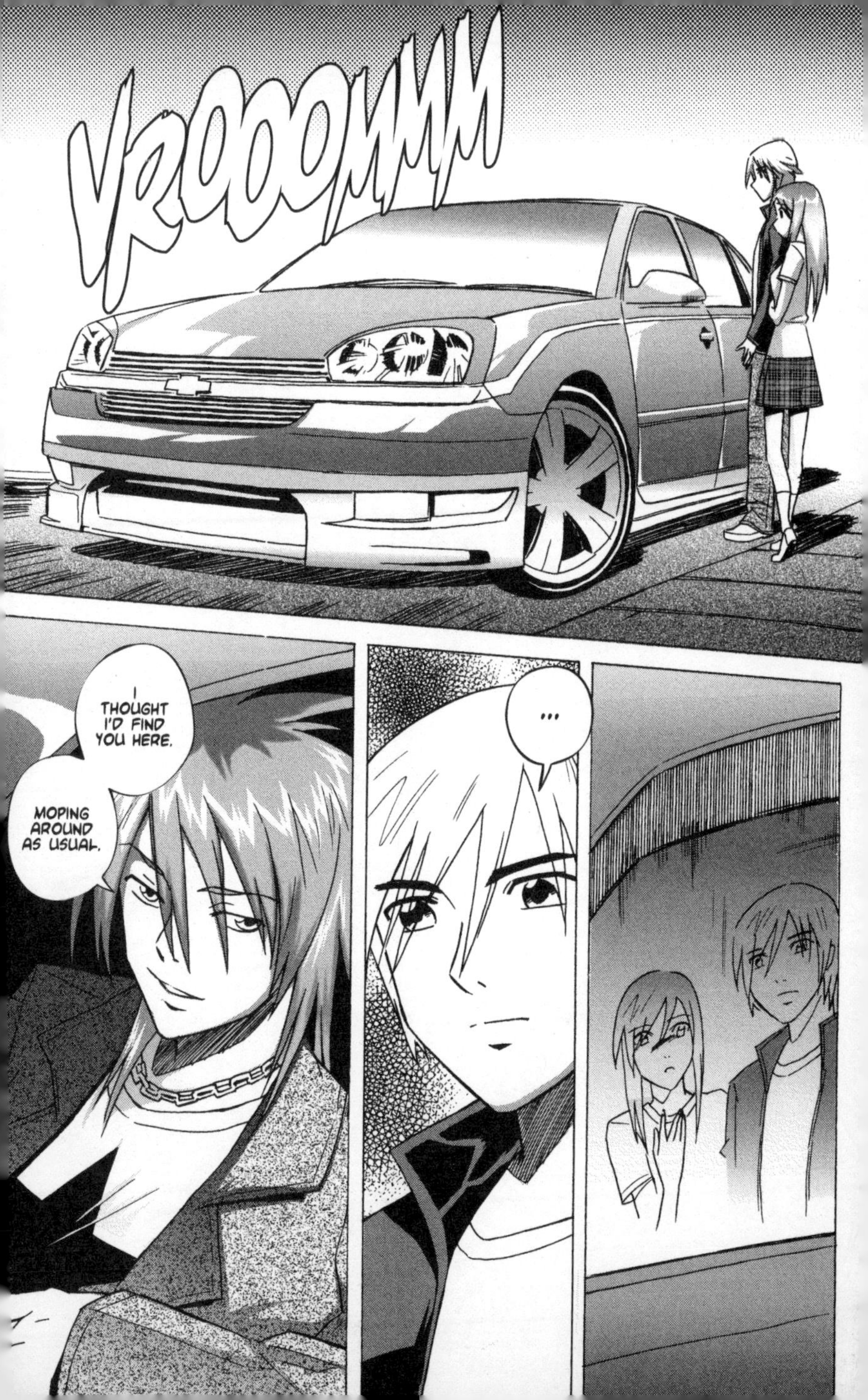
VROOOMMM
...
I THOUGHT I'D FIND YOU HERE.
MOPING AROUND AS USUAL.

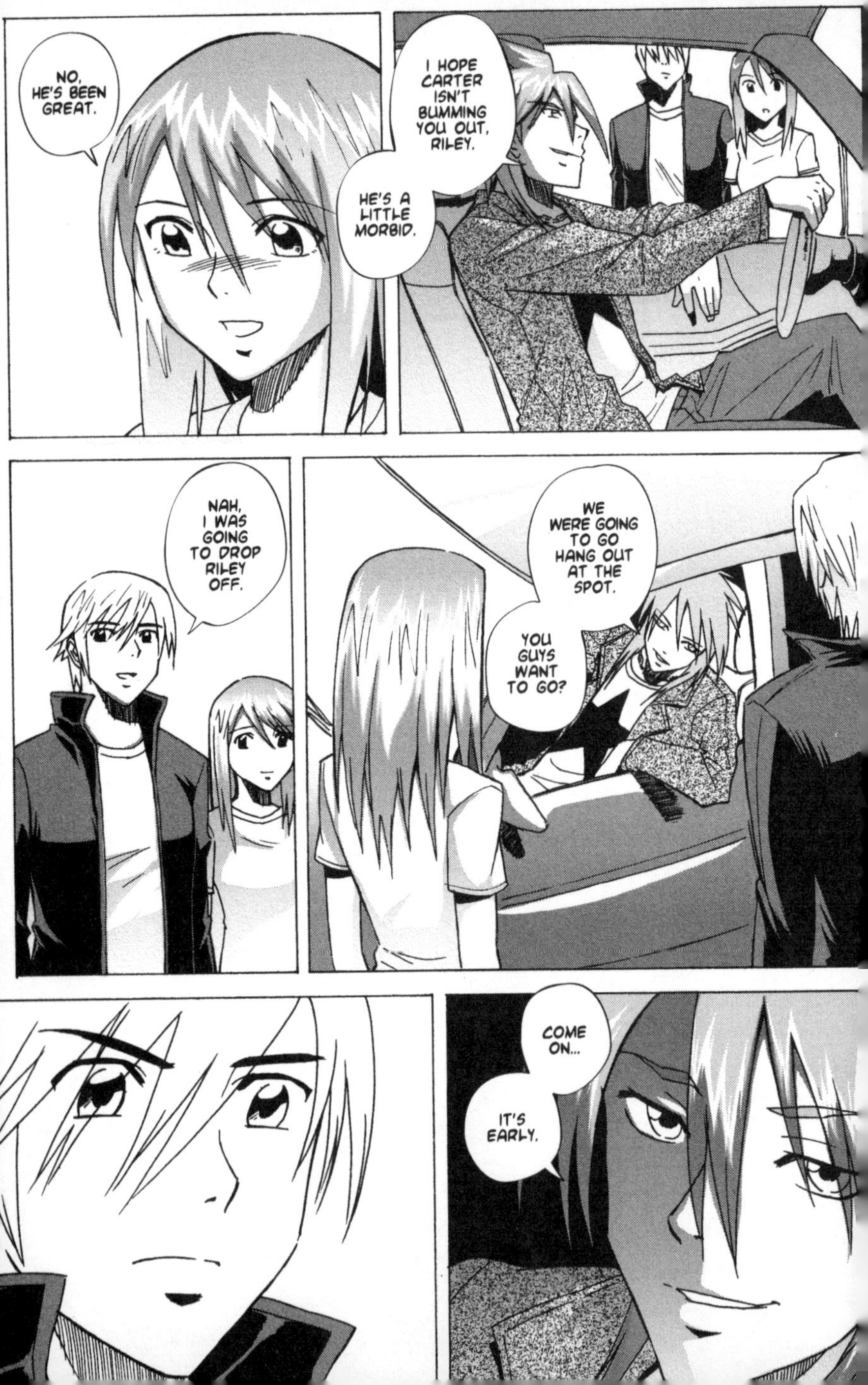
I HOPE CARTER ISN'T BUMMING YOU OUT, RILEY.
HE'S A LITTLE MORBID.
NO, HE'S BEEN GREAT.
WE WERE GOING TO GO HANG OUT AT THE SPOT.
YOU GUYS WANT TO GO?
NAH, I WAS GOING TO DROP RILEY OFF.
COME ON...
IT'S EARLY.

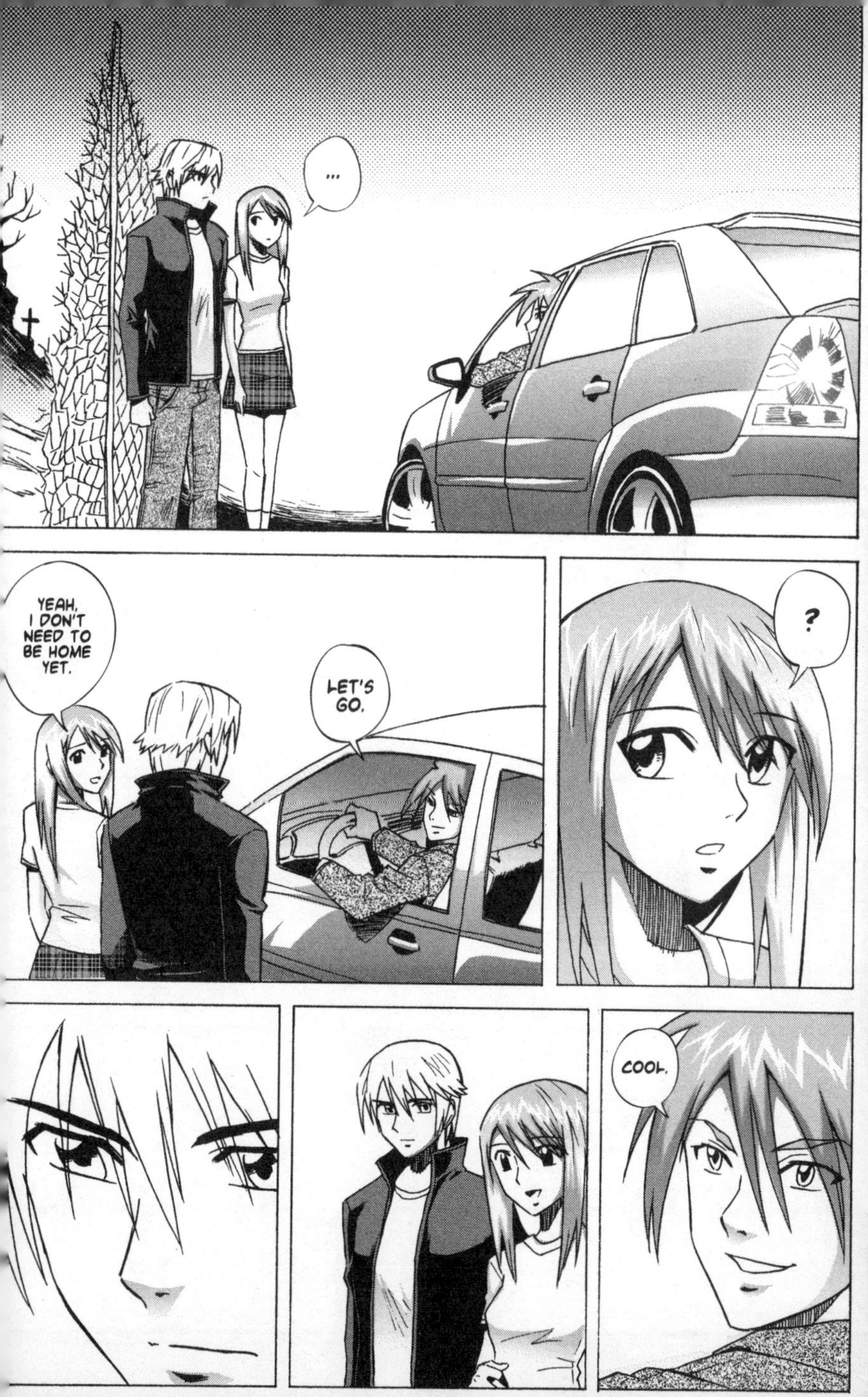
...
?
LET'S GO.
YEAH, I DON'T NEED TO BE HOME YET.
COOL.

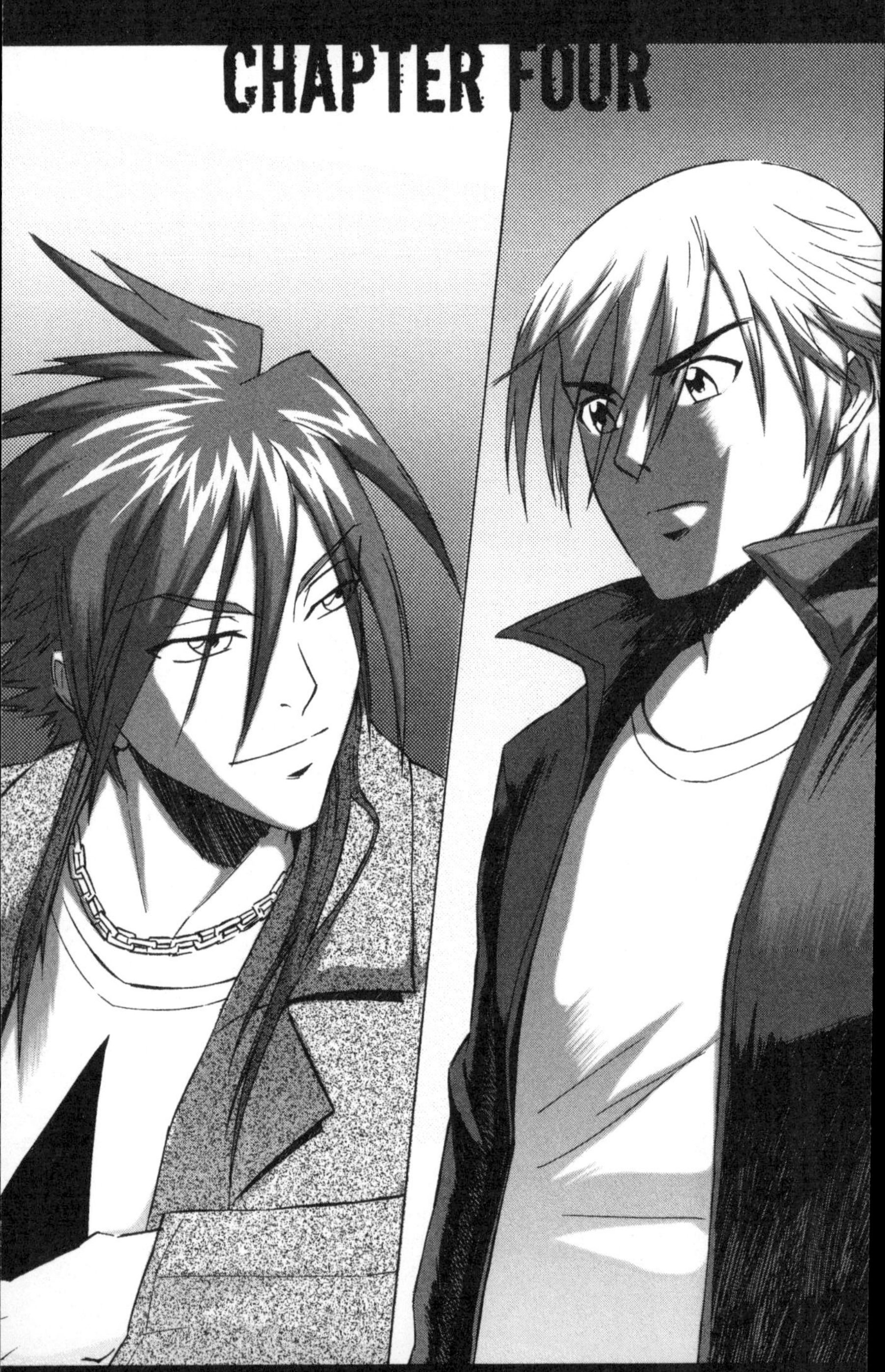
CHAPTER FOUR

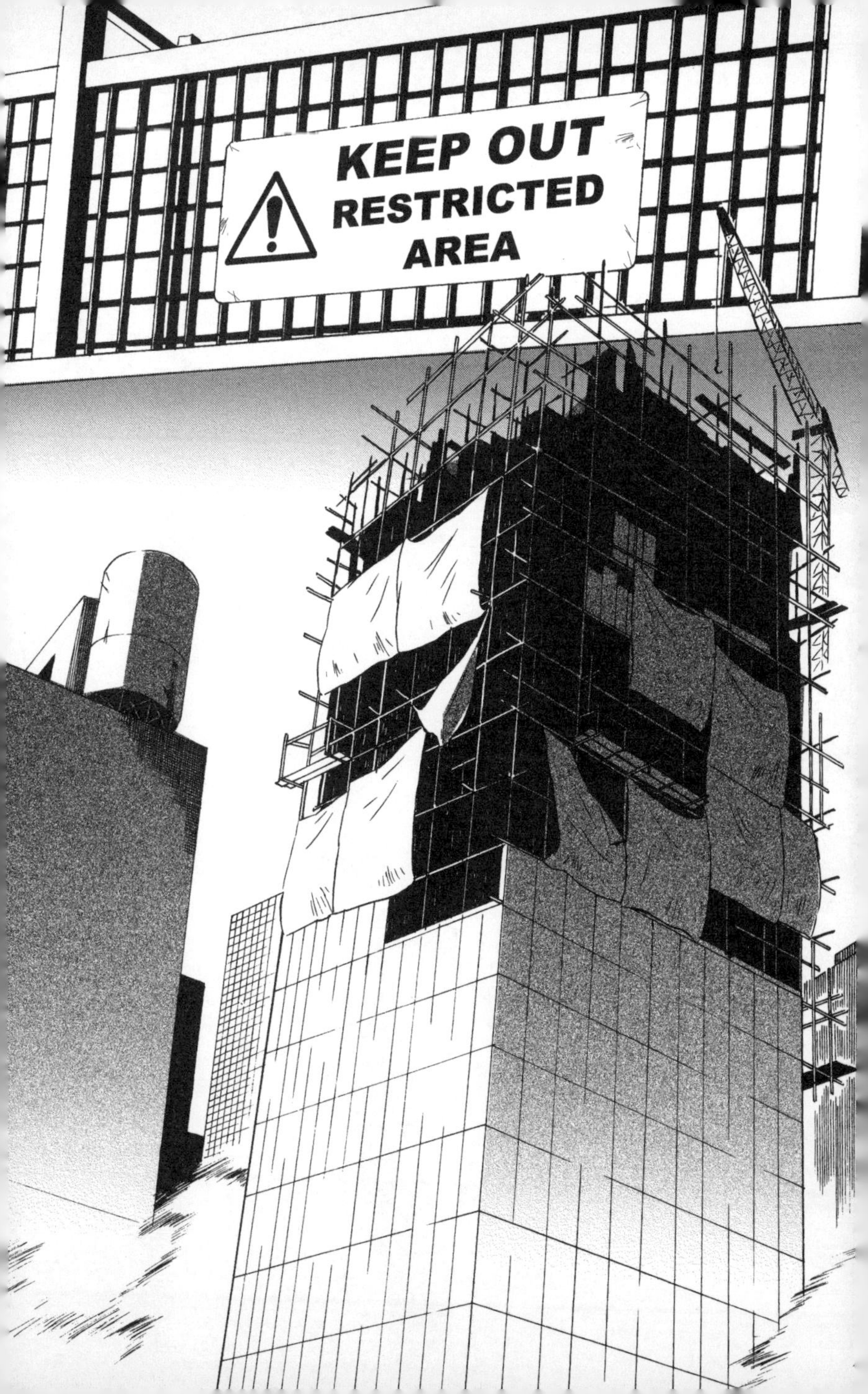
KEEP OUT
RESTRICTED
AREA

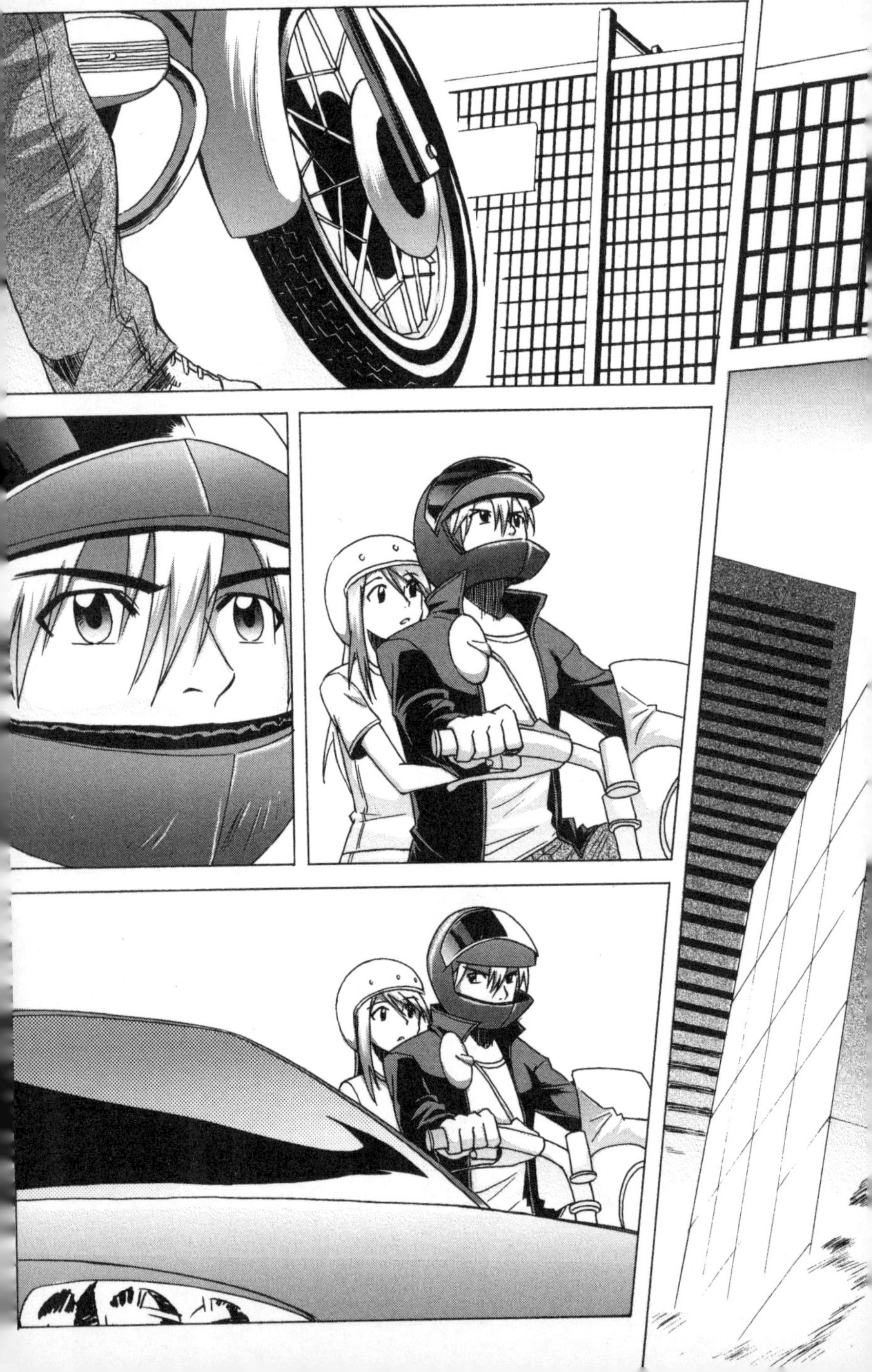

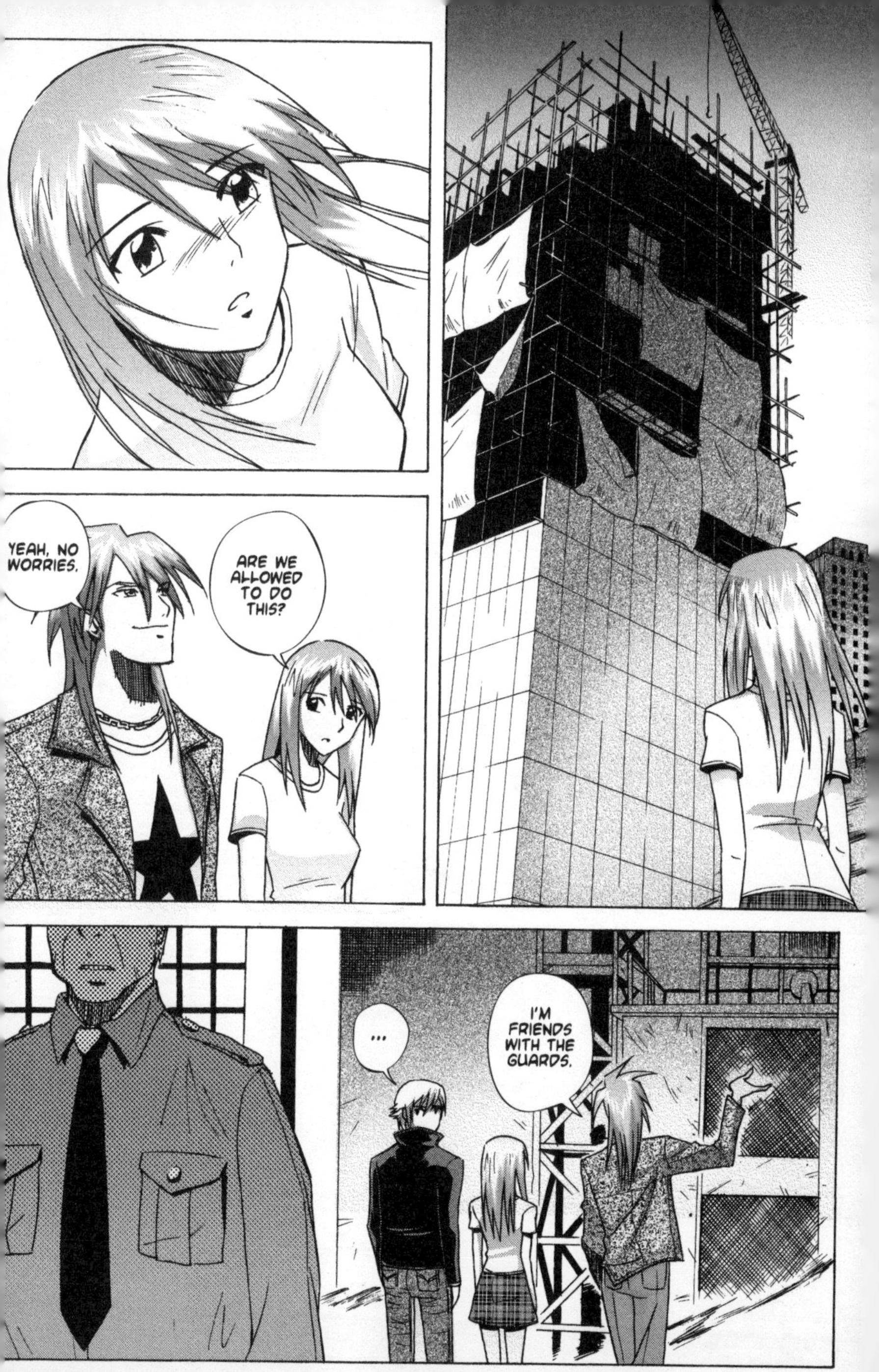
ARE WE ALLOWED TO DO THIS?
YEAH, NO WORRIES.
I'M FRIENDS WITH THE GUARDS.
...

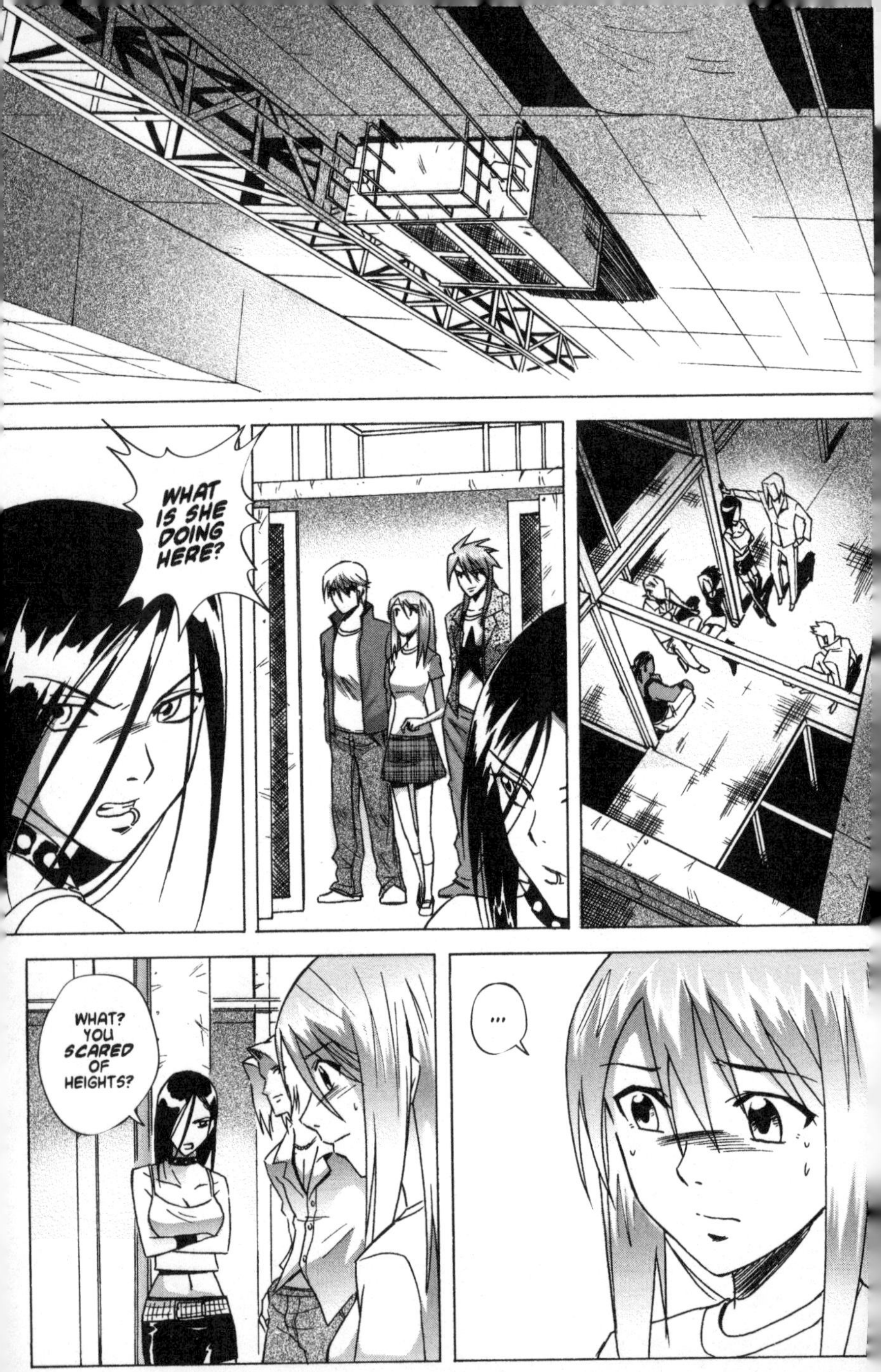
WHAT IS SHE DOING HERE?
...
WHAT? YOU SCARED OF HEIGHTS?

HEY, TAKE IT EASY, MAXY PAD.

WE'RE ALL FRIENDS HERE.

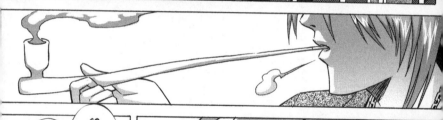

SO WHAT DO YOU THINK, RILEY?

BEATS THAT DREARY **OLD** CEMETERY PLOT ANY DAY, RIGHT?

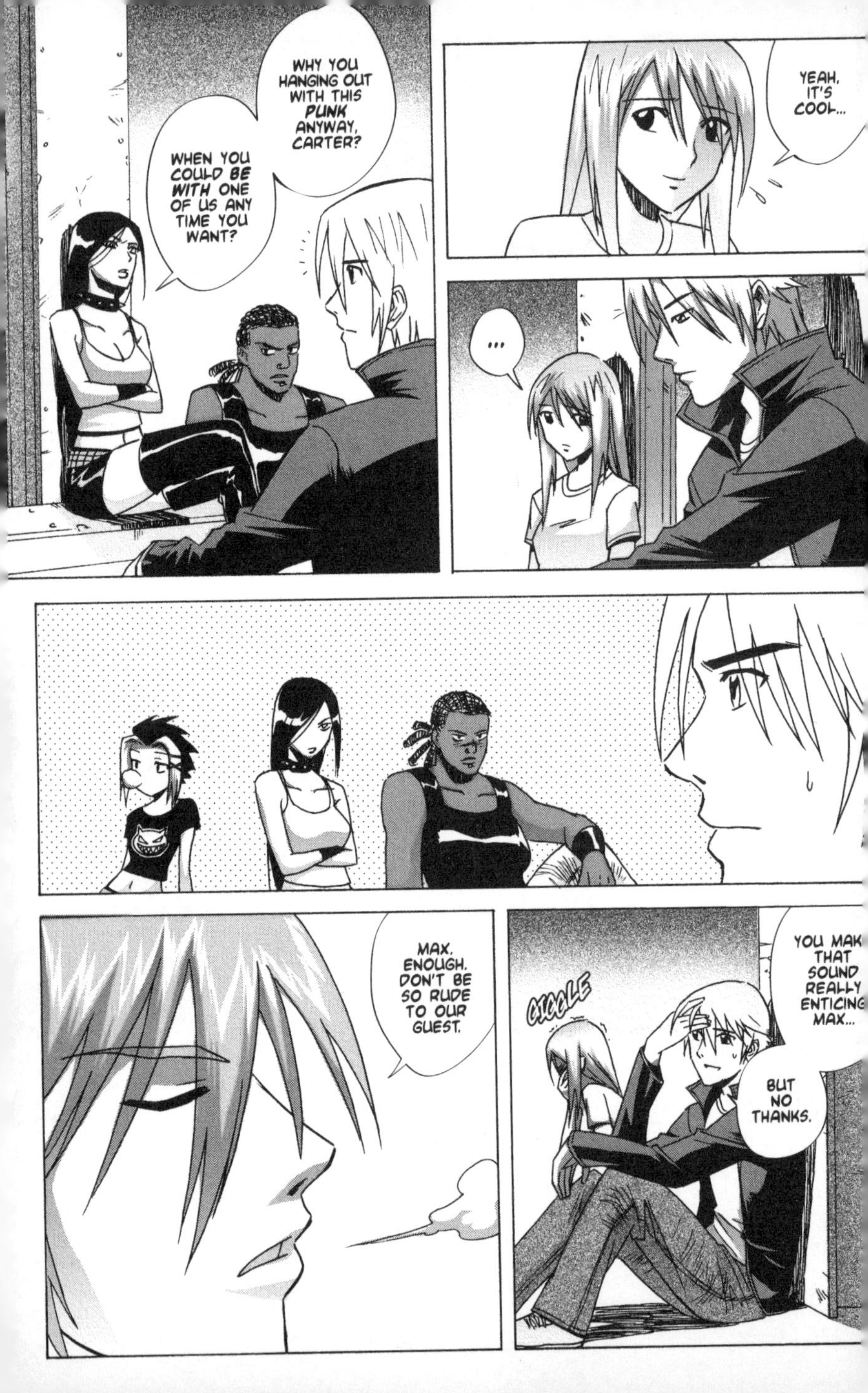

YEAH, IT'S COOL...
...
WHY YOU HANGING OUT WITH THIS PUNK ANYWAY, CARTER?
WHEN YOU COULD BE WITH ONE OF US ANY TIME YOU WANT?
YOU MAK THAT SOUND REALLY ENTICING MAX...
BUT NO THANKS.
GIGGLE
MAX. ENOUGH. DON'T BE SO RUDE TO OUR GUEST.

NO THANKS.

IT MAKES BEING UP HERE EVEN BETTER.

SMOKE?

WHAT IS IT?

IT'S NOT ILLEGAL. IF THAT'S WHAT YOU'RE THINKING.

AN HERB.

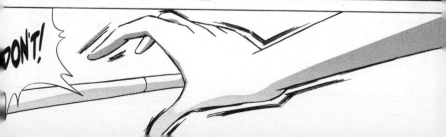

DON'T!

?!

DON'T!

IF YOU DON'T WANT TO.

?!

CARTER, YOU'RE AS NERVOUS AS A FAT LADY AT A BAKE SALE.

RELAX.

...

...

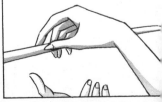

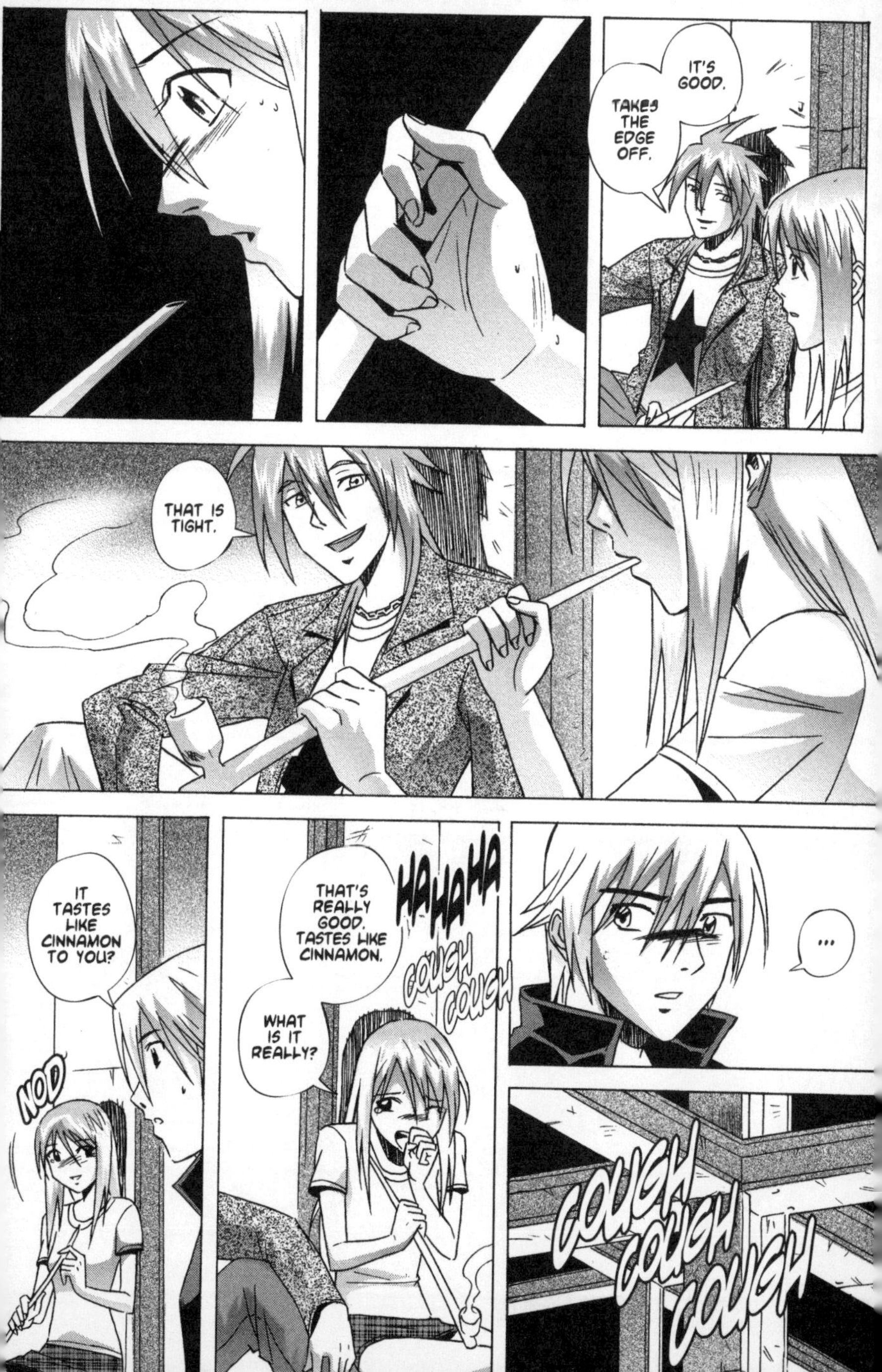
IT'S GOOD.
TAKES THE EDGE OFF.
THAT IS TIGHT.
...
COUGH COUGH COUGH
THAT'S REALLY GOOD. TASTES LIKE CINNAMON.
HAHAHA
COUGH COUGH
WHAT IS IT REALLY?
IT TASTES LIKE CINNAMON TO YOU?
NOD

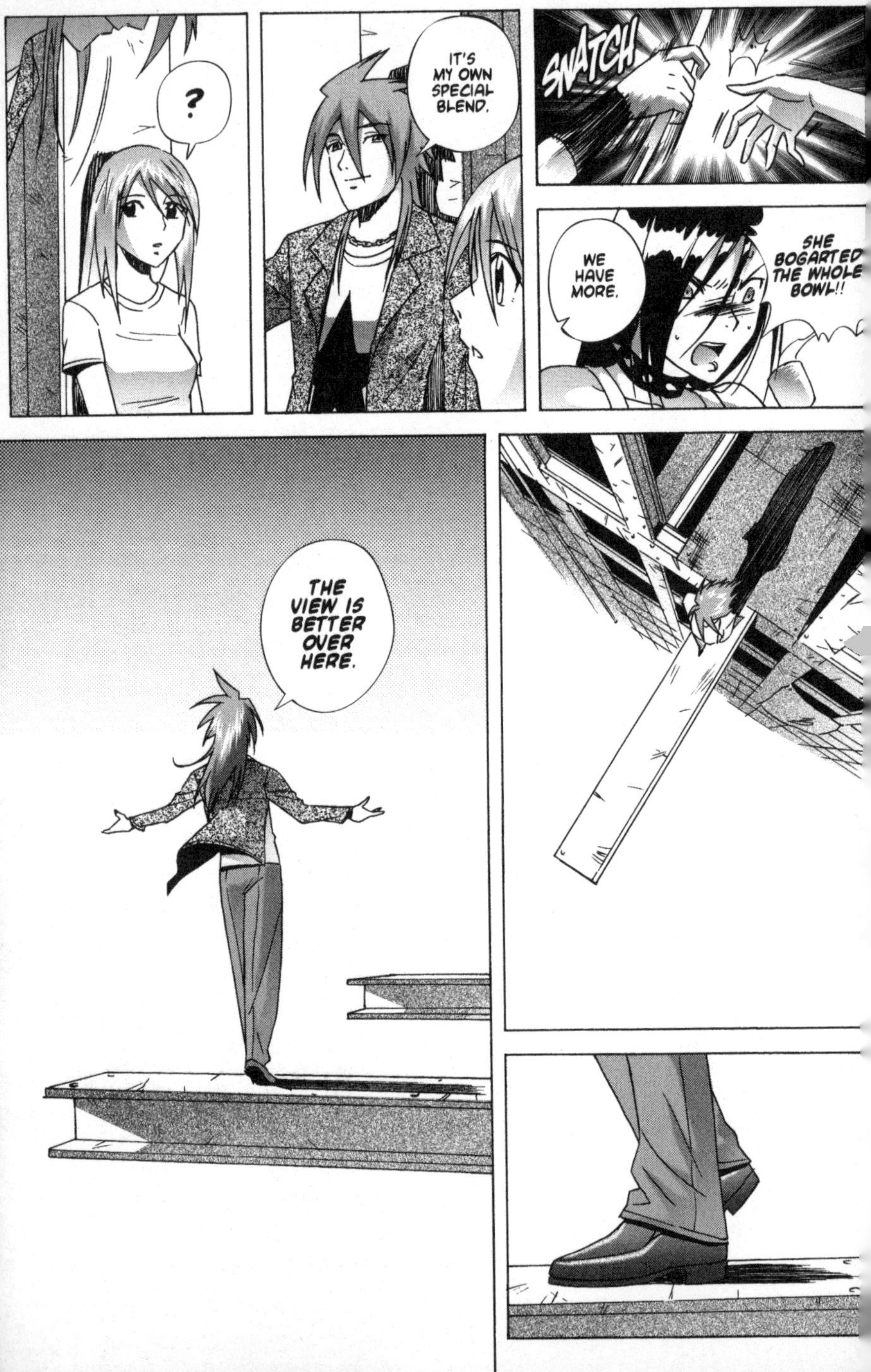
SNATCH
SHE BOGARTED THE WHOLE BOWL!!
WE HAVE MORE.
IT'S MY OWN SPECIAL BLEND.
?
THE VIEW IS BETTER OVER HERE.

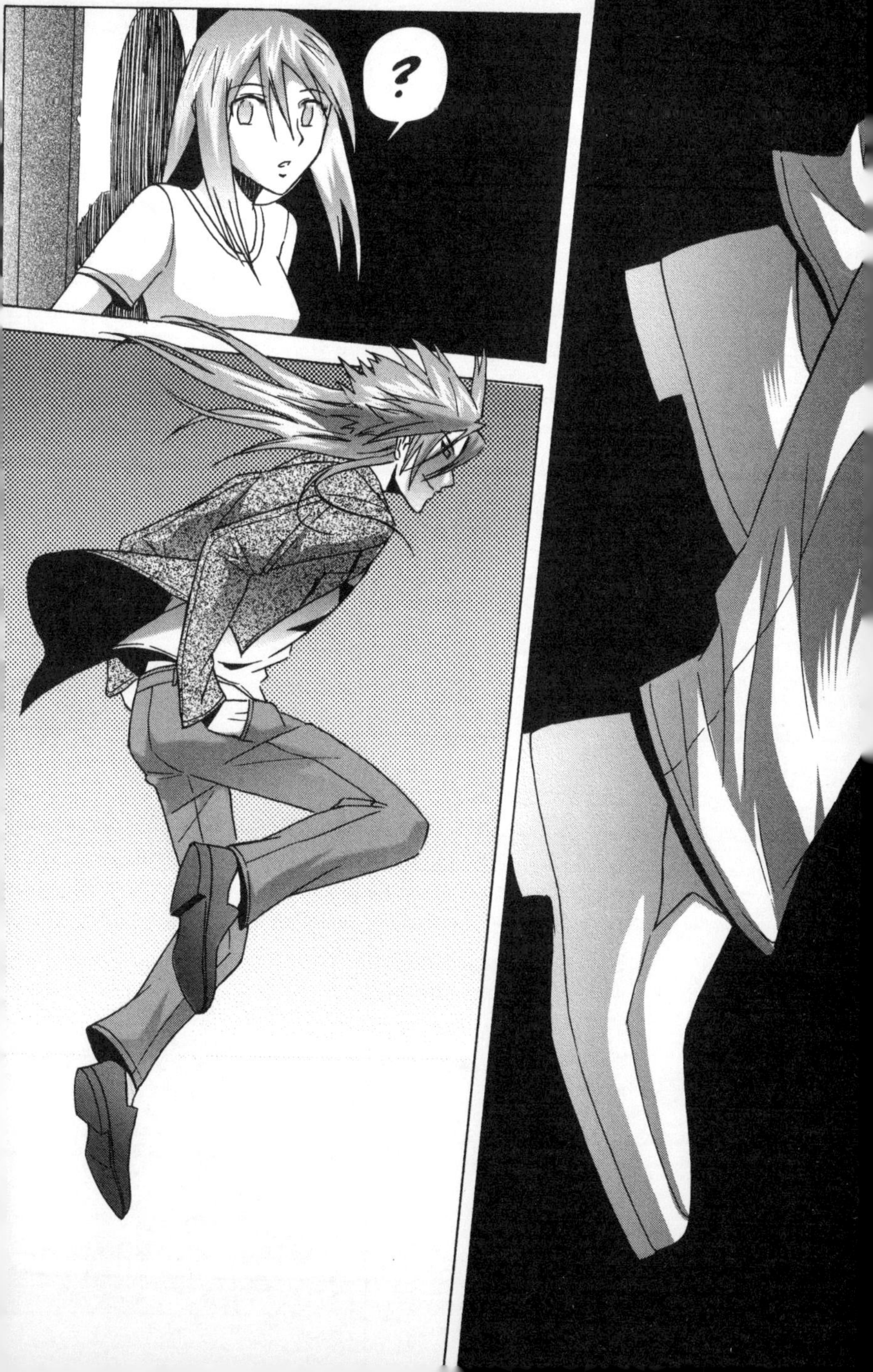
?

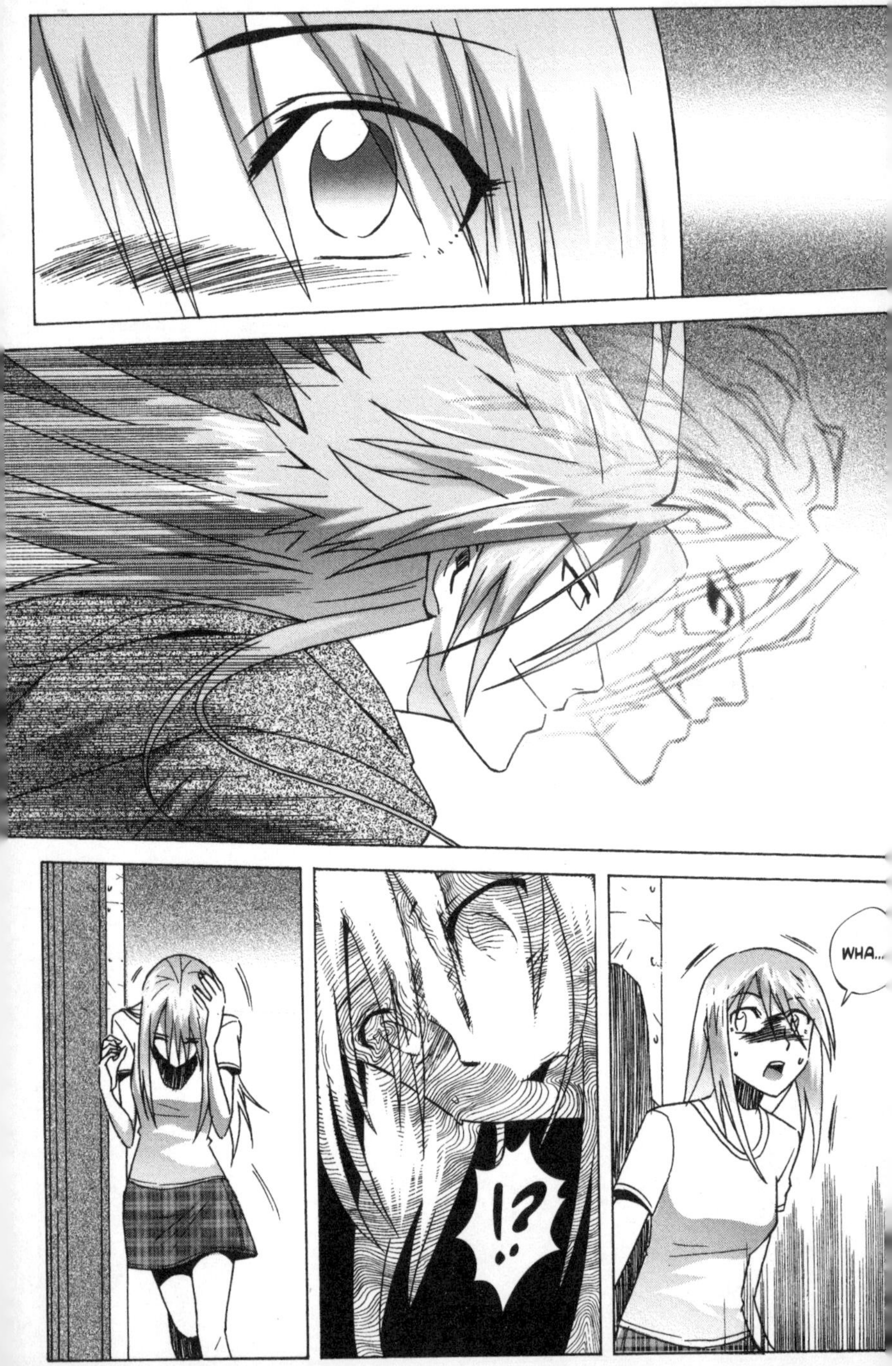
WHA...
!?

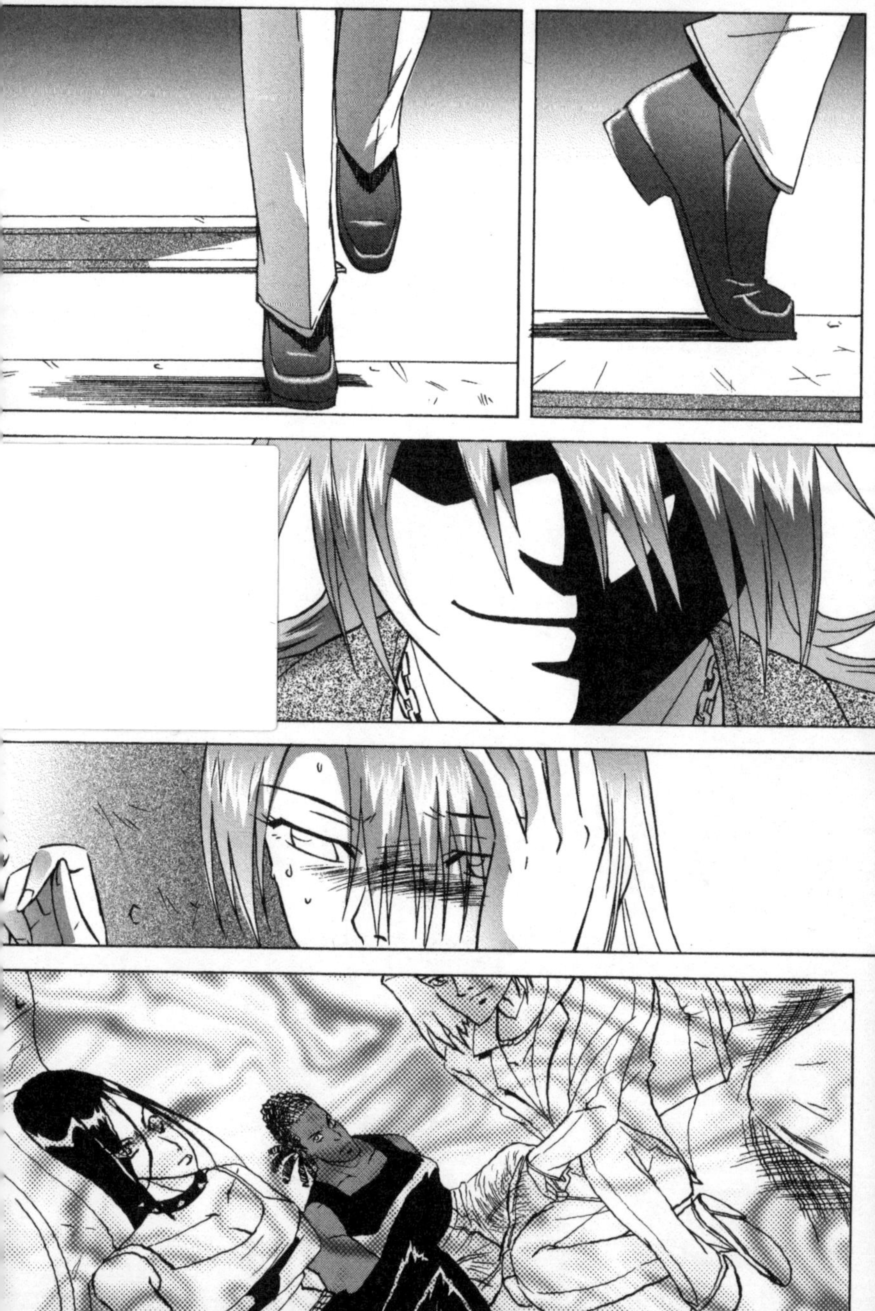

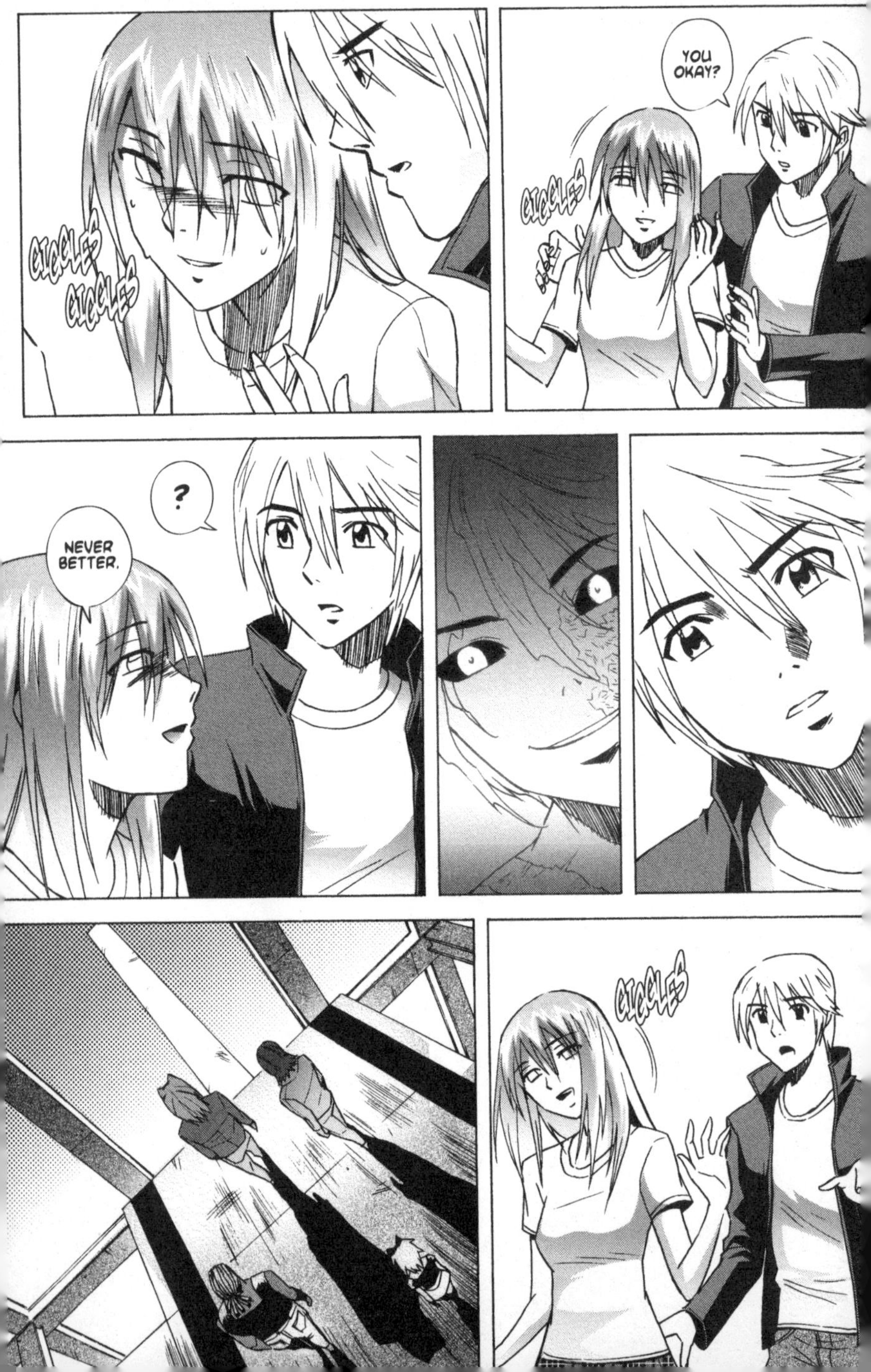
YOU OKAY?
GIGGLES
GIGGLES
GIGGLES
?
NEVER BETTER.
GIGGLES

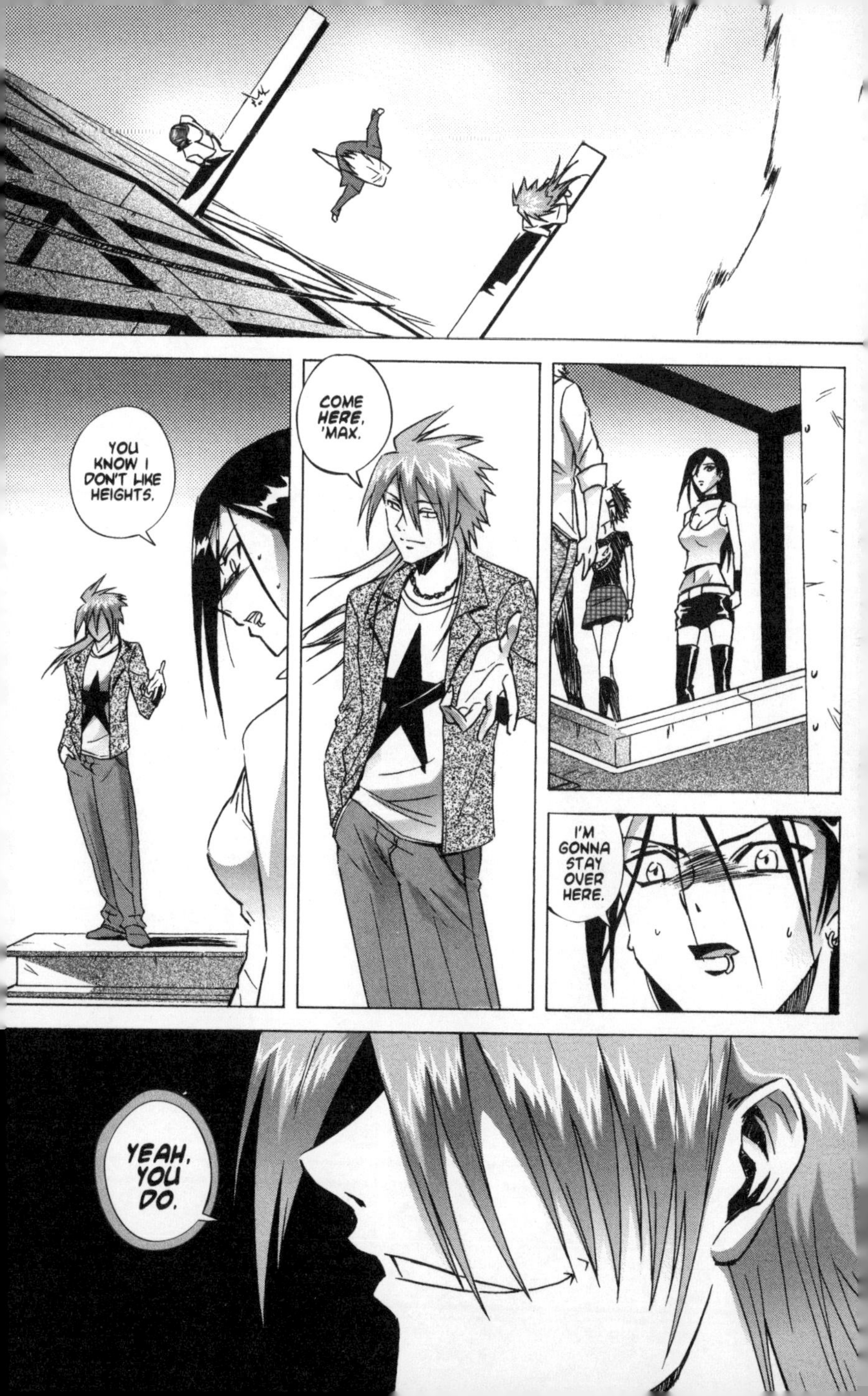
I'M GONNA STAY OVER HERE.
COME HERE, 'MAX.
YOU KNOW I DON'T LIKE HEIGHTS.
YEAH, YOU DO.

THOMAS, COME ON...

SHE DOESN'T *WANT* TO DO IT. LET IT GO.

THEN SHE'LL MISS THE FUN.

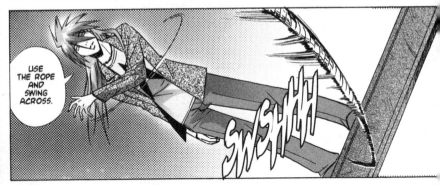

USE THE ROPE AND SWING ACROSS.

SWSHHH

...

IT'S NOTHING.

GRAB!

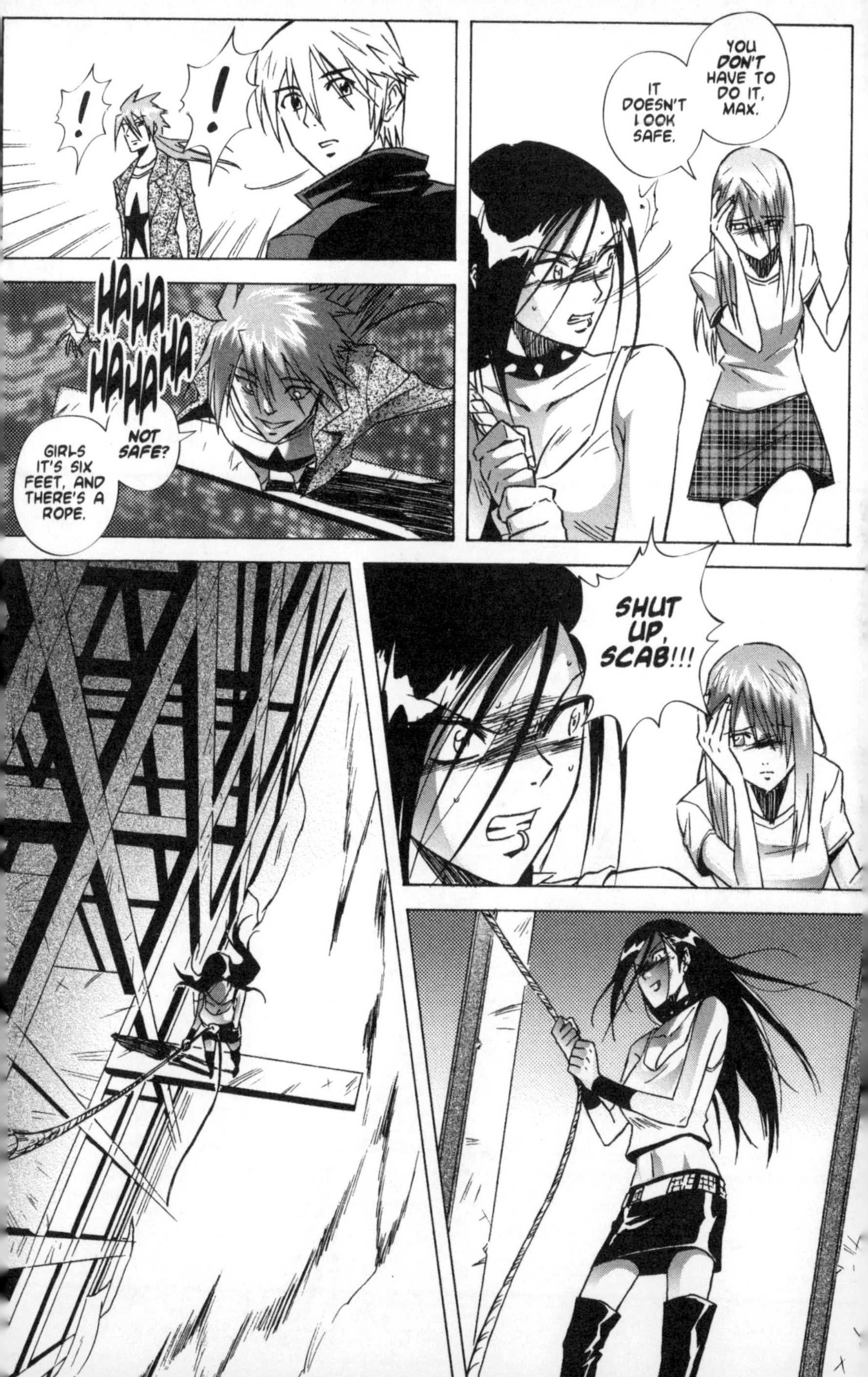

YOU DON'T HAVE TO DO IT, MAX.
IT DOESN'T LOOK SAFE.
!
!
HAHAHAHAHAHA
NOT SAFE?
GIRLS IT'S SIX FEET, AND THERE'S A ROPE.
SHUT UP, SCAB!!!

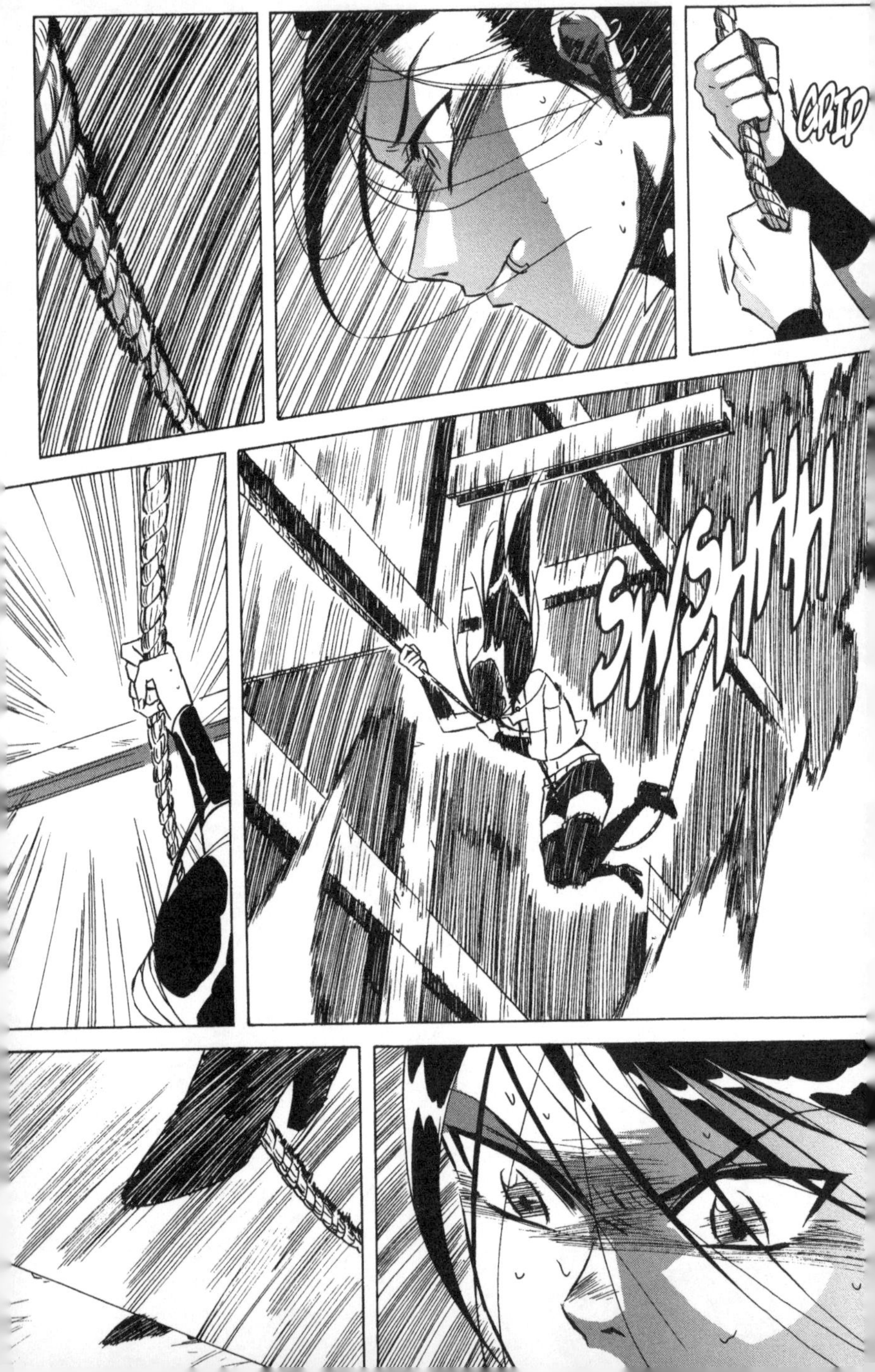
GRIP
SWSHHH

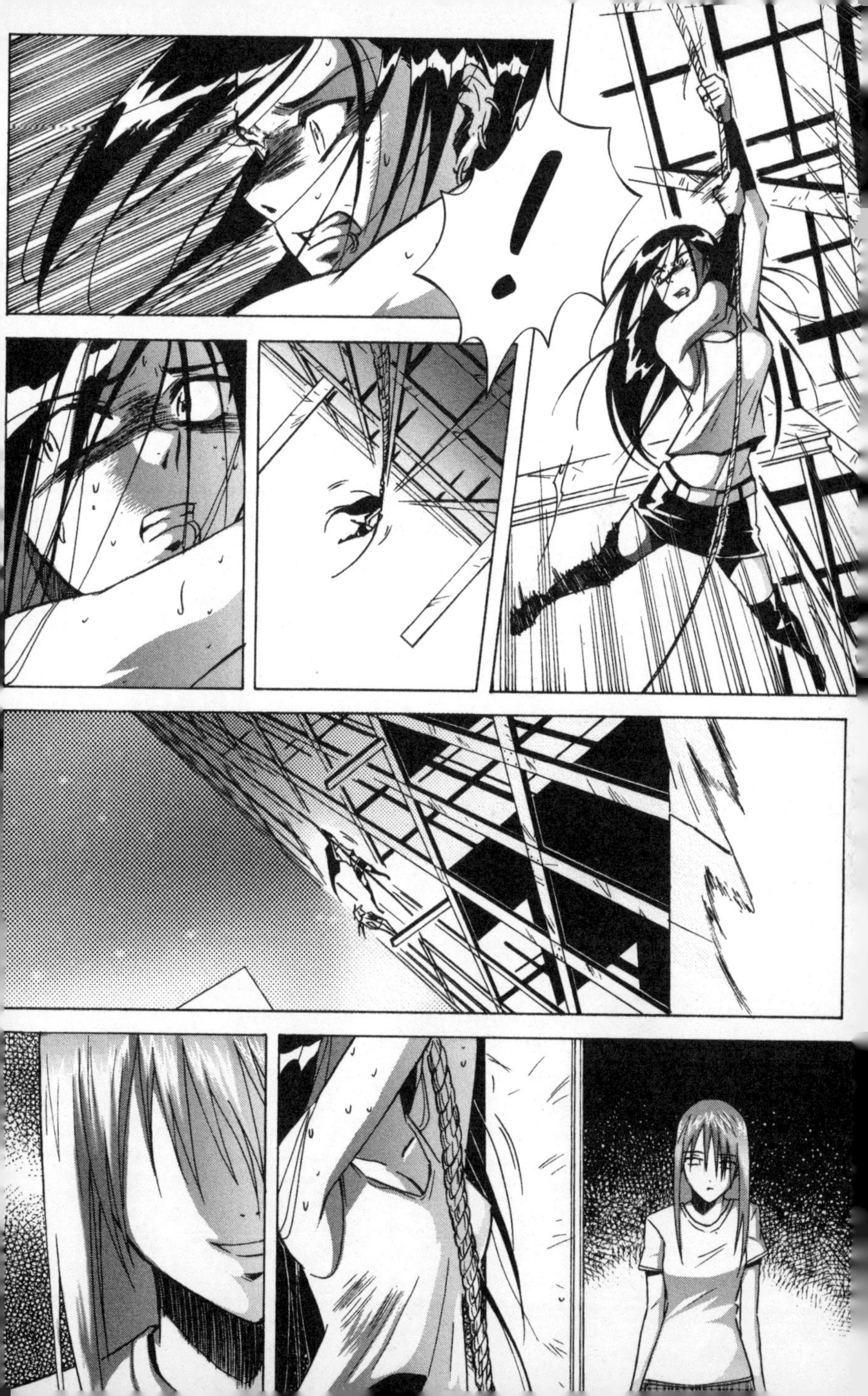
!

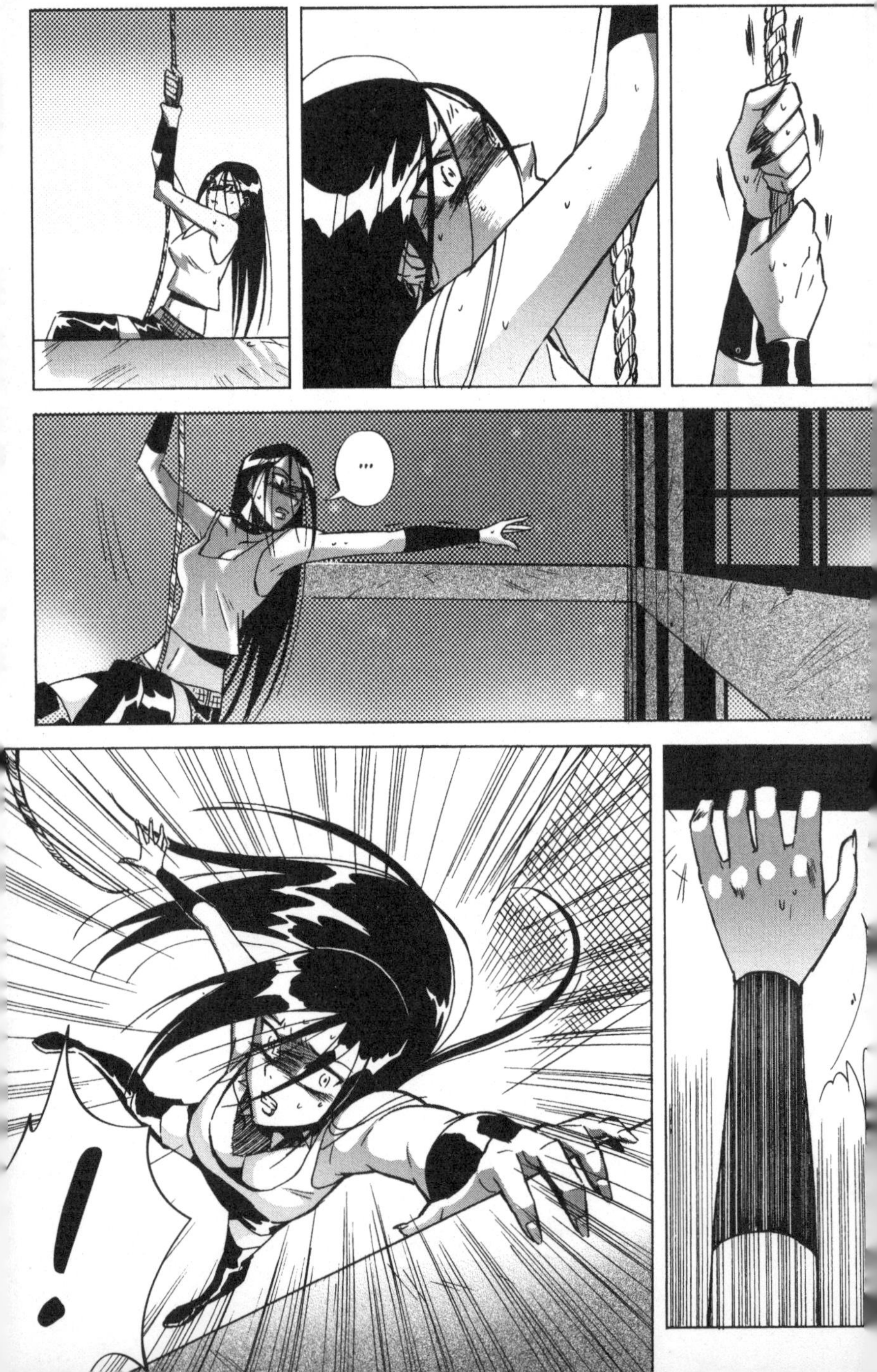
...
!

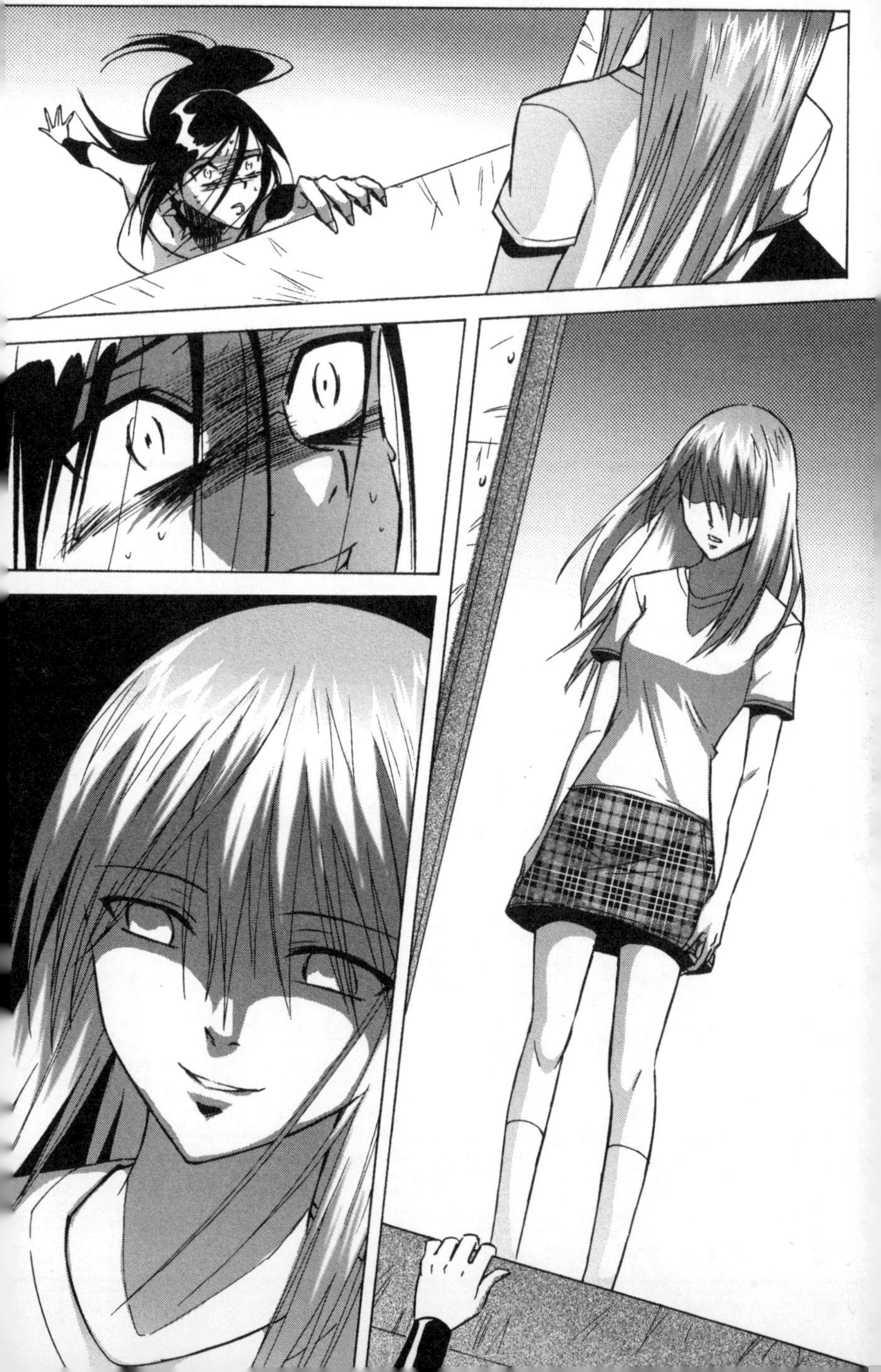

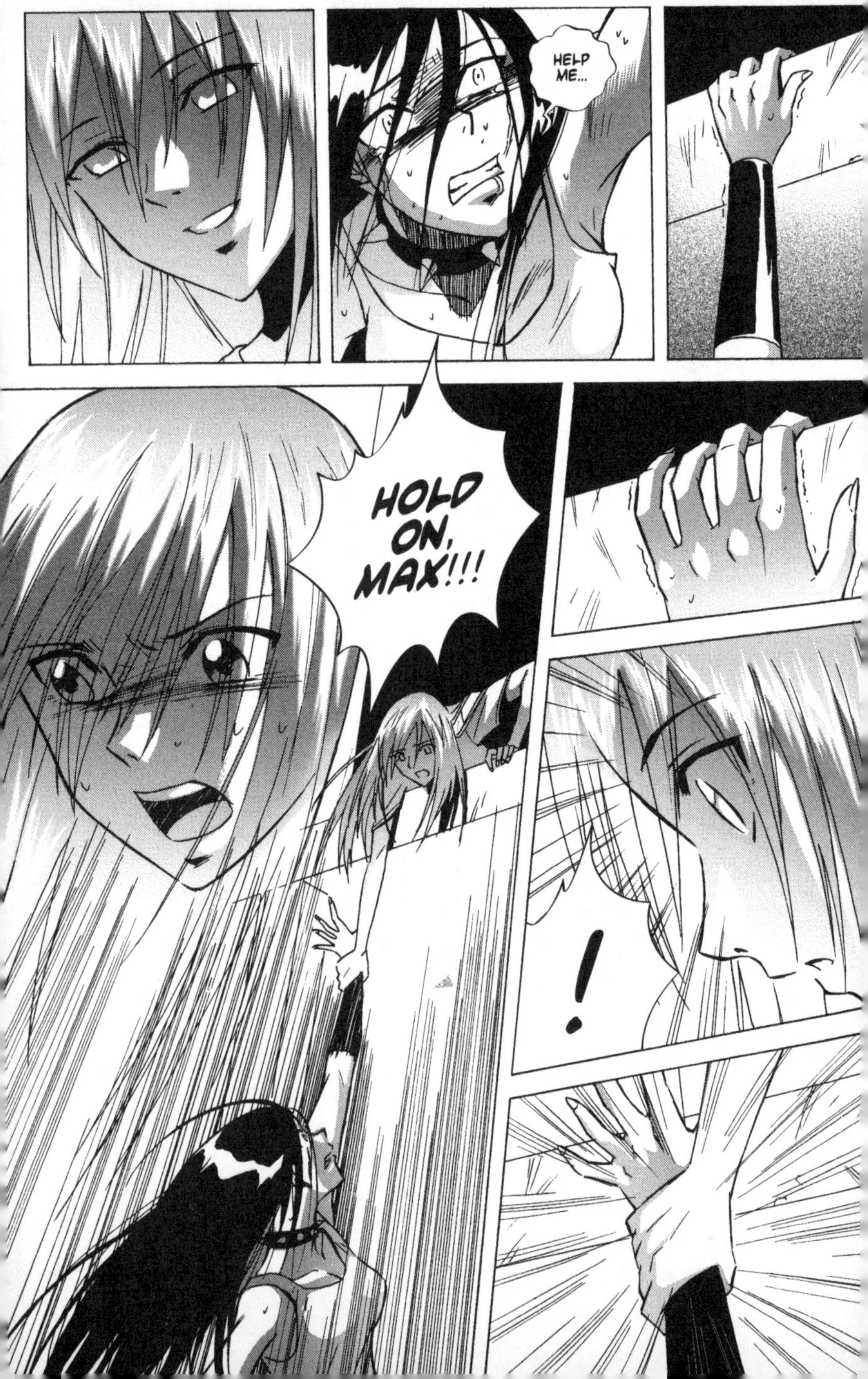
HELP ME...
HOLD ON, MAX!!!
!

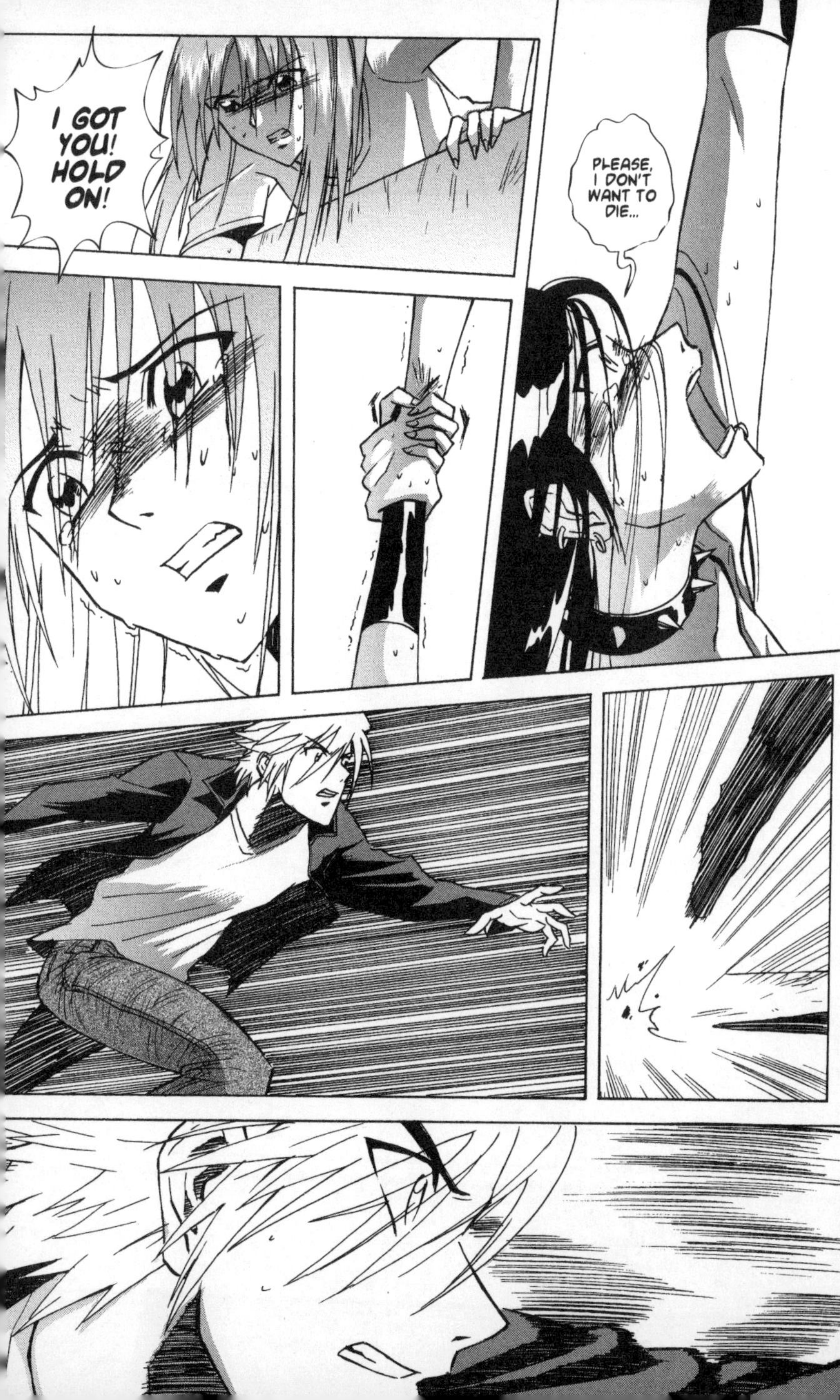
PLEASE, I DON'T WANT TO DIE...
I GOT YOU! HOLD ON!

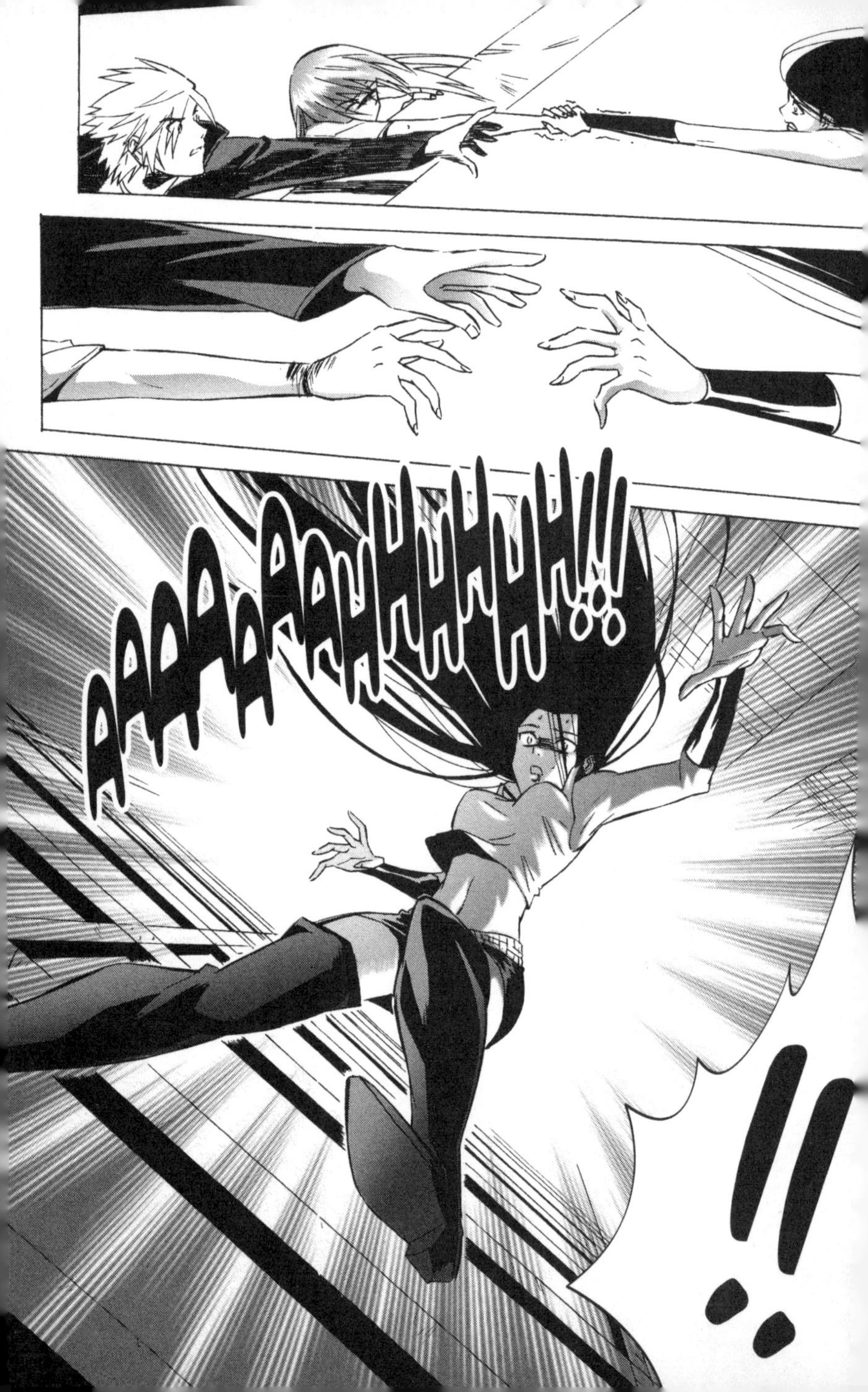
AAAAAAAHHHHHH!!
!!

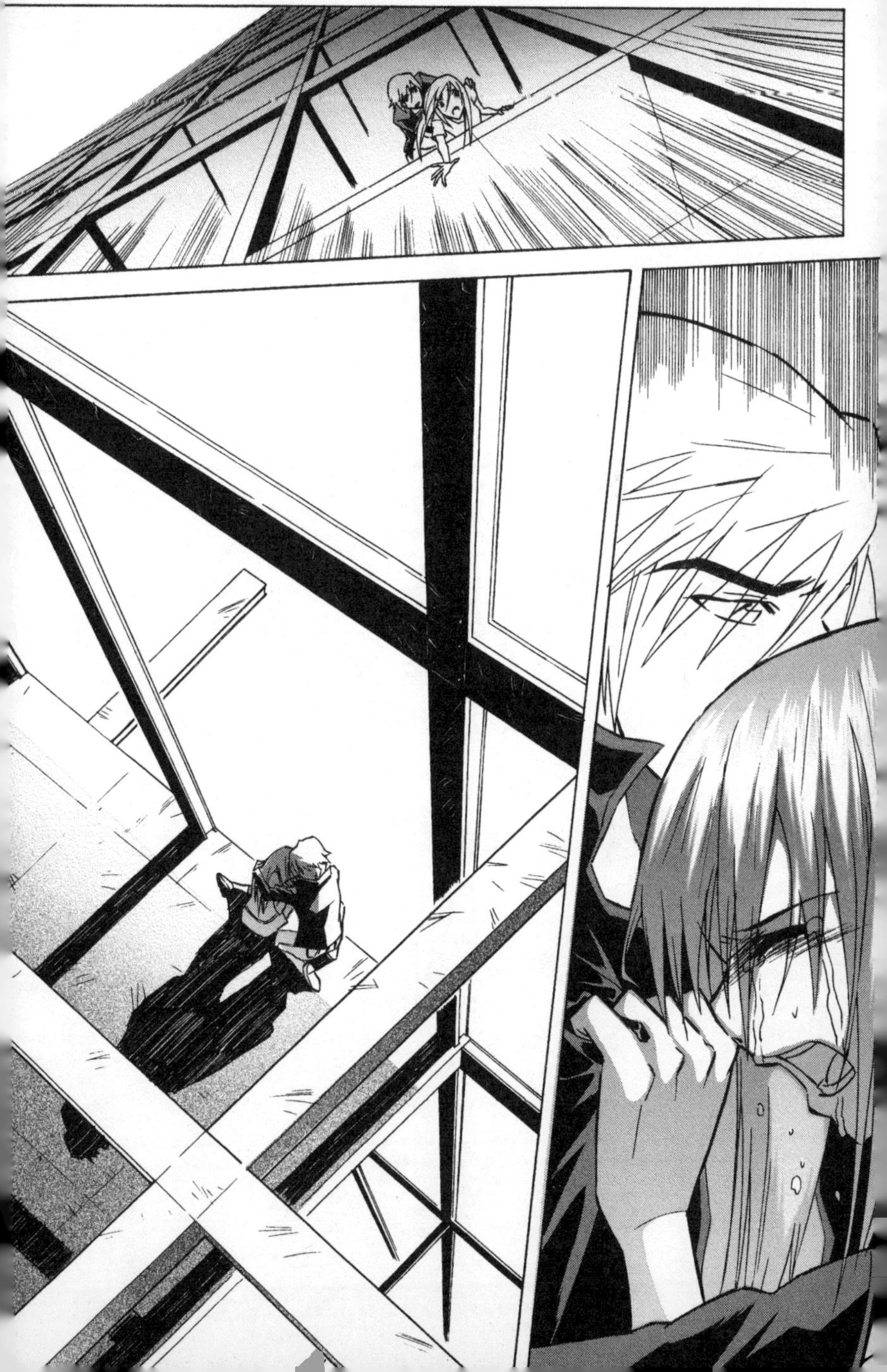

CHAPTER FIVE

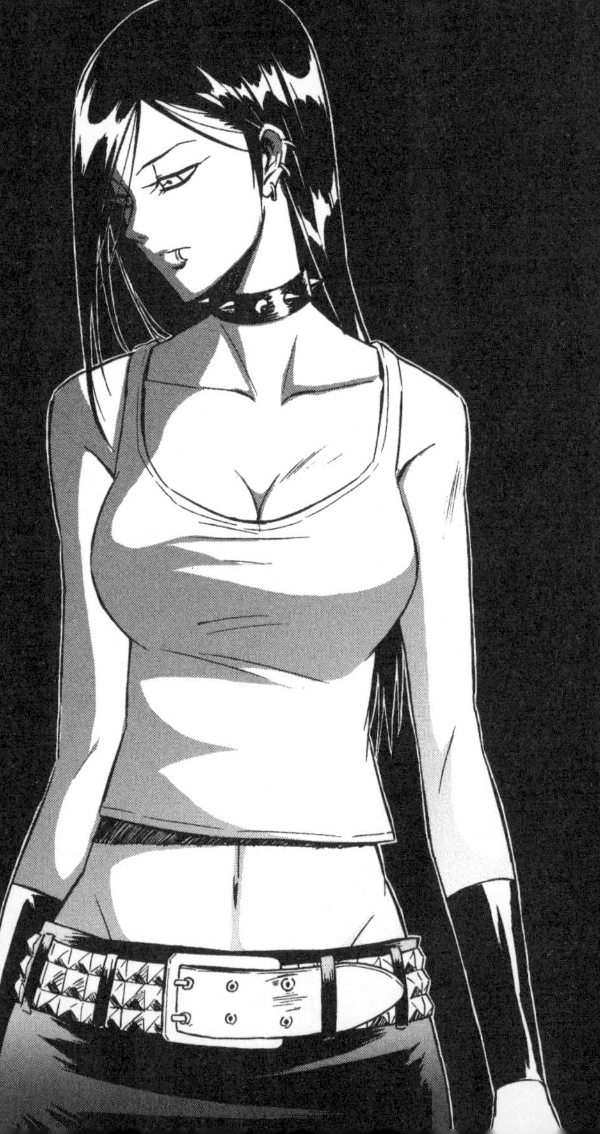

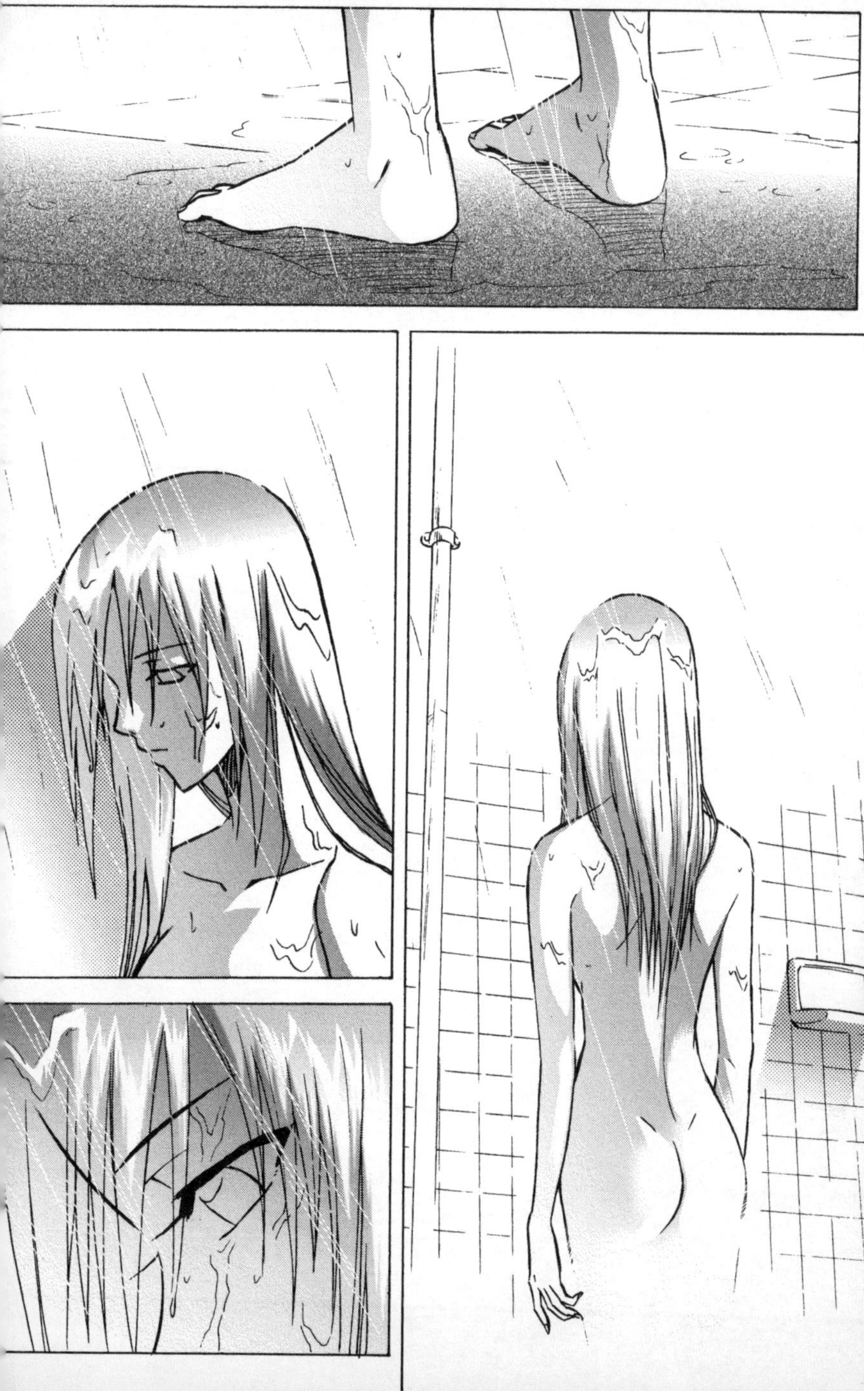

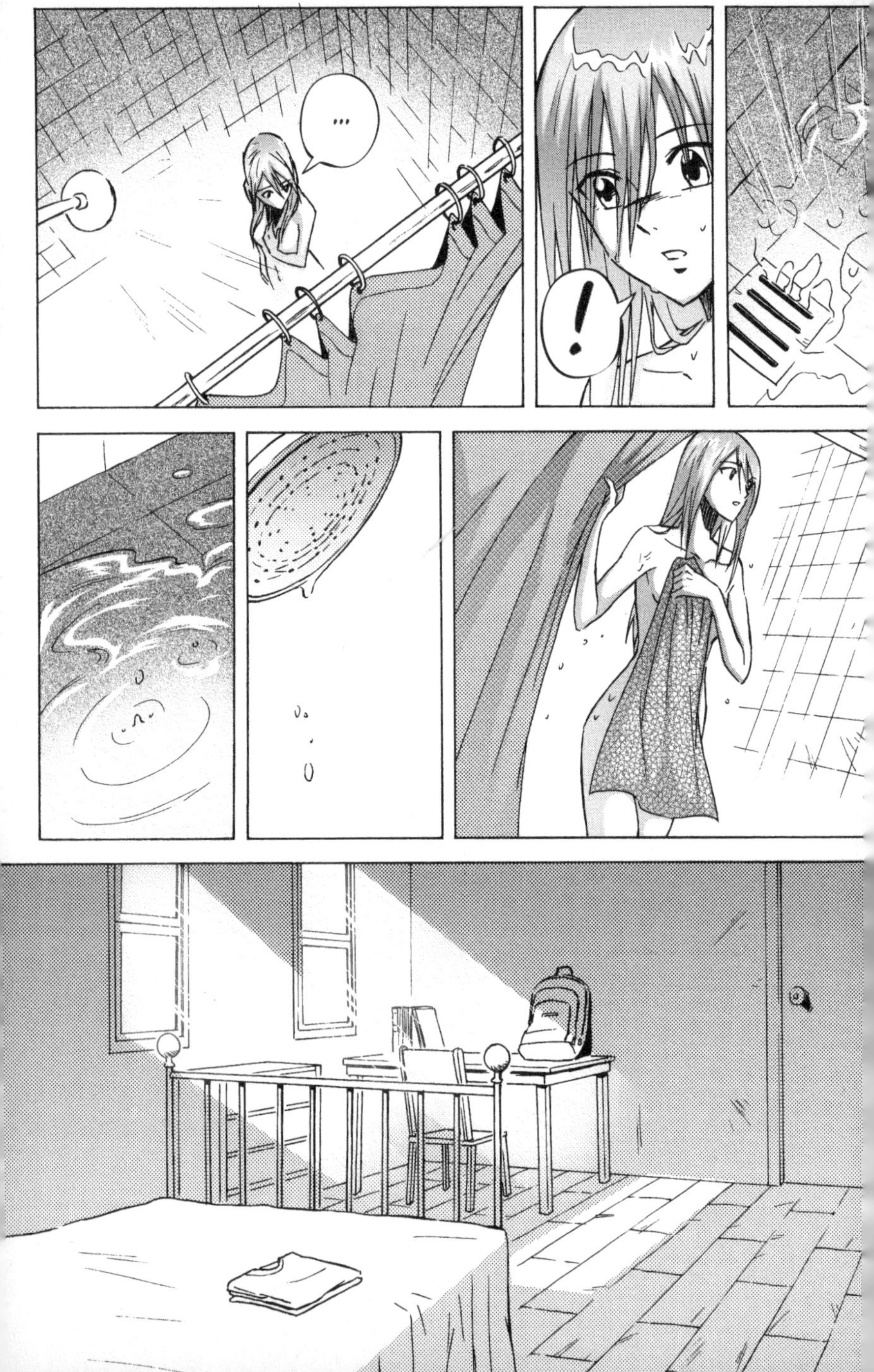
!
...

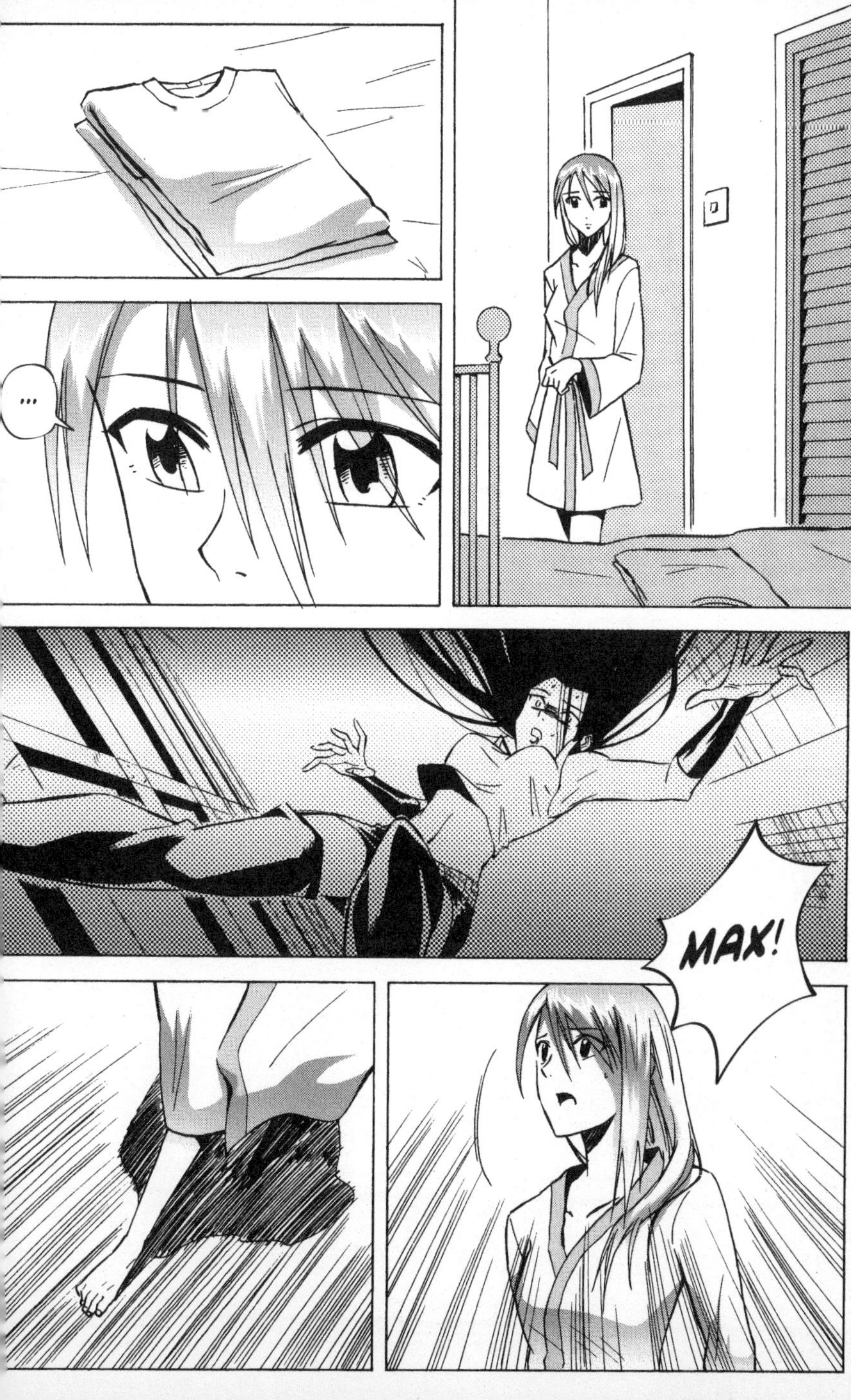
...
MAX!

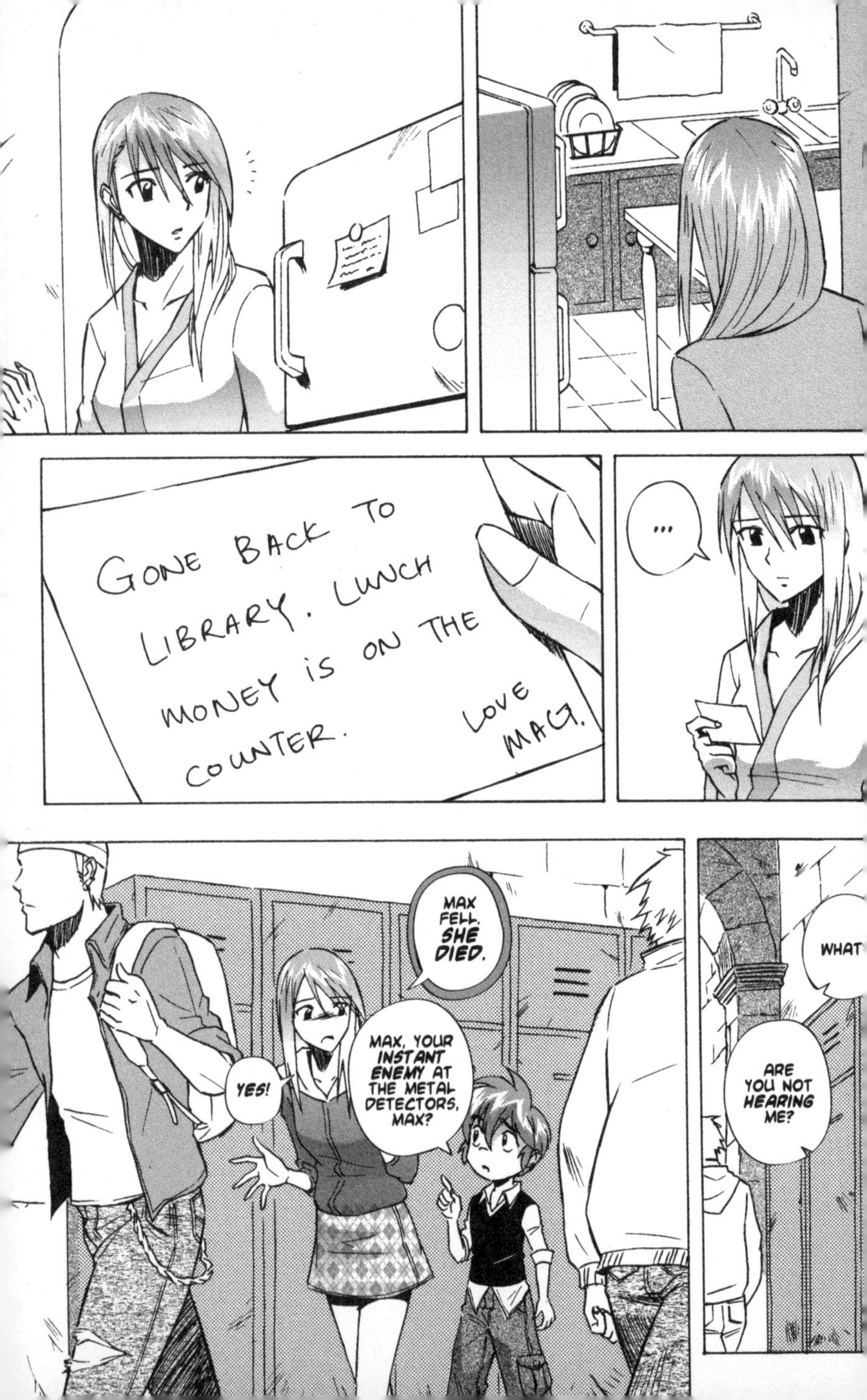
...
GONE BACK TO LIBRARY. LUNCH MONEY IS ON THE COUNTER. LOVE MAG.
WHAT
ARE YOU NOT HEARING ME?
MAX FELL. SHE DIED.
MAX, YOUR INSTANT ENEMY AT THE METAL DETECTORS, MAX?
YES!

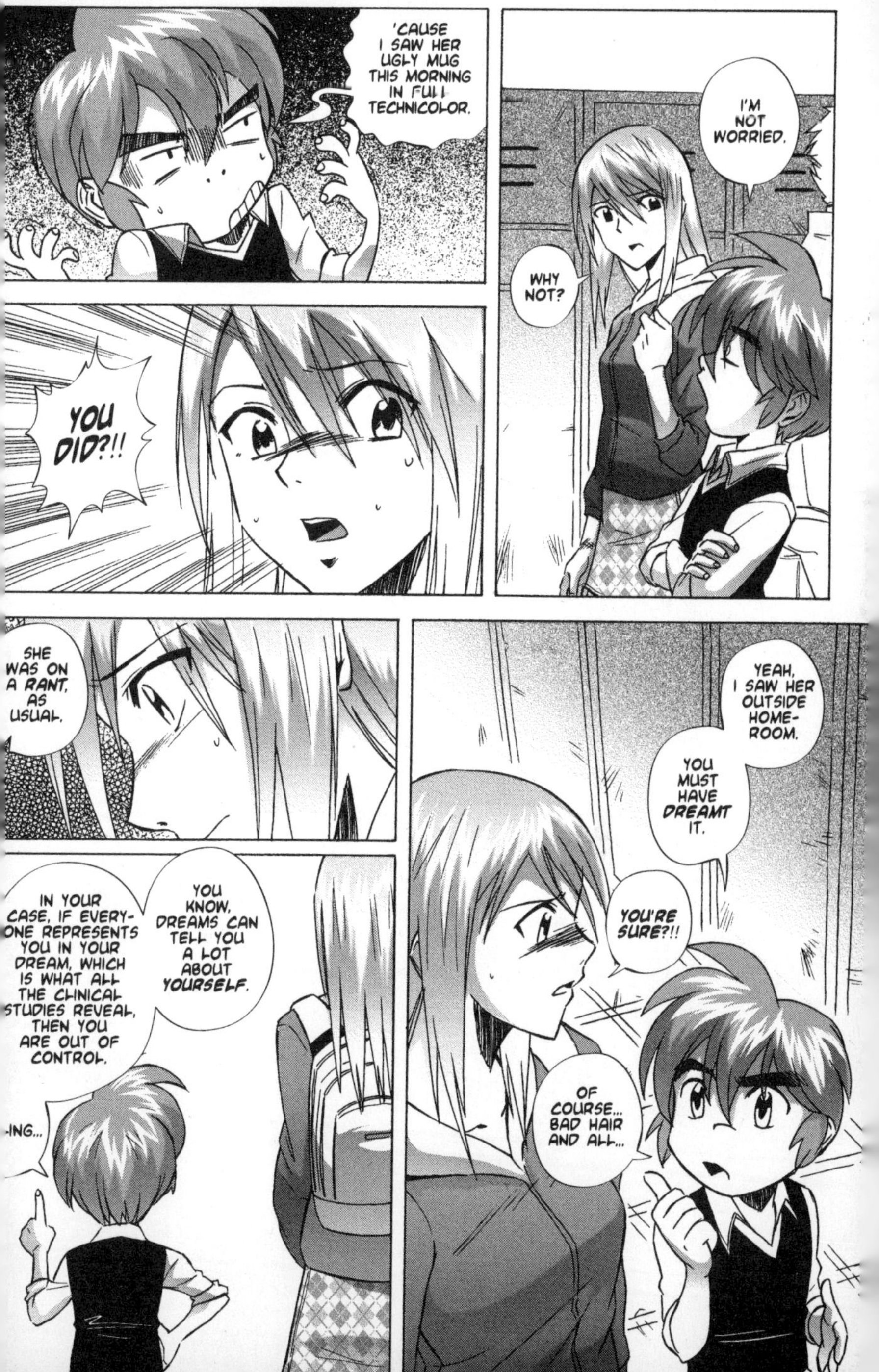
I'M NOT WORRIED.
WHY NOT?
'CAUSE I SAW HER UGLY MUG THIS MORNING IN FULL TECHNICOLOR.
YOU DID?!!
YEAH, I SAW HER OUTSIDE HOMEROOM.
YOU MUST HAVE DREAMT IT.
YOU'RE SURE?!!
OF COURSE... BAD HAIR AND ALL...
SHE WAS ON A RANT, AS USUAL.
YOU KNOW, DREAMS CAN TELL YOU A LOT ABOUT YOURSELF.
IN YOUR CASE, IF EVERYONE REPRESENTS YOU IN YOUR DREAM, WHICH IS WHAT ALL THE CLINICAL STUDIES REVEAL, THEN YOU ARE OUT OF CONTROL.
ING...

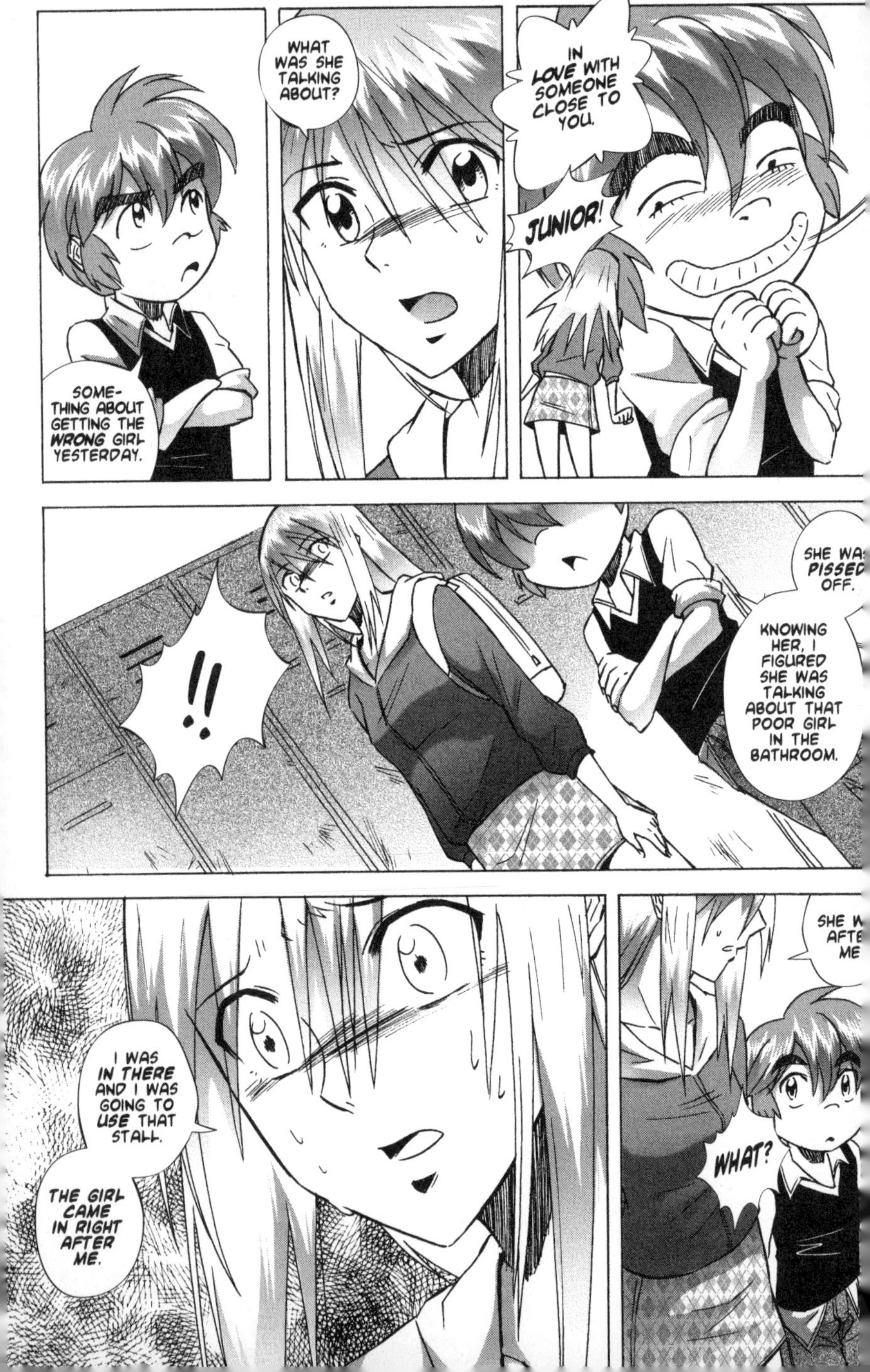

IN LOVE WITH SOMEONE CLOSE TO YOU.
JUNIOR!
WHAT WAS SHE TALKING ABOUT?
SOME-THING ABOUT GETTING THE WRONG GIRL YESTERDAY.
SHE WAS PISSED OFF.
KNOWING HER, I FIGURED SHE WAS TALKING ABOUT THAT POOR GIRL IN THE BATHROOM.
!!
SHE W AFTE ME
WHAT?
I WAS IN THERE AND I WAS GOING TO USE THAT STALL.
THE GIRL CAME IN RIGHT AFTER ME.

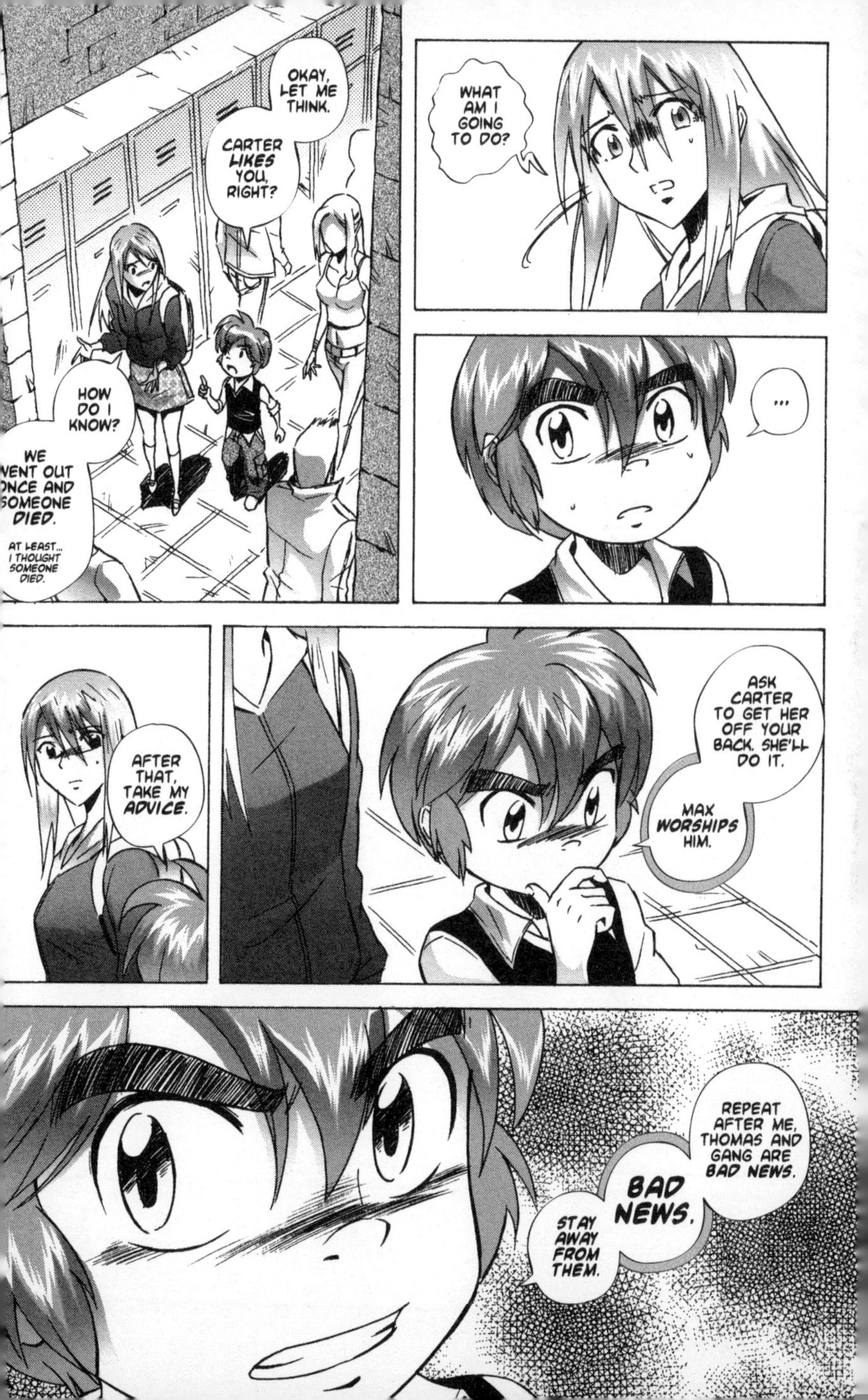
WHAT AM I GOING TO DO?
...
OKAY, LET ME THINK.
CARTER LIKES YOU, RIGHT?
HOW DO I KNOW?
WE WENT OUT ONCE AND SOMEONE DIED.
AT LEAST... I THOUGHT SOMEONE DIED.
ASK CARTER TO GET HER OFF YOUR BACK. SHE'LL DO IT.
MAX WORSHIPS HIM.
AFTER THAT, TAKE MY ADVICE.
REPEAT AFTER ME, THOMAS AND GANG ARE BAD NEWS.
BAD NEWS.
STAY AWAY FROM THEM.

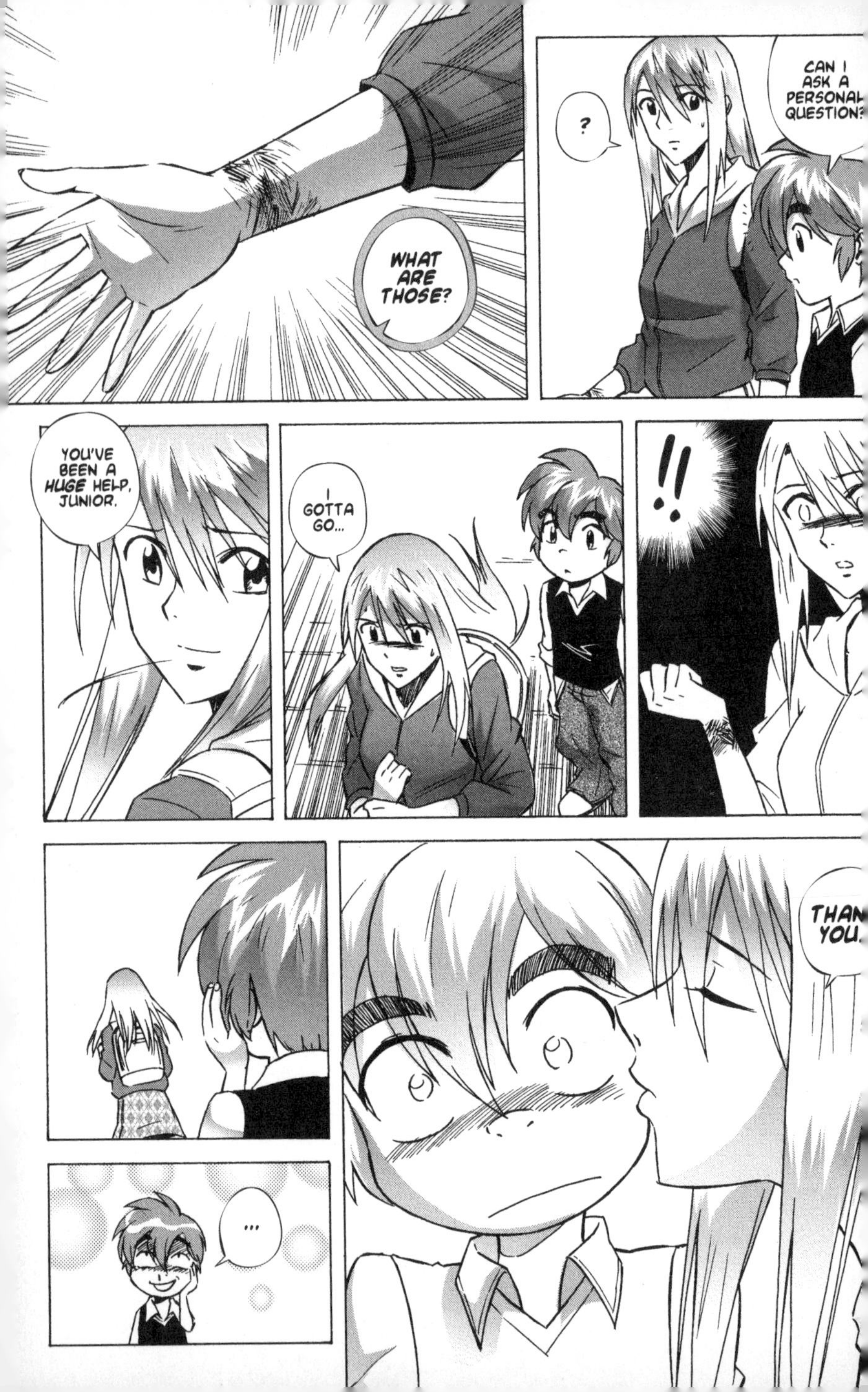
CAN I ASK A PERSONAL QUESTION?
?
WHAT ARE THOSE?
!!
I GOTTA GO...
YOU'VE BEEN A HUGE HELP, JUNIOR.
THAN YOU.
...

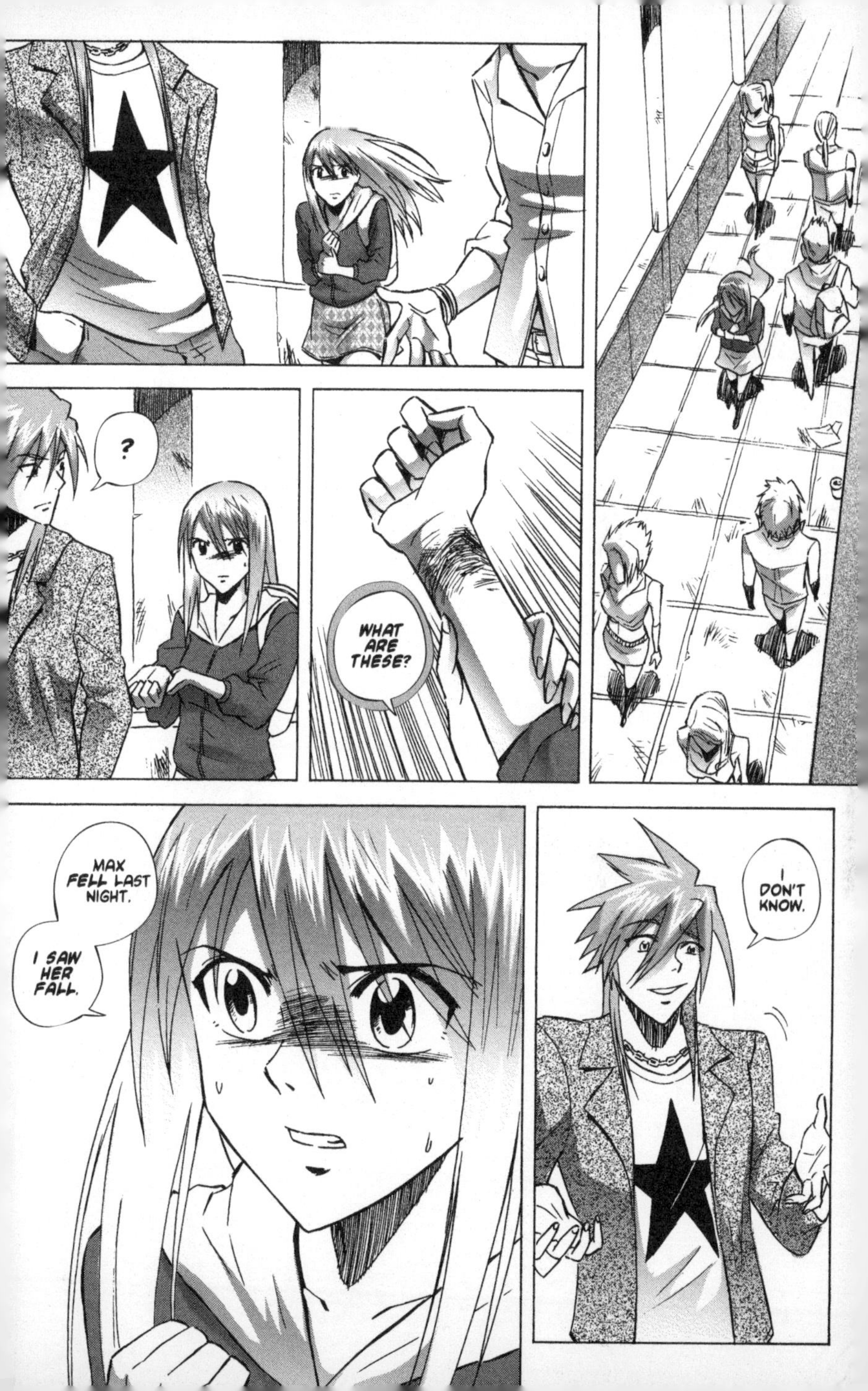
WHAT ARE THESE?
?
I DON'T KNOW.
MAX FELL LAST NIGHT.
I SAW HER FALL.

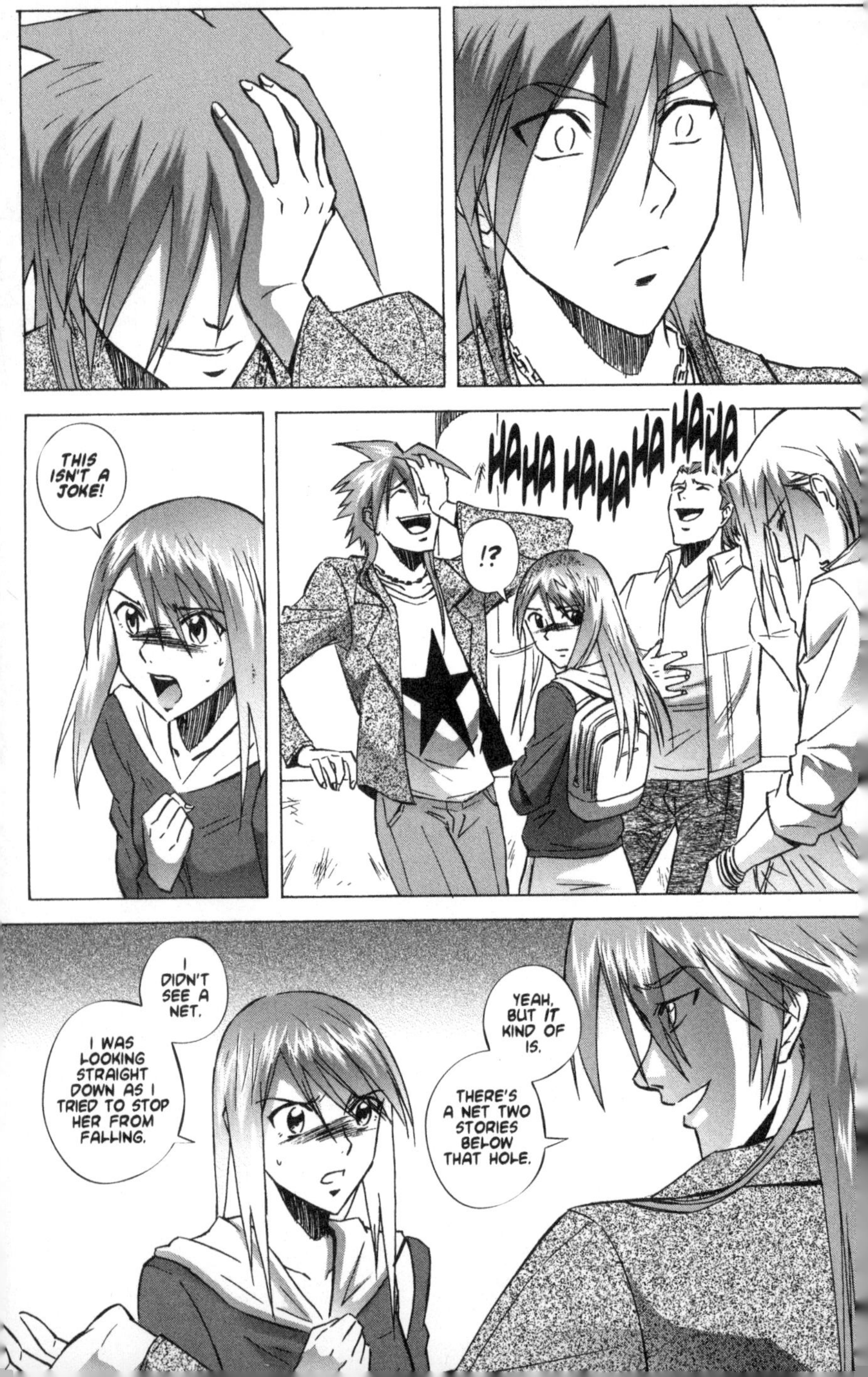
HAHA HAHAHA HAHA
!?
THIS ISN'T A JOKE!
YEAH, BUT IT KIND OF IS.
THERE'S A NET TWO STORIES BELOW THAT HOLE.
I DIDN'T SEE A NET.
I WAS LOOKING STRAIGHT DOWN AS I TRIED TO STOP HER FROM FALLING.

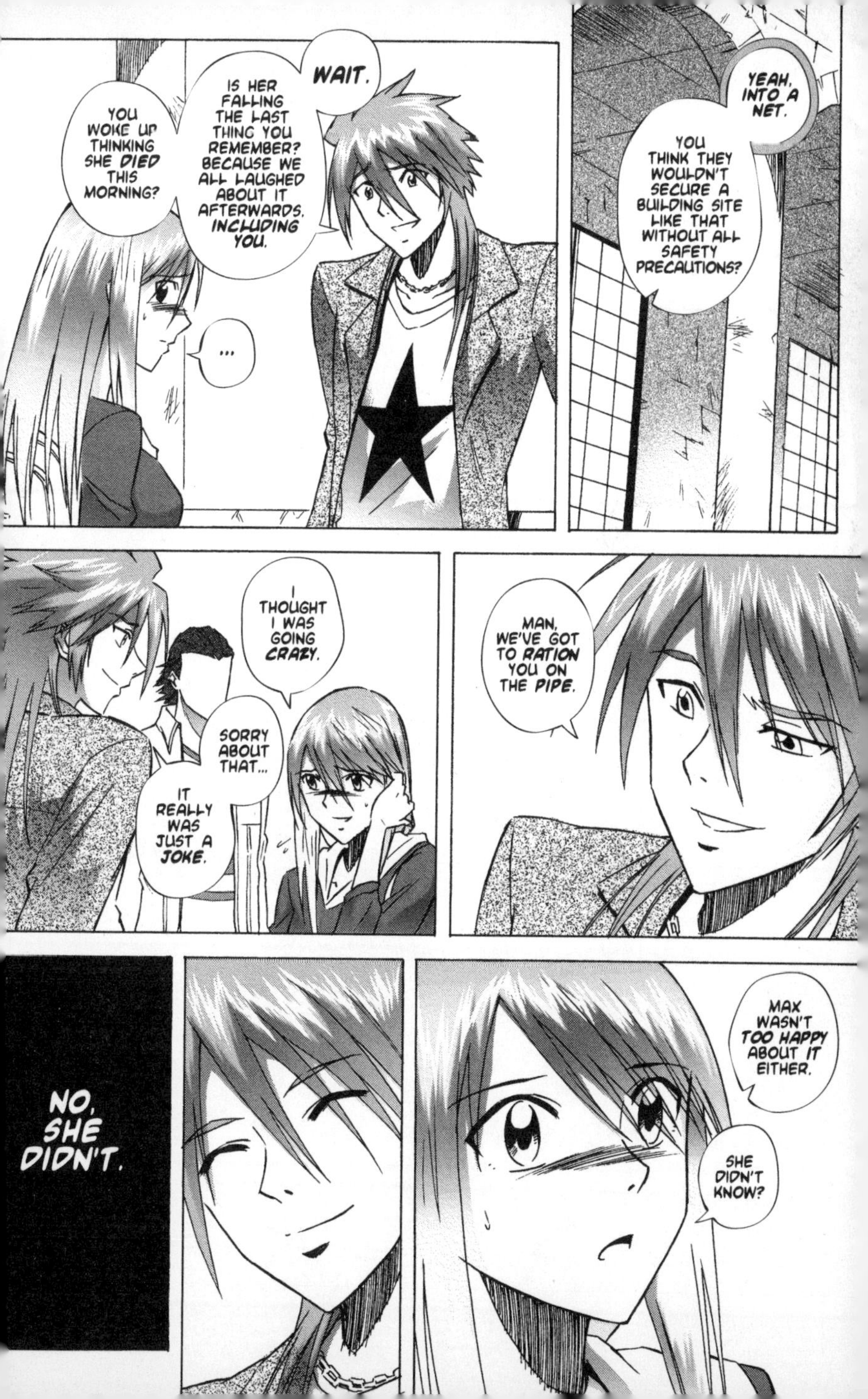
YEAH, INTO A NET.
YOU THINK THEY WOULDN'T SECURE A BUILDING SITE LIKE THAT WITHOUT ALL SAFETY PRECAUTIONS?
WAIT.
IS HER FALLING THE LAST THING YOU REMEMBER? BECAUSE WE ALL LAUGHED ABOUT IT AFTERWARDS. INCLUDING YOU.
YOU WOKE UP THINKING SHE DIED THIS MORNING?
...
MAN, WE'VE GOT TO RATION YOU ON THE PIPE.
I THOUGHT I WAS GOING CRAZY.
SORRY ABOUT THAT...
IT REALLY WAS JUST A JOKE.
MAX WASN'T TOO HAPPY ABOUT IT EITHER.
SHE DIDN'T KNOW?
NO, SHE DIDN'T.

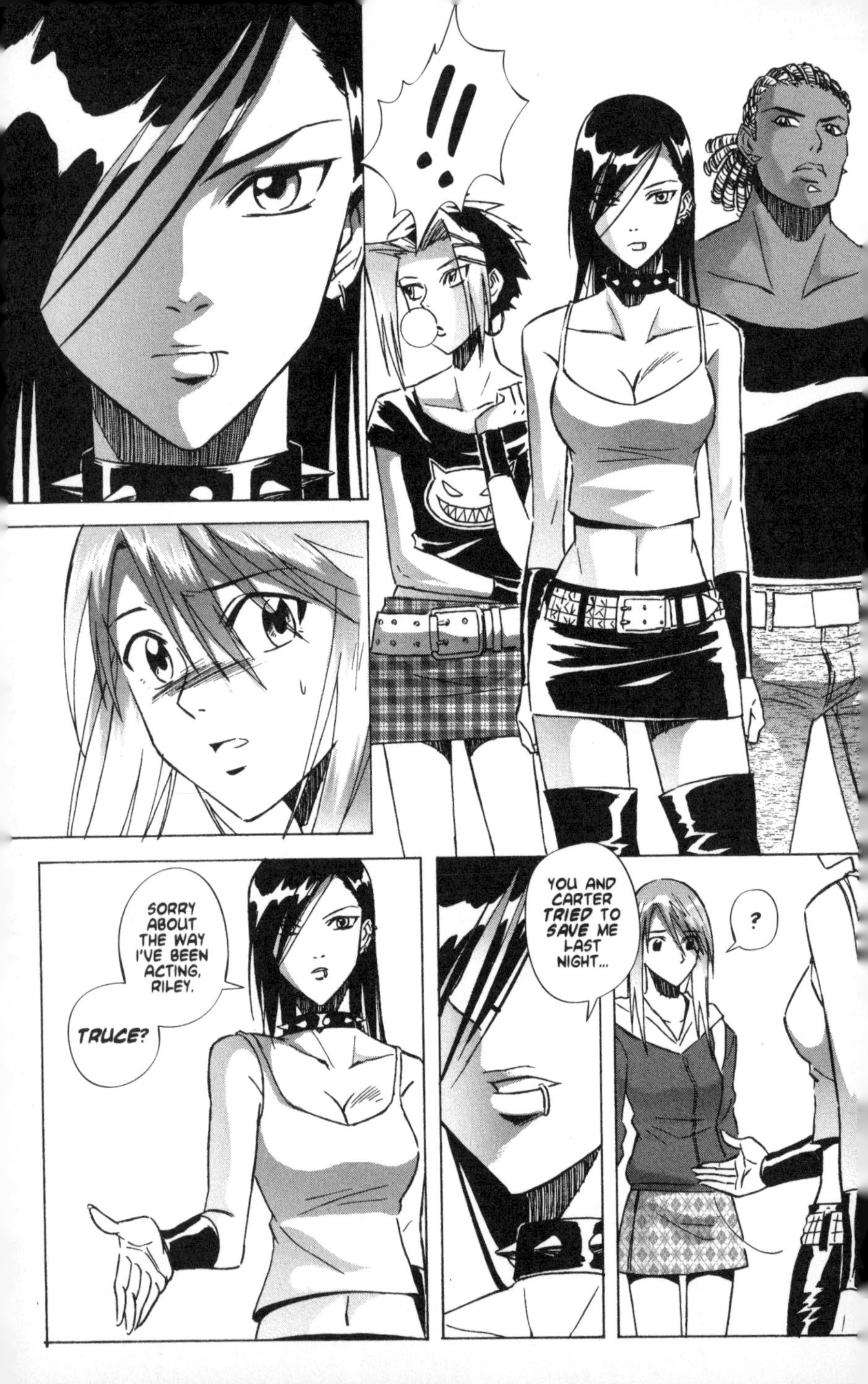
!!
?
YOU AND CARTER TRIED TO SAVE ME LAST NIGHT...
SORRY ABOUT THE WAY I'VE BEEN ACTING, RILEY.
TRUCE?

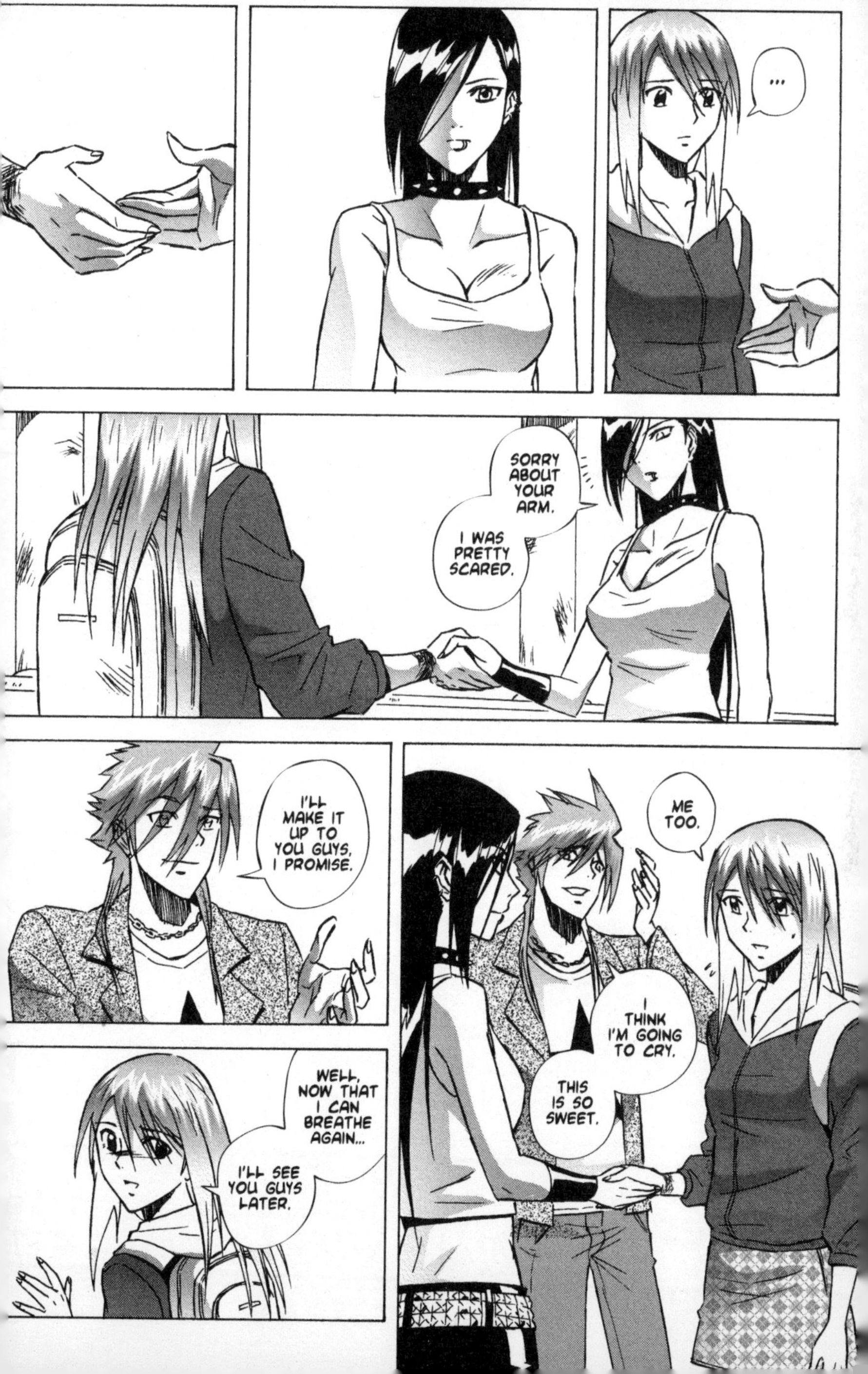
...
SORRY ABOUT YOUR ARM.
I WAS PRETTY SCARED.
ME TOO.
I THINK I'M GOING TO CRY.
THIS IS SO SWEET.
I'LL MAKE IT UP TO YOU GUYS, I PROMISE.
WELL, NOW THAT I CAN BREATHE AGAIN...
I'LL SEE YOU GUYS LATER.

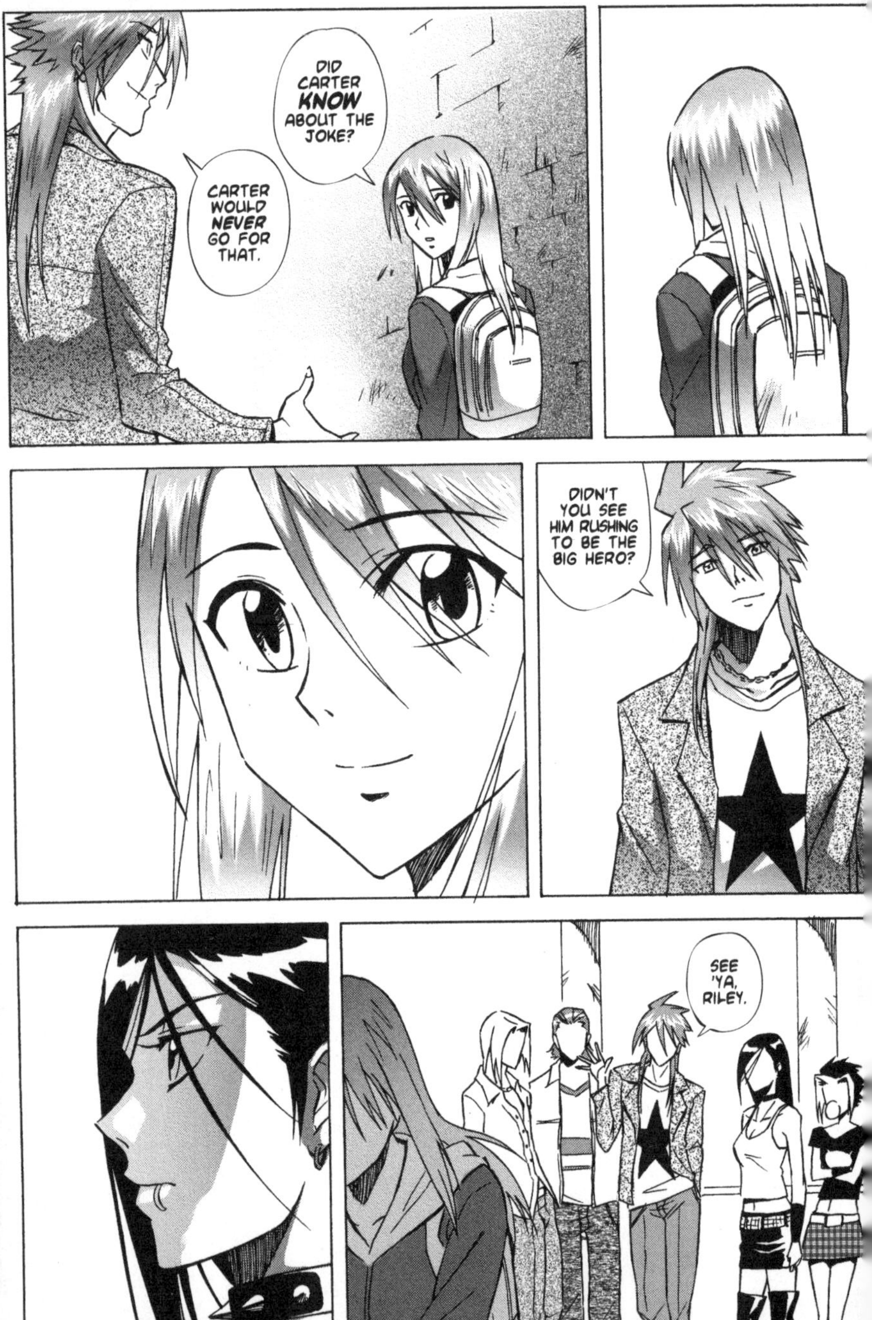
DID CARTER KNOW ABOUT THE JOKE?
CARTER WOULD NEVER GO FOR THAT.
DIDN'T YOU SEE HIM RUSHING TO BE THE BIG HERO?
SEE 'YA, RILEY.

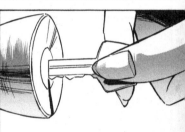

HORTON TRUMBOLD.

NICE TO MEET YOU. I AM TAKING OVER MANAGEMENT OF THE CO-OP.

OH.... HELLO.

HELLO.

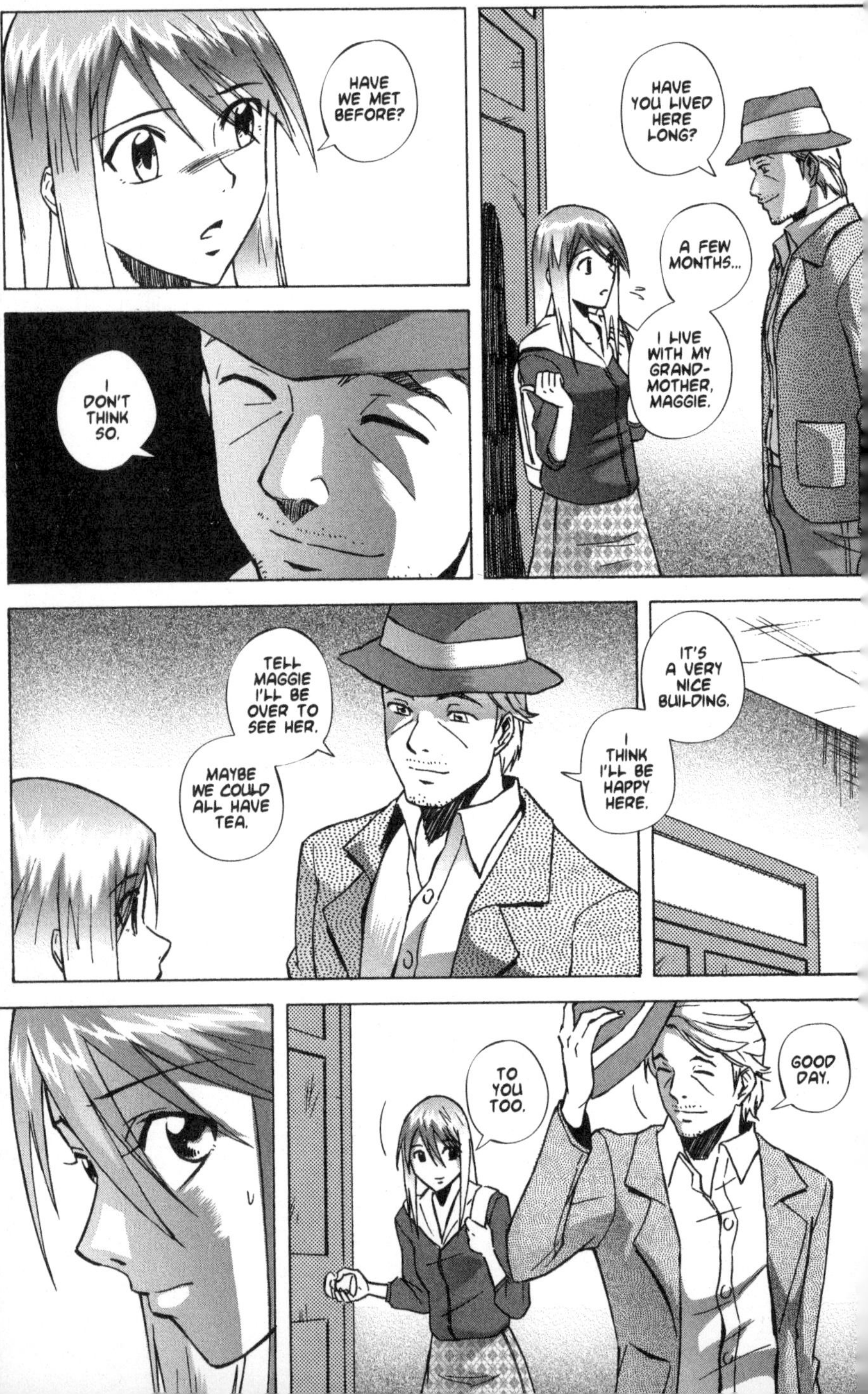
HAVE YOU LIVED HERE LONG?
A FEW MONTHS...
I LIVE WITH MY GRAND-MOTHER, MAGGIE.
HAVE WE MET BEFORE?
I DON'T THINK SO.
IT'S A VERY NICE BUILDING.
I THINK I'LL BE HAPPY HERE.
TELL MAGGIE I'LL BE OVER TO SEE HER.
MAYBE WE COULD ALL HAVE TEA.
GOOD DAY.
TO YOU TOO.

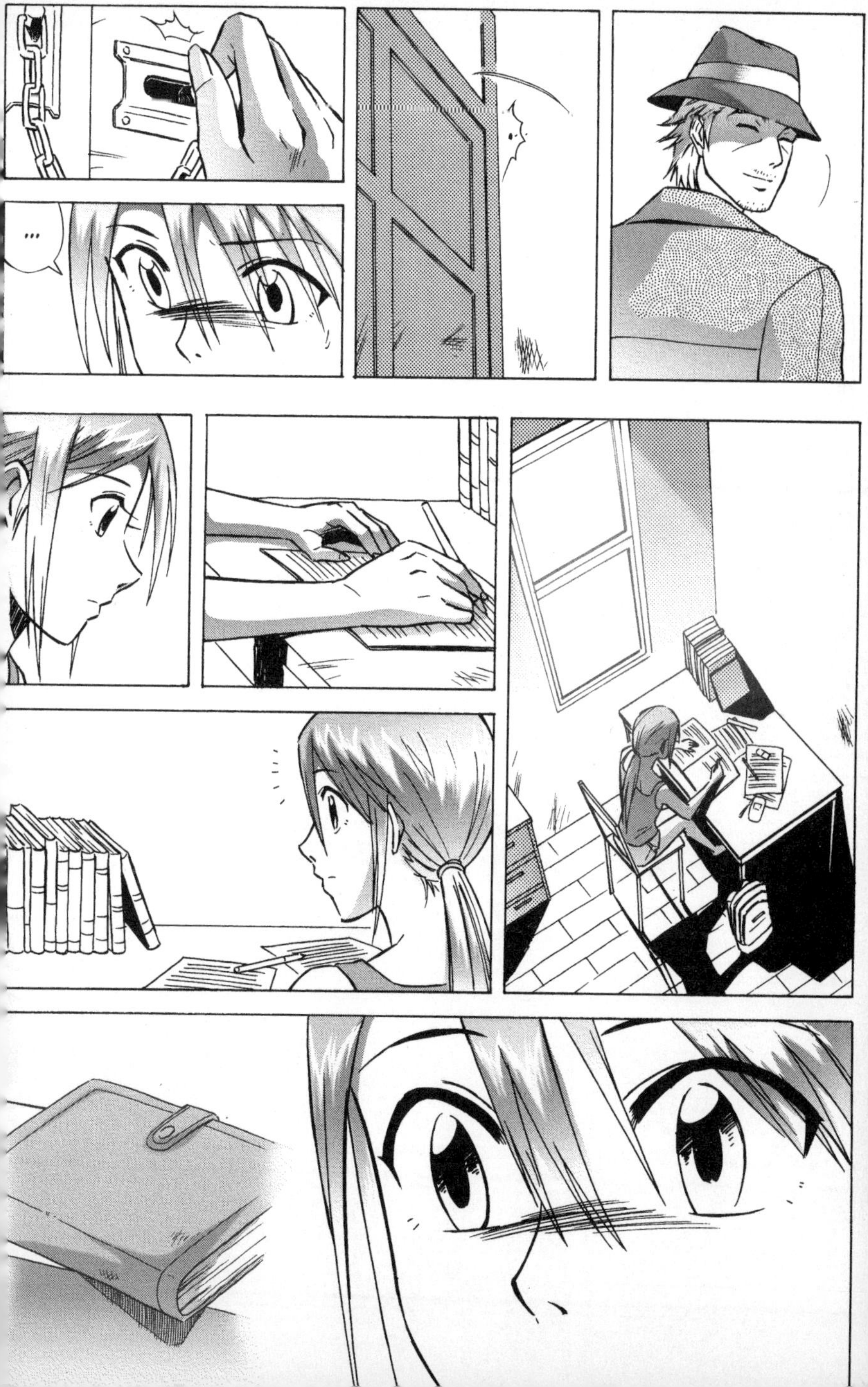
...

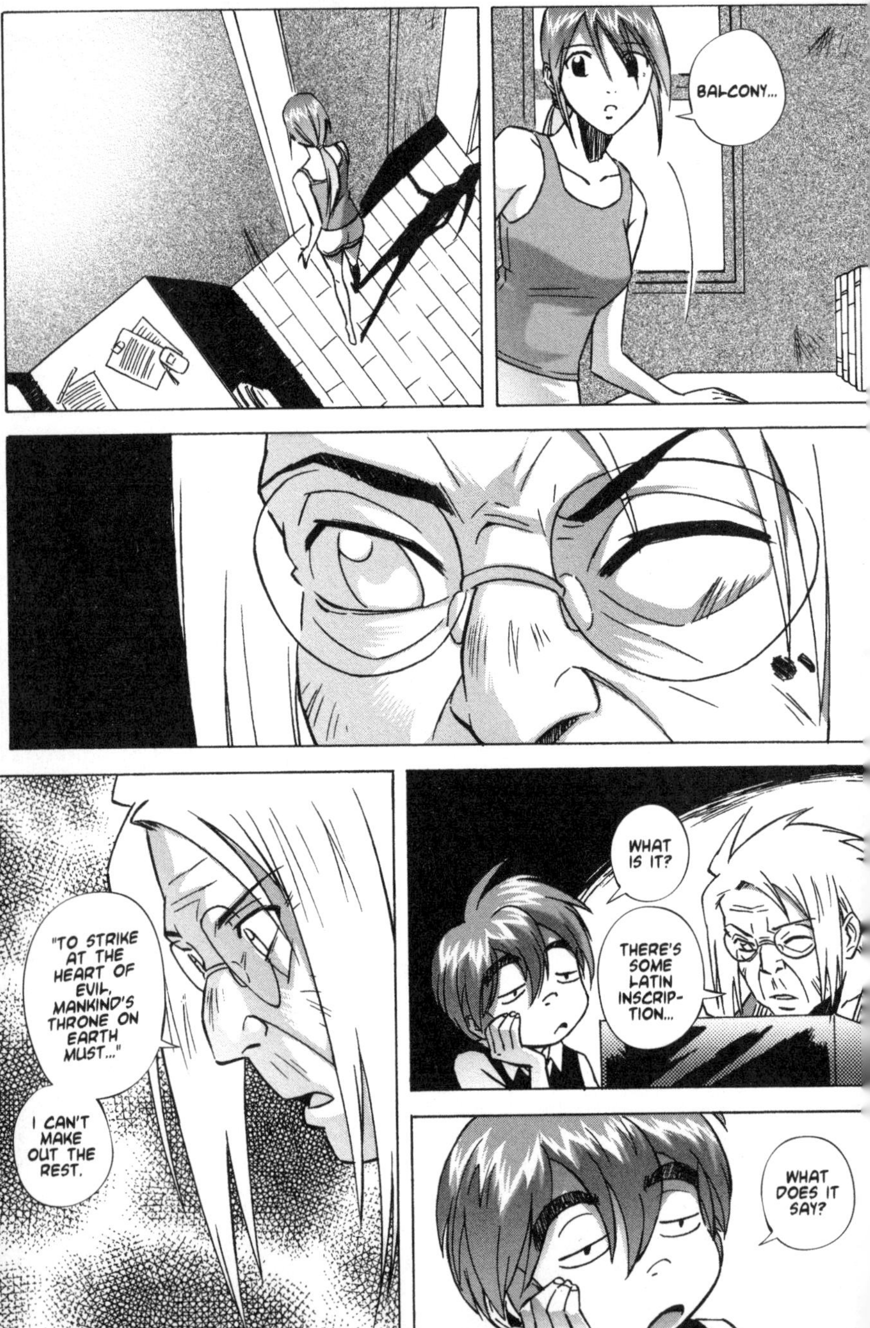
BALCONY...
WHAT IS IT?
THERE'S SOME LATIN INSCRIPTION...
WHAT DOES IT SAY?
"TO STRIKE AT THE HEART OF EVIL, MANKIND'S THRONE ON EARTH MUST..."
I CAN'T MAKE OUT THE REST.

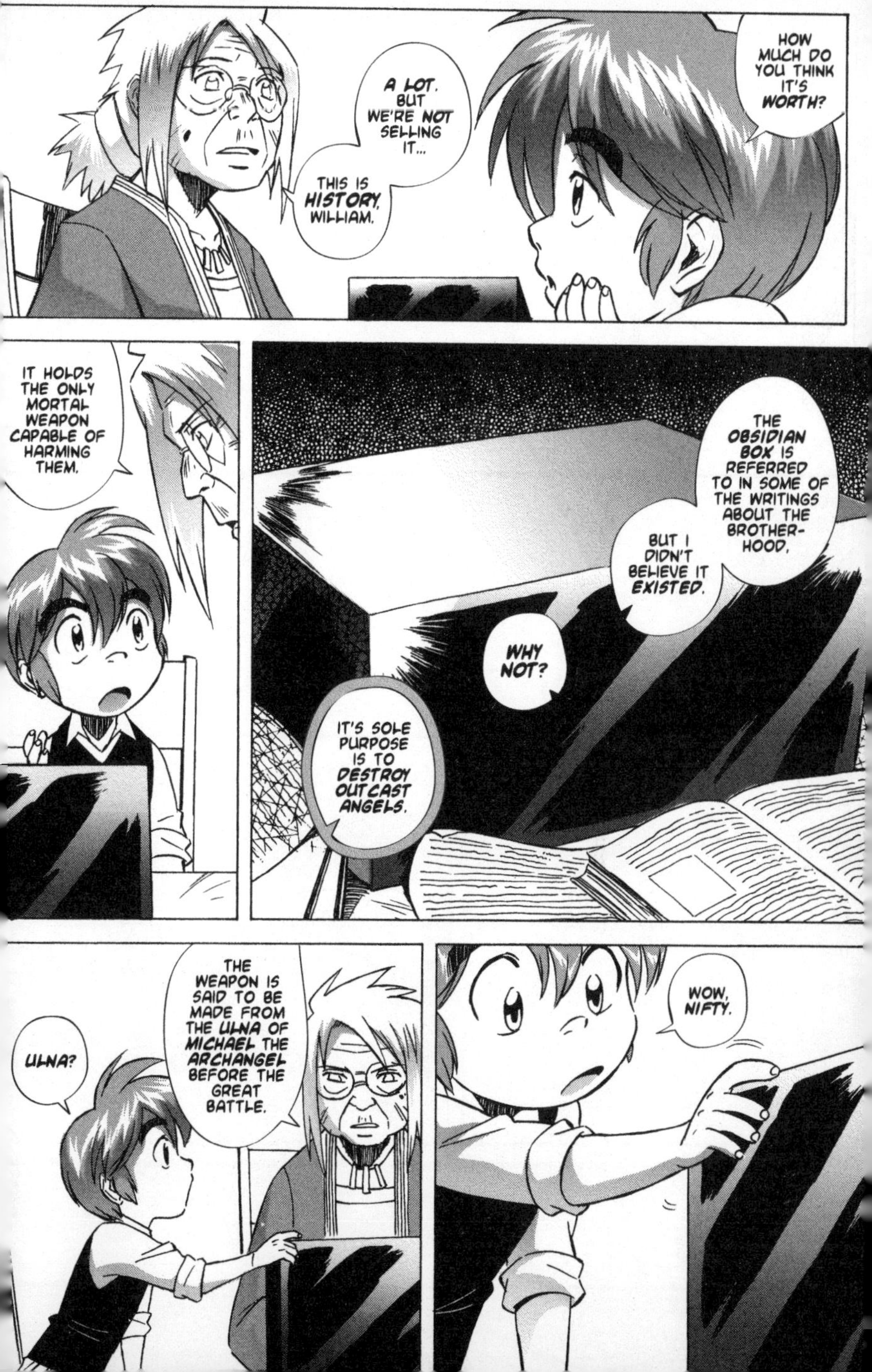
HOW MUCH DO YOU THINK IT'S WORTH?
A LOT. BUT WE'RE NOT SELLING IT...
THIS IS HISTORY, WILLIAM.
THE OBSIDIAN BOX IS REFERRED TO IN SOME OF THE WRITINGS ABOUT THE BROTHERHOOD.
BUT I DIDN'T BELIEVE IT EXISTED.
WHY NOT?
IT'S SOLE PURPOSE IS TO DESTROY OUTCAST ANGELS.
IT HOLDS THE ONLY MORTAL WEAPON CAPABLE OF HARMING THEM.
WOW, NIFTY.
THE WEAPON IS SAID TO BE MADE FROM THE ULNA OF MICHAEL THE ARCHANGEL BEFORE THE GREAT BATTLE.
ULNA?

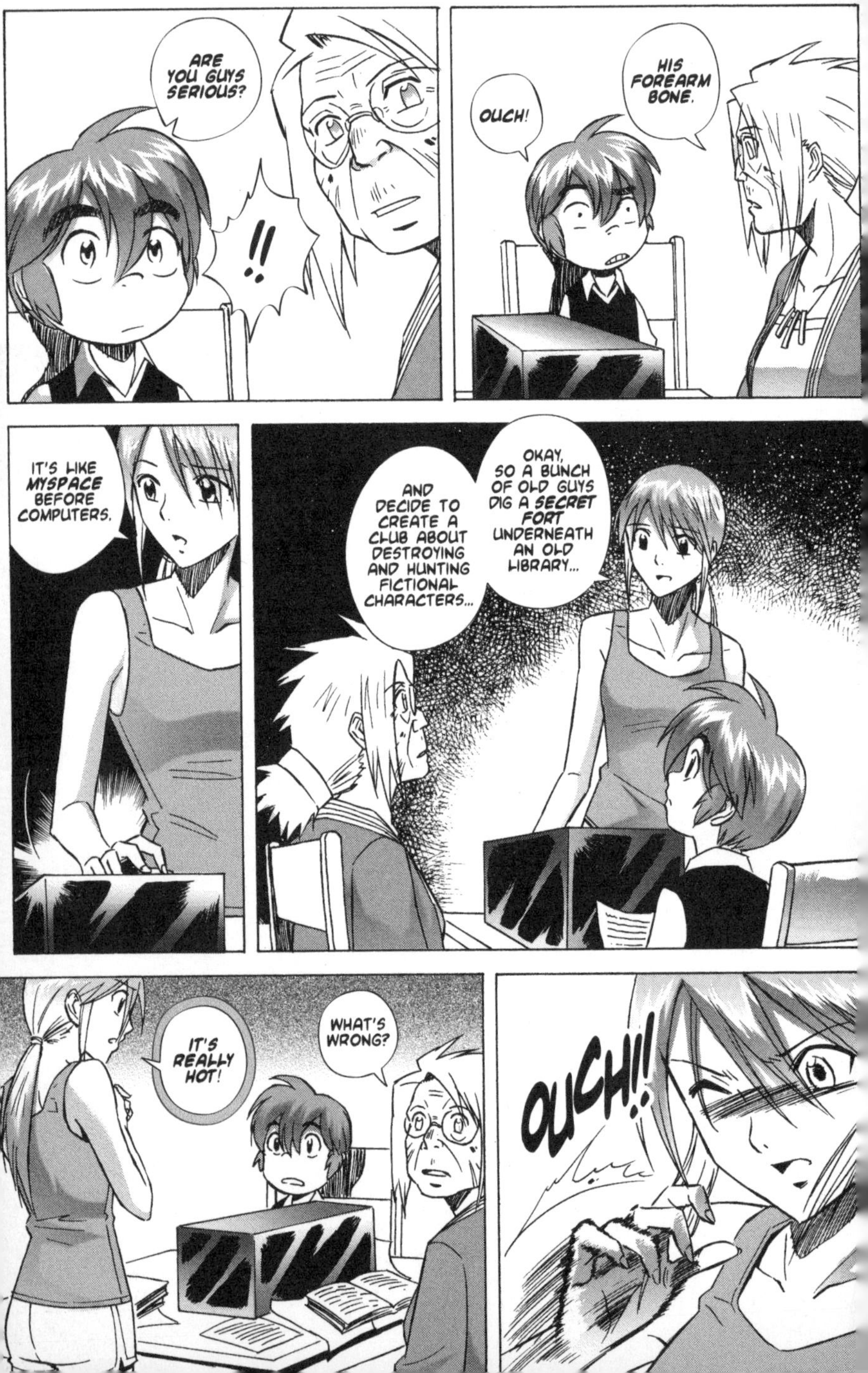
HIS FOREARM BONE.
OUCH!
ARE YOU GUYS SERIOUS?
!!
OKAY, SO A BUNCH OF OLD GUYS DIG A SECRET FORT UNDERNEATH AN OLD LIBRARY...
AND DECIDE TO CREATE A CLUB ABOUT DESTROYING AND HUNTING FICTIONAL CHARACTERS...
IT'S LIKE MYSPACE BEFORE COMPUTERS.
OUCH!!
WHAT'S WRONG?
IT'S REALLY HOT!

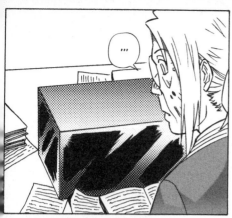

IT'S ACTUALLY QUITE COLD.

I'M GOING TO BED.

OH YEAH... IT IS.

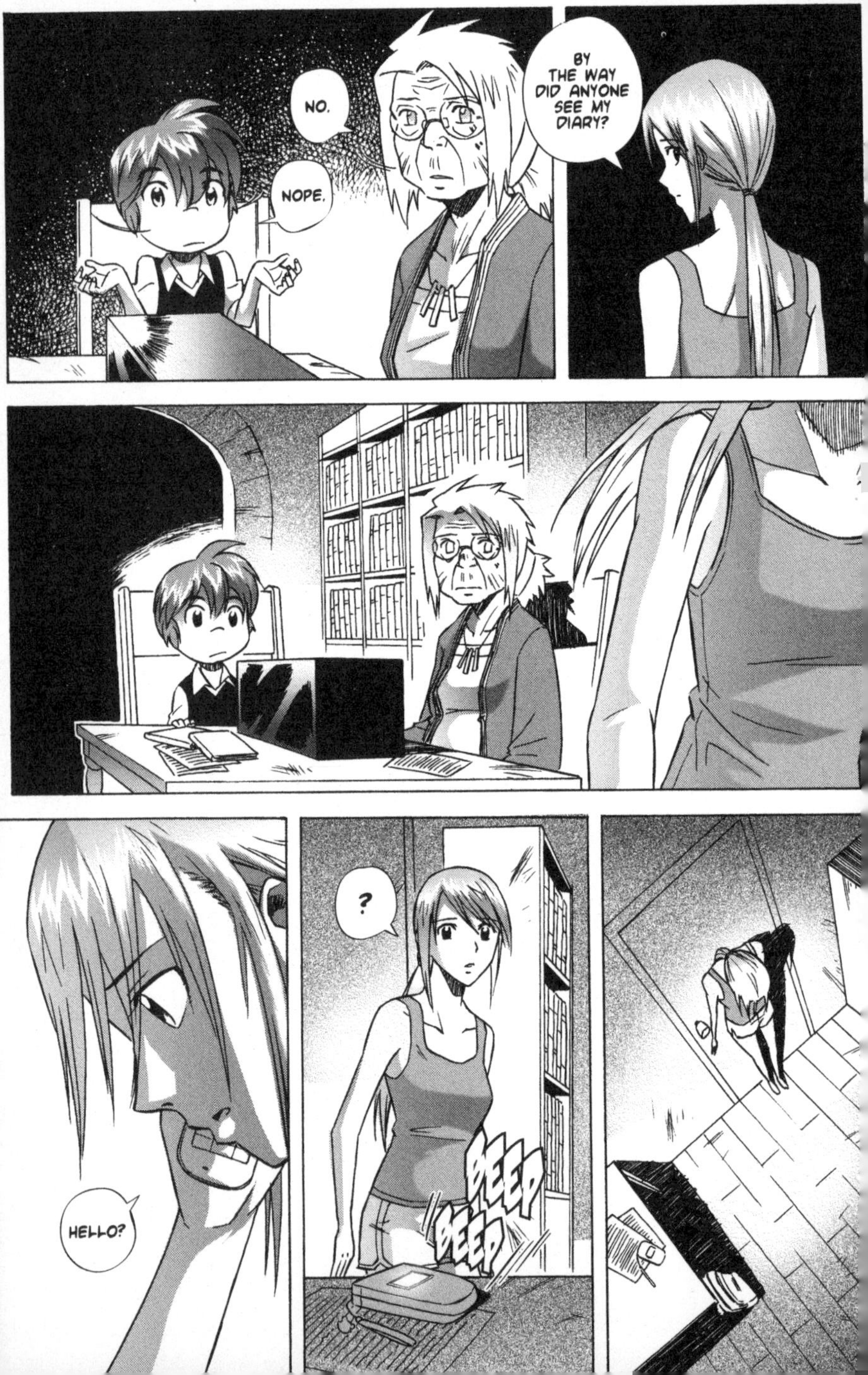
BY THE WAY DID ANYONE SEE MY DIARY?
NO.
NOPE.
?
BEEP
BEEP
HELLO?

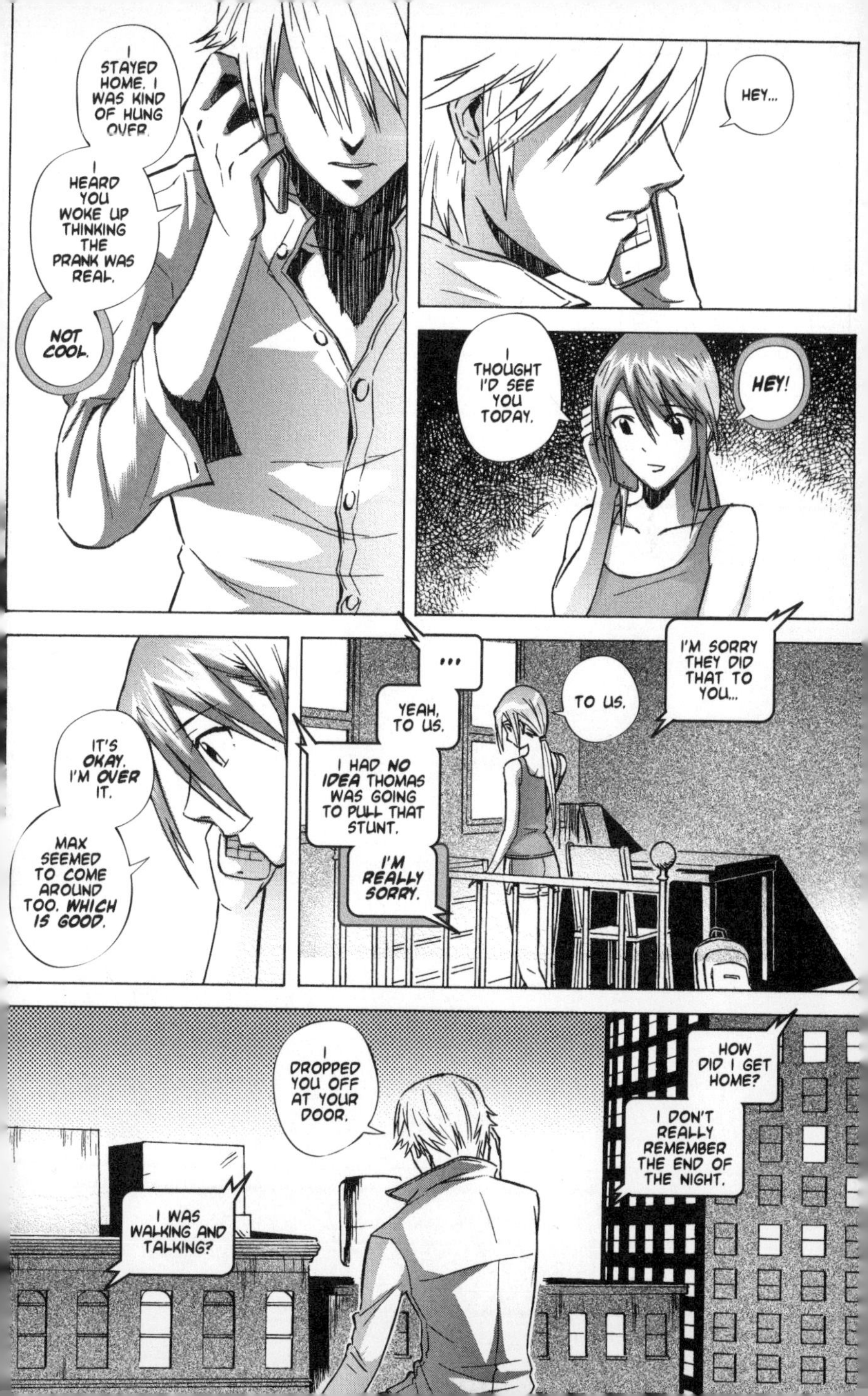
HEY...
HEY!
I THOUGHT I'D SEE YOU TODAY.
I STAYED HOME. I WAS KIND OF HUNG OVER.
I HEARD YOU WOKE UP THINKING THE PRANK WAS REAL.
NOT COOL.
I'M SORRY THEY DID THAT TO YOU...
TO US.
...
YEAH, TO US.
I HAD NO IDEA THOMAS WAS GOING TO PULL THAT STUNT.
I'M REALLY SORRY.
IT'S OKAY. I'M OVER IT.
MAX SEEMED TO COME AROUND TOO. WHICH IS GOOD.
HOW DID I GET HOME?
I DON'T REALLY REMEMBER THE END OF THE NIGHT.
I DROPPED YOU OFF AT YOUR DOOR.
I WAS WALKING AND TALKING?

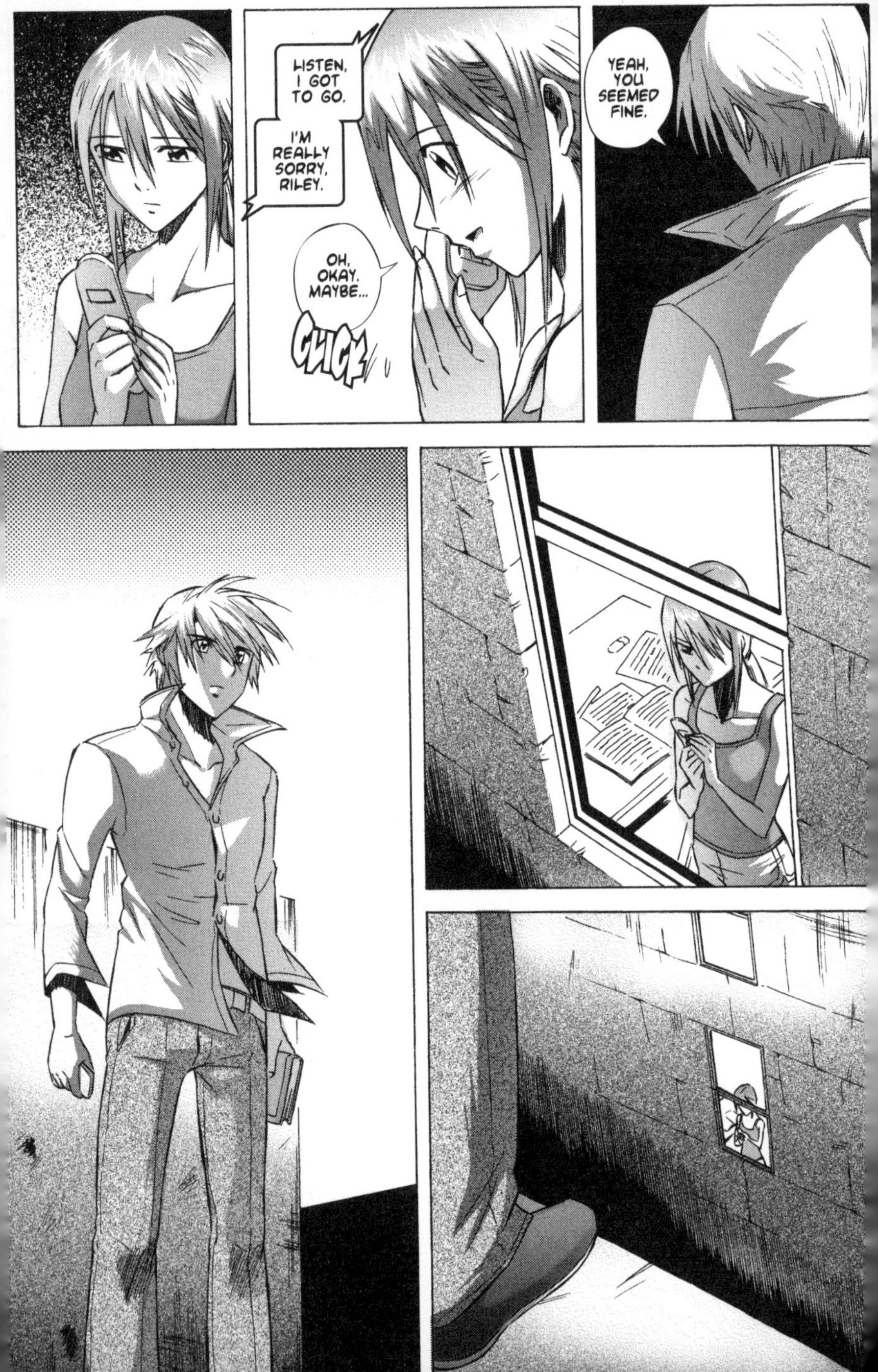
YEAH, YOU SEEMED FINE.
LISTEN, I GOT TO GO.
I'M REALLY SORRY, RILEY.
OH, OKAY. MAYBE...
CLICK

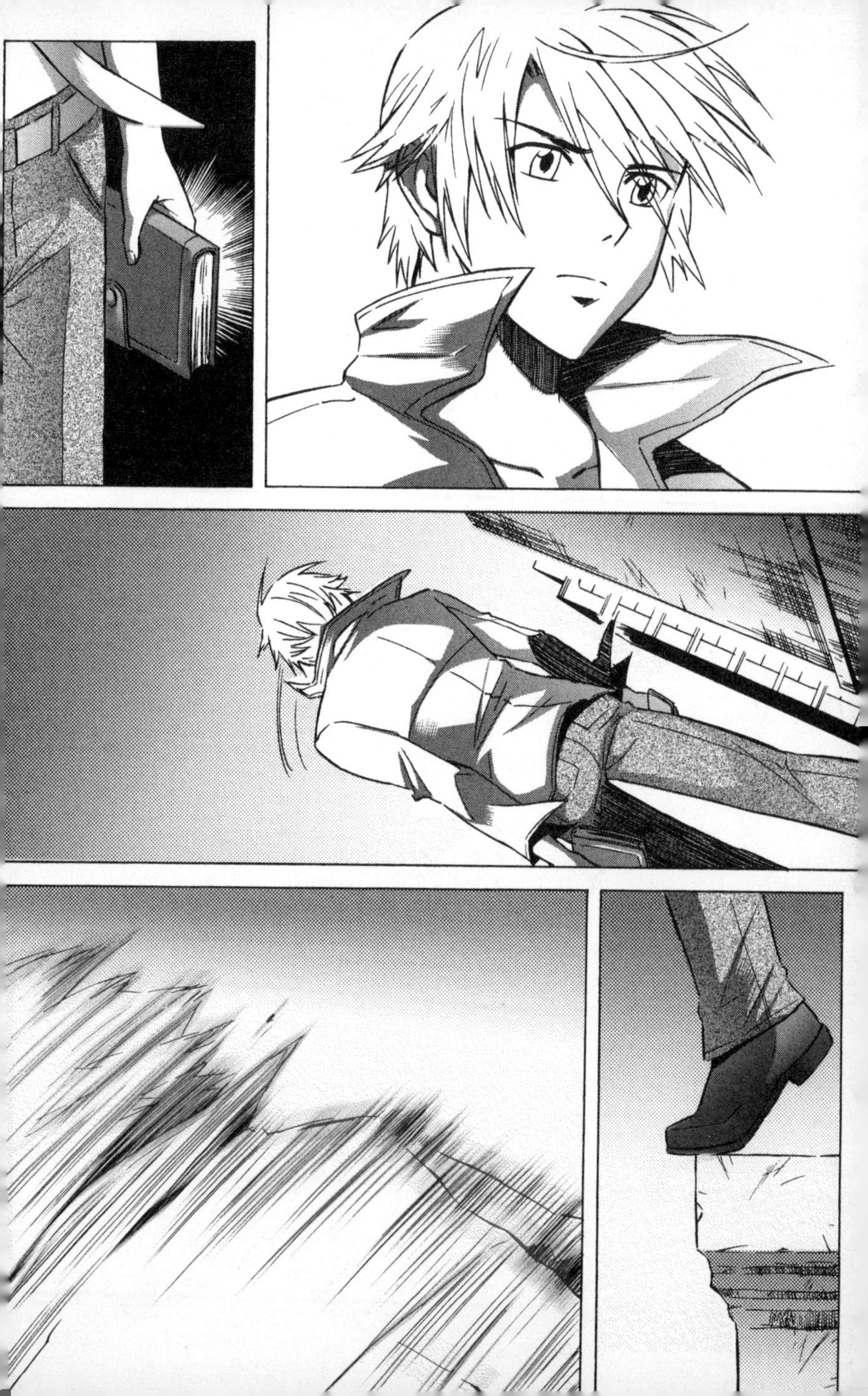

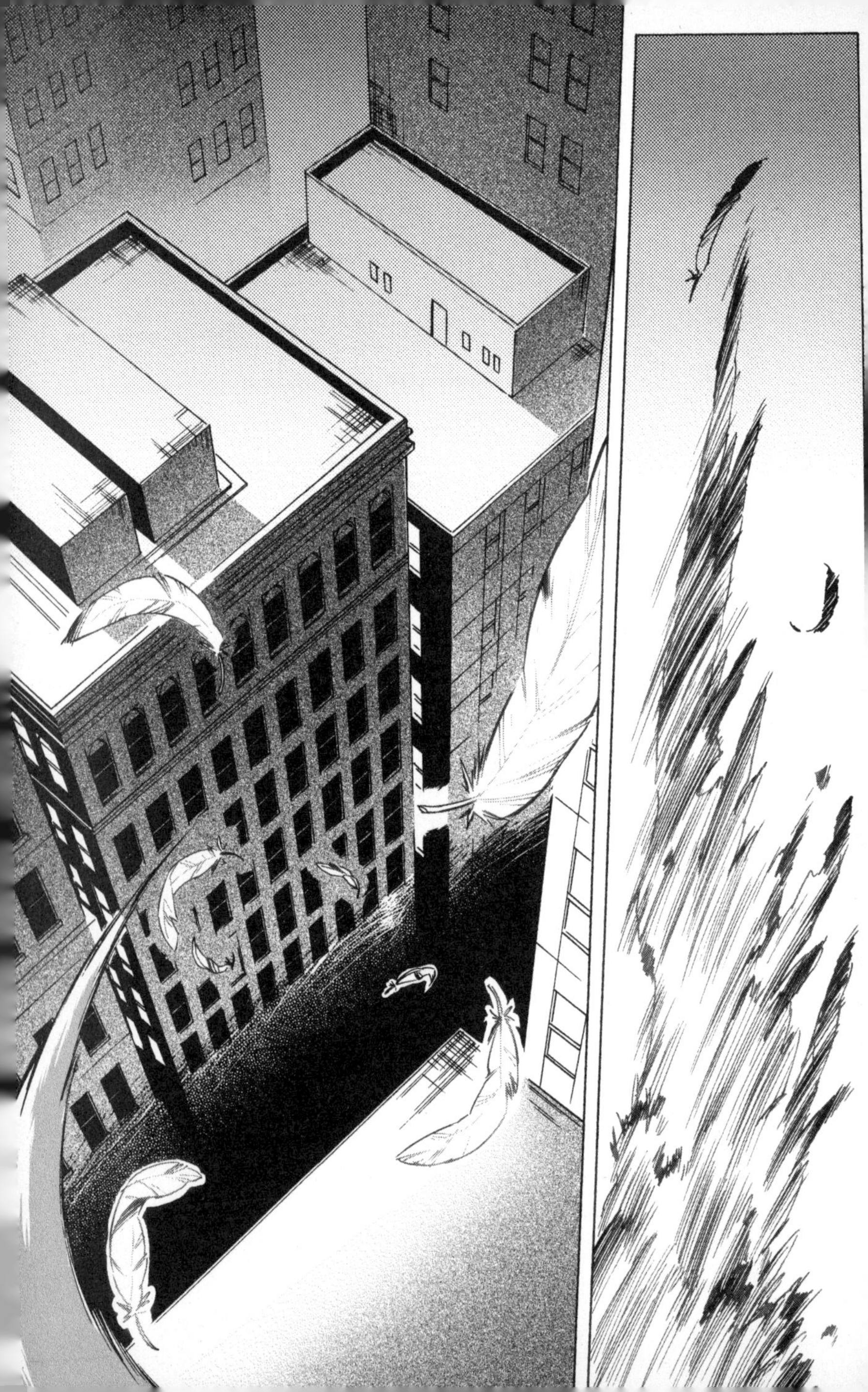

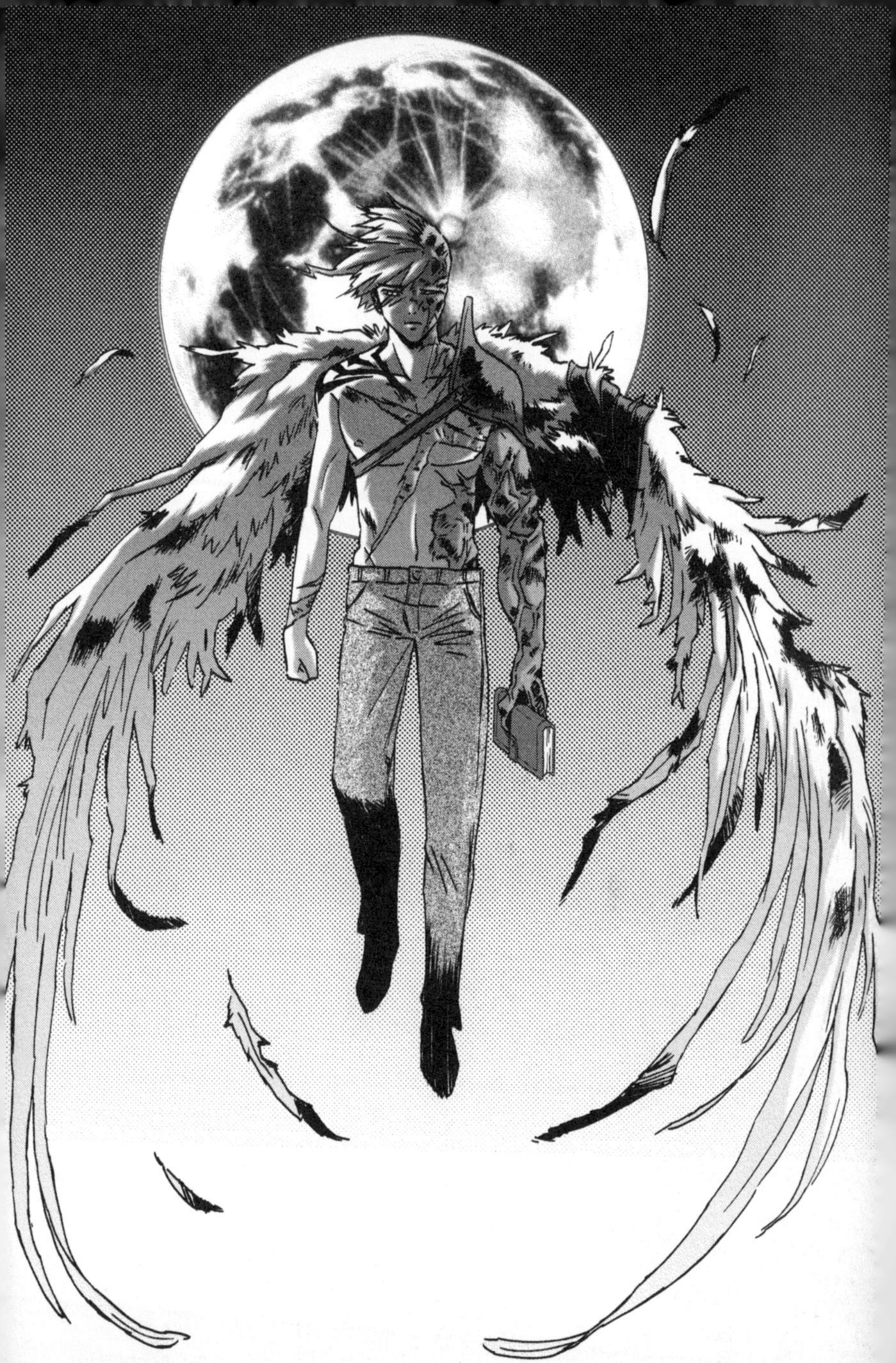

TO BE CONTINUED...

THE ✝ OUTCAST
· SKETCH PAD ·

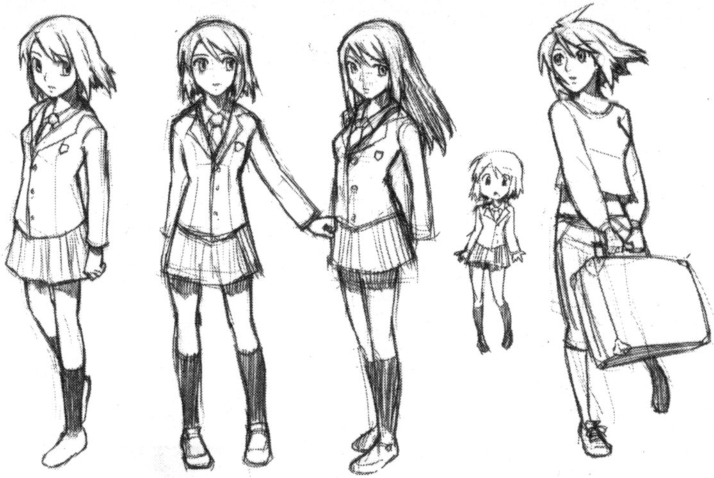

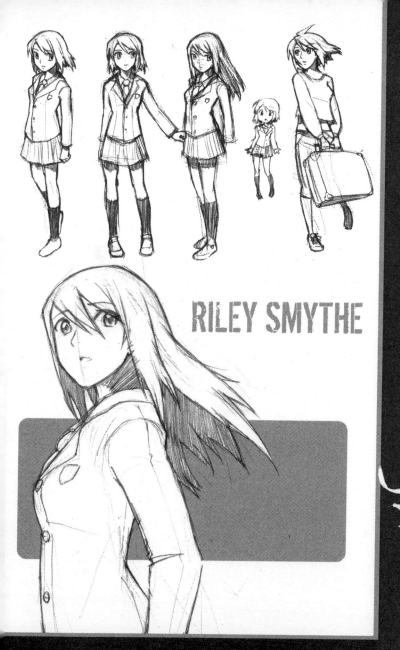

RILEY SMYTHE

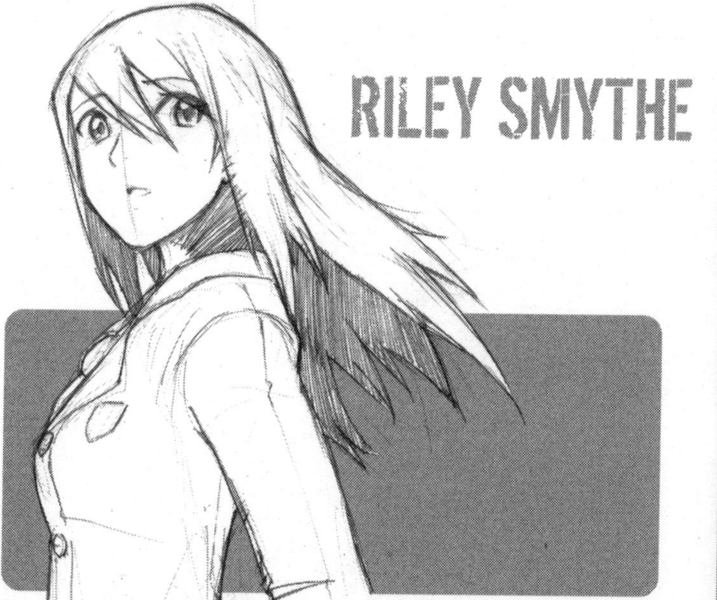

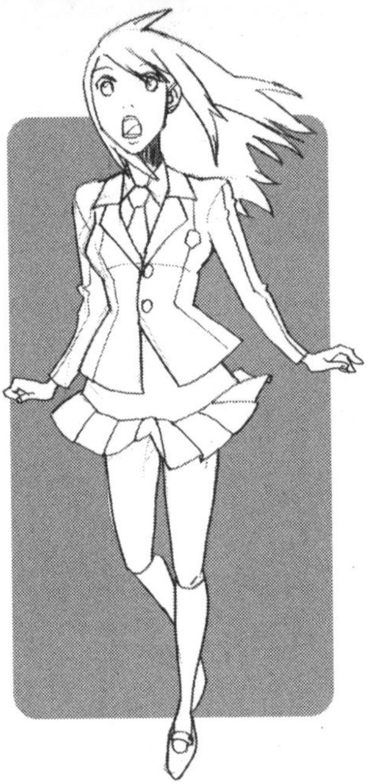

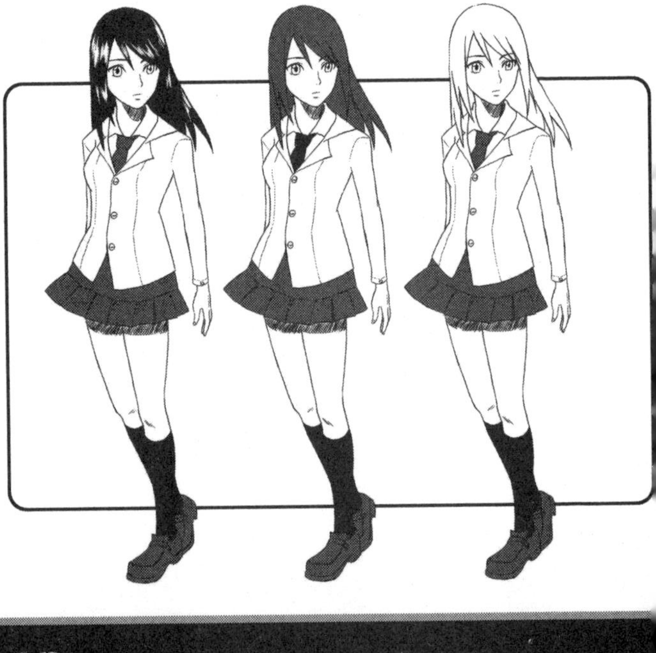

SKETCH PAD

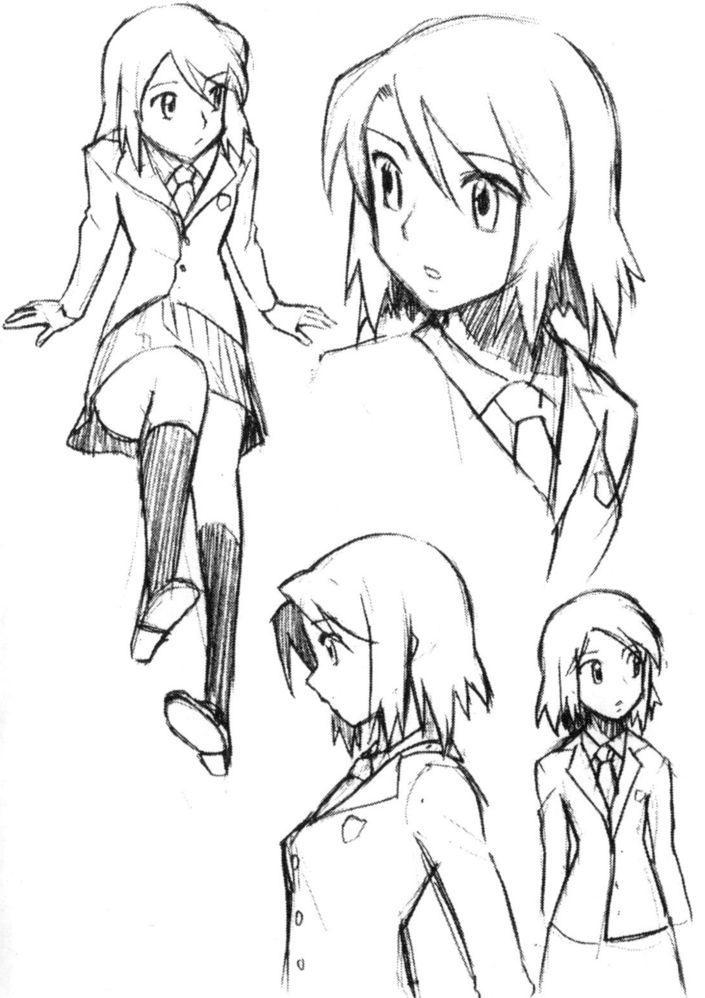

SKETCH PAD

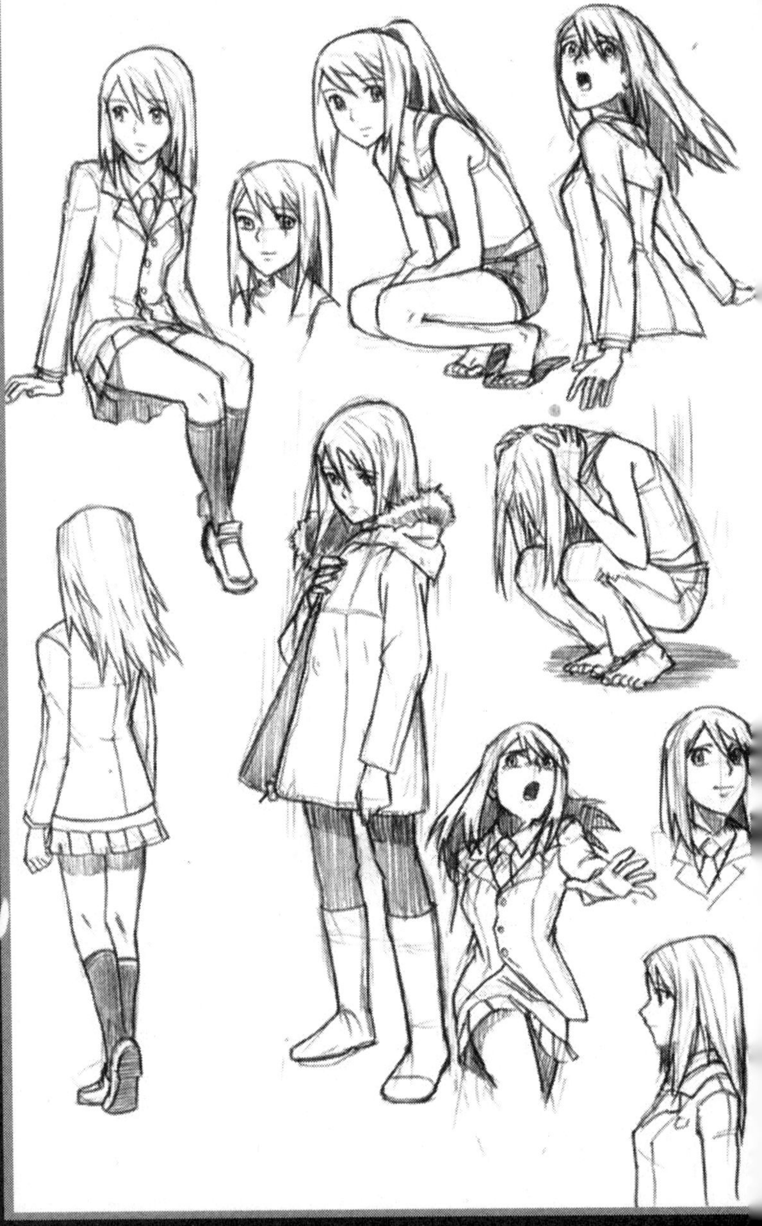

SKETCH PAD

Riley Smythe

SKETCH PAD

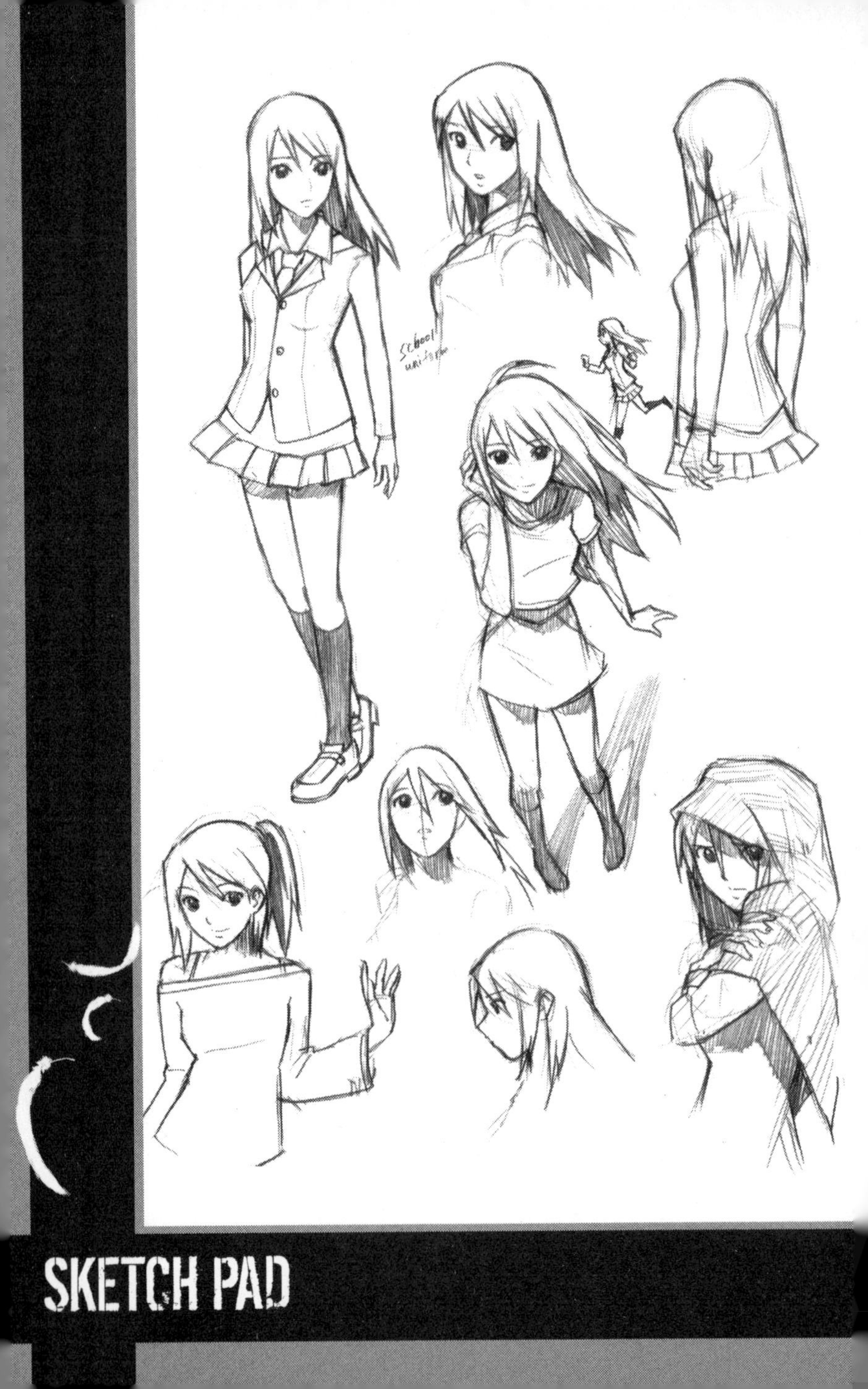
School uniform

SKETCH PAD

WILLIAM LANG
AKA JUNIOR

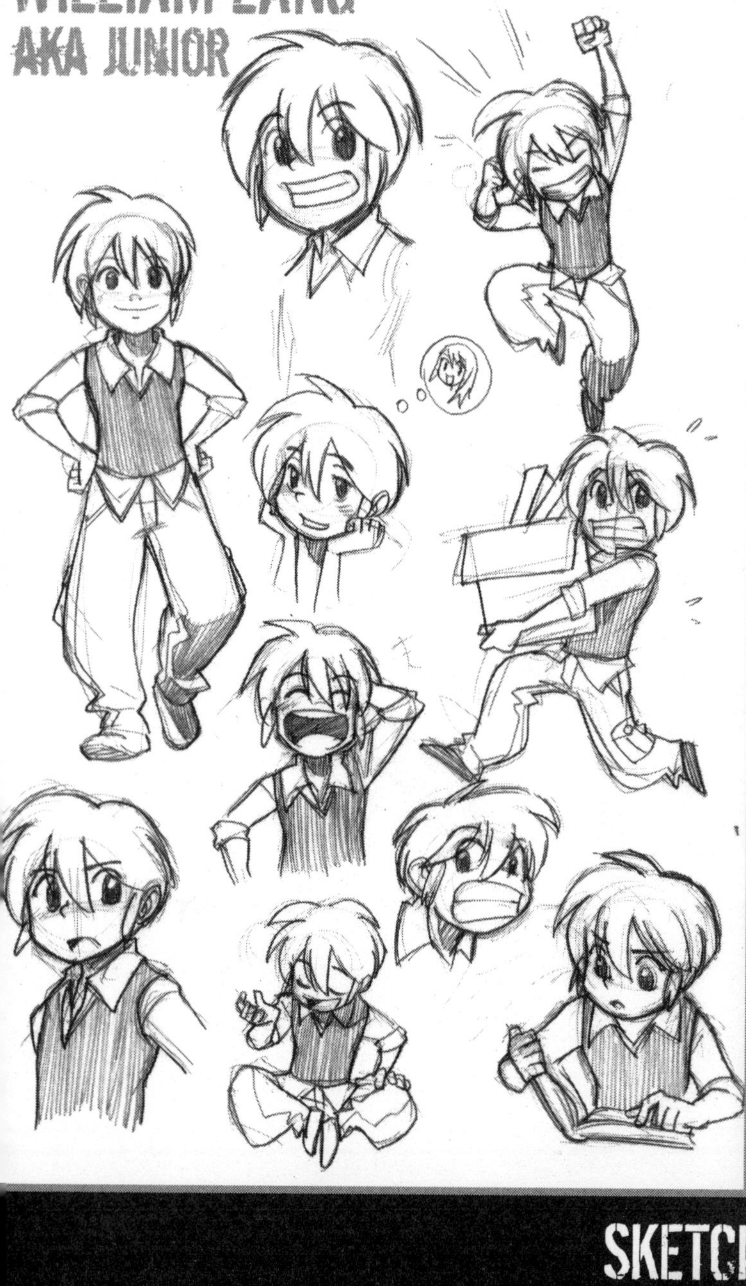

SKETCH PAD

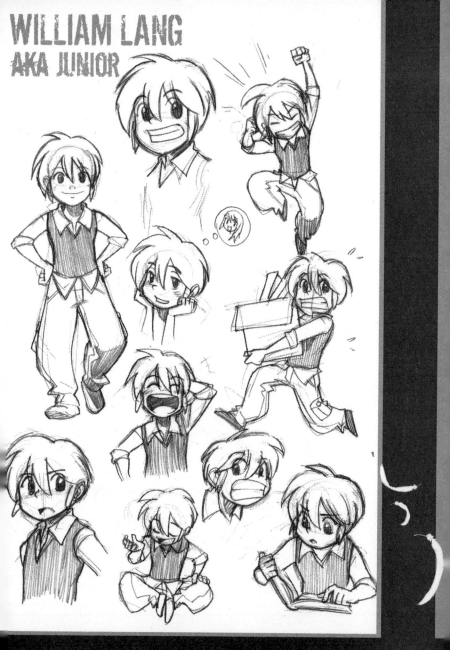

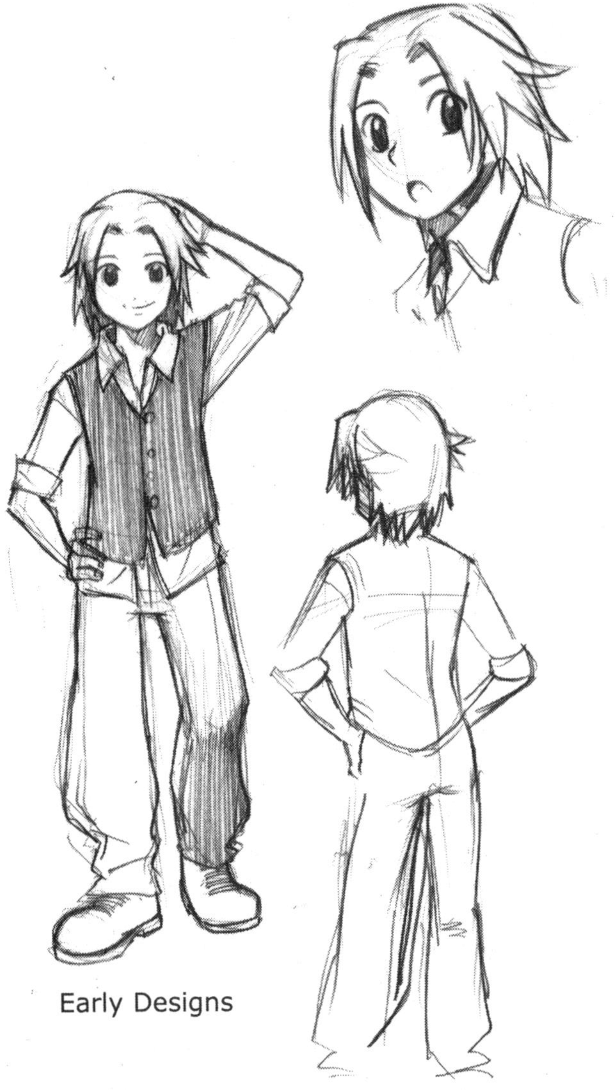

Early Designs

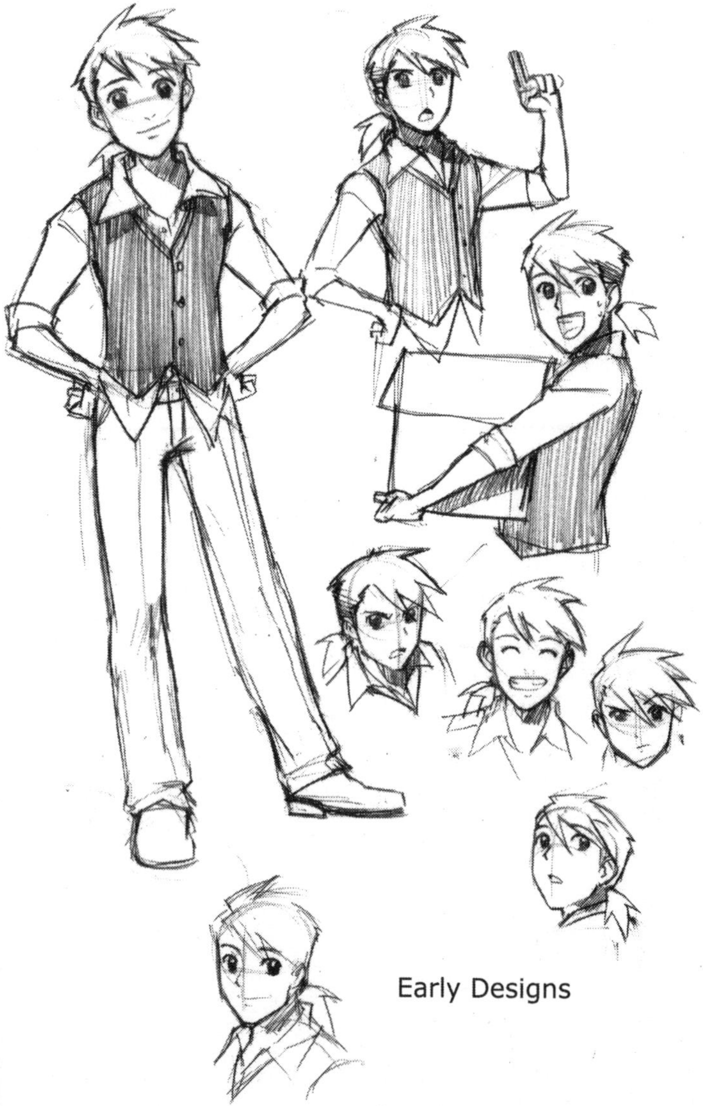

Early Designs

SKETCH PAD

GRANDMA MAGGIE SMYTHE

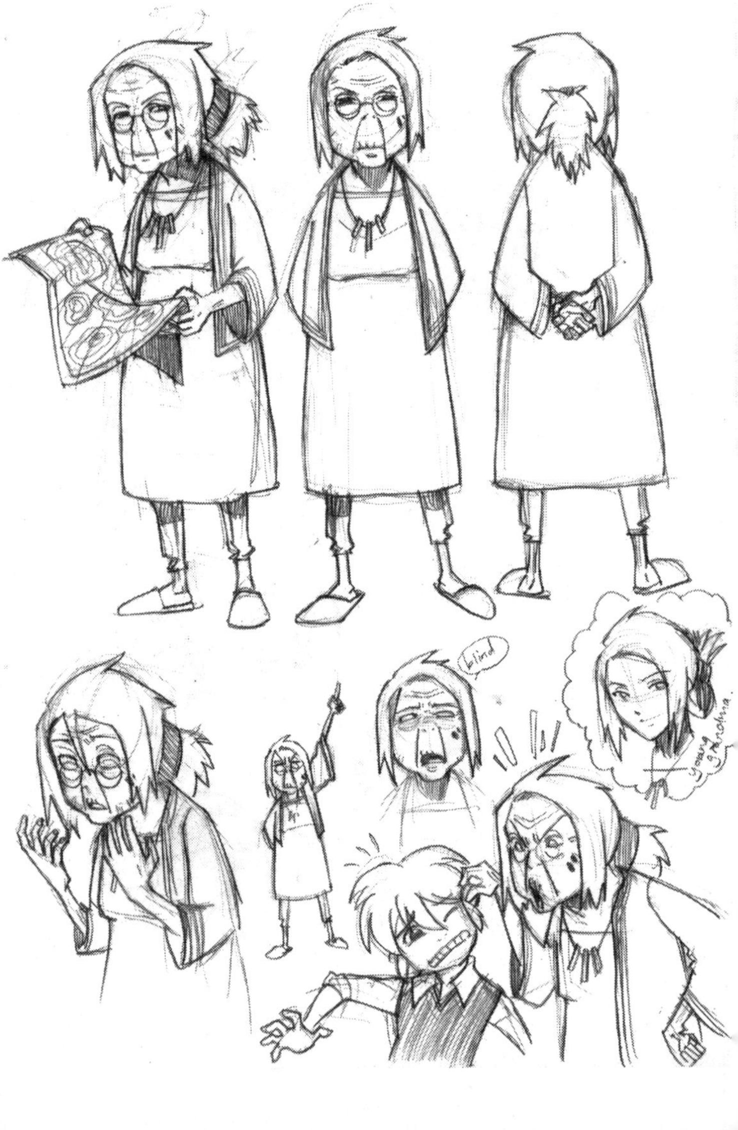

blind
young grandma.

KIT WILLIAMS

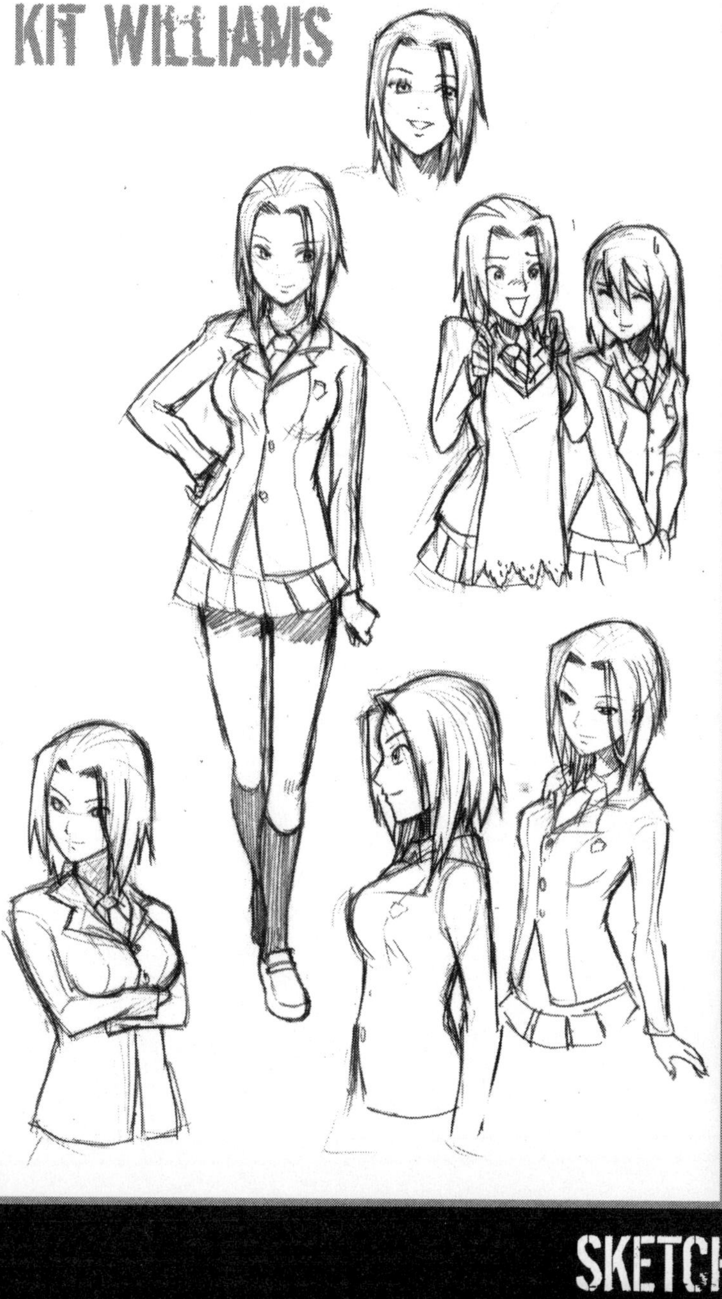

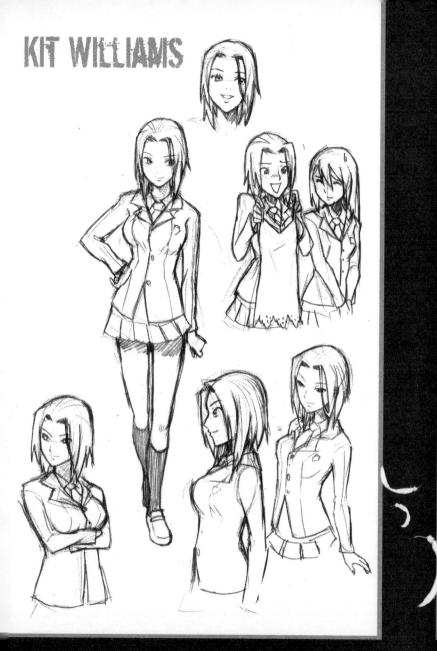

MAX TILDON

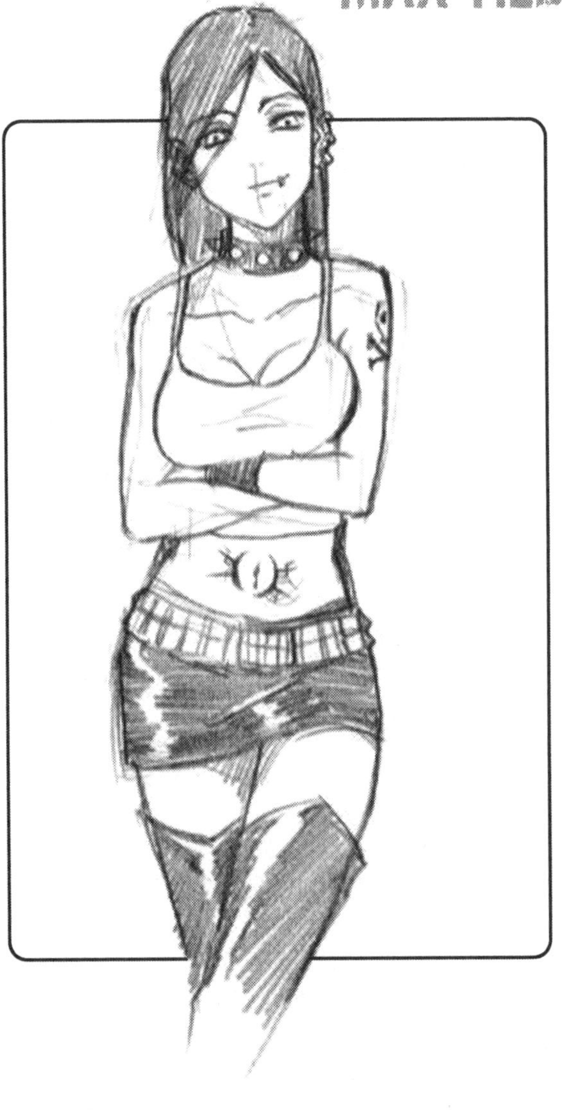

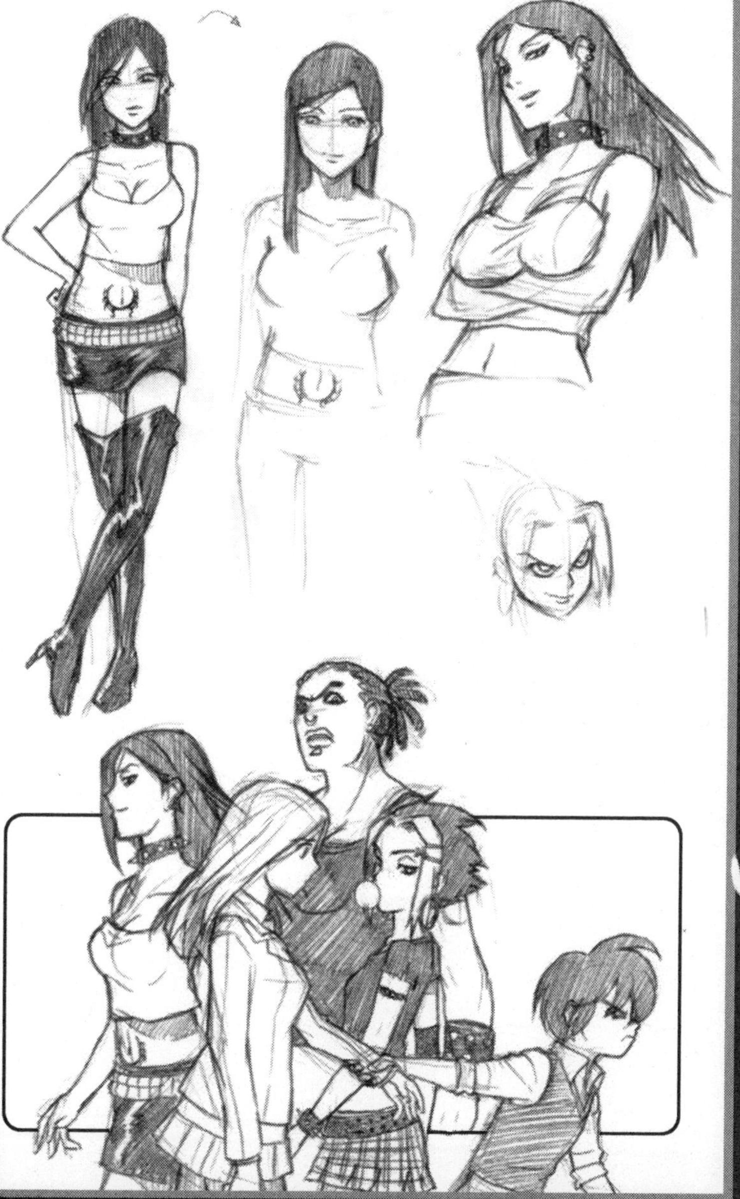

SKETCH PAD

CARTER MORSE

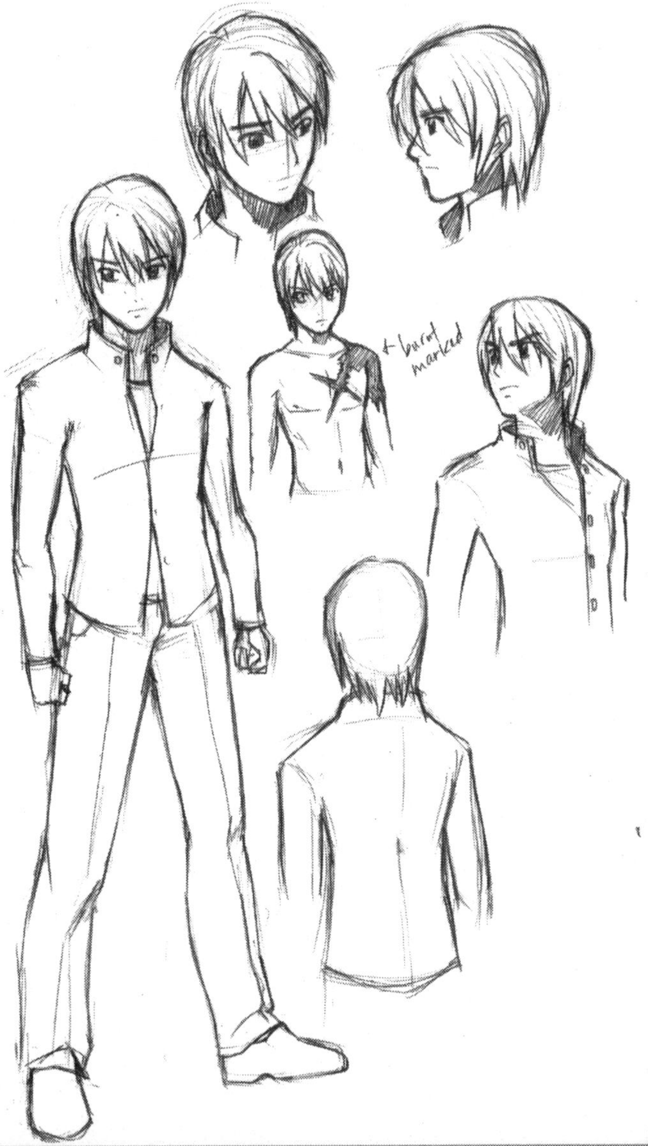
burnt marked

SKETCH PAD

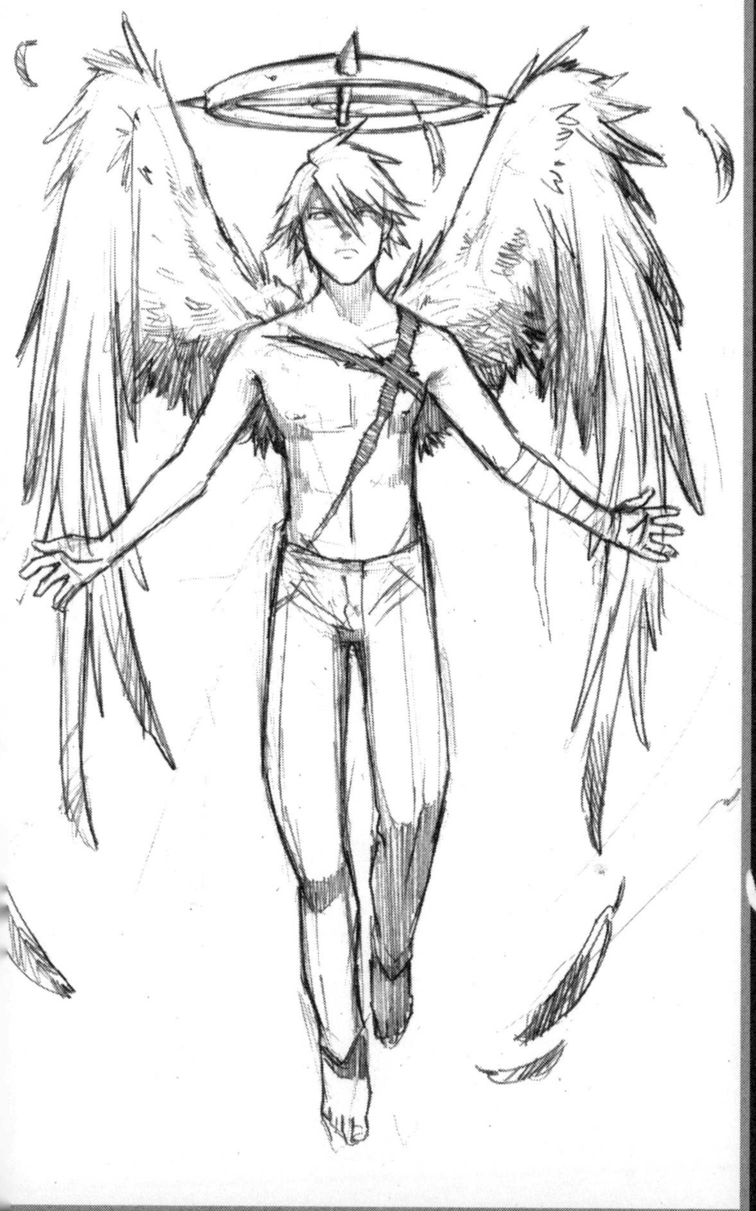

SKETCH PAD

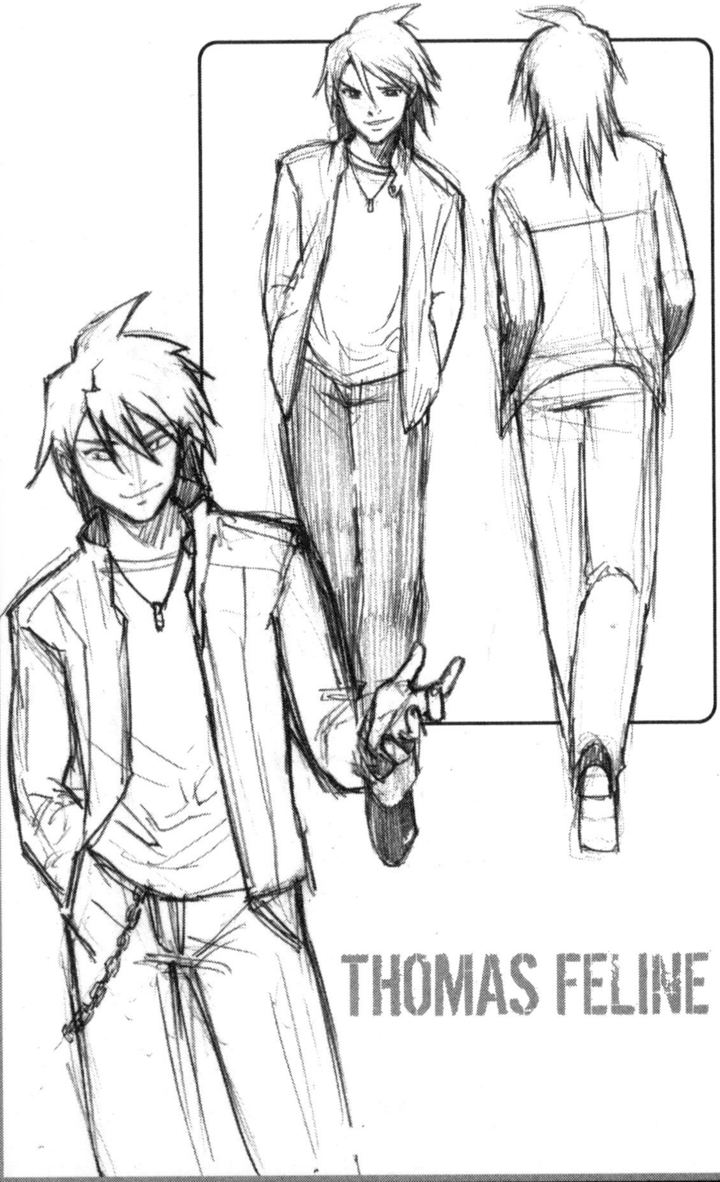

THOMAS FELINE

SKETCH PAD

PAGE THUMBNAILS

- Hey, are you alright?
- help
- help me

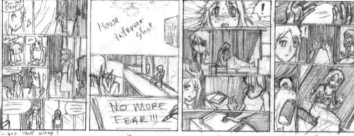

- you can't escap?
- No
- same dreams?
- school not bag
- I don wanna go, I'm not ready
- Riley, you've been holed up out for months. It'll do you good

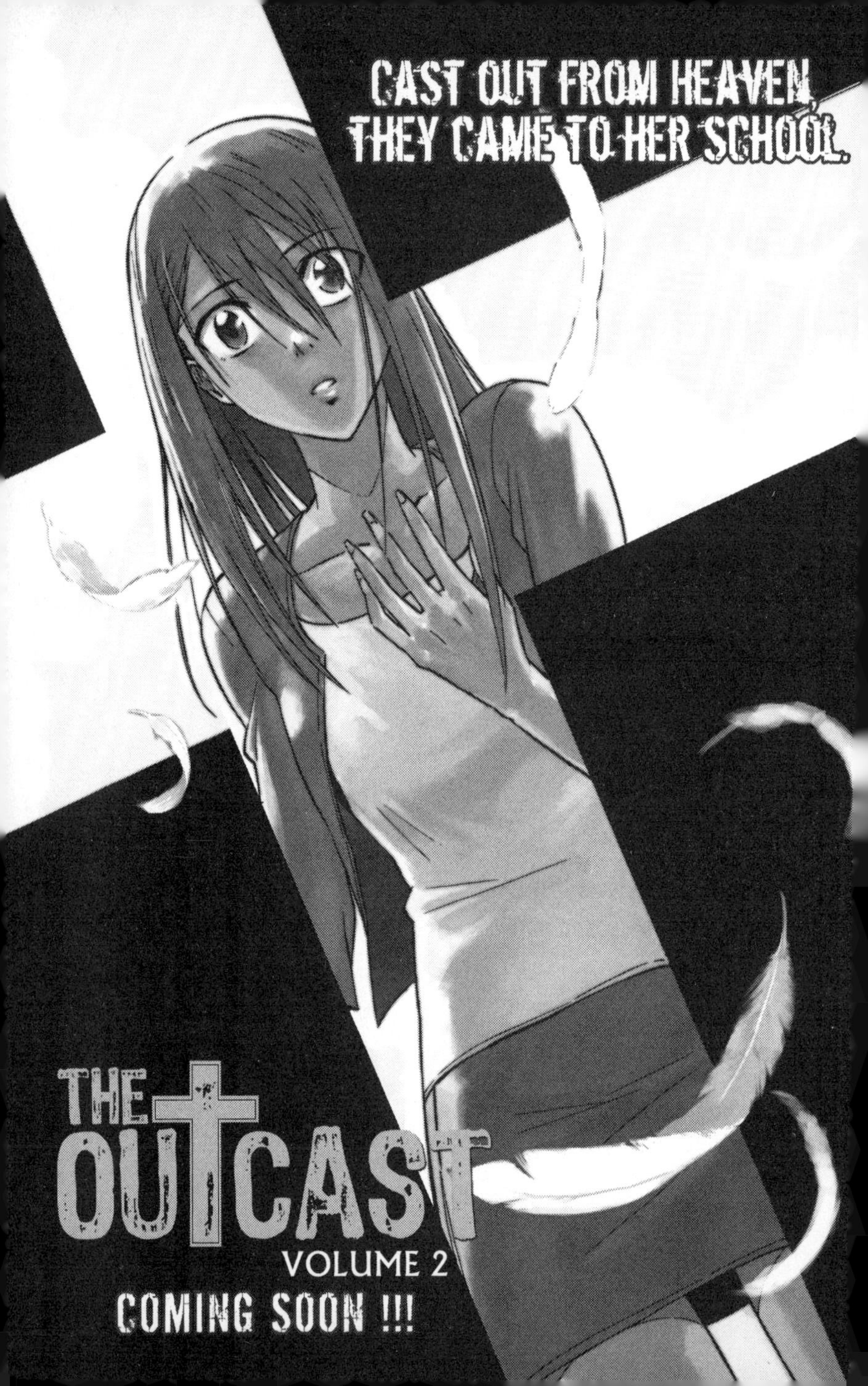
CAST OUT FROM HEAVEN,
THEY CAME TO HER SCHOOL.
THE OUTCAST
VOLUME 2
COMING SOON !!!

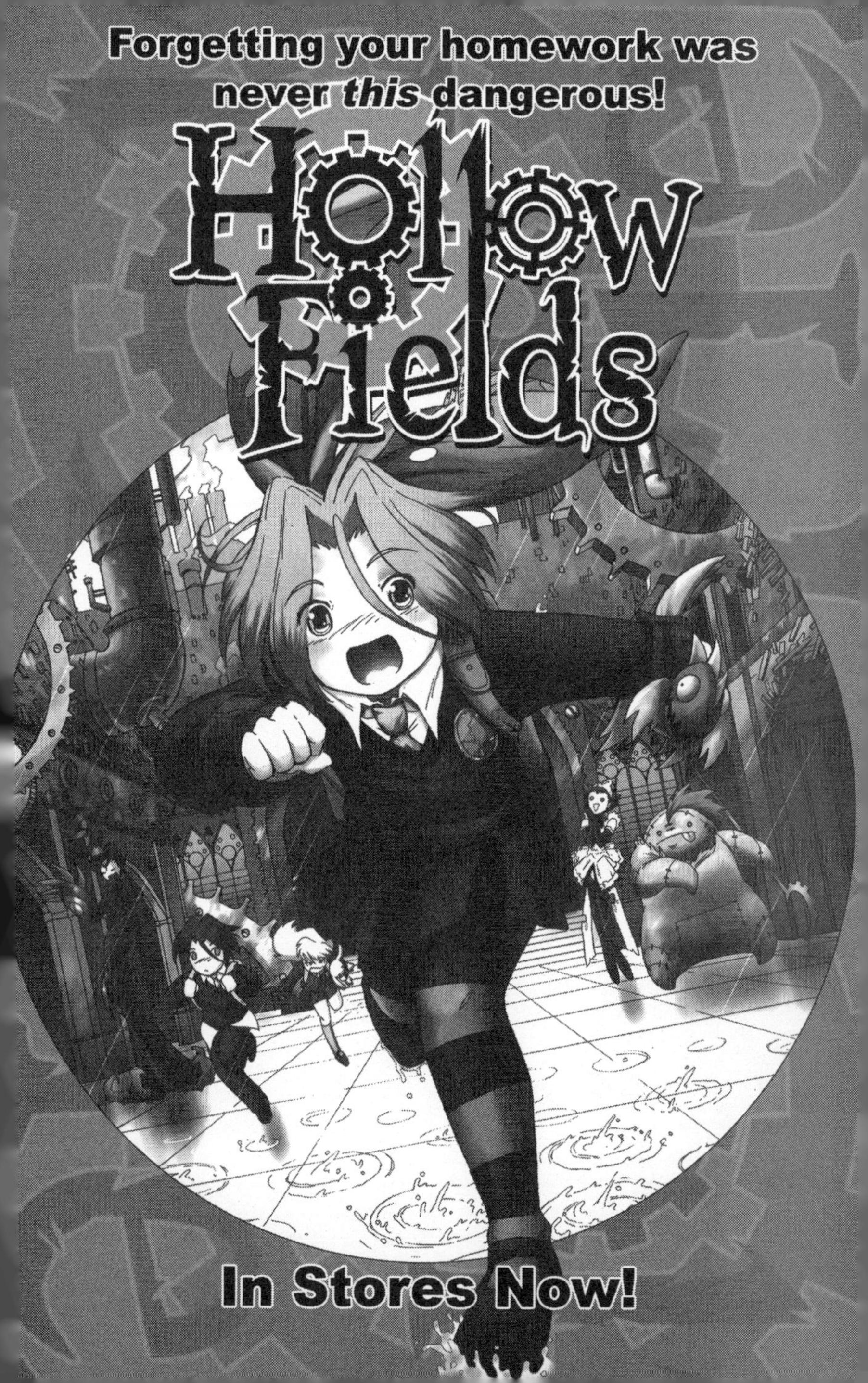
Forgetting your homework was never *this* dangerous!
Hollow Fields
In Stores Now!

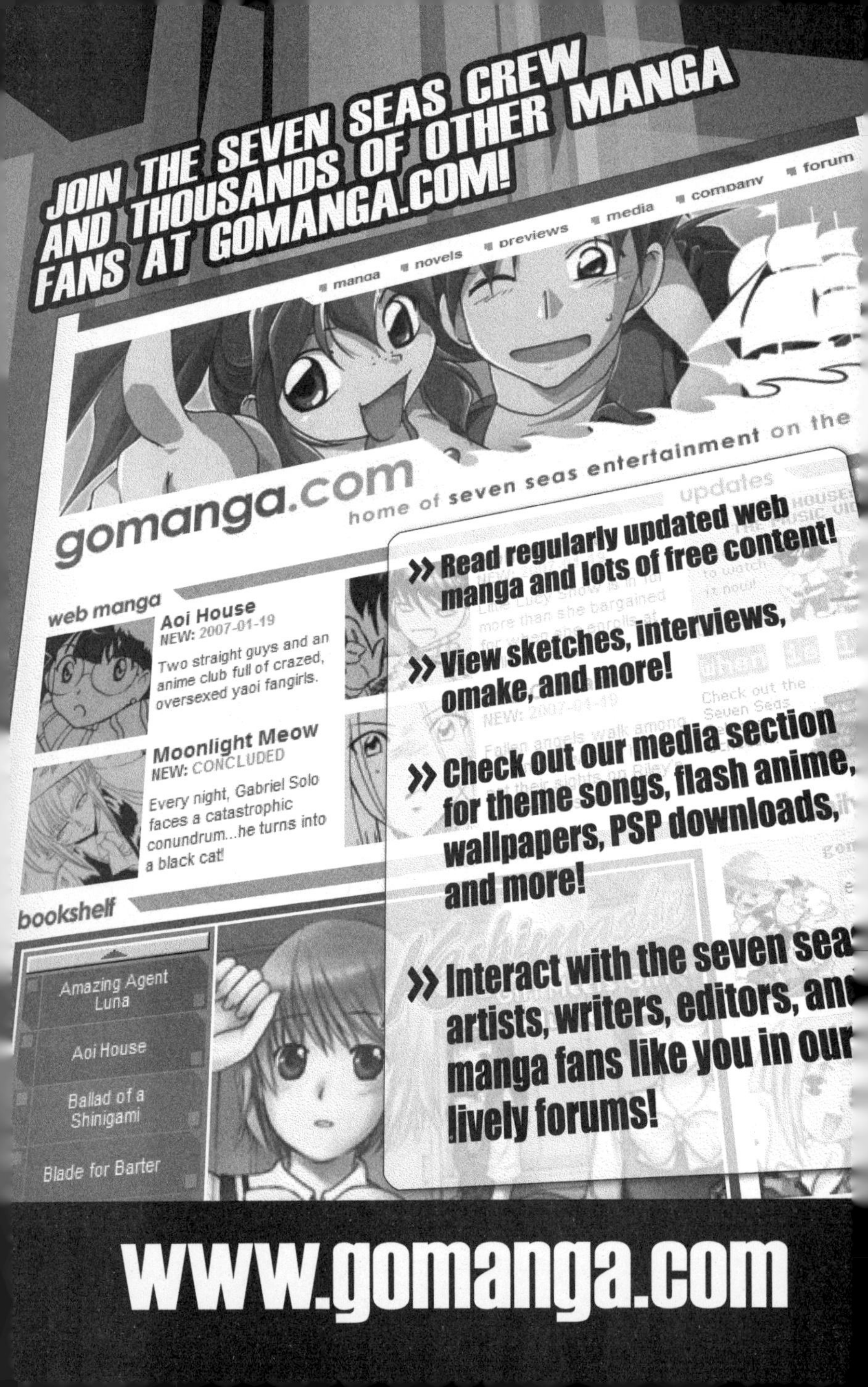
JOIN THE SEVEN SEAS CREW AND THOUSANDS OF OTHER MANGA FANS AT GOMANGA.COM!
manga
novels
previews
media
company
forum
gomanga.com
home of seven seas entertainment on the
updates
web manga
Aoi House
NEW: 2007-01-19
Two straight guys and an anime club full of crazed, oversexed yaoi fangirls.
Moonlight Meow
NEW: CONCLUDED
Every night, Gabriel Solo faces a catastrophic conundrum...he turns into a black cat!
bookshelf
Amazing Agent Luna
Aoi House
Ballad of a Shinigami
Blade for Barter
» Read regularly updated web manga and lots of free content!
» View sketches, interviews, omake, and more!
» Check out our media section for theme songs, flash anime, wallpapers, PSP downloads, and more!
» Interact with the seven seas artists, writers, editors, and manga fans like you in our lively forums!
www.gomanga.com

YOU'RE READING THE WRONG WAY

This is the last page of
The Outcast Volume 1.

This book reads from right to left, Japanese style. To read from the beginning, flip the book over to the other side, start with the top right panel, and take it from there.

If this is your first time reading manga, just follow the diagram. It may seem backwards at first, but you'll get used to it! Have fun!